BICHE

BICHE

Stephanie Theobald

FLAME
Hodder & Stoughton

Theobald, Stephanie
Biche
I. Title
823.9'14 [F]

ISBN 0 340 76841 X

Typeset by Palimpsest Book Production Limited,
Polmont, Stirlingshire
Printed and bound in Great Britain by
Mackays of Chatham plc, Chatham, Kent

Hodder and Stoughton
A division of Hodder Headline
338 Euston Road
London NW1 3BH

For Dick Olive

Acknowledgements

Special thanks to Adam Jones, Farah Nayeri, Jody Johnson and Peter Rook. Thanks also to Randy Koral for the commissions, to Alison McNaught for finding me an agent while I went on holiday, to Saskia Sissons for sticking her neck out, to Anne-Marie Harper for French consultancy, to Darian Leader who spurred me on by claiming my advance would be enough to buy me several villas on the Cap d'Antibes, to Victoria for the heartache, to Elisabet for the desk in Barcelona, to Madame Valienne with apologies for the moonlight flit, to Pincus for the hair, to my agent Mary Pachnos and her collection of how-I-nearly-got-deported-from England stories, to my editor Kate Lyall Grant for being incredibly nice to me all the time, to all the odd people I have ever met and above all, to Veronica and Roy Theobald for always being there.

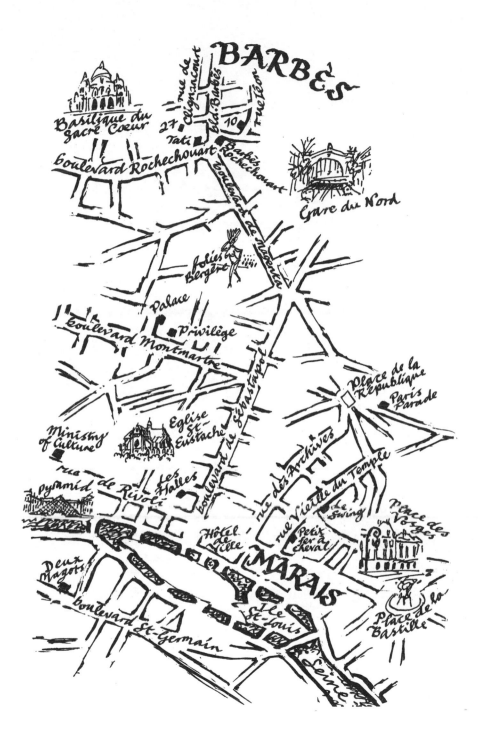

FRENCH GLOSSARY

banlieu	suburbs
BCBG (bay say bay jay)	*bon chic bon genre*. Yuppie. Very *seizième arrondissement*
beignet aux pommes	apple doughnut
BHV	*Bazaar de l'Hôtel de Ville*, semi-grand department store in the Marais
biche (beesh)	female deer. Used as a street chat-up line in the 'hello gorgeous' sense
bienvenu	welcome, as in 'Bienvenu Cocktails'
bise (beeze)	kiss of greeting or goodbye
bricolage	DIY
brocanteur	antiques dealer
chambre de bonne	literally, 'maid's room', situated in the attic of a building. Now used as the cheapest form of accommodation in Paris. The hole-in-the-floor toilet (*toilette à la turque*) is usually located on the outside landing and there is often no running water
chin	cheers (drinking salutation)
clochard	tramp
copines	female friends
cul sec (coo sec)	literally, 'dry bum'. Down in one, a slammer (alcohol)
décontracté	relaxed
dégueulasse	disgusting
demi	half a pint of lager
Diana Vreeland	eccentric editor of *American Vogue* in the 60s
grave	serious. In a rave context, *grave* means 'really cool'
harissa	hot red sauce important in North African cooking
HLM	*habitation à loyer modéré*. Council house
il y a du monde sur le balcon	literally, 'there are lots of people on the balcony', figuratively, 'you have very large breasts'
incroyable	unbelievable
Inès de la Fressange	famous French model of the mid-1980s. Muse of Chanel designer Karl Lagerfeld
informatique	computer-related work

Jean-Paul Gaultier	eternal enfant terrible famous for putting men in skirts and conical breasts on Madonna
Les Négresses Vertes	punk accordian group
mal baisé	literally, 'badly fucked'. Used as noun or adjective of someone who hasn't had sex in a long time and is consequently miserable and grumpy
mairie	town hall
merde, merdique	shit, shitty
mignonne (min-yon)	cute
morpions	crabs (genital)
Mouton à Cinq Pattes	the five-footed sheep. A chain of discount designer clothing stores
nul	stupid
ouais (ooo way)	yeah
pavé	paving stone/thick piece of steak
pédé (pay day)	gayboy
poulet	chicken/cop
profession libérale	the antithesis of the sitting-in-an-office-all-day job. Supposed to require some creative output which can span from poetry writing to porn-film making
putain!	(exclamation) fuck!
pute	hooker
quartier (cartier)	neighbourhood
ras le bol	literally, a 'full up bowl'. Fed up
religieuse	nun. Also, a nun-shaped choux pastry bun filled with chocolate or coffee *crème pâtissière*
salope	slapper, bitch
seizième arrondissement	sixteenth *arrondissement*. The poshest of Paris's twenty districts or *arrondissements*
soixante-huitard	middle-aged French person claiming to have been active on the Saint Michel barricades in May 1968
stage	course or internship
sucer	to suck
Tati	chain of bargain clothing shops situated in the poorest districts of Paris
Thierry Mugler	designer who reached the height of his fame in the 1980s. His muses include vampires, amazons, androids, witches and insects
tout à fait	totally
un petit service	a favour

CHAPTER ONE

The Sleeping-Bag Dream

For three days I have lived off four cans of green lentils, two baguettes and a 20 franc pork chop cut up into three rations so that I can budget for the research of a deed which, to be honest, I have been dreaming of ever since I was eight years old.

In those days it was my English teacher, Mrs Kant, who was the object of my desire and the protagonist in a logistically dubious yet persistent fantasy scenario which involved freezing cold weather conditions, a one-man tent and one member of the wrong sex.

Mrs Kant and I would be doing the Duke of Edinburgh Award in mid-winter Cornwall. We would get stuck on Dartmoor in heavy snow and we would have only one sleeping bag between us, but we would have to take our clothes off before we got into it because an unorthodox doctor's report had recently shown that you kept warmer that way.

I think the outside of the sleeping bag was blue in colour but what I remember distinctly is that the inside was dark and secret and vaguely slippery. The deed never became very concrete; after ten minutes of immersion in that dark, secret place the sleeping bag would disintegrate in my mind like a wisp of smoke, like the slow closing of theatre curtains on an act that I was too young to imagine in any more detail.

It has taken me three solid nights of keyboard slog on the

Minitel to find out what happens behind the curtains. It has taken me so long because sex with a woman seems surprisingly hard to come by. Most of the people on the Minitel women-only sex lines are men promising endless cunnilingus or world-weary lesbians accusing you of being a man when you ask what their bodies look like. The Minitel is like an electronic Yellow Pages which also doubles as a sex contact service. You tap a code name into the tiny computer, chat to people in real time and then, if you are lucky, they give you their phone numbers and you call them up to arrange a rendez-vous. Of course, using the Minitel sex lines is like shopping by post. Like shopping by post it is expensive (4 francs 30 per minute for the X-rated numbers), and you don't know what you are getting until it is too late. What I got when I arrived for my rendez-vous at the Holiday Inn in Place de la République was a spongy-looking woman wearing a ruche-necked blouse over a spongy sort of body. Even beforehand, sitting at a table in the bar, wondering whether to gaze at the bowl of salted peanuts or the nervous smirk plastered all over her spongy face, I wished I was back on Dartmoor in my slippery sleeping bag in the arms of Mrs Kant.

When the métro suddenly jolts forward out of Belleville station I am thrown out of my reverie and nearly into the lap of a powder-grey mink coat, with badger tails hanging off the shoulders and criss-cross leather bits laced up the lapels, worn by a woman who looks like she has come back from the dead five times. When I sit back and close my eyes I see a shawl made of raw rabbit embroidered with chicken giblets and pig-trotter shoulder pads. My eyes are sticky and cold from lack of sleep and it feels nicer to keep them closed than contemplate the passengers who sit around me. It is 6.30 a.m. and the métro carriage is filled with grim Parisian death heads on their way to work. Their faces, grey and drained of blood, look nauseous as they sit in their blue overalls in the stuffy air and the sepia light. I fold my arms, rest my head on my shoulder and try to rewind to the situation that is responsible for my current post-promiscuity high — a mixture of panic, sexual satiety and ha! ha! ha! how's about bloody that then!

If you haven't had sex in a while you can forget what a compulsion it is. You can get into solitude and gardening and making cakes. But once you have five orgasms in one night from a one-night stand you want to do the same thing the next night with someone else. You want to have five orgasms with someone with brown hair, then try it with somebody tall with curly hair and then with, say, someone with broad shoulders and artistic hands. You kid yourself. You think that you are going to discover some monumental truth about life, about yourself, by having some stranger thrust their genitals against yours after a few glasses of cheap wine. Sex is placed on a pedestal, as if it were more important than gardening or cake making.

For those minutes of searing oblivion you can pack up your troubles in your old kit bag and throb in physical ecstasy as your brain turns to pap and loads of carefully thought-out fantasies spring up in your delirious head: you shagging the baker and his wife from over the road, Donatella Versace whipping you lightly while wearing the silver diamanté cocktail dress from this month's *Vogue* cover. (And the frontal zip has to be two inches higher than her right knee before you can come.)

Whereas all the time you're rubbing less than one-sixteenth of your body in a very ungainly style over your partner of the night — who you went off ten minutes after copping off with — and who now has the facial expression of somebody having their wisdom teeth extracted.

Like Sisyphus pushing his stone up the mountain, you think that any minute now there'll be an end to it. The thrill of promiscuity will wane. One day, the prospect of the desperate set piece of kissing, followed by blow job, followed by 69, followed by orgasm, will make you feel like a doomed contestant on the *Generation Game* conveyor belt. You'll be ripping your victim's clothes off and you'll have a terrible vision of what's coming next: the teasmade, the Persian rug, the badminton set, the bathroom scales and the awful inevitability of the cuddly toy.

When you feel grim the next day, you'll console yourself with the thought that once you've popped your latest fantasy (sex under the desk with an American TV executive in smart clothes), then that'll be it. Promiscuity over. Back to the straight and narrow.

But of course the cursed stone always comes rolling back down to the bottom of the hill again. I am at the bottom of the heap now. I am irritated because I can think of no way of getting sex within the next twenty minutes with some new body and my head is beginning to throb.

Luckily, the Paris métro is lit like a bedroom so when the train stops at La Chapelle station I close my eyes even tighter and find myself back in Sponge's house last night. We were stoned by the time we got to her bedroom (vermilion in colour with a four-poster bed), although certainly not stoned enough for me to find interesting her tale of how her husband probably wouldn't be back until morning. When she kissed me it sounded like a dog lapping water and the sight of her in a flannelette nightdress (with ruff collar) wasn't exactly sexy. But when she flashed me a look of cruelty and started rustling around manically under the bed, things began to look up. She pulled out a grey shoe box, removed the lid and began to peel away sheets of white tissue paper that wrapped some sort of object. From the elaborate packaging it seemed likely that the object was some precious Easter egg and my heart sank as I thought she might be going to suggest a midnight feast instead of sex. But when the last sheet of tissue paper had been unravelled, she pulled from the shoe box a 12-inch double-headed dildo with all the exuberance of Mr Punch pulling a string of sausages from the mouth of the crocodile.

4

*　　*　　*

It struck me at the time what great story-telling potential that detail held for the Gang. I'll call Holly when I get home. Fill him in on events. Holly is the devil on my shoulder. He is the most selfish, most charming boy I have ever met. He ducks out of sight at the merest whiff of trouble but he has filled me with the cocky faith that I am a slate that can be wiped clean *ad infinitum*. He says that we are living a chunk of life that doesn't matter. 'Life doesn't start until you're at least twenty-six,' he says. 'And here we are, still perfect twenty-twos.'

I believe that when I am about twenty-six, someone will cruise into my louche street in a red MG wearing a T-shirt that says 'The One' in pink neon lettering, and the whole *arrondissement* will reverberate with the rubbery 'boi-yoi-yoing' sound of love at first sight. We'll drive off to our love nest where the love of my life won't get cross if I eat food in bed and will say things like, 'It's never been like this with anyone before.' And when we can bear to be parted I'll drive a Harley Davidson over to my new job as editor of the *Herald Tribune* where I'll have a black leather swivel chair and lunch delivered every day from Fauchon, and I'll go to a local *brasserie* where the head waiter will treat me as if I am Inès de la Fressange. Most importantly, both in my office and in my bedroom I will have a Philippe Starck-designed control box: one button when pressed will summon the presence of 'The One' when I need comfort, and the other I'll press when I want 'The One' to disappear.

Not that I don't know anybody in Paris who is romantic. There is Raoul, Alex's boyfriend, who likes sex but who says he prefers flirtation and the measures that are necessary to arrive at the bedroom door. 'Better than orgasm is the moment in your tête-à-tête when you pass from "vous" to "tu",' he says, extolling the advantages of the rigid French language.

'You are having a conversation with a man you have met in a bar. The way his eyes are looking at you tells you that he wants nothing better than to sweep you off to the nearest bushes of the Tuileries. But he continues to address you as "vous" with all the formality of François Mitterand addressing the Assemblée Nationale.

'Then, the ice starts to break: he tells you a witty anecdote from his childhood, you brush his hand as you reach for the ashtray, you catch him looking at your crotch as you tell him the story of an argument you had in Comme des Garçons.

'Now you don't feel so embarrassed. Now your heart feels high and he hands you another beer and says the words: "T'es drôle, tu sais".

'And you are thrilled and slightly sad at the same time.'

I was thrilled and sad at the same time with Sponge's double-header. Up until now there had certainly been no love at first sight, no lust at first sight, no lust at first kiss, not even that much lust at first sight of nakedness. But the mere fact of her possessing a portable penis that she kept in a shoe box under her bed seemed exciting proof of a sexual knowledge far beyond my ken. Who would have thought that this was what had been lurking down at the bottom of the sleeping bag all these years?

As she brandished the double-header aloft, my libido thrashed around like a fish out of water. Her flannelette second skin, folded up virginally over an Ikea chair at the end of the bed, now began to breathe like a leatherette cat suit. I reached out and touched her big, round breasts as her eyes held me with that big, mean look and a panic of pleasure ripped through my body. I wanted to do everything and grab everything and shake it all and lick it all and smell it all and as I slipped up and down her oily thighs I thought how the nuns at my school would be furious if they knew what I was doing and for a millionth of a second I thought of what would happen if her husband walked back in through the door at that minute, and best of all I didn't think, I just saw waves and waves of red red lust in a red red sleeping bag that throbbed in and out, scalded by the bars of red neon light glowing in from the *tabac* shop across the street.

There was no stopping me now. Goodbye dim, dull cave, goodbye to all that. Goodbye dark shadows that block the view – the sweating top lips and the shifty eyes, the mummified sex drives. Rise up and heal thyself: chin up, legs apart, into the light. Unzip your old life like a shedded snake skin, toss it aside like an A-line skirt. Give your shiny new wrapper a treat: a plastic love rocket, perhaps, a carpentry tool or two, some glitter dust upon the midnight hour?

Burping, slurping, snuffling, snorkelling eye of a geyser in downtown throbland. There was no time to think, just to be: neon red, snake writhing, humping sinner, a desperate, lecherous, lip-sucking flower.

Unfortunately, when I finally managed to grab hold of the magic baton that she continued to wave around, it turned out that it was as hollow in the middle as a strap-on party nose and incapable of taking either of us anywhere near pleasure mountain. She fumbled around with it for a while but it was about as hard as the finger of a rubber glove. After a few hissed '*zut*'s and '*merde*'s she finally gave up and flopped down next to me. She grabbed me to her and started cuddling me – which is completely the wrong end of the stick for a one-night stand. As I lay locked in her doughy grip while I waited for the first métro home, I wondered if my love life is destined to be quirky all the time or if it is just that Holly and I always look for quirky elements in our evening encounters to make our stories for the Gang more interesting.

We are rather going against the grain of the typical French experience. Like the best food, the French believe that carnality should be invested with intimations of the '*au delà*', the transcendental. Buggery, for instance – a staple of the French one-night stand – isn't just buggery. Done in the correct poetic framework it becomes Fauré's *Requiem*, Renoir's *Umbrellas*, the Versailles Hall of Mirrors, *Last Tango in Paris*. When Ann got off with a forty-year-old man from the *profession libérale* last Beaujolais Nouveau night in Le Petit Fer à Cheval (The Horseshoe), they ended up going back to his studio in the Marais where he did it to her up the bum. Afterwards, she said that he climbed down from the mezzanine bed, put on some Dvorak and made some leek soup which they both ate cross-legged on his wooden floorboards by the light of a candle.

Ann's life is much more *Pauline à la Plage* than mine is, but Paris has nevertheless brought out the poetic in me too. For instance, there is something about promiscuity that makes me feel pure. This stands to reason: if you go out purposefully to scrape the bottom of the barrel, then when you come home you feel purged and cleansed. The world goes back to degree zero, like it has been washed clean with dew. It is full of possibilities. The French call staying out all night a 'white night' and that seems a good description to me.

One or two people get on the train at each station. When the doors are about to close there is a clarion sound – like a mischievous school orchestra – and when they finally come together you hear a Miss Marple 'ping', like an old-fashioned till being snapped shut. Things are starting to come up roses again. The carriage even smells quite pleasant at this ridiculous time of the morning – a smell of detergent-soaked croissants as opposed to the 6 p.m. warm meat smell of office workers who've gone without soap since morning.

My morning-after-the-night-before routine is about to be put into action. I will go home, stuff my clothes into the cupboard, take a shower, climb into my bed, eat an apple doughnut and drink a cup of black coffee. I'll look at my watch and luxuriate in the fact that I don't have to get up until the afternoon. I'll feel like a young grape with dew still frosting my skin, an eight-year-old just lifted from my evening bath and wrapped up in a clean white towel. (When you live at 27 rue de Clignancourt, clean white towels can only ever exist in the imagination.)

At Barbès-Rochechouart I leave the métro station and wade my way through the streets of this rundown part of Montmartre – the section where the little old ladies and their poodles end, and the crippled Algerian beggars and butchers' shops selling sheep's heads begin.

I walk up towards 27 rue de Clignancourt, past the men setting up for a day of 10 franc V-neck bargains at Tati, past the Algerian man at the Sandwich Grecque stand who makes the usual snaky hissing sound as I walk past and into the *boulangerie* opposite the apartment for my daily apple doughnut.

I smile at the woman behind the counter and say, '*Un beignet aux pommes, s'il vous plaît.*'

I have been coming here for a year now, but Madame Dupont (I only know her name because it is written on the bags) still insists on the French habit of slamming the change down on to the plastic ashtray on the counter instead of straight into my palm. Still slow and hazy I put my hand out for the change by mistake and Madame Dupont glares at me sternly. I feel a twinge of guilt for the first time in twenty-four hours.

CHAPTER TWO

27 rue de Clignancourt

Twenty-seven rue de Clignancourt is my home. It is a place I need as much as my hectic nights. I am more fond of my thinning brown sheets and my piece of sponge mattress which rests on three large, wooden fruit crates than I am of any of the people I have met on my night errands.

After I shower and climb into my bed with my *beignet aux pommes* and my cup of coffee, I pass my hands reassuringly over the moth holes in the brown cotton sheets, like reading Braille. My bedclothes have been a constant in my life ever since I stole them from my last sub-let.

The two men who live below us are quiet this morning. Their bedroom is directly underneath mine and sometimes I am woken up by the sound of their arguments. Sometimes I am woken by the sound of one of them coming. It is a whining note similar in pitch to the sound they make when they raise their voices in argument. But it is shorter and sharper, like a sleazy alarm wake-up call.

That puts me in a bad mood for the first few minutes of the day. I feel angry with my sheets and wonder how long it will be before I am editor of the *Herald Tribune*. Madame Valence, our landlady, thinks I am editor of the *Herald Tribune*. Thanks to some forged letters of recommendation on *Paris Parade* headed notepaper (the magazine where I try to scrape a living), she signed Clignancourt over to me instead of the couple of genuine accountants who also wanted to live here.

I wonder if Madame Valence knows what a lofty position my fantasy job is. When she comes round to collect the rent she never asks why the editor of the *Herald Tribune* has eight pieces of scrubby furniture in her whole apartment: a fruit-crate bed, two tables made of scuffed planks, a camping oven permanently latticed with melted Emmenthal and strands of hair, a dented fridge and three chairs which look like they were found on the street – which of course they were. Our saucepans are on loan to us courtesy of a friend. Bits keep flaking off and I read somewhere recently that cooking with cheap aluminium can give you Alzheimer's disease, but that is a risk I am taking. I hope that the ill effects of the cooking utensils will be counterbalanced by the health-giving properties of the 240 franc liquidiser I and my two flatmates – Bet and Ann – all have equal shares in. At least once a week, we fill it with edible bits of the rotten fruit we buy from Barbès market that costs less than 10 francs a kilo.

My brown cotton sheets are the last give-away of my pretend lifestyle, although the kitchen floor is another clue. The yellow-tiled floor is sticky under foot because we never wash it. Bet and Ann and I have developed a special rue de Clignancourt walk: four paces, stop. Wipe left foot against right shin or right foot against left shin. Carry on until all lumps of grey squashy stuff have fallen off respective feet, walk on.

Bet and Ann share the main room of the apartment – with a fusty white sheet nailed up on the ceiling in the middle of the room for privacy. Actually, the sheet is nailed up three-quarters of the way along the room and Bet rules the three-quarters. Bet is possessed with a character that the French call '*très speed*', and indeed, she seems to have found the perfect country for her finely tuned sense of the dramatic.

She usually goes *décolleté* and favours short skirts – a brave choice for this neck of the woods – but her pace is stalwart and her chunky high heels are in league with her. Sometimes the metal tips click gently but sometimes they sound like toppling skittles as she stomps up the stairs to the seventh floor and I know that her bank manager is going to get a flea in his ear. She comes in, snatches up the phone which she takes into her three-quarters and slams the door shut. She has lots of phrases of indignation up her sleeve like '*Je trouve ça dégueulasse*' and '*Ecoutez-moi bien, Monsieur, c'est tout à fait inadmissible*' which torpedo through the sheet into Ann's quarter. I think her attitude is pretty brave considering that she only has 300 francs in the bank. She comes out looking relaxed as if she's just had a nice cup of tea and then, only then, she will say: 'Hi, had a good day?'

Bet's battling spirit has been nourished from her time working as a temp in a variety of French companies. Hanging around with so many secretaries she has learnt that while the English comment on the weather in a wittery fashion, the French talk about it as though it augurs World War Three. In the summer, most secretaries will start the day concertina-ed up with misery about the state of the temperature:

'*Quel chaleur, j'en peux plus!*' ('This heat, I can't bear it any more!')

'*Ah, mais c'est pas vrai!*' ('God, I can't believe it!')

'*Putain! Qu'est-ce qu'il fait chaud!*' ('Fuck, it's boiling!')

They chorus tragically as if they bear the weight of the world (and the solar system) upon their size 6 shoulders.

Ann, Bet and I all knew each other vaguely from French lectures at university, but we didn't meet properly until our year-out in Paris. The week before I returned to England, I bumped into Bet and Ann at a party at the *Institut Britannique*. All I remembered of Bet from university was the sight of her sitting scowling on the wall outside her college, chewing gum and wearing a completely orange outfit and earrings like hubcaps. At the party she was downing sangria and engrossing the other English *assistants* with daring tales of her flirtation with Yannick, one of her sixth formers at the *lycée* where she had worked.

When we went back to university for our final year we became good friends. When Bet came to visit me, she'd flop herself down on my bed and recite her favourite lines from *Les Fleurs du Mal*, '*Ah Seigneur, donnez-moi la force et le courage de contempler mon coeur et mon corps sans dégoût*', which means, 'Oh Lord, give me the strength and the courage to contemplate my heart and my body without disgust'. Then she would scowl and tell me how traumatic her personal life with Steve had been ever since she sent him a Valentine's day message which said, 'irresistible force meets immovable object' attached to a packet of Bakewell Slices wrapped in black paper. I would sigh and say that I wished *I* had a personal life.

Soon we were having twentieth-century French literature supervisions together. After one on 'Metaphors of the circle in *A La Recherche du Temps Perdu*', Bet bolted out of the room in her scarlet bull skirt — a memento from Paris when she'd found herself with fifty francs to live on for a week and had decided to blow it on a scarlet felt mini skirt from the *pute* shop in Chaussée d'Antin. Although Bet was the most brilliant student the professor had had in years, he had scolded her for handing in her essay late. When I was trying to cheer her up afterwards she said she didn't care anyway because she was going to go back to Paris when she'd graduated and carry on working at the Rex nightclub where she'd been cashier for the *Soirée Goa Boa*. That is exactly what she did do when she first came back — until the day the promoter ran off down the street with the night's takings in her bra and went to Barcelona in a truck with a group of performance artists called Mutoid Waste.

Whereas I feel like I've ended up here almost by accident, Paris has some magic hold over Bet. She loves the city against all the odds. The night after the *Soirée Goa Boa* incident, I stood in a phone box with her in Saint Michel to give her moral support as she pleaded with her mother to send her fifty pounds so she could afford to stay for a bit longer. And she couldn't even hear what her mother was saying because there was a man outside rubbing his penis against the glass door, shouting, '*Sucez-moi, salopes!*' And Bet had only had a packet of processed ham, half a baguette and three *demis* all day, and there wasn't even any running water in the louche *chambre de bonne* she was living in at the time, and I just thought, what's the point? Bet, on the other hand, thrives on adversity.

Ann came to Paris because her ambition is to be a great juggler and France has some of the best circus schools in Europe. We think that maybe her upbringing in Hay-on-Wye accounts for her irrepressible *joie de vivre*. Every day is a party for Ann. She spends her days teaching English and her nights doing clown *stages*. These are physical theatre courses given by François Jolier who is famous for teaching the ways of New Theatre – how to play washing machines, enact a jug of water, that sort of thing. Once he invited Ann back to his house and gave her a tour of the premises, bedroom included. She just nodded nervously and said how nice the place was and left quite quickly. At the following class he'd knocked her clown and informed the others that she was failing to seduce the audience. 'Acting,' he pointed out predictably, 'is all about seduction.'

Ann likes to throw parties at the weekends for her fellow physical actors and actresses. Sometimes the evening starts with the chocolate game. The chocolate game consists of kissing the person next to you with a mouth full of chocolate. The flat fills with Israelis, Germans, Swedes, Brits and French wearing bright-coloured leggings and chocolate smeared all over their faces – boys with girls, girls with girls, but no boys with boys as Holly and his flatmate Alex always point out in disgust. At some point, Ann will rush up excitedly to Bet and me in the kitchen and exclaim in agitated Welsh tones something like, 'Lord! I've been snogging a woman for the past half an hour. Lord! And some of the boys want to join in too!'

I get all cynical about it and tell Bet that it all seems a bit sixties, but actually I quite like having the clowns around. It is usually Bet who puts a stop to Ann's clown parties at about 2 a.m., when she stomps into the joint bedroom filled with ovens, washing machines, hairdryers and deep freezes, takes her shoes off and dramatically begins nailing the sheet back to where it was before it was dismantled for the party in a fit of *entente cordiale*.

Ann is a good flatmate, upbeat and happy most of the time and she has only ever raised her voice at me once – ever so slightly – when I fried bacon in her vegetarian frying pan for the umpteenth time. Unfortunately, an innocent smile on a face and a gait that looks like a carefree stroll in the country works against you in the rue de Clignancourt. Her day is often blighted on her way up from the Barbès métro by snake sounds made by the Arab men. She thinks they are provoked by her blonde hair and large breasts – a rarity in France – and she is probably right. Not that harassment is limited to this *quartier*. On the Champs Elysées she has been bothered by white-collar lawyers who offer to buy her perfume and whisper 'My compliments on your bosom, *mademoiselle*' or 'Your balcony is very crowded, *n'est-ce pas?*' as they glide past her with their pig-skin briefcases and their folded copies of *Le Figaro*.

In the early days, Ann used to give our Clignancourt phone number to men in the street who came up to her telling her they worked in video. One day, a man with a voice like a porn film called up and asked to speak to Ann. The voice claimed to have met her on the Champs Elysées and when I said that she wasn't at home he asked me if I myself was in the *milieu artistique*. I said 'No' in a huffy voice and thought afterwards how difficult it must be to get it going as an actress.

* * *

Paris was the last place I thought I'd end up when I was a child. When most of the girls from my convent school were taking posh holidays in Scotland and the south of France, I'd go to bed on hot summer nights memorising the formula for knickerbockerglories: syrup, green jelly, ice cream, fruit cocktail, red jelly, cream, chocolate sauce, nuts, cherry.

Unlike Ruth Worthing's parents, mine knew nobody who lived in France. I spent the holidays working in my father's fish and chip shop in Cornwall and my best friend Ruth would return from her six-week stay in the hills of Montpellier to inform me that the French ate snails and rabbit every day and sometimes they ate crisps which they called 'sheeps'.

By the time I was fifteen, I had met five French people. One of them was an exchange student who came to the convent during the summer term, and the other four were a French family who came into the chip shop one Easter. They looked maliciously at the plates of fish cake, chips and beans that were placed before them, trilling: '*Mais c'est quoi ça, alors?*' But it was the exchange student who made me wary of the whole French business.

As we hadn't done anything in our lives, all there was to talk about with her was the difference in educational systems in our countries and the rise of the National Front. The exchange student would force her mouth into the shape of a flabby sea creature and say 'ooh la la' and 'sooo-paire' in an irritatingly frilly blouse sort of way. I had no intention of sounding like Mary Poppins; if this was French, you could keep it.

And then, one day, at the end of year assembly, Mother Clare ordered me to stand up in front of the whole school. She had just delivered her usual morale-killer speech: 'Now girls, I have been informed that some of you have been spotted in the company of boys from the comprehensive school. I have prayed for you but I warn you all: if there are any more stories of any of you flinging your bodies around dance-hall floors, serious action will be taken.'

She finished off, as usual, by announcing that chocolate and crisps were morally corrupting and that we must all learn to sit with our shoulders back and never to cross our legs. (Our music teacher told us never to cross our legs as well, but she said it was for varicose veins.)

Then came my turn. There was a silence and then my name came booming at me like a cannon ball shot from Mother Clare's mouth. I stood up in front of 400 girls whose eyes all seemed to be boring into me. They knew the Last Judgment had come.

'I have made my views clear on girls who go against nature,' she hissed at me.

I gulped.

'You know well my feelings on girls who adorn themselves with ...' She shuddered as she spat the word from her lips: 'Perms!' She erupted. 'Devil's work! Sin of vanity and pride! The Lord died on the cross to save us from our sins ...'

'But, but Mother,' I stammered, 'my hair's natural ... I've been here since I was five years old and I've always had curly—'

'Devil's work!' thundered the voice again. 'Sit down and don't let me see it again.'

It was my French teacher, Mrs Woods, who managed to comfort me afterwards. She was a cheery, scruffily dressed type who lived on a farm and always had specks of mud on her knitted green tights. She wasn't a Catholic and sometimes I'd seen that she mimed to the hymns we had to sing at compulsory mass on Wednesdays. 'Don't worry,' she consoled after I'd sobbed my way through indirect object class. 'You can't do much when you're up against a loony.'

I stopped crying abruptly and looked amazed into Mrs Woods's sparky eyes. She became my hero from that moment and French became my lifebuoy.

*　　*　　*

I have the kind of body the French describe as a *boudin* or a black pudding. I don't consume coffee and cigarettes compulsively and by their standards I am about ten pounds overweight. When I walk past men, pushing my bicycle, wearing holey jeans, fake DMs and a scowl, they cannot think what word to use and usually end up by shouting '*sportive*' lasciviously after me.

I suppose I must be an odd sight for them in a city where most shops have strips of mirror down the side of them so that you never have to spend more than five minutes at a time without looking at yourself. In the rich *arrondissements* you have even more of a duty to be beautiful. Words like '*sublime*', '*splendide*' and '*merveilleux*' pirouette from the mouths of stony-faced women who gaze in windows of *confisseries* and *chocolateries* that have been decorated to sponsor the Second Coming of Auguste Escoffier.

The calorie patrol is even worse at the rue de Clignancourt juvenile delinquent supermarket. Sometimes the man behind the till tut-tuts when I buy a *Milka* chocolate bar or a packet of French Jaffa Cakes which are called *Pims*. He points a finger and winks, 'Watch out for your figure, *mademoiselle!*'

In general, nobody has a chance to say anything to me as I whizz past them on my bicycle, plugged up with Walkman and shades, icy wind blowing through the holes in my jeans. Flying down the boulevard Barbès on my metal friend, as Holly calls it, to deliver my latest freelance article to *Paris Parade* magazine, I am at my happiest. I feel so happy all words fly from my head and all I can think of is sky blue. Being a foreigner has given me an extra lease of life before my life has really begun.

Sometimes I see silverfish scuttling from under my bed. But silverfish are okay. It's spiders and cockroaches that have to be squashed and luckily it's too cold for cockroaches at 27 rue de Clignancourt. I like the cold, and the way the wind blows in an arctic gale every time you open a door, although

Bet complains she doesn't see why she should pay 1,500 francs a month to share a room with Ann when she has to go to sleep every night with a towel wrapped around her head. We have tried to talk to Madame Valence about insulating the windows, and at least getting the place rewired, but seventy-nine-year-old Madame Valence is obdurate.

Sometimes we call her up to discuss the condition of the flat and she turns up at our door with a plastic bag tied like a scarf on her head. We explain to her that every time we put a plug in a socket, big sparks leap out. She always answers the same thing: that the place was rewired in 1945. When we point out that this was rather a long time ago she always says: 'The English bombed the Gare du Nord during the war, you know,' and taps her nose.

One day when she came round she looked distraught and her plastic bag hung limp on her head. We were about to start the usual line of wiring requests when she came out and said that her son had committed suicide. She said that in his last days he would strip himself naked, flagellate himself and say Hail Marys with the window wide open. The neighbours didn't understand the nature of schizophrenia, and indeed, neither did she until a few years ago. Now he'd hanged himself. I sat her down and made her a cup of tea. I felt bad when a tongue of fire leapt out of the socket when I plugged the kettle in.

If we were living in London we would be considered very considerate tenants, but in Paris many people are suspicious of us. The Yugoslav concierge is always telling us off for leaving the front door open and making noise when we come in late and leaving our washing to dry outside the window (in Paris there is a law against hanging your washing to dry out of the window). The concierge must only be in her mid-thirties but she is very pale and her hair looks like it's been toasted. Luckily, most of the time she is too exhausted from screaming at her extended family, who keep coming over from their troubled country, to scream at us.

In fact, our only real enemy is the woman who lives on the third floor, code name Ship Ahoy. She wears glasses as big as windshields and billowing cream blouses with sleeves like sails and collars like wings. When you meet her on the stairs you say to yourself, 'Ship Ahoy!' and she says, '*Bonjour, mademoiselle,*' in a disdainful way where '*mademoiselle*' is a put-down. It means, 'Watch your step, young missy. You are too young for anybody to take you seriously.' We believe that Ship Ahoy is the one who slashed my bicycle tyres. At least, she's the prime suspect. Once, a guest at one of Ann's parties — code name Legs Apart — was sick outside Ship Ahoy's front door on the way down the stairs. Even though we'd put up a ridiculously formal *avis* the day before, warning of the party, and even though we apologised profusely the next day, the bike was a write-off before the week was out.

Ship Ahoy is a typical example of your Joan of Arc-worshipping, Le Pen-voting, Vichy government-supporting, *mal baisée* French woman — even though I don't normally like to use that word because smelly men with coffee-stained teeth use it against women who don't want to get off with them. But you can just imagine it; while Madame Valence was out carousing with the British soldiers on Liberation Day in Paris in 1945 — not being a woman to bear grudges even over the Gare du Nord incident — the lunatic from the third floor was probably in the cellar with a bread knife doing her best to nobble the wiring in the whole building.

Everyone we know who has a proper job keeps on telling us that the air is filled with optimism and that now is the perfect time to be young: the Berlin Wall has just come down, Rick Astley is making secretaries swoon all over France and Jack Lang, the Minister of Culture who wears pink shirts and once got thrown out of the Assemblée Nationale for wearing a Thierry Mugler jacket, is obsessed with *les jeunes*. Personally, I get fed up with hearing about the latest grant he's given some university for some graffiti spray-painting course. I sit in the kitchen feeling hard done by and staring at grafitti-ed lumps of Berlin Wall that the clowns keep bringing round. Jack Lang has been no help to me on the job-finding front.

Contrary to popular belief, it is not easy to be a writer in Paris. There are only two options open to you if you want to be a journalist: *Paris Parade* and the *Herald Tribune*. *Paris Parade* magazine is filled with wide-eyed Americans doing *stages* and editors who only drink fizzy water when they go out. Plus, nobody reads it.

The *Herald Tribune* is the light at the end of my tunnel. It is an American paper based in a BCBG district of Paris called Neuilly. It has become a Paris institution ever since that scene in *A Bout de Souffle* when Jean Seberg strolls down the Champs Elysées in tight, black, *nouvelle vague* trousers selling copies of it. In reality, the paper is not sexy at all. The people who work there are a lethal combination of preppy American, BCBG Parisian and Queen Elizabeth I. (According to a woman I once met in Le Petit Fer à Cheval, Elizabeth I is the nickname of the features editor and that sounds about right because she has never answered any of my letters.)

My French friend Sophie has a full-time journalist's job writing for *Time* magazine about Exocet missiles, the preparation for the single currency, and France's *rapprochement* with the Germans. Political journalism is not my interest. This month, sardine sandwiches are my interest. The article I wrote most recently for *Paris Parade* began: 'Food-sellers are being swept from the streets of night-time Paris after the chief of police decreed that take-away crêpes and sandwiches were a major cause of public disorder.'

I stumbled upon this story when I came back from a club in the early hours and went to the couscous take-away shop at 29 rue de Clignancourt. Here, you can buy half a two-day-old baguette filled with deep-fried sardines and chips served by a grizzled man in a sweaty fur Cossack hat which he wears even in the summer. The sardines and the chips are so old they are tough, but with a good helping of *harissa* you are just aware of a warm comforting feel in your mouth. The whole thing costs only 12 francs which is good value considering that my spirits are lifted by the sound of frying every time I go in there.

This time, the man in the Cossack hat looked a bit shifty as he handed over the greasy package and told me I'd better make sure there were no police around. Apparently, the *Mairie* of the eighteenth *arrondissement* was cracking down on late-night food consumption because it was causing trouble in our *quartier chaud* — which means the dodgy area where we live. This seemed a bit rich because the other week a North African *jeune* was shot in the head by a policeman in the *commissariat* of the eighteenth *arrondissement* and nobody made much fuss. (Also, maybe the *Mairie* should be cracking down on sandwich hygiene; I once found a half moon of toenail in my chips but I never said anything.)

The next day, I called up the president of the National Union of French Bistros and Brasseries who I quoted as saying, 'Beer causes aggression, sandwiches do not. Forbidding food after 2 a.m. is all part of a big clean-up operation in the more bohemian areas of Paris. It's shameful. Imagine Edith Piaf going home at 1 a.m.'

It is obvious that nobody round our way is going to take a blind bit of notice of this new food law and I know that the police will not enforce it, but I hyped it up and sold it anyway. You always have to hype things up a little bit if you want to earn a living. *Paris Parade* rates are very low. In a good month I can earn 4,000 francs from writing, of which 2,500 must go on rent. That means 200 francs per week on food. The sardine and chips sandwich is only for special treats and I do realise that I have my health to think about. So each week I spend 100 francs at the Barbès market for potatoes, broccoli, bananas, spinach, wet fish — one plaice and a few sardines — and leeks which I will cook in various permutations along with products bought with the other 100 francs: cheese (Bleu d'Auvergne — the poor man's

Roquefort, and Comté), milk, bread (5 baguettes, one *pain intégrale*), plain yogurt.

Bet, Ann and I have been waiting for our lives to take off in Paris for a while now, but while we sometimes perceive dribs and drabs of light at the end of the tunnel, our self-sufficiency always verges on bankruptcy. Because of this, we have become entangled with a formidable woman called Madame Bourse who has skin like filo pastry topped with a light dusting of icing sugar and who dresses like Juliette Gréco in her heyday. She spends lots of tax-returnable money taking heads of companies out to lunch because she wants their staff in her cowboy language school.

If you need quick money in New York you wait tables, in London you work as a temp and in Paris you teach English. There is a ruling in all French companies that you have to spend a big percentage of your turnover on *formation continue* which means continual training. The easiest way to keep this ruling is to send all your workers off to learn English once a week.

I learnt that English teaching was not for me during my year-out in a Paris *lycée* working as an English *assistante*. I thought my pupils would like me if I tried to keep the lessons fun. For the whole year I taught from three articles from the *National Enquirer*: Michael Jackson and his oxygen tent, Madonna and how she'd survived from 'the pickings of trash cans in her down-and-out New York days', and an illustrated quiz. One of the questions was: What would you do at a party if you bent over and suddenly your trousers split? Would you a. Go home, b. Pretend it hadn't happened, c. Burst into tears. Meanwhile, the German *assistante* with yellow plaits and a smile like the lesbo sadist in *From Russia With Love* was teaching about Greenpeace and kibbutzes. In the first week, one sixteen-year-old boy in the top stream *premier* class told me it was *nul* to say what he'd do if his trousers split at a party and why couldn't I teach about Northern Ireland.

Teaching in Madame Bourse's school is even worse. It feels

like being a prostitute. You go in to work and Madame Bourse will say something to you like, 'Room number 6 with Monsieur Ruffier: French tickling and English polishing.' At least, that's what it sounds like because if she doesn't like you she makes you start at seven in the morning when your head is still in last night's silly season mode. Really what she says is, 'Room number 6 with Monsieur Ruffier: definite articles and numbers one to ten.' Definite articles and numbers one to ten means that Monsieur Ruffier is really dense and before you go in you hope that he hasn't got the morning horn because room number 6 is half the size of the kitchen at rue de Clignancourt. Starting the morning trying to explain how you pronounce 'one', 'two', 'three', five million times until cheap, black felt-tip pen is running down your arm and you wish you'd worn a higher necked T-shirt, is really not a healthy way to start the day. Madame Bourse gives Ann quite a few pervy pupils because she comes across as bright and sunny with her beaming smile and her lilting Welsh accent, even though she has been up all night smearing chocolate over the faces of half of Europe's aspiring actors. Surprise, surprise, men really get off on this virginal image and Ann often comes home complaining that her pupils have been pestering her to teach them 'dirty words' all day.

Because Madame Bourse doesn't like me, she always gives me the 'definite articles and numbers one to ten' pupils and the dumb students are too nervous to have time to be lechy. Secretly, Madame Bourse does quite like me because I naturally speak very quickly and very unclearly and all my pupils come out worrying that they are really bad at English and ask Madame Bourse for extra lessons.

My favourite pupil is Madame Vendôme, the wife of the managing director of a famous yoghurt company. She comes in for English lessons on Monday mornings before she has her weekly treatment at the *Institut de Beauté* on Avenue Montaigne. She has that Saint Tropez skin, that Saint Tropez expensive smell and she lights up cigarettes in the classroom without asking permission. She wears one of those big, silk Hermès scarves draped over her shoulders like only French women from the *seizième arrondissement* know how to wear. (*Seizième arrondissement* women look like rehashes of Munch's *The Scream*, with jewels. They think most things outside the *seizième* are '*vulgaire*', eat celery sticks as appetite suppressants with their *copines* on *terrasses* and cross their legs in a manner which they hope is reminiscent of Catherine Denude in the 1970s.)

Madame Vendôme crosses her legs like Catherine Deneuve and gives me goose pimples. Sometimes, I'll say something like, 'I think we'll do some grammar today,' and she will blow out a languid line of smoke and say, 'We will do nothing of the sort.' Then she will start to talk about how *ras le bol* she is with cocktail parties and how life was much more exciting when she was a *soixante-huitarde*. We talk in French all the time these days. She says she can't be bothered with English any more because the Australian swimming instructor she was having an affair with recently ditched her.

Teaching English is a terrible thing because you have to rub shoulders with expats who have been living in Paris too long and who now speak strange English – like saying 'the green light is on' instead of 'yes'. But the worst thing is that we can't ever be really rude to Madame Bourse because every few months, when we are bored of living off the bare essentials, Bet, Ann and I have to go back with our tail between our legs and ask for work. Even when we leave Madame Bourse in the lurch – like Bet has done now that she has decided to try her hand at temping – we always get our jobs back because, cleverly, Bet has made friends with the secretary, Joséphine.

It's not easy to be ugly in a city like Paris and frankly that is just what Joséphine is. She is cross-eyed, skinny and her two front teeth bend in opposite directions. She speaks as if she is constantly exposed to a lot of laughing gas; not that she ever laughs. She sits there digging her sharp pencil into her *agenda* and brewing bad thoughts. Some time ago she brightened up and started talking about a man. She started to take Fridays off for long weekends in Normandy and big bunches of flowers began to arrive on her desk in the mornings. She bloomed. When Bet commented on how young she was looking, Joséphine gave her lots of afternoon shifts in big rooms with pupils who were happy to sit reading *The Times* all lesson while Bet wrote letters to her friends. This lasted for about three or four weeks until Madame Bourse wanted to leave a message at Joséphine's house one Friday when she was away with her boyfriend in Normandy. Joséphine's mother answered the phone and snapped that *of course* her daughter wasn't in Normandy, that she'd never been to Normandy in her life. What boyfriend was Madame Bourse talking about? Joséphine had been here at home every weekend for the past year, at this moment she was at the market buying an *entrecôte* for their lunch and why had Madame Bourse given her the day off anyway?

Madame Bourse regaled Bet with the tale of Joséphine's non-existent boyfriend one evening. She did this because Madame Bourse is mean and twisted and only hired Joséphine so that *she* would look good in comparison. Now that Madame Bourse's Juliette Gréco scaffolding looks in danger of falling down any day, she is very pleased that the discovery of the fantasy boyfriend is making Joséphine look even ropier than ever. All in all, Madame Bourse's school is a bit sordid and sad-making.

We often make ourselves a few glasses of kir when we get home from our shifts and this usually de-stresses us and puts us in the mood to go out. Much of our monthly budget is reserved for *demis* that cost about 20 francs each, even in the cheap places where we hang out. This is why we always make sure there is a bottle of vodka in the house to top up with before we set out for the evening.

I have yet to find my perfect drug. Heroin is scary, cocaine is hard to come by and hashish is expensive – nearly a week's living allowance for a piece of dope the size of a dice. Beer bloats, red wine gives acid tummy, tequila is too trippy and Champagne leaves you with terrible bad breath and a meringue head in the morning.

There is something cheap and cheerful about vodka. It can make you feel like you're strapped to a racing-car seat going hundreds of miles an hour. Of course, vodka isn't really that honest. The good thing about vodka and orange is that it doesn't even taste of alcohol. Without the orange, vodka tastes of gasoline. But add some juice and it sounds like purring when you order one in French: *un vodka orange, vodka'ronge. Un vod korange, s'il vous plaît. Vod kor ronje,* with the velvety rumble of orrrange – *rrrange* – it could be the tender beginnings of a Jacques Brel song.

Vodka does not merely pump up your derring-do; it absorbs any ounce of reason from your brain and blasts you to a world of hyper reality where nothing seems shocking and where everything is sexy: trees, bicycles, men, more glasses of vodka orange.

It is every man for himself when the Gang is in a vodka-overload situation. One night Holly, Bet, Ann, Holly's flatmate Alex and I were so drunk that we stumbled into Joe Allen's, the hub of expat American power dining. The waiter stood impatiently for our order as we laughed cruelly about the American magazine editor whose *soirée* we had just finished terrorising. I had brought the Gang along to help me do some networking and in the course of the evening we found out that the editor only had one testicle. I ended the night pogoing round his flat singing, *I Fought The Law And The Law Won.*

'He deserved it,' Holly scoffed, 'how can you expect to have a good time drinking fizzy water all night!'

'Yeah, fizzy water,' I scoffed.

'Yeah, when you've only got one testicle, you might at least *try* to get it going!' Holly scoffed some more, banging his fists on the table like he was going to accompany me in another Clash number.

Alex bounced up and down in time to the fists. 'Yeah, and it was really good when you fell against his bookcase and it nearly collapsed all over his Tiffany lamp collection!'

'Lord, yes!' Ann giggled. 'He looked really scared!'

'Can't help but think, George,' Alex added, 'funny sort of networking you do . . .'

'Tiffany lamps!' Bet spat. 'How awful! And what a pretentious bookcase! Filled with Auden. As *if* he's ever taken Benzedrine in his life!'

Holly grabbed a chip from the plate of the executive type giving him the eye at the next table. 'Yeah, Auden,' he munched. 'A poet who got it going.'

'Ball zac!' Alex chuckled.

'What's Benzedrine?' Ann asked.

'It's what Bet's going to take when she has sex with a woman,' Alex announced like a naughty boy.

Bet went red and clipped Alex lightly round the head. 'Stop being such a gayboy! I don't want a woman, I'm seeing Sam.'

'Charming!' Alex said, prodding Bet's breasts with his fork. 'I think you'll find that you made a pledge last Beaujolais Nouveau night to do it with a woman before you were forty. She did, didn't she, George?'

'Well, I'm only twenty-three so I've got ages yet. Anyway, look what I've got,' and Bet opened her velvet purse and took out an embossed card. 'One Testicle gave it to me! He said he was going to Rome next week for a story. He said maybe I'd like to come with him. Can you believe it! He said I was a "funny little thing".'

There was a collective shriek of laughter. And then I vomited all over the table. Naturally, the fierceness of the vodka suffocated any feelings of mortification as I watched the watery green wave studded with peanut shards and orange blobs spread across the cloth towards the waiter who was speechless with horror.

Bet said: 'Oh my God.'

Ann said: 'Oh poor George.'

Alex said: 'Cool.'

Holly went very pale, folded his serviette up daintily like a perfectly trained footman and said, 'I hope you all have a very nice evening.' He staggered almost gracefully to the door as Bet screeched furiously after him, 'Holly, you're so bloody ineffectual!' while she tried to dam the swell of sick with a wall of sodden napkins.

CHAPTER THREE

The Gaultier Party

———————>•◇•<———————

Holly is beautiful. He has blue eyes that want to be loved. Of course, they are contained in a body encased in spiky wit and bitchy bonhomie, and when I first met him I thought him a spiteful gayboy who would hurt anyone's feelings for a good one-liner or a ripple of laughter from his uglier and better behaved group of admirers.

My first meeting with him was down to Bet. During her first week in Paris she spotted Alex on the métro and thought she recognised him as the boy with blue hair from her school in Bournemouth. When she introduced herself, Alex recognised her immediately as the catty girl from the upper fourth who used to make other girls cry. She invited him to the *Soirée Goa Boa* and told him to bring someone interesting. 'You're not going to frighten him, are you?' Alex said with a slight glint in his eye, and Bet smiled back and said, 'We'll have to see about that.'

But it was Holly who frightened me. That night at the Rex I was wearing my cherry skirt. I had bought it from Dorothy Perkins just before I came to live in Paris. It was very short, black checked and covered with a red fruit print. It was nice for Dorothy Perkins. When Holly arrived he looked really snooty. He made me feel fat and uncomfortable when he looked at me and he seemed more interested in talking to Bet.

So with the feistiness of spirit of my twenty-second year, I decided he was just a shallow fashion person and I went home early. He called me a week later sounding slightly cross. 'Hello, it's Holly. I met you last week at the Rex. I've got a spare ticket for the Gaultier party if you want to come. It's tonight. Should be good.' He sounded very formal. Like a protective older brother who feels obliged to take you out for dinner on your birthday. I could tell that he'd only invited me because his intended guest had dropped out at the last moment. But I was bored and curious and convinced my future lay just around the corner.

'Okay,' I said, smiling down the phone line. 'But I warn you, I haven't got anything to wear.'

In the event, it was Holly whose outfit proved unsuitable for the Jean-Paul Gaultier party where the theme was the Wild West. As we waited in the queue at Le Palace nightclub, listening to a man in front of us talking about another man who wanted to pee in his mouth ('with him, there was something weird about it'), we became aware of crowds of people pushing against the barriers on either side of us. In the absence of invitations, these people had decided that jeering the invited guests was the best option left open to them. 'Eh!' a pale boy on the other side of the railings started shouting at Holly. 'That's no cowboy, it's Snow White!'

I turned to look at Holly's second-hand Jasper Conran blazer and his cream cashmere trousers with 10-inch turn-ups. Like the pale boy, I too wondered what kind of cowboy he'd come as. I knew that his trousers were cashmere and that his jacket was second-hand Jasper Conran because that was the only conversation we'd had when we met outside Bonne Nouvelle métro. Someone had put chewing gum on the métro seat where he was sitting and he mumbled moodily all the way to the entrance of Le Palace about what a vulgar city Paris was.

Now, Holly found himself flanked by vulgarity. Le Palace

is an old music hall where Maurice Chevalier and the French stripper Mistinguet began their careers and it still lives off the reputation it had when the likes of Karl Lagerfeld, Yves Saint Laurent and Andy Warhol turned it into the Studio 54 of early 1980s Paris. These days it welcomes fans of contemporary musical heroes like Sam Fox and Rick Astley, and the surrounding Bonne Nouvelle area has become tacky – crêpe stands serving up stale hot-dogs and dried-up pizzas, car loads of cruising men up from the suburbs, tourists with big maps asking for directions to the Folies Bergères. If you are going to Le Palace the thing is to get in as quickly as possible. But the queue had stagnated and the competition on both sides of the barrier to see who could jeer the loudest at Holly's outfit was growing in intensity. Holly blushed deeply and kept flicking his head – as if he had some hair there and it wasn't covered with a blue checked scarf. This prissy movement, of course, occasioned more hilarity until the atmosphere became what the French call *une galère* – meaning 'a real bugger of a situation' – an image drawn from the slave galley ships where, you are supposed to imagine, all hell was let loose down below in a haze of sweat and tears and puke and whips and the mother of all hullabaloos.

I was starting to get nervous. I stood on tiptoe to crane over the heads of the other cowboys and see how much longer we'd have to wait. Just behind the bouncers I noticed a porky cherub wearing a pink Shirley Temple wig, a rhinestone-encrusted Stetson, a black rubber mini skirt, a transparent pink blouse and glittery red moon boots. I breathed a sigh of relief. It was Kiki.

I met Kiki at *Paris Parade* where she was trying to sell some illustrations. She told me how she was planning to become a famous gogo dancer or a painter and make her gynaecologist parents back in Stockholm proud of her. She is addicted to diet pills, gay men and latex clothing of all types.

Once, she'd invited me back to her flat in the Bastille together with four gay men friends. She served four bottles of chilled vodka and a portion of Marks and Spencers *Pommes de Terre Dauphinoises* between the six of us, rushed off to the bathroom with a pill bottle in her hand, and came back buzzing with the news that she'd run out of talcum powder and would therefore be unable to perform the promised rubber fashion show. But like the trooper she was, she agreed to slake our disappointment by showing us some of the prized paintings she had been working on for the past months. Her favourite was of a Siamese cat standing on its hind legs outside a monastery, rubbing a pink feather boa between its thighs.

I began waving at Kiki. When she recognised me, she squealed and rushed out to grab my arm and pull me through the long line of impatient cowboys up to the very entrance of Le Palace. Holly held on to my arm and was pulled up too. 'Okay! Okay!' Kiki sang in the direction of the bouncers as she marched us past the main doors. When we were standing inside the dark entrance hall, Kiki said, 'I'm so sorry I didn't get you in before! I didn't recognise you.' By way of explanation, she added, 'There are things going on in my head.'

The *Soirée Wild West* was not the Wild West in the strictest sense of the term. The lobsters clawing their way out of silver *bain maries* seemed to have come to the wrong party and so had many of the guests. Most of the men in the room looked like pumped-up Tintins with white T-shirts and a little lick of gel on the tiny curl at the front of their cropped hair. Instead of hatching plots to rescue buried treasure they expatiated with men of similar aesthetic market value about concepts: concepts for hair, concepts for making money, concepts for sexual positions. To every concept their friends came up with, the Tintins would swizzle their hands in the air gasping, '*Mais, c'est la folie!*' which means 'that's madness' in the ordinary world but at a fashion party it is a concept referring to the trivial goings on that make life worth living.

When we entered Le Palace, Holly looked slightly dazed at the abundance of beautiful waiters and beautiful food. He announced that he was going to 'flamboyantly not eat', and scooped up two glasses of Champagne from a tray being carried by a waiter dressed as Roy Rogers. He swigged them both back as he stared at a man brandishing a couple of banana pistols, clad in silver leggings and a Stetson, posing for a photographer. I went over to a never-ending *bain marie* counter where a white-coated waiter asked me if I'd like a half or a whole lobster. I said that I'd like a bit of everything if that was possible and the waiter handed me back a plate filled with all manner of splayed crustacea. When I'd fought my way back over to Holly's side, he was being topped up again by another waiter dressed as Roy Rogers. '*That* is the best looking man in the world, ever,' Holly said slowly when Roy had gone. 'Even the ugly ones look like the beautiful ones at this party.' He watched me pick at some corn bread on my plate and said, 'Rule number one, Calamity Jane, you feel much sexier on an empty stomach.'

He offered me one of the glasses of Champagne and sighed. 'The only time I ever let myself go is when I'm out to dinner with an ex. Going out with your ex is a sign of complete social incompetence but at least it means you don't have to order fish and salad off the menu.'

He picked a peeled prawn from my plate, bit the tail off and put the rest into my mouth. Our eyes met for the first time all night and we both grinned with relief.

'Meanwhile,' Holly said, 'I mean to make this evening a *soirée* of complete social competence. I'm just wondering who'd work best on the conversation front.'

His gaze suddenly stopped in the middle of the room. Barely moving his lips, he said, 'There's a man with a school-teacher haircut and a shirt under his waistcoat talking to that woman with really bad skin.' I watched the man's eyes darting over towards Holly as he nodded distractedly at the woman's animated conversation.

'Puh!' Holly snorted, holding his gaze. 'He's hardly super-sonic trade but he looks like a good one to warm up with. I'm not sure, but I think there might be something quite sexy about ordinariness, in the right context.'

Holly says that because we're younger than most of the people we go to parties with, we come at the top of some sort of hierarchy. The fact of our topping this ill-defined hierarchy also makes it okay for us to stagger around being rude to people. 'Stagger' is a key point in Holly's world. He is always 'staggering home', and 'staggering to a rendez-vous', and 'staggering to a job interview', although he doesn't do that much of the latter. Holly wants to be the next Yves Saint Laurent but in his honest moments he will admit that he has a fatal flaw. An ex of his – a Dickensian Dutch boy called Nicolas – is nearly a famous fashion designer because, as Holly says, he doesn't live life as if he will turn into a pumpkin if he doesn't have anonymous sex every night. As well as making up far-fetched tales about illustrious roots, Nicolas chooses to spend at least three evenings a week eating elaborate *pâtisseries* in *deuxième empire* rooms filled with old Russian ladies, antique lace antimacassars and the smell of poodle farts in the cause of rustling up a few future *couture* customers.

'Hi ho, Silver!' Holly pronounced in an exaggerated northern English accent as he took my hand and led me across the odd-looking prairie to the man who looked even less like a cowboy than Holly.

'Hello,' Holly drawled to the man with the school-teacher haircut. Knowing his own power, he stood almost directly in front of the woman with bad skin and a bleached bob that moved like a helmet, completely blocking her view of the school teacher. She stuttered, '*Bah, alors . . .*' but the school teacher merely bid her a curt, '*A bientôt*' and feasted his eyes on Holly.

'*Bonsoir. Vous travaillez pour Gaultier?*' he said quickly.

'Puh! Talk about work when we're at a party! We want to know what kind of cowboy you've come as.'

The only bit of French Holly claims for his English speech concept is the 'puh!' sound that punctuates most of his sentences when he is on a roll. His 'puh!' is a bastardised form of the contemptuous French 'puh!' — a brief exhalation of air passed through briefly vibrating lips which, when accompanied by a shrug of the shoulders and a slight raising of the hands, denotes an elegantly streetwise *ennui*.

As the man opened his mouth, Holly held his collection of Champagne glasses in the air and signalled again to one of the Roy Rogers.

'Oh, you know,' he said in clear English, 'I am just a bit player.'

'You play with bits?' Holly slurred theatrically, swinging a hip towards the school teacher.

'I have played many things in my time.'

'So, you'll know what the three Rs are then.'

The man looked Holly in the eye with the nearest thing to a twinkle that I have ever seen.

'I think you are about to tell me,' he said softly.

'Rogering, rimming and rooting,' Holly pronounced.

'You'd better tell him what rooting means,' I chipped in, gaining confidence as I watched Holly at work.

'Rooting,' Holly carried on, 'is that long vein thing that lies between the cock and the bum hole. You have to nibble on it lightly like this,' and he mimed eating a hot piece of corn on the cob.

Holly has the knack of knowing who will enjoy being abused by him. He instinctively knows which men will not kick his head in for saying the things which are well beyond the boundaries of acceptability. I had no experience of being this rude to anyone before but Holly made it fun.

'Do you like Holly's trousers?' I looked the man in the eye.

'I think your friend is very beautiful,' he smiled, looking Holly straight in the crotch.

In his attempt to react with cool, Holly spilled the rest of his Champagne on the cream cashmere trousers. He gave a loud, horsey 'puh!', linked his arm through mine and made a big stage exit towards the bar. Once there, he looked slyly over his shoulder at the man.

'Oh, well, if nothing else turns up,' he sighed, looking pleased.

Sitting at the bar I asked Holly why he had a girl's name. He said that Holly was a nickname short for Holly Golightly. 'Or rather, "Holly-scrape-the-bottom-of-the-barrel-at-3 a.m.-in-a-clammy-nightclub-when-you're-looking-for-a-husband."'

He said that at 3 a.m. in a clammy nightclub, everyone wished they were married and then he told me other things. That the small loops on the back of a jacket meant that it was by Gaultier, that Valentino was divine, that Thierry Mugler was demented, that Marithé Girbaud was for florists and hairdressers, that *Chevalier de la Rosette* meant botty bandit or, literally, horseman of the ass hole, that real models walked – as he demonstrated – by placing their feet like they were walking on a tightrope, that the correct way to apply lipstick was 'lipstick, blot, powder', 'lipstick, blot, powder', 'lipstick, blot, powder' – three times – so you could snog the whole of the football team and it would still stay on, and that you could get a whole bottle of La Villageoise red wine for only 5 francs at the ED supermarket.

Then he turned all his attention to the barman. Now that it was 3 a.m. and alcohol was no longer free, Holly was pulling all the stops out. 'Oh, that's interesting,' he was saying languidly.

'Yes, I learnt many things there,' came the barman's voice.

'Mmm. Can't say I've ever been to Clacton.'

'You know, in France, they fail to recognise the art of the great cocktail.'

'Yes, but you've obviously mastered the art of it. I think I might have to try another of your very fine Margueritas.'

'Margueritas! *Tu sais*, the first time I make one of these in the college of Clacton, they suggest to serve with a bowl of fruit and nuts. Never have I forgotten that.' He tossed an empty tonic bottle in the air and caught it by the neck in a quick-draw cowboy manoeuvre.

'Really?' Holly said weakly, pushing his glass back towards the barman. 'Fruit and nuts?'

Then the barman hissed in a deep, oily voice, 'In Clacton they call tarts to people like you.'

Holly made a loud 'puh!' and said in a peevish voice, 'Let's drink to Clacton then, chérie.'

As he clinked glasses with the barman, a middle-aged man and a young woman with a palm tree of blonde hair came up to stand next to me. The man squeezed the woman on the arm and said, 'We believe that if Renoir were alive today he would be working for *Playboy*.'

The man had glazed eyes that hadn't been to sleep for at least two days. They looked like halved berries that had been left out in the sun or under the glare of disco lights for too long. The man and the woman kissed each other on the cheek and the woman walked off into the crowd. As the man waited for the barman's attention he hummed to the song playing in the background.

Been around the world and ay, ay, ay, I can't find my baby ...

His surfeit of hair gel suggested a lack of sincerity. When he smiled at me, he revealed a set of teeth stained the colour of the worst by-products of the alimentary canal.

'*Bonsoir, charmante mademoiselle*,' he said.

'Salut,' I nodded, taking another swig of drink.

'I have seen that you are an observer of life,' he said. 'This, I like. This, it pleases me. You are a philosopher perhaps, like myself?'

I don't know when, I don't know why ... why he's gone away and ...

'You could say that I was in the *milieu artistique*,' I said, noticing that his mouth was shaped like a fish's.

'*Ah, mais c'est parfait!*' he exclaimed. He took a brief sip of whisky through a straw and said, 'Let me introduce myself. I think of myself as an old Cartesian – despite my brief dalliance with Zen Buddhism during my *soixante-huitard* days. I currently specialise in charm photographs. I think that this type of work will be very interesting for you.'

When I said that I preferred Sartre to Descartes, he began to laugh wistfully and said, '*Mais oui! La Nausée*. Nausea, Nausea, Nausea,' as if Nausea was a long-lost friend. Then he said, 'Beware the fungus, *mademoiselle*.'

'Fungus?'

'Mushrooms and moss and dark, rank things that swell and proliferate. Consider the tree that Roquentin ponders, the tree trunk that suddenly explodes with the contingency of being, the terrible tree which takes on new and terrifying life and sprouts inexorably. Consider that, *mademoiselle*.'

I did too much lying, wasted too much time, now I hear him crying . . . ay, ay, ay . . . been around the world and ay, ay, ay, I can't find my baby . . .

I wondered whether, in so many words, the Old Cartesian was asking me back to his place for a session of charm photos. Then he spoke again. 'Only the other day, I felt a fungus patch growing in my stomach. A patch of fear that radiated red despair to my very belly. "What if this is all there is to life?" I asked myself. "What if death is like a plug being yanked out of an electric socket and this is how I have spent my days?"'

Been around the world and ay, ay, ay . . . Been around the world and ay, ay, ay . . .

'That is why I have dedicated my life to an area that burns bright, that scorns the shadow of the valley of death. I have always been outspoken. We are all free human beings, yet freedom is a terrifying prospect for some.'

He swayed slightly as he turned to pick up his whisky. 'You have heard, perhaps, of the Theatre of Sexuality?'

'No,' I said, thinking that Ann had probably already met the Old Cartesian on the Champs Elysées.

He hesitated momentarily before putting his hand on my leg and saying in a thick voice, 'You have the thighs of a dancer. They would be very well received on the international charm market.'

I was considering which part of him could be considered in any way attractive – his lips maybe – when I suddenly realised that I felt quite sick. On top of the Nausea, all the Old Cartesian's talk of red mould reminded me of the quantities of red lobster claws I had downed not two hours ago. I no longer saw his eyes or nose or mouth. I looked at the Old Cartesian's face and I just saw bristly shrimp whiskers and sopping clam shells and orange crab meat swilling around in a soup of vodka and orange all over his porridge-crust skin, and then I saw toilet bowls there.

I lifted his hand off my leg, put my index finger into the middle air and mumbled something about coming back in a minute. He raised his glass to me as I slid off the bar stool and began the monumental task of walking down the stairs towards the toilets.

Downstairs was quite like soup too. A soup of blurred colours and thumping base line bubbling with chunks of shiny face and muscly arm and luminous T-shirt. When I finally located the toilets, the queue was so long that I groaned and crouched down on the floor to reflect on my next move. Then I saw a glowing green sign that said 'Exit', quite near to where I was. I threw myself against the bar of the door and soon found myself in a narrow back alley vomiting lobster flesh over a row of plastic rubbish bins. As I surfaced for air and wiped the last string of sticky green bile from my lips, I glanced further down the alley and saw a couple of men getting it going – one had his face buried in the zipper of a blond man's trousers.

I was glad to see that this party seemed to be taking off.

Throwing up had made me feel jubilant and it was refreshing to step back from the alley through the emergency exit into the cauldron of soup the other side. On my way back to the bar, I stopped at the bottom of the stairs to watch Kiki who was now performing on a podium near the dance floor. She was dressed in leopard attire, leaping around like an unbalanced cheerleader, lashing her tail at the men watching her, panting rhythmically as she blurted out a strange chant:

'Skin gleam, thigh high,
sex god, green light,
slick back, hot shot
fuck
me
skin
deep.'

After a while she was joined by a boy who suddenly leapt up next to her and started to dance. It can't have been an easy leap since from his neck down to the top of his thighs he was wearing what looked like a huge, padded, red yoghurt pot. Around his neck was a green velvet ruff cut into spiky leaf shapes and on his head was a black cap stuck with dozens of ping-pong balls. On top of that a pair of deely boppers flashed and cast red shadows over his face which was plastered in white foundation and crimson lipstick. The pot of – presumably strawberry – yoghurt danced with its back to Kiki although she, her sweaty face now streaked with black mascara and dripping whiskers, did her best to get its attention by digging her claws into its squashy red middle.

As I swayed from side to side watching the performance, a pair of big wiry spectacles suddenly loomed up in front of my face. The pair of eyes behind them looked as screwy as a couple of coiled springs and the figure's anorak, blighted all over with zips and flags and badges, rustled like a tent as it came towards me. It seemed strange how we'd both focused in on each other just at that moment so I closed my eyes and waited for his mouth.

The kiss was dark and warm and slippery. I pulled away when it began to get lizardy.

'Ça va, toi?' his stringy voice enquired, kind of pointlessly. I was already tugging at his zip. Just as I made contact with a pair of clatty boxer shorts I felt a claw scratch my arm. I turned to see Kiki's anxious face.

'It is terrible,' she burst out, her top lip wobbling.

Then the huge pot of strawberry yoghurt came up and grabbed her by the tail. In a big, nancy-boy French accent he started screaming at Kiki: 'Eh alors! Et alors!' His rouged lips twisted with fury and his deely boppers flashed. 'Where was the fruit ensemble for goodness sake? Was it totally beyond you to remember the fruit ensemble? How many times did I tell you this morning that we were fruit this evening? How many times? Me strawberry, you peach! Even you shouldn't have found that too difficult. So where is your peach, Kiki? What is this leopard shit? This leopard shit is for Wednesday evenings as you know very well!' You expected that any minute he was going to say that he'd never had to put up with this when he danced with Nureyev but he just spat, 'You're so . . . so—'

Kiki began to whimper hopelessly but luckily there was no time for the yoghurt pot to come up with an adjective because he was suddenly grabbed from behind by one of the Tintins. When Tintin's pumped-up arms had turned the padded pot around and pulled him to his white T-shirt, he kissed him violently on the mouth. Tintin took the yoghurt off by the hand and soon they vanished, swallowed up by the furious dancing soup. Kiki started to tremble.

The man in the anorak was, I saw, now swaying to and fro. He seemed even nearer to unconsciousness than I was so I put my arm around Kiki's hot, rubbery shoulders, staggered past the swaying man and started levering her upstairs.

When we reached the bar, I sat her down next to Holly who raised an eyebrow when he saw me. Kiki grabbed Holly's gin and tonic and gulped it down. Then she burst into tears and began telling Holly about the scene downstairs.

'I know I should have brought my peach costume, my peach costume is beautiful. It is orange PVC. But you know, ever since my yeast infection it is no good for me to wear it. How many times have I told Stéphane this. I have told him: the press-studs come very high up – up to here.'

Holly's lip had curled when Kiki mentioned her yeast infection but when she offered him a swig from the hip flask that she drew out of one of her moon boots, he straightened his face and decided to try to shut her up with a piece of advice.

'Listen, luvvie,' he said. 'I know that in Sweden you all walk around with no clothes on talking about vaginal discharges and measuring out how many dessertspoon-fulls of blood you lose every month but you have to understand that you're never going to win an argument with a gayboy with that sort of talk. Gayboys find that sort of thing very frightening indeed. All they want girls to do is wear more make-up and get drunk with them in bars until a better-looking boy comes along.'

Kiki's eyes were becoming bigger and bigger. She said: 'You think that Stéphane is gay?'

Holly made a big Hilda Ogden 'puh!' before fishing around in his pocket and pulling out a serviette with a phone number scribbled in one corner in blue biro. He gave it to Kiki who dabbed her hot cherub cheeks. The melting leopard whiskers were soon replaced with faint ink smudges.

It was almost a relief when the Old Cartesian came over and handed me a glass of vodka and orange. I threw him a smile and left Holly to deal with Kiki.

'*Alors*, and how is *La Nausée*?' he said.

'Okay,' I smiled. Then I said, 'How old are you then?'

Something like terror shot into his eyes and he said, 'I see that you are sharp, sharp as a knife, *mademoiselle*. I think that we were meant to meet this evening.'

He looked at my dancer's legs again and said, 'The trappings of youth are on loan to us, *mademoiselle*, but nobody tells us that until the letter comes through the post on our fortieth birthday. You may not choose to open it, but the bailiffs always come round in the end to take away the beautiful things.

'Today I saw a glove on the rue de Rivoli. A woolly red glove that had been dropped and abandoned. The thumb was twisted grotesquely to one side. And people just walked over it. Just walked over it. It makes me sad when I see abandoned clothes. Very sad. So sad. I felt the mould growing again and everything grew fuzzy.'

The Old Cartesian was rapidly turning out to be a lunatic so I glanced over to Kiki and Holly who were still chatting at the bar together. Judging by the shivery rises and falls of Kiki's shoulders, Holly's efforts at cheering her up weren't going very well.

'So, what about the Theatre of Sexuality?' I drawled, turning back to the Old Cartesian who I reckoned was about fifty.

'Talk rather of the Cuisine of Sexuality,' he said with a slight rise of the eyebrow. 'Tinned vaginas,' he continued. 'Tinned vaginas would be my dish of preference. Snap them up, buy in bulk, take them home and suck at your leisure.'

I wasn't sure quite which level of reality the Old Cartesian was operating on but now seemed a good a time as any to see what he was made of. My right hand shot out like a bullet and hooked on to his testicles which I began squeezing sceptically as if they were under-ripe avocados, not yet ready for the plucking.

Pathetic, I thought, as he lifted my hand away in a panic and said with a flicker in his eye, 'Let us discuss things more clearly in another place.'

Suddenly, the man downstairs in the anorak seemed a very

attractive prospect. I headed back towards the stairs as the Old Cartesian clutched his straw and whined incoherently behind me.

I didn't see him immediately. The fresh alcohol on an empty stomach had made my vision start to go blurry again. What I most wanted to do was dance, to be the best dancer on the dance floor and I knew I would be. Aside from my new rave dance technique I was wearing my special hooded purple rave top with silver zigzags, bought from Mr Byrite, and my 40 franc fake DMs – bought from the theatre converted into a shoe cash and carry just off the rue de Clignancourt. A nail started to come through the sole of the left boot a week after purchase but with two pairs of socks on you almost didn't notice. Tonight, I could have been standing on a bed of nails and I wouldn't have felt a thing. Tonight, I knew that the whole room was jealous of me and my fantastic dance technique. I knew that the gayboys were thinking of changing sexuality as they watched me from the corner of their eyes and the straight boys would see a blade of individuality in me that would make them want to cast off their women of the night and come home with me. And the women. The women would by now all be wishing that they were wearing zigzag rave tops and army boots instead of mini skirts and skinny heels. They would probably try subtly to integrate some snaky arm motions and lolling head movements into their boring hip thrusts and stupid lip pouts.

Never gonna give you up, never gonna let you down, never gonna run around and desert you . . .

I closed my eyes and saw myself being Rick Astley at the Parc des Princes stadium in front of thousands of people, a hairbrush at my mouth and a mirror to look into when I tired of looking at so many people. I glanced around occasionally to check I was still in the middle of the dance floor, to check that my technique was still changing the lives of the people all around me.

*Never gonna make you cry, never gonna say good bye, never gonna tell
a lie and hurt you ...*

When I opened my eyes I saw him there, standing in front
of me, looking the same strange mixture of the unremarkable
and the sinister as he had the last time I'd seen him. He was
jogging from one foot to the other like he was waiting for a bus
in the rain. When he moved his legs I saw flashes of faded red
and blue boxer shorts through his zipper which was still open
from the last time.

Never gonna give! Never gonna give!

When he saw me looking at his flies he moved nearer,
slapped his hands down on my buttocks and pulled me towards
his open zip. I liked it. I liked his confidence and I liked the
ache which started to grow between my legs. Now I wasn't
even looking at his face. My chin nestled in the hollow of his
neck, my hands massaged his buttocks as I looked out to the
undulating dance floor. All the energy from his rain dance had
rushed to his groin as he thrust himself against me. We pressed
and squashed at the crotch until I spread my legs wider and
gripped his buttocks harder as he slammed his stiff cock into
the groin of my jeans and through my jeans I rubbed myself
closer into him. Even Sam Fox's latest record couldn't put me
off this one and when in frustration I realised that he was never
going to get inside me, I put my hand through his zip and felt
the warm thickness through the worn cotton of his boxers.

Touch me now! Touch me now! I wanna feel your body!

I slipped my hand through the narrow gap and felt his
cock. The whole package inside was warm and soggy like a fish
supper choked to death in a pall of salt and vinegar. When I slid
my hand down towards the root and began tickling his flaccid
bollocks they felt icy moist with disco sweat. Remembering
Holly's definition of the root I trained two fingers under his
balls towards his ass hole. Whatever it was I located didn't
feel like corn on the cob but when I brushed it, back and
forth, Holly's prediction seemed about right. Anorak brought

his head back from my shoulder and, with a look between awe and terror in his swirly eyes, began to whimper.

I ripped open my own zip and grabbing hold of his swelling cock I rubbed it up and down and all around my lathering bits. Our breath became harsher as our hot genitals battered against each other with increasing urgency.

Your heart beat next to mine ...!

I closed my eyes. I was no longer wanking off a trainspotter in the middle of a nightclub floor, I had a desirable stranger on my brown sheets on my bed at rue de Clignancourt and I was going to make him my slave. When I occasionally opened my eyes I saw the alarmed faces of the Tintins and the bopping girls in mini skirts looking at us with frowns and open mouths. I knew they thought we were really cool and just to show off I raised my right hand to my mouth with a flourish, licked my palm with the gravitas of a magician about to yank a rabbit from a hat, then brought it back down to his weeping penis and listened to him moan even more helplessly as I jerked him off with such force that I elbowed a man next to me in the stomach. The man said, 'Eh! Eh!' as if I'd really upset him and when I turned I saw that he was wearing an orange-lined black bomber jacket — the uniform of Parisian nightclub bouncers.

The bouncer's Etcha Sketch eyebrows and his monstrous bulk made him look like a Sumo wrestler. I couldn't really hear what he was saying, but he pointed dramatically to the Anorak's sticking-out penis. Anorak tucked himself in and started to slope off but the huge bouncer grabbed him by the hood and brought him back, rustling, to stand by his side. Then he started waggling a furious finger at me in a rush of words. The only ones I could determine were *dégueulasse* and *police*. And then, incredibly, in the middle of the bouncer's furious spiel, Holly suddenly appeared in the company of another big man wearing an orange-lined bomber jacket. The Sumo wrestler grabbed a handful of my rave top and most of Anorak's hood and hauled both of us up through the crowds which parted like a jagged rip in the dance floor. When we arrived at the place where Holly was standing, another doorman appeared from nowhere so that by the time we reached the exit we each had personal bouncers to take us by the scruff of the neck and chuck us from the Gaultier party into the dirty street ouside.

Although Holly is normally very good at being rude to people and getting away with it, when he is drunk he is an expert at misjudging the mood completely. I only realised that Holly had misjudged our current predicament when the sound of a wet fish smacking a slab hit the early morning air. When I turned to Holly I realised that he had been punched on the cheek by his personal bouncer. Holly had made the mistake of looking the bouncer in the eye and saying, 'Take your hands off me you big, fat git,' with an emphasis on the word 'fat'. The only positive thing to come from the situation was that the kerfuffle gave Anorak the time to bolt from the scene. Holly and I watched him scarpering in a wobbly zigzag motion in the direction of the Folies Bergères.

Luckily, Holly was more outraged by Anorak's escape than he was by the slap to his face which had merely served to sober him up. 'Can you credit it!' he said. 'Trust my luck that some ugly, good-for-nothing anorak wearer gets away Scot free while the most fantastic pair of cashmere trousers ever to grace the Palace end up sitting wounded on the steps of a pizza kiosk.'

It wasn't entirely unpredictable that he and I should find ourselves sitting on the grubby steps of a pizza kiosk. It turned out that while I had been trying to re-enact the fall of Babylon on the downstairs dance floor, Kiki had become paralytically drunk at the bar with Holly who had then allowed her to wander off into the Parisian night when his famous five-second pull technique suddenly worked with the cowboy with the banana pistols and silver leggings. Kiki ended up passed out on the back seats of a coach taking a load of student clubbers back to Manchester. As the coach hit the Périphérique, she was woken up by the sound of taut latex being snapped back on to soft flesh (her own), by a group of students who recognised her from her leopard number earlier on in the evening. Unfortunately, the bus driver refused to turn back no matter how loudly she protested that Stéphane would be waiting furiously for her on her podium in only five minutes.

The Clacton-trained barman denounced Holly as the one responsible for Kiki's absence since, he said, Holly had been the one talking to her all night. The barman couldn't care less about Kiki. What he cared about was the fact that Holly had started calling him a 'naff old queen', under the influence of several of his Long Island Iced Teas, a little too heavy on the tequila for Holly's own good.

But Holly's mind was still dwelling on the Anorak. 'He had those beer bungs tied on to his button holes,' he said incredulously, rubbing his jaw and looking more like a real cowboy than he had done all night. 'Those beer bungs with metal bits on the side that plug up bottles of ale. Dangling they were! All over his rancid anorak!' and he made the loudest 'puh!' that I had heard him make all night. Then he sighed, cradled his jaw in his hand and said contemptuously, 'Anorak.' Then again, he said, 'Anorak,' before adding out of nowhere, 'my anorak got set fire to on a bus once.'

The rowdy pizza kiosk suddenly seemed to go quiet. Holly made his statement so matter-of-factly that I wasn't sure whether to enquire first about the style of anorak or to ask where the bus was going at the time. 'Bus' seemed the interesting point so I said, 'What bus?'

'The school bus.'

There was silence again. I said, 'Why did they set fire to you?'

'Why?' Holly glared as if it was obvious why they'd set fire to him. He lit a cigarette and drew on it.

'I was wearing one of those Parker anoraks – green with grey rabbit fur around the hood. Not overly trendy, you'd have thought, to wear in a Yorkshire comprehensive in 1978.

I was sitting on one of the back seats at the time. It was the only place left on the whole bus. I sort of wanted to sit there because of its dangerous connotations but I was scared too because the seats next to me were filled up with the meanest boys in the school.'

'And what happened?'

'Somebody sniggered, "There's a funny smell." Then I put my hand to my neck and burnt my hand.'

'But who did it to you?'

'A really sexy boy, actually. Greasy yellow hair. Always with a fag in his mouth. King of the back of the bus. I pretended to be unconcerned so that he'd think I was hard. But then I realised that the hood was burning up quite quickly, so I had to whip the coat off and thrash it about like mad on the back of my seat.'

He started to straighten his blue bandanna. 'It has to be said though,' he sighed, 'I was very impressed. As I flailed around with my anorak for the best part of five minutes with all the bullies in the school laughing their heads off at me, I remember thinking that I wish I'd been cool enough to set fire to someone's coat.'

Holly smiled shyly then stood up and started picking at the stains on his trousers which now included chewing gum, Champagne, Long Island Iced Tea and back-alley muck around the knees.

CHAPTER FOUR

The Gang

Holly and Alex live five minutes down the hill from rue de Clignancourt at number 10 rue Léon. In every city in the world there are a handful of streets where taxi drivers refuse to go and where people with routine lives shudder and tell you never to set foot. In Paris, the rue Léon is just such a street. It intersects with the rue Goutte d'Or whose profile has changed little since the nineteenth century when Zola evoked it in *Nana* as a heartland of washer women, benighted robbers and tarts with hearts. Today, it is still home to hotels that charge by the hour, but most of the shops reflect the needs of the new inhabitants.

The area is a maze of streets lined with sheep's heads, pigs' trotters and chucked-out furniture; the air is filled with smells of coriander, stale piss and *merguez* sausages which mingle with sounds of arguments in Arabic and rickety rai music played on cheap stereos. Hair shops catering for afro hair predominate. Their windows are filled with polystyrene women's heads in nylon wigs and they don't stop at hair. Next to boxes of *Main de Fatma* henna with drawings of belly dancers on the front, you see fading tins of imported Bird's custard with packaging from the 1970s and sticky trays of syrupy Algerian buns. Sometimes, when taxi drivers are driving tourists through Barbès they tell them that the area is '*le Paris folklorique*'.

The backbone of the area — the boulevard Barbès — is filled

with warehouses selling every variety of kitsch object and cheaply designed household appliance imaginable. On sunny days, the streets wink with the fake gold and brass of pans and kettles and trinkets and knick-knacks and teeth. On rainy days when every pore of the *quartier* is waterlogged and the wind slaps you around the face like a wet nappy, then the boulevard Barbès feels like a Magrebin Scarborough.

Ten rue Léon has been heavily influenced by boulevard Barbès. There is a 3-D Jesus cuckoo clock and a Koran-themed rhinestone tissue-box holder as well as a brunch bar which Alex picked up in the Clignancourt flea market for only 300 francs. It has a fake Fraggonard front showing some lambs watching an idealised peasant on a swing although I personally am more impressed by the washing machine that stands next to it. It is Alex whose budget has chiefly financed the décor of 10 rue Léon. Holly only works two days a week teaching pattern cutting at the Parsons School of Fashion and Alex seems to subsidise the rest of his life. Because of this power dynamic, it is Alex who sleeps in the flat's one bedroom while Holly sleeps on a thin mattress down by the cooker and gets up every morning looking, he says, like he had a stroke in the night.

Alex has curly hair, sexy eyes and a complex about having a big bum. He can come across as puerile, but the truth of the matter is that he is the only person in the Gang with a proper job so he relaxes by acting like a toddler prodigy as soon as he gets off work. The first time Holly took me to rue Léon, we bumped into him in Barbès market. He gave me a brusque once over, nodded a polite 'Hello,' then turned to Holly and said worriedly, 'Can't get any Jimmy coriander.' When he shot off in the direction of the *moules* stall Holly raised his eyes to the sky and invited me back to dinner.

The Jimmy coriander was for *Moules Marinières* because Alex's drive doesn't stop at wanting to be the best designer in the world, he is also determined to be an accomplished cook. During dinner at their apartment in 10 rue Léon, I said how impressed I was with the *moules* and Alex began reciting the recipe – garlic, onion, a glass of white wine, salt and pepper, boil for five minutes and make sure you don't eat the ones that don't open up – when suddenly he stopped and said, 'Show us yer boosies then.'

Alex looked over at Holly, and like two tear-away eight-year-olds they yelled, 'Get her!', pinned me to the ground and started to dig blue pencils into my eyelids. They said they were going to transform me into Bette Davis.

Alex having a proper job in fashion (he is a knitwear designer at a famous Japanese fashion house) does have its advantages. It means that he gives me clothes that he doesn't want. Alex says that although his boss was an innovative fashion force in the 1970s – when his famous flower prints were worn by the Saint Germain left bank set – he now spends much of his day taking pills and walking into walls.

His boss is also incontinent. Every few months he brings in a battered black suitcase full of clothes that he no longer wears and distributes them to the staff. Alex gave me a blue linen jacket faded at the elbows and a pair of linen trousers with yellow piss stains on the inside of the left leg. By the way the jacket pinches under the arms and pulls tightly around the body when the front buttons are done up, it seems that Alex's boss is a good two sizes smaller than me. The trousers are a good fit if I leave the top button undone – although Alex says they look like half of the Japanese man's relatives have died in them and I have to remember to grab the inside of my left thigh at all times to cover up the butter-coloured stain. I have never been so smart, although when I wore the outfit for a temping interview, the personnel manager of Interjob took one look at me and said, '*Mais, vous avez un problème avec votre look, mademoiselle.*'

Although Alex is going steady with Raoul, it is as if he demands lurid stories from Holly and me. He urges us to outrage to keep him amused. For our part, Holly and I need the Gang because it makes us fearless; the more feats we perform the more cocky it makes us, and the more cocky we are, the more cocky we feel the need to be. Holly is delighted to be invited to act irresponsibly since it means he can feel less guilty about sponging much of his material life from Alex; Alex too is happy about the state of affairs since it gives him ultimate control over the relationship.

Alex's desire to see the world as a kinky fairy tale has been a heavy influence on the Gang's speech patterns. Our sexual vocabulary is more interested in comic narrative than it is in gynaecological detail. In fact, we make no secret of our distaste for gynaecology and the whole Gang has ended up adopting Alex's Famous Five sexual vocabulary which stipulates that sex must stay on an adventure playground level.

And so it does. Not for us the cool of 'fuck', 'cunt', 'dyke', 'shag', 'make love', 'tits' or 'dick'. We say 'todge', 'vage', 'licky', 'get it going', 'do it', 'boosies' and 'bits'. By using words like these, our sexual experiments become funny and harmless. With the Gang there is no such thing as sexual sophistication; only sticky anarchy and no moral hang-ups. We don't talk of what we feel, we talk of events: what happened, with who, which way, how big, how old, what charm, what hair, which shoes. Sometimes, the morning after the night before, my stories sound more like Enid Blyton than something I am going to go to hell for.

Holly goes as far as to insist that mixing business with pleasure is the only viable option for people like us in the *profession libérale*. He says we are much more likely to find our dream jobs through our night errands and our getting it going on the town. 'No use looking for some ludicrous career ladder to get us out of the bottom of the barrel,' he says. 'The bottom of the barrel is exactly where we should be.' He can cite a whole list of people who have got on in the world by chance meetings in nightclubs and louche couplings in back rooms. 'Just about everyone in the fashion industry, plus whole sections of the pop industry . . . the writing industry . . . everyone.'

Sometimes, when I ask Holly how long it will be before

these magical encounters start happening, he snaps and says that I shouldn't be so obsessed with money. He says that wealthy without taste is social suicide. 'Who wants cigars, bidets and cruises to Australia?' he scoffs.

So far, my plans for when I am rich only get as far as buying black T-shirts with dye that doesn't come out when you wash them, being able to afford real Roquefort instead of Bleu d'Auvergne and only using tea bags once before throwing them away. Holly, on the other hand, is already thinking big. One day, I saw a piece of paper on the brunch bar with his handwriting on. It said: 'milk, bread, art déco ice bucket'. He admitted that it was quite a demented shopping list, especially when you hadn't paid the rent for three months.

So we put our energy into getting it going.

On Saturday afternoons, Ann, Bet and I will gather round at 10 rue Léon. Holly and Alex will then make me call up a string of people I hardly know and ask them if they've got any parties going. Many people are shocked by such a forward approach and that is the reason why we often have to put Plan C into action. If Plan A is a party in someone's house and Plan B is a night in the Marais – at Le Swing or Le Petit Fer à Cheval – then Plan C is a night out in Barbès. On a Plan C night we eat Chicken Maffei from an African restaurant on rue Myrha for 40 francs or we eat cheap, quite good curry (a rarity in Paris) on the street perpendicular to rue Léon. Here, there is an Indian restaurant called The Navel that gives us free *bienvenu* cocktails that are pink and taste like Fairy Liquid. After this, we might walk up to the quaint, Montmartre end of the eighteenth to see our 'good friends in the *quartier*'. We have no good friends in the *quartier* but we like to say it because it makes us feel above everyone else for being so anonymous. Up on the outer edges of *la butte* – or the hump, meaning the hill of Montmartre – we stop in at Le Progrès. The interior of this café looks like a French Martini advert on its good days, although sometimes there are a group of Algerian buskers who play a medley of Simon and Garfunkel songs all night and then come up and want to talk to you in English about The Beatles and Benny Hill. They speak in that urgent Arab way. They say things like, 'George, you must understand that I respect you, George. George, you think that I would lay one single finger on you if you invited me back to your apartment? On the life of my mother, I swear that no harm would come to you, George.'

Sometimes, Plan C nights mean just going to the Jupiter bar round the corner from rue Léon. The Jupiter looks like a police station and smells slightly of a public urinal, but at least it is not lit like a police station like most of the bars round our way are. The Jupiter is certainly not a gay bar, but the clientele – young and old Arab men with scarred faces – participate in the kind of eye contact with Holly and Alex which suggests that they are not raring to get back to their wives at home. Alex and Holly are two obvious *pédés* but Saïd, the owner, has taken a shine to them because sometimes Alex brings English girls from work to the Sunday afternoon lock-ins. They wear vintage 1970s Japanese designs stolen from the archive and they smile a lot. Even when Holly and Alex bring nobody in at all, Saïd will chat to them. He chats about how Arab boys often prefer goats to women. Holly says this is Saïd's strange indirect way of making a pass at him.

I listen, and sometimes I comment on how unfair women's position is in society – including Arab society. And Saïd will smile at me and reply that Arabs respect their women and that I have had too much education. Alex will joke that I am about to blow up my inflatable soap box again so I laugh and shut up a bit, but when I look round the Jupiter I sigh and wonder if I will ever find my goat.

*   *   *

It was after one particular Saturday spent with Holly, Alex, Bet and Ann that I realised it might be down to the Gang that I have still not become editor of the *Herald Tribune*. My French journalist friend, Sophie, had invited me to a party in the Bastille thrown by one of the paper's staff writers. Naturally, I felt the need to take the Gang with me and to prepare for the Plan A Saturday evening we all met up at 10 rue Léon early in the afternoon.

At two o'clock I knocked at the front door clutching an ED bag containing a bottle of cheap red wine and a plastic bag of squid for Alex's promised paella afternoon. As I waited for someone to come and answer, I observed the usual rue Léon ambience consisting of a pissed *clochard* in the courtyard standing on a piss-stained mattress shaking his fist at nobody in particular, shouting, 'Bring out your menfolk! Bring out your menfolk!' And then Ann opened the front door and there was a man sitting at the brunch bar who looked like Alan Whicker.

When I walked into the room he hurriedly buttoned the front of his chocolate tweed blazer, wiped a limp hand over his pale face and trotted off into Alex's bedroom. Immediately, the bathroom door opened and Bet and Alex peeked out, sniggering. Holly was pacing up and down behind the brunch bar looking something between traumatised and embarrassed.

'Go on then!' Alex was bossing him. 'You have to do it! We can't have him coming round here any more and that's that!' Then he slammed the bathroom door shut until Bet opened it a few minutes later to say, 'Poor Holly!' in an attempt at sympathy that wasn't entirely convincing. Holly folded his arms in a helpless gesture and mumbled, 'What's wrong with him?'

'He's awful!' Alex said, poking his head out and there was another stifled laugh from Bet.

I knew exactly who the agitated man was. I had last seen him two weeks ago at four in the morning in the rue Léon courtyard. He was waving a white silk scarf up at Holly and me and yelling out, 'Lolita . . . Lolita . . . Loliiita!'

✶　　✶　　✶

A lot of very attractive men are drawn to Holly and you would think that Holly would have developed a rigorous quality-control system because of this. In reality, Holly is as uninterested in quality-control valves as I am because quality is not always what you feel like. If you have this approach to life it is inevitable that one day you are going to find an Alan Whicker look-alike on your doorstep.

The man with the white silk scarf and the chocolate tweed blazer was the result of a 2 a.m. Minitel session at rue Léon. To start with, Holly and I logged on to 3615 CUM looking for a *soirée bisexuelle* and we ended up with a man called 'Motorbike'. Within half an hour of giving him our phone number a 5-foot 6-inch weed brandishing an enormous crash hat turned up at the front door. Holly went polite with horror and started buttering and jamming slices and slices of baguette. Making jam sandwiches is one of Holly's many ways of burying his head in the sand. He says that eating too much – even just enough – truly nobbles your sexual appetite and I could tell he wanted to get out of going to bed with Motorbike. When Motorbike announced that his real name was Pierre, the terrible ordinariness of the situation made Holly start cramming as much into his mouth as he could. Luckily, in the nick of time, Pierre slammed his tea cup down on the table and in a sloppy *banlieu* accent said, 'Where's the bedroom then?'

When Pierre had gone into the bedroom, Holly announced that he was going out to Le Swing because Pierre wasn't anything like a Hells Angel.

'I'd rather die than sleep with him!' he spat and then added quickly, 'I mean, not literally.'

I said, 'Don't you dare cop out,' and pushed him towards the bedroom where we found Pierre already undressed and under the covers. We got in too and lay staring up at the ceiling with the sheets pulled up to our chins like virgins. Pierre kissed me briefly on the mouth and then hoiked himself up on top of me, straddled my knees and started giving me head. Holly was doing precisely nothing, so I took his hand and placed it on Pierre's rabbit ribcage whereupon Pierre flinched and demanded to know what Holly thought he was doing. I said, 'Well, we did say we were looking for a *soirée bisexuelle*,' but Pierre just looked over at Holly who was polishing his nails on the sheet in a sulk and said, 'Him! He's no bisexual!' Holly stood up in a huff and stomped off to the kitchen mumbling about the disgrace of being queer-bashed in his own bed.

Considering his looks, the size of Pierre's ego was fairly large. Afterwards, when he was pulling on his corduroy trousers, he said blankly, 'You were nervous. I used to be nervous but through the Minitel, I have slept with so many women there is no longer any need to be nervous.' He slipped his packet of condoms back into his shiny Perfecto and added, 'Paris is filled with lonely women who are looking for sensuality.' And then, 'Some of the women I sleep with are very beautiful.'

Pierre slamming the door and leaving us alone with two tall plates of buttered and jammed baguette was not the end of it. Holly had just bunged Alex's bedclothes in the machine for a rapid white wash before Alex came home from Raoul's house, when we heard a crazy hollering coming from the courtyard outside. When we looked out of the window we saw a man in a blazer and a white silk scarf crooning, 'Loliiita!' which was the code name Holly and I had been using all night on the Minitel.

Holly looked at me and went pale. It's not that he worries about sleeping with people so much lower than him on the market value scale. His worry is that Alex might throw him out if he gets too bad. I think Alex is beginning to wonder why there are freshly laundered sheets on his bed nearly every day, and things are not helped by the ever-rising Minitel bill and the fact that Holly's wages barely cover his *demi* habit.

Even by Barbès standards, the sight of Alan Whicker and

his hollering and his outfit would strike the neighbours as a bit of a funny business. So Holly had to go down into the courtyard and sort the situation out. He returned ten minutes later and announced sheepishly that Alan Whicker had asked him for a date. Holly insisted he'd had to say 'yes' because otherwise Alan Whicker would never have gone away.

Holly suddenly left his position at the brunch bar and stormed into Alex's room where Alan sat pale on the bed. Holly muttered, 'Bugger bollocks,' under his breath as he rushed past, so I went back to sit by the brunch bar with Ann. Bet and Alex came out of the bathroom and Alex poured us some sangria in silence, then carried on tending to the paella.

After a few minutes of low-volume conversation, Holly and the man appeared in the kitchen. The chocolate tweed blazer had its back turned to us, but you could see it was upset because its shoulders were shivering up and down. A pale hand waved a feeble goodbye in the direction of the brunch bar as Holly escorted Alan Whicker gravely to the door. Holly gave him a brief *bise* and then closed the door gently. Immediately, he swung round to face Alex and with as much drama as he could muster, puffed, 'Well thank you very much!'

Alex handed Holly a big tumbler of sangria.

'I thought that the whole point about *trade*,' Alex said calmly, 'was that you did them once and then you never had to see them again.'

Holly looked into his glass and made a big, sulky 'puh!' If he was honest, he was slightly surprised that Alan Whicker had ended up becoming his sugar daddy for the past fortnight. Deep down, he could see that the concept wasn't really him. It really wasn't funny when you were stuck in a restaurant with him on another Saturday night, cutting your way through another plateful of deep-fried Gascony *foie gras* with caramelised apples. Fried *foie gras* and *boudin* were Alan Whicker's favourite foods and left Holly feeling like he'd force fed his own liver and it was going to burst at any minute from over-stuffing.

Plus, Alan Whicker's topics of conversation were: a. his mother – who he lived with; b. the great year he had spent in Scarborough in 1966; c. how food was more than just food.

'Look at this pig,' he'd say, waving a piece of *boudin noir* over Holly's plate. 'Its life on earth was ignoble. It snorted and rummaged in the stinking, dirty mud. Ah, but its life after death is a thing of nobility since it was created by a chef who has sacrificed twenty-five years of his life to the cause of *haute cuisine.*' His forehead would start to sweat and he'd yelp something like, 'Bowls of sacrificed youth!' or 'Platters of human worth!' His voice would rise and other people in the restaurant would turn around to stare. And then his chunk of *boudin* would fall from the end of his fork and land with a little splash in Holly's bowl of soup leaving a circle of congealed pig's blood curdling on the surface.

'He was sweet though,' Holly sulked, downing the glass of sangria in three gulps.

'He gave you *morpions!*' Alex said, indignant.

'It wasn't him that gave me *morpions!*'

'Well then! *Suggest* you're sad when you've got boyfriends with *morpions* all over Paris!'

'Not all of them!' and Holly's eyes stared dreamily into the middle distance. 'Just Marcel . . .'

'Is he the one who chucks you out of his car in the middle of the Périphérique?' Bet asked.

'Not all the time,' Holly sulked.

'*Morpions!*' Ann shivered.

Holly went to the bathroom to go to the mirror. 'Nothing wrong with a few *morpions,*' he shouted back. 'That *pharmacie* near Chateau Rouge métro is the cleanest shop on the whole of boulevard Barbès. I quite like going in there for my powders.'

'Nothing wrong!' Alex snorted. 'And what if I catch them off you and give them to my boyfriend? Then I'll get chucked and it'll all be your fault.'

Holly came out of the bathroom grinning. He patted Alex's cheek with his hand whereupon Alex shrieked, 'Get off, crab hand!' and ran off into his bedroom to hide under the white-washed sheets.

After several more bottles of cheap red had been emptied into the sangria bowl and consumed, we left rue Léon and began our walk towards the métro for our big, Plan A night out in the Bastille at the *Herald Tribune* party.

On the way, Holly and Alex bumped into a Jupiter regular called Jean-Paul, a fifty-something ex-fashion designer – so he says – with a poodle, a moustache and what looks like mascara on his eyelashes. (One night, he invited Holly and me back to his flat to give Holly a pair of Thierry Mugler trousers but we ended up rushing out laughing, without even saying goodbye because Jean-Paul had made the trousers conditional on Holly doing '*un petit service*' for him.)

As the three of them chatted away, a man with a face like he went round killing prostitutes at night came up to Bet and hissed, '*Ça va, ma biche?*' ('Biche' means female deer). Bet twizzled round in her black platform sandals stolen from the archives at Alex's work. Slapping her hand on her scarlet bull skirt, she shouted, '*Ta gueule,*' which means 'shut your mouth', and the man kicked her and shouted '*Pute,*' which means 'whore'. Bet was so shocked he'd kicked her, that for a few seconds she was speechless. Then she opened her mouth and a mad hornet's nest of French and English shot out. The man looked like he wanted to knock her block off, but he glanced briefly at the Gang and Jean-Paul and seemed to think better of it. Odd why. Alex and Holly would probably have run a mile and it is doubtful whether Jean-Paul's free trousers offer would have saved the day. Bet would have stomped off home in a fury but luckily she was buoyed up by the knowledge of the date she had later that night with Sam.

When we arrived at the party, it was my turn to be furious. The place was filled with the sound of American expat journalists saying things like, 'I think your piece was right on the ball,' and, 'Peter, let me introduce you to Mark Korall. Mark lectures on Medieval French at the British Institute. Mark, this is Peter Finley. Peter writes about automobile innovations for the *Trib*.'

Some people were talking about that morning's *Le Monde* which had a story by Julia Kristeva on the front page. ('I mean, it's amazing. Can you believe it? Some obscure feminist literary critic writing some story about "The Self" on the cover of *Le Monde*. Don't you just love France? I mean, it's amazing!')

There were various dog-shit conversations going on too. You can always tell how long an expat has been living in Paris by their take on the dog-shit conversation. If they have just arrived they might start a conversation with a stranger by saying something like, 'You know, in a city like this you'd have thought that they'd clean up all that dog shit. On my way to work this morning, I stepped into shit three times.'

Then there are those expats who never seem to give up on dog-shit conversations, finding them an endless source of mirth. An advanced dog-shit conversation will go something like: 'You know, when I was back in New York this summer I noticed that they've come down really severely on dog littering in the streets. A friend of mine in the seventeenth was telling me that City Hall are thinking of introducing fines . . .'

The minute I hear this kind of talk my fake DMs start tingling. Paris is all right if you're sixty years old but sometimes I itch to go around and kick everyone with my boots. I'd start off with the duchess I interviewed the other day who said that she couldn't understand why her daughter wanted to wear a leather jacket because at her age she should be showing off her beautiful neck. I'd kick her. Then I'd start kicking all the French people whose idea of a good night out is to sit for hours on a terrace over one beautifully coloured drink and then finish off the evening queuing to watch a film where people say things like, 'But love doesn't exist, only proofs of love exist.' But I'd really get to work on the expats. A lot of the expats I know are forty-somethings who make crummy money and live in *chambres de bonne* in the hope that gatherings like the *Herald Tribune* party will give them their big break. Sometimes they hang out in Shakespeare & Co in Saint Michel and listen to some grisly American expat reading anti-Vietnam War poetry upstairs. School teachers from Canada come to Shakespeare & Co for their summer holidays and listen to hyperactive sales assistants with bad dye jobs talking about the 'bohemian life' and trying to palm off over-priced copies of their vanity published beatnik poetry anthologies. The first time I went there, the man who runs the place – who looks like Steptoe and who reckons he's a descendant of Walt Whitman – came up to me and said, 'Are you a rasta?' and added that I could sleep there for a couple of days if I wanted to.

The other sort of expats are the ones who have good enough jobs to allow them to fantasise they're living in a Henry Miller or a Hemingway novel. They like the word 'syphilis' and dream of 'whores' squatting over *bidets* in buggy hotel rooms. They get all hot under the collar when they go to red-light areas like Pigalle – as if there's something more artistic about French prostitutes than American ones. Not that I have anything against age. I'm sure that I too will be having sex on car bonnets in the middle of the road when I am forty. What annoys me is standing in their living rooms – with their walls hung with New Mexican rugs and their shelves heaving with African carvings and tax-return forms – and being congratulated by them on 'your bohemian neighbourhood'. They always go, 'Hey that sounds really interesting. An African restaurant, you

say, with *plats*' (which they always pronounce trying to sound
French) 'with *plats* for 40 francs? Yeah, you know, Barbès is
really bohemian.'

Alex could see I was getting hot under the collar so he grabbed
hold of my hand and, singing, 'Ridicule is nothing to be
scared of ...' under his breath, walked me over towards a
sixty-something man with a shaggy grey beard. I later found
out that the man was one of the *Herald Tribune*'s leader writers.
He was talking to an American girl whose face seemed painfully
concentrated on him.

The Great Old Man of American Journalism (as he liked to
be known at the *Trib*), was waving his hands round in the air and
speaking with such animation that the hairs of his beard were
weighted down with a horrible spitty dew: 'Of course, you have
to understand that walking is very important to the Parisian; it
is a practical way of manoeuvring around the city but you have
to remember that the manner in which the Parisian walks also
reflects his state of mind.'

'Oh really,' the American girl was saying, smoothing her
hair down nervously.

'Yes,' he frothed, taking another sip of red wine, 'the
Baudelarian *flâneur* stroll, the agitated Surrealist amble and
the clipped Situationist swagger have marked out generations
of men ...'

They both turned to us when Alex tapped him on the
shoulder and, with a cheap vodka wobble, said, 'Hello, I'm
Alex. Are you a journo?'

The Great Old Man looked at us with thinly disguised irritation. But he didn't quite know if we were being rude so, winking
at the girl he said with a smile, 'You could call me that.'

Alex poked the hole in the left sleeve of his Aran sweater
and sniggered: 'Are you doing research on moths for your
next article?'

I thought it was quite a funny thing to have said but the man just muttered, 'Sure' under his breath and pointedly turned his back on us to resume his weighty conversation with the American girl who looked like she was in ten times more pain than she had been before.

The Great Old Man looked as if he was immune to any further goading so Alex and I left him alone and went to rescue Ann who was being crowded by a circle of expat men with more beards and more bobbly jumpers, all dying to know about the shapely blonde juggler's bohemian life. 'Here you are, Ann,' Alex shouted over the expats' heads. 'We've got your crab tablets here. You've only taken one dose today!'

'Bohemian!' Ann sighed afterwards. 'One of them said it was the glamour of not being normal.'

'Pathetic,' Bet agreed, downing some Champagne she'd liberated from the fridge. 'Bohemian's just another way of saying poor. Poor means fried food, utilitarian wardrobes and semi-absorbent toilet paper. Bohemian means vegetarian mulch, old fridges as wardrobes and semi-absorbent toilet paper.'

'Yeah,' I said, polishing the toe of my right boot against the back of my left jeans calf, 'the only good thing about bohemian is that it means you don't have to wear tights and a skirt to earn a living.'

Then I saw my friend Sophie standing in a corner saying, 'I mean, he just busts my goddam balls!' in a perfect upper east side New York accent, and I thought I'd go over and say hello because even doing that might somehow make tonight useful. Sophie really throws herself into the journalist role. There is always somebody busting her balls, somebody who is kicking her ass, someone who is driving her fucking crazy. Sophie is the daughter of a French diplomat but she has lived in Paris for twelve years and bears the signs of having been educated in the best schools around the world. She is the most accomplished person I know – she speaks twelve languages, can say insightful things about the political intrigues in the socialist party, knows the difference between Alain Finkelkraut and Bernard-Henry Lévy and when you go into cafés with her she'll nonchalantly order something chic you've never heard of – like a *noisette* (an espresso with a dash of milk) – in a manner that makes the waiter jump to it and bring a glass of water without you even having to ask for it. When the waiter arrives with my *noisette*, Sophie doesn't just say, 'It's for her'. She will gesture to me with a confident, cupped hand and say, '*C'est pour Madame*', in the correct French manner.

I am Sophie's idea of what a mis-spent youth looks like. It makes her feel rebellious to be around me. Even when I turn up at her *hôtel particulier* office at *Time* magazine opposite Hermès and next door to Valentino on the Faubourg Saint Honoré, fresh from my bike in cut-offs and a sweaty face, she doesn't seem to mind. She says she enjoys 'pissing off that goddam bitch of an editor'. Once, she introduced me to the bitch – one of those chalky-faced *Parisiennes* with a *particule*, who look at you like they feel sorry for you and hate you at the same time even though they are making a passable attempt to smile. Sophie said, 'This is George Quentin, a top journalist at *Paris Parade*.' Sophie always introduces you with your surname and an exaggeration of what you do.

The Gang has a complicated relationship with Sophie. Sophie's catch phrase is, 'Goddam, my life's such a mess' and then, for half an hour or so she'll tell you why this is the case. You can always tell when it's Sophie who calls up rue de Clignancourt because if Bet picks up the phone, she walks immediately to my room (going 'yes, yes' or 'did you?' or 'never mind' in an unenthusiastic tone of voice), and when she sees me she'll point dramatically at the receiver with a big pointy finger and make grotesque shapes with her big, red lips so I know it is Sophie at the end of the line. Sometimes, I run out of the room, doing a neck-slicing gesture with my right hand and mouthing, 'No, I'm not here,' so that Bet has to listen to Sophie for a while longer. Being Bet, she doesn't put up with her for long. When she's got rid of her, she'll come stomping into the kitchen where I'll be cowering to say, 'I'm fed up with being a bloody psychiatrist down the phone to bloody Sophie.'

Sophie's sheltered upbringing means that she is hopeless when it comes to men. Her fantasy is eating steak tartare in La Coupole with an ambitious son of a politician before retiring back to his house to discuss the merits of Picasso's blue period. So far nothing like this has ever happened.

I am quite fascinated by knowing someone so establishment. I don't mind that much about being a psychiatrist to Sophie down the phone. Optimism is by far the best angle: the man who hasn't called for two weeks will call her any day now; the married man friend who invites her to his Christmas parties every year *must* have ulterior motives. And all the while I'm wondering at what point I can cut her off and say, 'Have you got any cuttings on Vanessa Paradis?' without sounding too insensitive. Sometimes, when I chip in with requests for people's phone numbers or research material when she's on a neurosis roll, she gets all huffy and says, 'Goddam, you only want me for our contacts. I think you ought to rethink the nature of this friendship.'

Obviously, this is a bit rich. Sometimes Sophie goes on for ages about what a mess her life is while I know that at *Time* she has access to one of the best clippings libraries in Paris. But unlike Bet, my policy is to be told off, shut up and bite my tongue until the red, burning feeling under the skin has passed. When it has passed, I will ask her if she fancies a coffee and we will meet up in the *brasserie* next to her office. If it's lunch time, she'll nonchalantly order a goat's cheese salad or a *croque monsieur* and a Badoit while she tells me about the goddam bitch in the office and what a mess her life is. I wonder if I dare order a *croque monsieur* as well because sometimes she pays for me and sometimes she doesn't and if she doesn't pay then a *croque monsieur* is more than a day's living expenses down the drain. It means green lentils with no bacon for tea or two Leffs less at Le Petit Fer à Cheval. You could say that my friendship with Sophie is a bit of a gamble.

I smiled when I saw her because she was squeezing the arm of a gawky-looking boy in Barber and Brogues. Thanks to me, Sophie's love life is not such a goddam mess any more. The gawky boy was Patrice Doisneau, an estate agent who worked on the Ile Saint Louis. A month ago I had taken her to a themed salsa party in a disused railway carriage at Quai de la Gare. She ended up outside snogging Patrice on a rubbish heap in fullest Moschino, having made the first pass she'd ever made in her life at a man. She'd said, 'Shall we go for a walk?' which Holly said he'd never heard described as a chat-up line in this century. Now she squeezed his arm again. She bellowed, 'Goddam, doesn't he look like a Greek God!' and started picking fluff off his jumper while he blushed to his roots.

The only person who seemed to be making any headway at the party was Holly. He was holding court in the middle of a group of giggling expat wives, twisting wire Champagne tops into miniature Louis XIV chairs and telling them how to lead more exciting lives. He said, 'What you have to remember is that the body is the most important fashion accessory. If your body's not up to scratch, then a good outfit is indispensable in the sense that it is important to remember what the person was wearing before you took their clothes off. Often, that is the only thing that sustains you through the night.'

Gales of laughter accompanied whatever Holly said, followed by soft-core revelations from the expat wives about the few minutes in their youth when they had crossed the line of good taste. Girls love Holly. He lectures them with utmost authority about fashion matters ('Galliano the new fashion genius! Purlease! What's Sao Schlumberger going to look like

in that collection? Like a demented drag queen, that's what!'),
and he always has tips about how they could improve their
personal appearance ('God, you've got fabulous breasts. You
should always wear *cache-coeurs*. They've got some divine ones in
Tati. Only 37 francs each!').

Holly excels in anti-charm. It was he who really livened up
the *Herald Tribune* evening when he took me up on my idea of
pouring Champagne into the shoe of the hostess. She was a
sour-faced American who kept giggling 'Excuse me!' every ten
minutes, before rushing out of the room and rushing back five
minutes later with freshly applied pink lipstick. Every time she
came back she'd giggle the same boring phrase: 'Now, I hope
nobody's been saying bad things about me while I was away!'

Some people doubled up with laughter as if she'd said
something funny. One time, she rushed back to find one of
her shoes had been filled with Champagne and wedged into the
top of her birthday cake. Her body became rigid with anger but
she just made a tight-lipped smile and said icily, 'So, someone
thinks they're real funny, huh?'

The only noise that could be heard was Holly's voice ('It's
true! Cold water! Ten minutes you dip them in there for. It firms
them up like nobody's business ...'), and the dying laughter of
his group of expat wives.

Nobody denounced Holly but the give-away was that he
had been speaking in a very loud voice all night about how
he was going to fill up the toaster with Cointreau. When Alex
announced that he couldn't bear the dull *Herald Tribune* party
any longer, we all trooped over to leave. Bet, Ann and Alex
all managed to get out, but the hostess closed the door when
Holly came level with her. In a voice as loud as she could muster
without sounding hysterical, she said, 'I guess I'll vet my guest
list more carefully next time,' upon which Holly blushed a very
odd shade of red, made a series of hair-tossing movements with
his bandanna and shot out of the apartment. Sophie gave me a
stern look as I prepared to follow Holly and I thought, 'Damn,

now I won't be allowed to go to *Time* on Monday for research material on Euro Disney.'

When we were safely in the lift, Holly announced what a complete disgrace the party had been. 'Really!' he said. '*Get* attached to some prissy, American pump with a horrible peeling-off sole because you're a ridiculous expat journalist who hasn't been able to buy herself a decent pair of shoes in twenty years!'

He was glum as we walked down the street and I was dwelling on the fact that yet again I hadn't managed to get any useful phone numbers for my future career. Ann had been pestered by too many randy beards to have enjoyed herself and as Alex's intoxication started to wear off, he complained that he would have been better off spending the night with Raoul.

The only person with a spring in her step was Bet because the one person on her mind was Sam. Bet had been seeing Sam for just a couple of months so they were still both in their honeymoon period. Bet seemed really serious about him and had so far refused to let us meet him. It was only because she was so drunk now that she was letting us traipse along with her to Le Swing. She was in such a good mood when we got there that she started the Tom Radish story.

Bet has always played true to Gang rules in relating intimate details about her relationships and encounters. Her Tom Radish story is about the session musician for the Cocteau Twins with a radish tattooed on his upper arm. She met him ages ago, before she started going steady with Sam, at one *Soirée Goa Boa* and they ended up sharing fourteen hours together in a seedy Place de Clichy hotel. The tattooed vegetable was about as interesting as Tom got, but luckily the denouement of the story provided ample satisfaction for the Gang. The day Tom went back to London, Bet went over to rue Léon where the Gang goaded her into telling them why she was so miserable.

'Come on! Tom Radish did something weird, didn't he!' Holly teased.

'Oh, shut up.'

'Charming!' Holly said. 'Been tiring you out in bed too much, has he?'

Bet allowed herself a reluctant smile.

'Bet! He didn't give it to you at all, did he? Did he, Bet? Come on now.' Holly made a noise, part laugh, part jeer which was a cue for Alex to start a boisterous chant of 'Bet didn't get it! Bet didn't get it! Bet didn't get it!' until the whole room sounded like a nervous breakdown and Bet finally caved in.

'All right!' she snapped. 'It's just that. Well. It's Tom. He didn't ...'

'He couldn't get it up!' chirped Holly in triumph.

'Yes he could!'

'He wanted it up the bum!'

'No!'

'He doesn't like ...'

'Girls!' Alex giggled until I nudged him quiet.

'He didn't like ... going down on me.' The words fled from Bet's mouth like a bat out of hell and I could see she regretted the revelation immediately. Holly and Alex both squealed, 'Vile!', Bet started drumming her fingers on her bull skirt, and Ann and I both laughed a bit before pulling ourselves together and saying, 'Poor Bet!'

Had this all come out at Clignancourt, things would have been much gentler. And indeed, later, Ann, Bet and I did talk about the situation one night as we sat round the kitchen table. There was a general intro about how awful men are, followed by a rant from me on how Bet should have gone on blow-job strike, followed by a speech from Ann on how cunnilingus is maligned in a patriarchal society, followed by more ranting about how awful men are, followed by a joint, followed by the munchies, followed by bowls of flour and water paste because there is never anything in the fridge, followed by a randomly choreographed performance around the apartment of 'You've Got To Pick A Pocket or Two', followed by banging on the ceiling from the men downstairs, followed by stifled giggles and chilly sleep.

Bet's shame is all water under the bridge these days. Now that Bet is going steady with Sam, she is glad that she has a past. She whips out the Tom Radish story like under-the-counter ham on rationing day.

When Sam finally walks into Le Swing the whole Gang has tipped back into drunkenness – mainly thanks to a quarter bottle of vodka that Bet keeps sneaking out of her velvet purse and passing round the table. Sam walks soberly up to our table and you can tell immediately by the look in his eye that he knows this is a bad idea. But it is too late. He has met the Gang. He sits down, bolt upright, next to Bet and with Sam as a new audience member, Bet decides to get Tom Radish going all over again.

This time round, her angle is more on Tom Radish's anatomical shortcomings and on her worldly wise mastery of the situation. Her face is fizzing with glee and she keeps accidentally elbowing Sam in the stomach as her elaborate arm gestures help tell the tale. It is only after Bet has finished her performance that the Gang notices the horrified look on Sam's face. When Bet finally realises that Sam looks like he is about to explode, she turns pale because she thinks she is going to be chucked. She dashes to the toilet with streaming eyes, wailing that Alex is always trying to nobble her and she can't bear it any more. It is no use us trying to tell Sam that Bet is over her cheap phase now because Sam is looking at us all like we're monsters.

He was so appalled at the beans he imagines Bet spills whenever she hangs out with us that he refuses to socialise with us any more. Bet now often spends her Saturday nights alone with Sam and she doesn't dare talk about her relationship with him. At least, not in any interesting depth. The only clues we have about Bet's happiness come from the state of her eye make-up: clogged lashes good, mascara dribbles bad.

CHAPTER FIVE

Back of the Bus

Thanks to the Gang I am now back of the bus stock. And not before time. At the convent, my position on the school bus wavered between two places from the front (even the front seat required a certain swot panache) all the way to three rows from the back. Never any further. I was afraid to even look at the seats at the very back and the girls who'd claimed them. Back of the bus stock had to have pierced ears, do their homework sloppily, lip synch to 'Love Don't Live Here Any More' by Rose Royce while looking out of the window in a strange reflective way. Most importantly, they had to profess to knowledge of sex.

On Monday mornings there was an extra tantalising forcefield radiating from the back seats as the five top dogs narrated in the most credible manner possible what they'd done with their Saturday night. There was no way I could compete with them. Nothing in my weekend involved love bites, smoking in cinemas or going to youth club discos. On Saturday nights I would lie on my bed, empty my orange plastic purse on to the lilac sheets, count up the coins and then imagine what I would buy to eat with 50 pence if I was stranded alone on a desert island for a week: flour and margarine to make a kind of dough, apples to prevent scurvy, onions because they were a cheap savoury and rhubarb and custard penny chews to keep my spirits up.

The king of the back of the bus was a beautiful fifteen-year-old called Louise who looked like Elvis. On good nights, she would come into my dreams and want to be best friends with me. But in real life, the only time she ever seemed to notice me was the morning after I'd tried to have my hair straightened at the hairdressers. I thought it looked quite convincing until I got on the bus. The hairs on the back of my neck stood on end as a rich Cornish voice boomed out from behind my head, 'Bloody hell, what's that girl done to her hair? She looks like Noel Edmunds.' From my mid-row seat I felt a prickle in my nose and knew that tears were coming if I wasn't careful.

Louise functioned as our surrogate sexy boy. She cracked jokes, she swaggered when she walked, she winked rakishly, she wore shoes we all agreed looked like men's shoes, she scored more netball goals than anyone else in the school, she had a cocky, swashbuckling laugh and in the end we hardly noticed her skirt any more.

Unfortunately, she never seemed to notice me. Even when I became known as the girl who could eat eight sausages in one sitting. These included mine and the ones that came from the plates of the other seven girls at the table who risked punishment if anything was left uneaten. The girls liked me for it, and although Sister Clare wasn't too pleased when she found out, I shocked myself by coming up with a brilliant on-the-spot excuse: 'I'm offering it up for Jesus, Sister.'

The nun hesitated and then congratulated me on my healthy appetite.

At that dinner table I learnt that Christianity, or the appearance of Christianity, could work wonders for you. I learnt charming deceit, convincing hypocrisy and mild ruthlessness. Before, I had eaten everything that was placed in front of me – stew and lettuce, ice cream that tasted like medicine, mashed potato with black lumps in, the pastry brush bristles I once found in my Shepherd's Pie – all in an unimaginative attempt to make the nuns love me.

The sausages were different. Through them I tasted the

excitement of power: I might eat my fellow pupils' sausages, but some days I would make one of them feel obliged to take a portion of slimy cabbage as a fair exchange.

My new roost ruling was nipped in the bud when the convent implemented packed lunches a term later. The new eating ritual served only to illuminate my true role in life. The other girls would bring neat sandwiches and individually wrapped foil triangles of cheese all arranged in different compartments of bijou Tupperware boxes. I lunched on brown bread doorsteps oozing with peanut butter that I prepared myself in the morning and that I had to wedge firmly in my mouth to fit. On the first day, it seemed that the whole of the dining room turned round to point furtively at George Quentin.

That was my first heady experience of rebellion, tinged with sadness. I was being singled out as odd, yet I knew it would be play-acting to pretend that I wanted foil-wrapped cheese triangles. I chomped self-consciously on my unlady-like lunch and a lifetime of being different flashed before me.

These days, thanks to Holly, I no longer think of sexual knowledge as rebellion. It is simply material. The tantalising forcefield that radiates from my story-telling seat the morning after the night before is almost as exciting as the idea of sitting in my leather swivel chair at the *Herald Tribune*. Sometimes, when Alex has friends who come to stay, he invites me over to his flat for Sunday brunch so I can entertain people who have spent all Saturday night in Le Petit Fer à Cheval doing nothing more than drinking Coca Cola and admiring the Art Déco ceiling.

The stories are always fresh because it is surprising how endless bed permutations can be. Each time I bed a stranger I come away with new strings to my bow, I gain extra spurs and earn more vouchers. I figure that soon I will have so many vouchers I will be able to trade them in when 'The One' cruises into town.

Holly agrees. He says that it is always good to have a few good tricks up your sleeve. Like eating spaghetti right, folding table napkins in interesting shapes, playing the spoons and playing Chopsticks without any mistakes, bed knowledge gives you an added dimension.

Some mornings when I return to my brown sheets, I take out my diary and write reconstructions. I think that maybe in years to come I will look back at my jottings and work out what on earth I was playing at.

Tuesday, 12 December 1989 (Told at breakfast to Alex's cousin Hugh from South Africa. Alex bought brioche.)

Standing vodka-soaked on the rue de Rivoli, I know I will be unable to reach the other end of the boulevard Sébastopol without having sex. I have just said goodnight in Le Petit Fer à Cheval to Sophie and the Greek God. Sophie asked if she could get me a taxi but I have so much energy there is no way I could sleep. I know there will be more to life, any minute now, and like a child let loose on a room full of birthday presents I sway off towards the light.

The beginning of the boulevard is filled with overspill from the Saint Denis red-light district. I walk past the neon signs which glow blue and pink on the hissing *banlieu* boys, the leery men on business trips and the couples who are putting off going home because they don't fancy each other any more. There's full-on eye contact if you want it, but stopping now would be too unimaginative.

Soon I am tottering into the second third of the street. Here, it is darker and there are less people. Occasionally you cross groups of very tall girls with large, laughing mouths, accompanied by men in leather jackets who don't even glance at you as they pass. These are models on their way to Les Bains, which is where Proust used to take baths in the nineteenth century but which is now an exclusive nightclub for models and rich men. It is so exclusive that it doesn't have bouncers, it has *physionomistes*. If you are female, the Open Sesame magic words are, '*Elle est mignonne*', grunted by the frightening door keeper Marlène to one of the *physionomistes*.

So I carry on up the boulevard Sébastopol. Two-thirds of the way up now and there are only dimly lit fur and leather shops lining both sides of the road. I prepare to cross the street to walk on the better-lit side of the boulevard. As I turn to check for traffic, a black man approaches on a green bicycle. This must be it, I think, as he stops the bike, dismounts and stands grinning on the pavement.

He is skinny in a thin blue blazer and I decide to go up to his apartment after the sticky kiss he has planted on my lips proves interesting – forgetting that in a vodka daze no kiss seems dull.

After the dark stairwell, which smells of hothouse damp, we arrive in a small, grubby room which functions as bedroom, kitchen and living room. The man rummages for something under the sink among piles of black nylon socks, greying white T-shirts and empty packets of potato purée. He stops rummaging, looks up and says in heavily accented French, 'My name is Mamadou. If my wife comes back, that is where you must go.' He points to a flimsy wardrobe. 'She works at the Gare du Nord. Sometimes she comes home early.'

I look at the wardrobe. It seems big enough.

'My name's Sarah. Roll a joint,' I say, drifting towards the bathroom and finding only a Turkish toilet which also seems to double as a shower and waste-disposal unit, judging from the carrot peelings and the piece of Dove soap lying near the foot rests. I do an expert balance job as I squat down to pee and when I return into the other room, Mamadou is already smoking. With a snaky smile on his face he pats the bed. After I've taken a drag of the joint I push him down on the bed, hovering over his cock. I hold his wrists with my hands, put my feet on his ankles and tease his hardening penis with my body. It is a position I perfected at the age of eight when I used to beat up boys in the woods. I'd only agree to get off when they shouted out, 'Get off, boy.'

But I am forced to release him without struggle when he announces that he hasn't been able to find the condoms he thought he had under the sink. I clamber off his chest.

'Come on. Put your clothes on,' I say. 'We're going on a journey.' I light the remains of the joint, put my coat on and stand in front of the door. 'Well, are you coming or not?'

'But where are we going?'

'Get your bike. We're going to an unusual chemist.'

It soon becomes obvious that Mamadou's thighs aren't up to the job of pedalling up hill with me balancing on the back. When we reach the end of boulevard Sébastopol I tell Mamadou to let me take over.

'*T'en es sûr?*' he pants.

'*Sans problème,*' I snap, pushing him aside and waiting until he sits side-saddle on the back so I can start pedalling off up the boulevard Barbès. Cycling up a steep hill is a very sporty thing to be doing at three in the morning and, to top it all, I am being tailed by a group of men in a car who keep shouting out of the window, 'Eh, *ma biche*, is there room for us?'

When we finally arrive at 10 rue Léon the other people on the streets at this hour – the odd prostitute and huddles of Arab men wearing lots of gold jewellery – look at me pummelling the metal doors with my fists as I shout, 'Holly! Holly! Stop shagging and open up.' Babies in flats start to scream and Mamadou looks frightened until a few minutes later the door opens and there is Holly whose face is one big dilated pupil. That's the good thing about Holly. He thinks it perfectly normal that someone should turn up banging at his door at three in the morning asking for condoms.

His bleary eyes give Mamadou the once over. As we troop through the damp courtyard and walk up one flight of stone steps to his flat he says, 'You on Africa already then?' He turns the key in the lock of his front door and says, 'Well you'll be pleased to know that I've already started work on North America. And I've already covered fifty per cent more ground than you have.' When the door opens, I catch a glimpse of two naked men with bottles of poppers up their nose. I know that Alex is staying the night in Raoul's *chambre de bonne*. Holly pads out and gives me a handful of condoms. 'Don't use them all at once,' he hiccups, closing the door.

Half an hour later I am wondering if it is all worth it. I do object to bed acrobats. Those men who flip you around like an omelette all night and expect you to give them a round of applause the next day. It is the element of being told what to do that always gets to me. Having sex with one of these men feels like you are the tent that they are erecting: 'Put that over there, now move that a bit to the right, this goes up here, come on, it'll be good when we get there.' Flip, flop, flip, flop, a chicken escalope being dipped in egg and then hoist over to be rolled in the breadcrumb tray. 'Okay, now we can go for the wheelbarrow. Just hang on a bit. It's a bit difficult, this one.'

Mamadou decides to give up on the wheelbarrow. 'I can't remember if this bit goes here, or if this goes here,' he says, looking at a pile of limbs. The next thing I know, there are a pair of hands around my neck. I think: 'I wonder if he's trying to strangle me or if this is that new technique Holly was telling me about – about cutting off air supply to increase orgasm pleasure.' I think it is the latter, yet all that cycling seems to have worn out my responses; the orgasm comes like the last dregs of toothpaste squeezed from the tube, sluggish and unwilling and dragging its feet. All I can think of is housework. I never normally think of housework, but I am niggled by the certainty that there are loads of alien pubic hairs in my bed by now. I hate that. I don't normally bring people back to my bed for that very reason – and also for the reason that the ghost of cheapness always lingers a day or two in my bedroom afterwards. I'll have to go to the launderette tomorrow and that is always a typical Clignancourt experience; if there isn't a man shooting up by the powder dispenser there is a man with three teeth and perma-stubble giving you the eye.

Mamadou smiles stupidly and starts prodding my stomach. This is becoming really irritating. One, I am no longer drunk, two, I am exhausted from all that cycling, three, you'd have thought that a man could tell when a woman had come, and four, if I'm not very much mistaken, Mamadou has already yelled like he's falling off a cliff twice since we got started in this cement-mixer sex session.

At times like these I wish I had my control box so that I could press the button and make him disappear. Maybe I'll make him disappear anyway.

'Listen, you have to leave now.'

'But, it's only 5.30 in the morning.'

'Yes, but I am a journalist. I have to go and do an interview at 6.' This line is almost as effective as an ejector button. It has worked before on several occasions.

'But Sarah,' he says, pressing himself even closer, 'I can make you happy, you know. Very happy.'

Now, I'm really bored. 'Mamadou, I'm happy already. Sex is over for the night, you understand?'

'No, no, not over.' More prodding.

'Mamadou, I'm dry, you understand, dry as the proverbial bone. There is no more lubrication around my bits. I am unoiled, arid, drought-ridden, it's no longer possible for me to have sex with you.'

Pause. Cease of prodding.

'You have some Vaseline?'
'What?'
'You have butter?'
'What?'
'Butter. Or jam. Jam. You have jam? Or chocolate spread? Come. I make you feel good.'

Sunday, 4 March 1990 (Alex's sister-in-law came to Saturday afternoon drinks at 10 rue Léon. She didn't say much afterwards.)

I went for Chester because he was wearing a pinstripe suit. We were at the Bourse, the French stock exchange, for the glittering launch party of *Boulevardier* magazine. I'd decided to wear an antique black lace flapper dress given to me by my long-lost godmother when she found out I'd escaped the world of fish and chips and made it to university.

But I was only going half-way. I was wearing the dress with some 20 franc Alice in Wonderland shoes from the Barbès shoe cash and carry. They looked like cardboard and the back of the hem was snagged due to maltreatment at my hands. Wearing it felt strange. Without the security of close-fitting denim it felt weird cracking jokes and striding around. I hankered for the protection of a pinstripe suit.

When I was eight, I thought my husband would wear a pinstripe suit. Men in suits were posh versions of Starsky; they had leather briefcases and bits of paper and everyone looked up to them; they travelled round the world and could fight off terrorists if any came to attack you. If you could snare a pinstriped man you'd be scooped up out of the mud and live in a way that you never could if your husband wore brown jumpers and sandals.

'Say, that's a great dress,' says a man in his early fifties wearing a pink shirt and a midnight-blue pinstripe suit.

He has grey hair, rough-hewn but distinguished bone structure and a raspy American voice that makes him sound like a New York Italian gangster.

'You know,' he says, 'I was down at a ball in Monaco last week and I saw a woman wearing one of those. But you know, you look even better.'

'You sound like a gangster.'

'Oh yeah? Yeah? You like that? You know, that's what I've put my success down to in advertising – the voice. It's all part of the image package, you know. You've gotta be able to project yourself. Projection, right?' He glints.

'Who do you work for?'

'Hey! Fast mover! Like it. Like it. You Brits are all so goddam kinky. You know, the woman who owns this dumb new magazine, I have it from a reliable source – and I mean a reliable source – that she wants me to tie her up naked in her office and then just, well, I don't know if I should be telling you this, but then just, you know – do the business.'

'Sounds pretty tame to me.' His lapels are nice. And that cut looks expensive. Must have a briefcase somewhere and lots of bits of paper.

'Now, you sound like the kind of girl I've been looking for all my life. What do you say to some dinner?'

'George! The guy's a goddam asshole,' says Sophie as I wait by the cloakroom for Chester to fetch my denim jacket. 'He's strung a couple of my friends along. Says he's a Grimaldi but that's all bullshit. The Monaco royal family would run a mile if they ever met him. He knows a few criminals in Argentina. He's a loser, man.'

But no pinstriped man had ever wanted to talk to me before. Although Sophie was right about Chester being an asshole – at the restaurant, he orders from the menu like he is selling oil shares and he sends his fork back twice claiming, each time, that it is dirty – his inordinate confidence persuades me to go back with him for his 'act' as he keeps calling it with a wink (the same wink he used when talking of the magazine owner being tied to the chair in her office).

At two in the morning we enter a large door on the boulevard Beaumarchais and climb the polished stairs covered with red carpet and brass stair rods. My stomach sloshes with a gloopy soup of strawberry *petits fours*, chocolate truffles and endless Taittinger top-ups added to the recent arrival of greasy *steak au poivre* from the restaurant. Chester leads me by the hand through a sun-bleached green room filled with overstuffed furniture to a dusty little box room.

'I have a Swedish student room mate,' he says. 'She's cute. I guess she's not coming back tonight.' He leaves me sitting on the corner of a single bed covered only with one fusty sheet. A few minutes later, wearing a shirt and a pair of white baggy boxer shorts, he tiptoes back to turn on a crackly radio and to lay his trousers and jacket over the back of a spindly chair. He winks and runs off.

His second coming is much more Shirley Bassey. His entrance is heralded by a hand snaking around the door, gripping the end of a brown leather belt which appears and disappears in a sawing motion in time to the radio which has just switched from scratchy George Michael to scratchy 'I'm Bad' by Michael Jackson. Then the whole of the belt is revealed, followed by the whole of his naked body which is blotchy but well-upholstered, apart from a pink turkey-wattle effect flapping vertically down his neck. His body attempts a series of Josephine Baker positions with the help of the belt which he rubs lightly over his stiffening penis. He smiles, and every now and then he caresses the back of his neck with the belt in a neck-drying towel action.

He backs towards the bed and I cross my legs primly as Chester lies down on the sheet, raises his bottom and legs into the air in the bicycle exercise position and begins to stroke his penis up and down its length while moving his pelvis nearer his mouth. It is a complex manoeuvre; Chester is not particularly supple in the pelvic area – it is more that his neck is strangely bendy. His neck veins stand out like whip chords as his mouth strains to get closer to his penis which waggles, tantalisingly, two or three inches away from his mouth like a game of apple bobbing. As the mouth and the penis near one another, I watch his anus (green in colour), opening up ever bigger. I reflect that the colour is an interesting detail. Many of the Marquis de Sade's exploits are so thrillingly disgusting precisely because of his observations on unsavoury shades of genitalia.

This mixture of military precision and ludicrous detail reminds me of Mr Dunn, a rambunctious seventy-year-old regular to my father's chip shop. In a fog-horn voice he used to insist that his evening meal arrived shipshape and Bristol fashion on his plate: four sausages at twelve o'clock, three slices of ham arranged in fan formation at a quarter past the hour, chips positioned due south in an orderly curve stretching from four o'clock to eight o'clock. He was a man of tricks, too. One evening as Mandy the counter server was finishing off his order, Mr Dunn leaned over the counter and gently prised her plump hand off the vinegar shaker. He tapped his golf-umbrella handle on his nose and told her that if she came round to his house one night to hear him play the piano, he'd pay for the installation of her new kitchen units.

It becomes obvious that Chester has neared his goal when he stops pulling at his penis and concentrates on the trigonometry of lining it up with the correct angle to his mouth so that when the white eel of liquid finally spurts out it will hit the target spot on. Just before he comes, he props up his buttocks with his left hand so that there will be less of a strain on his stomach muscles. I think this is a bit of a cheat as far as his 'trick' goes, but it seems inappropriate to interrupt him now that the eel is shooting into his mouth and he is moaning 'maaaaan', (although given that he is now gargling with spunk it comes out more as a rich, bubbly, 'gaaa gaaa' sound).

When the dead weight of his legs finally crashes down on to the bed, Chester's mouth has adopted a little boy grin. He pants, 'Pretty crazy, huh?'

I try to think of an intelligent question. 'You swallow the cum?' I ask, looking at a smear at the corner of his mouth.

'Sure. Part of the trick. You want me to do something for you?'

I look down at the sweating figure lying on the sheet, eyes closed and slack skin running down his neck like melting ice-cream. His trick has certainly been entertaining, the flip side of erotic. Chester has taken me on a journey up to sex's grimy attic where the terrible portrait of 'making love' lies in hideous splendour. His is The Portrait of Casanova as a performing seal, a peek behind the scenes at the rabbit-out-of-the-hat – a terrible revelation of trap doors and hidden wires.

His eyes still closed, he begins to chat merrily about a deal he is on the verge of closing with an Argentinian banker, how only four other people have seen his 'act' and how he is starting to get a flashback of the *sauce au poivre* of earlier on. 'That stuff was amazing. Didn't you think so? Not too hot, you know, but piquant. Piquant,' he says, managing to turn the word sordid as he sucks it in his mouth.

The concoction in my stomach is starting to burn and looking down at his blissfully slumped body I feel the pain of excruciating boredom. Sex has curdled, leaving bum-hole green underneath a clotted layer of banal conversation and awkward silence. But the sight of the pinstripe suit folded over the back of the chair makes me feel warm again. I clamber on to his sweaty back, hitch up my 1920s lace dress, close my eyes and start to slam myself down on his runny buttocks, back and forth, to and fro. Somehow out of nowhere I am Mick Jagger buggering the Chairman of Crédit Lyonnais.

The next morning I wake up with loose antique sequins pricking into my cheeks. I climb out of bed, exhilarated and recharged, knowing that the day only holds purity and innocence after last night, even though I later spend twenty minutes walking along the boulevard Beaumarchais towards the métro, trying to ignore the men who smarm: '*Et alors, mademoiselle, on va danser le Charleston?*'

Saturday, 24 November 1990 (Told at Sophie's dinner party at *cul sec* time. The women liked it. Bet says I'll never become editor of the *Herald Tribune*.)

Henry Flash doesn't just look like a sperm in spectacles. He has a neck that looks like it belongs to ET. Those weren't my first impressions though. When I first saw him, it was on a photographic light box at *Paris Parade* in a series of pictures where he had been dressed up as three types of clubber: the naff clubber, the gayboy clubber and the millionaire clubber. My job was to write the story to accompany these nightclub shots.

Looking at the photos, it was difficult to choose between the gayboy Henry and the millionaire Henry. In the former photo you could see him on the dance floor doing some waggling hand movements in a black Perfecto and being hit on by a beautiful blond man. In the Lotus Eater shot he was wearing a cream suit and a tie clip, sitting cross-legged in front of a large potted plant, puffing on a cigar.

Henry cut out the millionaire picture and stuck it on

his computer. He said it was because of the Brogues. Brogues are one of Henry's pet subjects: he is French-American and his New York Jewish father used to run a shoe store in Manhattan. When we finally met in the flesh, Henry's conversational gambit was about tongues and uppers. 'It's in the stitching, the stitching, totally in the stitching. You want good shoes, you have to pay for them, and if you're going to feel guilty about fourteen-year-olds shitting their guts out in the Philippines making them then you'd better be prepared to pay good money for them. And don't even talk to me about the British market, the Brits want shoe heaven for a few shitty dollars and if that's your attitude . . .'

His plus points were that he was weak and puny. When he shook my hand, his was limp and he didn't feel obliged to give me a piercing stare. There was also something endearingly antisocial about the way he communicated in extremely long sentences filled with scato logical references and punctuated with hyperventilating indignation. You felt that by the time the end of the paragraph came something terrible might happen.

He suggested we dined together at a restaurant so he could give me some tips for the story. Yet his non-stop rant about money and persecution at the hands of Ralph Davidson, the Editor-in-Chief of *Paris Parade*, was so relentless when we arrived at the restaurant that I ordered shark's fin and duck's feet to try to inject some interest into the evening. He didn't seem to notice and ordered Chow Mein. The first time he seemed to take notice of my presence came when I admitted I didn't know what his job at the magazine was. He launched into a speech filled with sub-clauses and bile about how indispensable the job of the fact checker was. But by the end of the meal he seemed ready to explode with a sense of injustice. Even the taxi driver taking us back to his house was encouraged to express outrage at his lot in an absurd and over-taxed universe.

While Henry's speech was clipped and sharp when

he spoke English, he came into his own when he reverted to French which was laced with a string of curt expletives, of which the favoured ones were *'incroyable'*, *'dégueulasse'*, *'inadmissible'* and the inevitable *'merdique'*.

Henry: What do you think of Mitterand's talk about tax reforms?
Taxi driver: *Bah, vous savez*, the people in power always want to raise taxes . . .
Henry: Exactly! You're exactly right! It's utterly disgusting what he's proposed. It's *merdique* in fact . . .
Taxi driver: But the right wing are the same, *vous savez* . . .
Henry: Just because they're doing the same thing, it's still *inadmissible. Inadmissible! N'est-ce pas!*

I watched Henry's indignant ET neck twitch from side to side like a roadrunner, but I tried to banish such perfidious thoughts by thinking of Henry in the gayboy picture, his mouth seized in an arrogant pout, his crotch outlined in tight blue denim.

The sight of Henry's spartan flat – a gamut of grubby browns, and its smell – fermenting refuse bin, was so seedy that I pulled him towards me, kissed him and fumbled with his crotch (now outlined, alas, with baggy beige draylene).

He pulled himself away and said, 'Jesus Christ, did you never hear of holding yourself back! You're like a freak in one of those seaside competitions where you have to swallow as many hard-boiled eggs as you can within sixty seconds.'

I decided that Henry was trying to be funny and went and sat down on his sofa while he went over to his stereo. He fiddled with it and mumbled that the tape he wanted had been chewed up. When he came back to sit next to me, the voice of Dame Celia Johnson began to fill the room: '"My dear Mr Bennet," said his lady to him one day, "have you heard that Netherfield Park is let at last? It is taken by a young man of large fortune from the north of England; a single man of large fortune; four or five thousand a year. What a fine thing for our girls!"'

The brown decor seemed even browner. 'Henry,' I said bluntly, 'are we supposed to be feeling sexy about this?'

'You don't want to listen to *Pride and Prejudice?*'

'No.'

Henry stood up and went over to the stereo. 'You know, this is good stuff, this BBC shit. Words are always clear, pronunciation is always correct. Things like that are important to me, you know,' he mumbled as he stopped Celia Johnson in her tracks and switched on Radio 4. 'Radio 4 too. There's no bullshit like with French radio, you get straight answers. Sometimes it just serves to highlight what bullshit it is copy editing at *Paris Parade*. Ralph Davidson is just a bully, you know. He swaggers around the office and all those girls just love him and he doesn't know jack shit about jack shit but sure, come issue day, you can bet your bottom dollar he'll come up to me in front of my interns – my interns, if you please – and say in his whiny little voice—' (Henry's string-thin voice is pulled even tauter. '"So Hen" – goddam always calls me Hen – "so Hen, had some problems with cedillas this month huh?" Problems, he says! Can you believe that? I think: what about your problems with your D minus editorial content! Huh? Huh? I'll shit on your ugly Jewish face you short ass fat Jewish fuck. Course I don't say that, I just think it. You know, these guys know nothing. They just want to trample all over you. They've got no respect. It's unbelievable. And writers today, they don't know the difference between a cedilla and an apostrophe. Punctuation! Punctuation's something for Caspar frigging Milksop.'

Henry's face was red with oxygen depletion and I suggested putting Dame Celia back on to calm him down, but Henry said he was fine with the Radio 4 news. As he got up to fetch a bottle of wine and two glasses, he suddenly seemed quite like an apostrophe himself. That squinting little worm's head, shiny as a plum, a pedantic little thing that you weren't quite sure what to do with.

'Yeah well, Henry, punctuation's not my strong point. I was off sick the week they did grammar at the convent.'

Henry stopped pouring wine and turned to me, his face frozen with horror. Then the face cracked and laughter came out of his mouth.

'Hey! That was a joke, right? Hey, that's funny, "I was away the week they did grammar". That's good. A good joke.'

The wine was as heavy as the conversation, and the Radio 4 background programme droning about 'the remarkable tenacity of variegated cacti' made me feel like tying Henry up with ropes and burning his nipples with a cigarette stub. It was strange. The more boring he got, the more turned on I became. After the initial shock of realising that Henry was as much of a swish millionaire as I was the Queen of Sheba I began to warm to the challenge. Electric boredom reached a peak as he began to speak of his ambitions to be a copy editor on *Reader's Digest* and how he was currently learning Spanish – in the bath – twenty minutes every morning before he went to work. 'I file Spanish news ideas to *El País*. I can make $30 in a good week.'

Henry's eyes were dull and dusty – windows looking on to an old junk room. Behind the dusty brown doors you could see the room, clogged up with the ungainly furniture of ambition, envy and frustration. If you stared long enough, squinted and peered and scrunched your eyes up a little bit, you could see, parked at the back of the room, almost out of sight, a little tea chest that looked a little brighter, a little shinier than everything else. I decided to kiss him again to see if anything interesting lay there.

When I opened my eyes, his face was all pinched, like he'd been sucking a lemon. But at least he was now making a move towards the fold-away bed. Predictably, Henry had a fold-up bed which took a good five minutes to assemble – giving him time to resort back to his Macarthyite moral system.

'You know,' he said, yanking at some dislodged springs, 'you're really easy, aren't you? The French girls I see don't even talk about this until a few months down the line. I mean, I just asked you out for dinner and this is the first time we've been alone together and now you want to, well, now you want to . . .'

'Henry,' I said annoyed, 'do you want me to go home?'

'I never said that.'

'Right. So stop panicking. Okay?'

Something seemed to thaw and Henry's face suddenly lit up and there was that smile again. He swiped me gently on the arm with a limp hand and, looking just like his gayboy picture said, *'Mais, t'as la pêche, tu sais!'* which, in rough translation, means 'you're a bit of a one'.

I much preferred him in French. There seemed some point to him in French. At least I could learn something from him. He seemed less of an etiolated broad bean shoot and more urbane and handsome when he exclaimed in French.

He insisted on folding up every item of clothing he discarded and going off to look for extra coat hangers. Then he refused to get into the bed without first making sure that the sheet was tucked in properly with hospital corners.

I kept myself calm by remembering that the interest in having sex with a nerd is that you become a god for the night.

I pulled him on to the bed and began to laugh at the look of terror on his face.

Unsurprisingly, Henry had forgotten to buy in any

condoms so our options were limited, yet I flattered myself that I would be the one to turn him around, I would transform him, take him to bathe in the pool of sexual healing. I lifted up the blanket and plunged into the unknown.

I smiled as I felt his hips begin to wiggle and his dick begin to stiffen. I slipped off his boxers and prepared for action.

When there's been a plaster on your toe for a very long time, it's often shocking when you rip it off to see how pale and strange, how thin and defenceless the skin underneath has become. The sight of Henry minus boxers was shocking also but, undeterred, I decided to jump-start the pelvic wasteland by putting all my cards on the table and with the aid of the hair trick and the root trick I started to put all my effort into this sad piece of halibut. Tumescence finally trickled into him and, like a lilo with a faulty valve, he slowly began to inflate. His penis rose like the ticktock little hand of a clock coming up to 12 and on the stroke of 10 past 2 a little phut phut of white spunk burped out.

A good start, I thought, rustling round in the under-growth of bedclothes. I started to come up for air, imagining how happy his face would be now that I had put my life's work into his groin.

As I emerged into the light I saw Henry writh-ing around on his pillows. I immediately realised that this was not happy, post-coital writhing. *The World Tonight* seemed to have sucked him into a vortex of indignation.

'Those chicken-shitted little Arabs have fucking gone and walked out of peace talks again! I mean, can you fucking believe it. Everything has been done to favour them, everyone's on tiptoe around them and they go and shit all over everybody.'

Sneaking a look into his eyes, I noticed that several deliveries of ugly furniture had been off-loaded there since I had last seen them: chairs of injustice, wardrobes of wrath, job lots of sideboards stuffed with anxiety rattled round in the dusty brown junk room, obscuring any other emotion.

He called two days later. I agreed to give him one more chance and things started off well in bed when he pulled out a box of three condoms. But then he began to roll around on the bed mumbling something about 'bullshit condoms, too goddam small'. The truth was, he kept losing his erection. The only way he could get it back was by scrambling on to my back and rubbing himself up and down. I wasn't averse to buggery but poor Henry didn't really seem up to it. When he'd finished panting from all the scrambling, he couldn't find the right hole and he muttered like when he couldn't get his Dame Celia tape to work. Finally he squeezed in half an inch. He made the noises that people having a whale of a time at a funfair make and then when he slithered off, he croaked, 'Jesus Christ. You took me to the moon.'

The next week I took Henry to a big waiting room with yellowing walls and a stern receptionist. I'd summoned him there following a telephone call I'd made just two days after his cosmic experience:

'Hi, Henry. Having a good Sunday?'

'Sure. I'm kind of busy though.'

'Oh, busy? Sorry to disturb you. What are you doing then? Sunday things like listening to a spot of Radio 4, flicking through the Spanish press?'

'Sure, that kind of thing. You know, I think maybe we should call it a day. I've been starting to get a little bored, you know.'

'Oh, bored, oh really? Well, let me tell you something that will really un-bore you. This fine Sunday morning, I woke up to discover I had a genital wart. Fine and bloody dandy I'm sure you'll agree to get a genital fucking wart from a man who can't get an erection. Trust my luck to have sex with someone who can't spawn progeny, but can only spawn genital fucking warts.'

A slew of 'oh my god's swirled down the other end of the phone.

'You know, Henry, I hoped there was more behind that dull façade than just plain dullness but right now I just wish it hid a stockpile of TCP and genital wart plasters. Next time you want to take somebody to the moon go to the VD clinic first!'

I was so furious when I discovered the spot that I decided to drag Henry through the humiliation with me. But now that the doctor has told me it's just a common pimple which will vanish within the week and is unrelated to sexual activity in any way – although it may in some way be related to excessive consumption of fried sardine sandwiches – I'm not sure what I shall tell Henry. After the initial cringe of embarrassment I feel indecently excited at the realisation that I might be able to extract some pleasure from Henry after all.

I close the doctor's door and see him sweating in a chair; his threadworm qualities have never been as clear as they are now. What shall I tell him? The upstanding fact checker who knows more about punctuation than anyone alive can hardly breathe at the thought that the one thing he never dared rant about, the thing that has been dead to him for so long, is in fact the carrier of more ill than all the tax inspectors, all the magazine editors in the world.

He stiffens at my approach.

CHAPTER SIX

The Theatre of Sexuality

The theatre curtains that had trundled shut on my sleeping-bag dream when I was eight, opened again on my tenth birthday. They parted as slowly as they had closed and at first all I could see behind them was a big, cheesy grin.

I came home from school and there was a large black and white photo of a famous show-biz tap dancer on my bed. In exuberant red biro down the side of the picture were the words: 'To George, much love, L.'

I looked at the suspiciously ecstatic face but I didn't recognise the black and white man as one of my role models. My main role model was Mandy from the chip shop. She had skin that fell loose around her face like soufflé cashmere. She reminded me of my hamster who could turn round 360 degrees in his skin. Her code name was Mandy fag ash because her daughter was an alcoholic and her son was in prison and it was rumoured that she had sex in ditches after work with her man, Ronny.

If Mandy had cares in the world she never let them show. Once, when she was placing a pot of tea for four on a customer's table a cockroach climbed out of the spout. She chuckled, 'My Christ!' as if somebody had just surprised her with a bunch of flowers. One day, when Bernard Manning came in with a group of friends from the North for double cod, chips and peas, Mandy got him to sign an autograph for me and he left me an 87 pence tip.

My other heroes were Peter Purvis, John Pertwee and Bruce Forsyth. They all had something indefinable about them, but the common denominator was that I'd have died to spend a day with them, somewhere, alone. Say, out on bikes, having a picnic, going on the rubber dinghies at Swanpool Beach. In my fantasy they'd really like me and want to spend lots of time, just playing. Once I had a dream that I really did make contact with Bruce Forsyth. Out of all of my class, I was the one he chose to spend a day with at the Dolphinarium. Then I woke up and my heart sank as I realised he was just another unattainable figure from *The Generation Game*.

I looked at the grinning face again. The squiggly red ink that spelled out his name meant nothing to me.

'Mummy,' I asked, walking into the kitchen, 'who's this man?'

'You'll have to ask your father,' she replied, sounding exasperated in a way that she rarely did. 'Ray! Your daughter's got a question for you.'

My father came into the room and seemed unusually cheerful. 'So, what do you think then?' he said.

Even though I was an impressionable ten-year-old who didn't know anyone famous, I was less than wowed. This was the early seventies, the days before a cheap studio quiz game had made the entertainer into a household name again. I wanted my father to know a really big cheese like China Blackwell's father did. He ran the biggest hotel in Newquay and sometimes Ian Dury came to stay in the summer.

'Who is he?' I asked, looking puzzled at the photograph of the grinning man.

'You don't know who he is!' my father guffawed. 'You know, he used to do variety. He was on Jimmy Tarbuck for a while. He's famous!'

Later that night, making fruit salad in the kitchen with

my mother, I learnt some more. It seemed that the famous tap dancer had fallen on hard times and had come down to Cornwall to manage a quality clothes shop until bookings picked up. Being a theatrical kind of person, he had been welcomed into the Arwenack Street business fraternity by its chief players: my father, Richey who ran the sausage emporium and Gemma and Robin the hippies who ran the Indian jewellery shop opposite us.

They would all go out on Wednesdays – early closing day. Tap dancer in dinner jacket and patent shoes, my father in denim and 'Persuaders' suede jacket, Richey in medallions and solarium tan and Gemma and Robin with no bra and hairy chest. Sometimes my mother went too. She said that the tap dancer kept calling her 'darling' and if he liked something he called it 'divine'. Nobody said 'divine' in Cornwall.

My mother said she knew the real reason for the man's regular orders of haddock, chips and pickled egg. 'He thinks your father's a bit of rough,' she said, chopping vigorously. 'It's "Ray" this and "Ray" that and "Ray those jeans are fabulous on you" and "Ray take these tickets for *Mother Goose* at the Falmouth Pier."'

She got up to wash her hands.

'And they say his wife likes the girls too.'

I was quite astonished. My mother had never talked to me in such adult language before, let alone brought up the concept of homosexuality. Earlier that year I'd had a conversation with my grandfather concerning the Jeremy Thorpe sex scandal. On the ITN news the night before there had been an item about the politician and a 'tube of lubricant' that had been found by his bed. Helen Ringwall at school, who'd already had a boyfriend, said her mother had told her it was for 'lubricating the act'.

Sitting in the car that weekend with my grandfather, I said that I thought it a shame that Jeremy Thorpe had lost his job because he loved somebody who was a man. 'Ah, but you have to be careful,' my grandfather said knowledgeably. 'It's dangerous for official secrets. Homosexuals lay themselves open to blackmail.'

'But if people didn't think they were bad then they wouldn't be able to blackmail them, would they?'

'You don't understand these things,' my grandfather said darkly and fell silent.

By this time, the black and white photograph of the famous show-biz tap dancer had taken on underground status in my mind and I took it to school with me the next day. I showed Ruth Worthing on the bus. I explained the circumstances: 'He gave it to my dad. He thinks my dad's a bit of rough.'

'Who is he?' she asked, staring closely at the mug shot.

'He's been in variety and on the Jimmy Tarbuck show,' I said hopefully. Ruth's father was a 'professional'. He was a councillor and she wasn't allowed to watch ITV. She didn't know who Bernard Manning was. She might not even know who Jimmy Tarbuck was.

Luckily, it turned out that Ruth did know who Jimmy Tarbuck was and three or four girls in my class had even heard of the famous show-biz tap dancer. The person they were most interested in meeting however was my father. When I told them all that my father had become the 'bit of rough of a very famous variety performer' and that I thought I had seen this very famous variety performer coming in for chips with tubes of sexual-act lubricant coming out of his pocket, they all became very interested and I got to sit on the back row of the bus for a whole week. My father came home one night and asked me if I knew why groups of giggling ten-year-olds in Tremough Convent uniforms kept coming in and staring at him.

I shrugged and tried to make my eyes go wide.

The flap, flap of the theatre curtains has now begun to obsess me. Even when they open up a little way, there is still too much dry ice for me to have a perfect view. I want to see, but since Sponge I haven't met any women who want to sleep with me. Bet has pledged to sleep with a woman by the time she is forty but she hasn't even been putting out any feelers. I can't bear the thought of waiting until I'm forty before I do it again. My front-of-house night errands with men are starting to bore me and although Holly insists that there is a lesbian orgy going on behind the pillar in Le Swing every time he drags me there, he's always lying. He only says it because he wants me to hang around with him until he's copped off in a place that is only ever stuffed with gayboys.

Then one day, a blonde Californian called Dawn burst through the curtains at *Paris Parade* and I felt a jolt of desire. She did a Puss In Boots strut up to my desk and said, 'Hi, you must be George Quentin, I know your name from the mast head.' She glanced at the pot of Marmite standing on the desk and rolled into a delivery of the Marmite anecdote that all Americans tell you when they see a pot of the stuff: 'You know, when I first tried Marmite I thought you had to spread it like peanut butter? My mom kept saying how amazing it was. I'm like, standing there with this bagel loaded three inches high with the stuff and I take a bite and I'm like, "This is bloody disgusting".'

Her prologue over, she perched herself on my desk and moved into Act One, announcing that in the US she'd been making 'big money' in TV – lifestyle interviews, music vox pops – but she'd come to Paris because she longed to be a writer. With a flourish of a pink nail-varnished hand she concluded that, sure, sometimes she was asked to write for the *Herald Tribune*.

Over the next few weeks she would come into the office most days for half an hour or so. She would sit down next to me claiming that she was doing some research 'to get to Bardot'. I liked the way she scared me. She would be prickly and distant, snapping suddenly if I casually introduced a word into the conversation that she didn't know ('Wait. "Aftermath". Where did you learn that?'). And then she would suddenly lapse into mild flirtation. She would tell me that she was turned on by the smell of soap, that the worst turn-off she could think of was somebody who didn't use dental floss, that Paris had lowered the quality of her life because her apartment didn't have a trash compressor. And I struggled with all my might not to learn her phone number off by heart.

I was wary because she seemed to flirt mildly with lots of people. I was sitting typing next to her late one night when her phone rang and a typical Dawn conversation ensued.

'Yeah? Oh, hi, Pierre. Yeah, I'm sorry I'm late, I got kind of busy. Look, I have to pick up some film scripts from just around the corner and then I have to go to the sixth to brief the cameraman about the shoot tomorrow. I'll give you a call in about thirty minutes, okay? Yeah, look, I know I said I'd be ready at nine but things came up, you know? Look, let me call you in thirty minutes.'

She turned to me and sighed. 'God, that guy's gotta go. He's a pain in the fucking ass. Doesn't understand me, my work, you know?'

I nodded, expressionless.

'You're such a scum bag,' she said huskily, as she always did when we were on the verge of intimacy.

She picked up her things slowly and was walking down the hallway towards the door when she turned and said, 'Maybe you can save me from all these terrible guys. Maybe you want to have dinner with me tomorrow night.'

I counted to five. 'Yeah, maybe. Have to see how busy I am.'

*　　*　　*

When we met at the restaurant, she was late and incredibly touchy. I ordered a chicken crêpe. She ordered quiche and salad, and made a point of leaving the pastry and scraping all the dressing off the lettuce leaves. When my crêpe came, it turned out to be a special Algerian deep-fried pancake. It tasted of that sinking feeling I had on misty, dark Sunday evenings, sitting with the family eating Sunday roast and feeling sick because it was school the next day.

After talking non-stop for twenty minutes about her boy-friend in New York, she put down her knife and fork and said, 'You know, you'd be much prettier if you were thinner.'

I was mesmerised by her self-assurance. She talked confi-dently to the waiter in very bad French and did the equivalent of Oliver asking for more gruel: she sent back her *demi*, complaining that she didn't like the taste. '*Oh, vas-y chéri*,' she commanded in a big, fat, American accent that was half CNN dominatrix, half cutesy schoolgirl, and which sent the waiter running off with his tail between his legs.

As she drank more, she loosened up and her obsessive quest for self-improvement became clear. She wanted it all. Her own TV show, thinner upper arms, a pierced clit, a trash compressor, a wider vocabulary, a better apartment on the Ile Saint Louis, a film deal, a more productive day, more energy, more money, more respect, immortality.

The longer she talked, the more obvious it became that her life had everything mine was lacking. She leaned back in her chair and stared me in the eye, smiling. 'So,' she said. 'I hear that you're a regular bohemian.'

I was sure that what she really wanted to say was, 'I'd love to go to bed with you.'

The waiter brought the bill and smilingly told Dawn she could have the beer on the house. We split the 320 franc total and she said, 'Come on. Let's go for a ride.'

Outside, she put her half-face crash hat on along with some goggles which made her look like a butch Penelope Pitstop. She handed me another helmet and we jumped red lights all the way to her place. 'Hold me tighter,' she laughed loud as we sped off. I knew she wanted to go to bed with me because she did anything I said. I said, 'Let's go up to Montmartre,' and even though it was two in the morning and going over all those cobblestones must have been bad for her scooter, she did it. Then, without consulting me, she suddenly headed the bike back towards rue de Clignancourt. We drove down scummy boulevard Barbès, through the Sentier and its tacky leather shops, past the hookers on the rue Saint Denis, along to the twinkling lights of Châtelet, past the Town Hall and the camp, green knights standing to attention on its roof, over the Saint Louis bridge, past the snogging shadows and the beaming lights of a *Bateau Mouche*.

When we arrived in front of the green doors of her apartment building she stopped the bike and I felt her body tense. 'God,' she hissed, unlocking my hands from her waist. 'Your hands are so cold.'

I'd wanted to put them underneath her jacket and nestle them against her warm skin. I supposed it was warm at any rate. I could feel myself blushing in the dark but I thought I should feign irritation at being scolded.

'Look,' I said harshly, 'I have to go back to my house. I've got a deadline tomorrow.'

'Nooo,' she soothed, back to the foxy rasp. 'No, look, I'm having a good time. Aren't you? I've got some pot upstairs. Let's get a little high.' She kissed me on the cheek and I felt the warm inside of her mouth.

When Dawn opened her front door I presumed that sex couldn't be on the mind of a woman who kept an apartment like this. Everything was white and polished and every wall was stacked with photos of tanned faces and smiling white teeth. Always a balanced group of gung-ho males and big-haired females, always in smiling crowds in front of waterfalls, at picnics, in parks, on green lawns with blue skies and enthusiastic pink-tongued dogs in the background.

Everything in the apartment was stacked, piled, filed and labelled, including her record collection which could have come straight from a lesbian commune in San Francisco. I looked at the rows of Janis Joplin, Tracy Chapman, Joan Armatrading and felt optimistic.

Dawn's saving grace was that she liked to get stoned. We sat on her white settee staring at the framed collection of brown smiley faces while she talked about her strategies to get her film script to Jody Foster, and her recent enrolment in the American Church's book club. 'You know,' she said, lighting up, 'a lot of the people there are really dumb. I mean, they just don't get what the books are about. Like, the one we're reading at the moment is about these two women who go live on a farm on their own and I was like, "Those two are totally together", you know? I mean, I didn't say . . . well, you know . . . I didn't say the *word*, but then this other woman goes, "Which bit makes you think they're, like, *together*?" and then afterwards she was totally, like, "You're right you know?"'

My knee banged playfully against hers until I could bear it no longer. I turned to face her and my lips met hers. About twenty seconds passed before she pulled gently back and said voluptuously, 'You know, I don't know about this.'

It was pretty funny that I fancied her smile because when I finally got her into bed her look of sexual euphoria was expressed by a grimace that looked like she'd eaten something horrible. It was a closed mouth smile, different from a public smile. Attempting love making with her was like being an amateur trying to diffuse a bomb. Each area of her body was a tripwire which, between low gasps and stifled moans, triggered off elaborate explanations and heart-rending tales of woe. I thought her body was the most perfect thing I'd seen this side of a TV advert. It was tanned, without stretch marks, spare tyres, cellulite or blotches. The only marks on her were those the surgeon's knife had left on her breasts when she'd had an operation to bring her up to West Coast standards of perfection. These scars were an obvious landmine and I was in a sense prepared for the torrent of unburdening that followed: the schoolgirl taunts, the hindrance to a good game of tennis of a 38 double D cup, the therapy sessions with the private doctor. As I kissed her breasts carefully I murmured that I'd hardly noticed. Naturally, the scars looked to me like she'd had a traumatic encounter with a car windscreen, but I wasn't going to say that and anyway, I really didn't care. Even apparently problem-free areas like her arms were booby trapped and one kiss of them triggered off a pre-recorded message about how many hours each one was worked on the *musculateur* machine at the gym and what the arm's correct fat/flesh quotient was. By the time I got down past her belly I was beginning to feel the strain of the journey and I suspected that this new leg of the trip would prove even more testing.

I didn't get much lower than her belly. I brushed against a spectacularly wrong wire and the 26 per cent fat-free arms rose up like well-oiled machinery and clamped down on the waxed fuse box attired in a black satin G-string. I looked up towards her face and saw her smiling nervously. I felt like a pig shut up in a pen in front of a huge puddle of bubbling mud and never let loose.

'I've washed that this evening,' she said, heaving me up next to her and putting her arms round me in an affectionate hug. I couldn't care less if she'd washed it or not, so exhilarating was the overall effect of her toned, tanned, soapy body. (The all-pervading odour of Clinique Shampoo and Crabtree & Evelyn soap was making me wonder exactly what she did smell of. I expected her to tell me to step into a bowl of sheep dip every time I walked through her front door and having sex with her was like trying to get intimate with a plastic bag.)

Then, just when I thought she'd fallen asleep, a voice suddenly piped up from the other side of the pillow: 'You only like me for my body,' it said. Very unconvincingly I replied, 'No, I love your mind too,' and waited for the thunderbolt to come and strike me down. To fill in the gap I mumbled nervously that, anyway, I thought she was terrified of the idea of sleeping with a woman.

'What I say and what I really feel are two different things,' she murmured sleepily, reaching out for my hand and squeezing it.

In the morning she scolded me for leaving a wet towel on the floor in the bathroom all night. 'Gross,' she said. 'There's probably mould growing all over it.'

Monday, 25 March 1991

The act of sex makes you more alive than you have ever been, but its aftermath saps concentration. The memory of sex has incapacitated me. It's grooved its groin into my mind and stunned my most efficient thoughts. My day is seen through kaleidoscope vision whose brightest shards are fragments from last night's slutty jigsaw. I give Monsieur Bellier his English lesson, tied up over the table while Dawn whips me lightly with a leather belt. I hope my Japanese-designer incontinence trousers and too-tight blue linen jacket fooled him into believing that my mind was fully on 'Madonna and her pickings from trash cans in her down-and-out New York days'.

I wish I could get Dawn off my mind. The morning after we slept together she begrudgingly agreed to give me a lift – not back to my house – but to Châtelet where she had another of her business meetings. When we went out into the street to go to her bike, she kept turning around and saying, 'Don't walk so close to me. We have to be careful you know.' I told her that just because we walked in the street next to each other people would not necessarily suspect us of being lesbian lovers. But she just snapped at me to 'take it easy'. So I sighed and remembered that, after all, she was Dawn. She stopped the bike near Châtelet along the rue de Rivoli. I got off and put the crash hat in her top box. To my surprise, she grabbed my arm as I said goodbye and said that she'd call me. I got the métro back to rue de Clignancourt, lay down on my bed and stared up at the cracks on the ceiling for the rest of the morning.

After a week of X-rated attention deficit disorder and a series of non-committal calls, Dawn finally made a firm commitment. I was lying in bed hoping every time the phone rang that it would be her.

When she did call she seemed in good spirits. 'Hi flake, it's me — your fun-time secret admirer.' The part about having to go to another 'boring dinner' followed but she finished by saying that she wanted to go to see a film at the cinema that evening.

'Do you want to meet me at the Odeon in Saint Germain at 6.30? The movie starts at 7. Don't be late, flake.'

The prospect compelled me to the shower where I used my precious plastic mini-bottle of Radox bath foam. I'd stolen it from the Plaza Athenée washroom when I'd gone to interview a minor French film starlette the previous week. Afterwards, I moisturised my legs, applied some fake tan and pulled on my clean jeans that I'd been keeping for just such an occasion as this.

In front of the cinema we both put up a cool front and all our intimacy slipped back to nothing. I asked her what she'd had to eat at the dull man's house and she said it was a stupid question and she bet I'd eaten more than her anyway.

I asked her what was up and she became furious. 'God, this thing between us is getting obscene. You know what happened to me the morning after I left you at Châtelet? I was at a very important meeting and I put up my hand to scratch my nose and, well, I just smelled this ... this smell. It was, you know, it was the smell ... of you ... of you on my hand! I mean that's gross, right! Right? I mean, my boss would freak out if he knew. At one point he asked me if he could smell my new perfume because he was intrigued that I kept sniffing my hand. I mean come on, I'm a valley girl for Chrissakes. Things like this aren't supposed to happen to me!'

We went towards our seats in heavy silence. I wondered what I smelt like. She smelt like fried lamb chops. But I'd save that one up until we had a really big row. When we were sitting down she suddenly said, 'Everything you find funny, I find gross.'

I sat throughout the movie feeling the pain of not being able to be myself and wishing that I'd had the courage to buy some M&Ms and popcorn. When something scary happened in the film and she leaned slightly towards me I thought, 'Hooray, she's doing that because she fancies me.' But when it was finished and we came out into the street she said she didn't think we should see so much of one another. I said that I hadn't seen her since Tuesday because she seemed to be spending all her energy on her friends and not on me. My gabble came to a sudden stop and I couldn't think what else to say. I could feel that my face was red. Then I opened my mouth, not caring what came out. I said that she was mad; that she wanted me to tell her what I thought, but what was the point if she only wanted to see me once a week, as if I could just cut off my affections. I blushed again when I said the word 'affections'.

Out of the blue, Dawn smiled. *Faux* sulky she said, 'I'm not going to give you your present now.'

I smiled, in spite of myself. 'You're lying. You're too busy seeing very important business contacts to buy me a present.'

'God,' she laughed, rolling her eyes to the sky. She put on her irritating English accent and said, 'You think I'm so shallow, don't you?'

She handed me a paper bag that had a white T-shirt inside.

On the front was a black and white cartoon of a stretched person and the words 'New York State of Mind'.

I felt strong enough to be sarcastic. 'So, you went back to buy it in New York, especially for me?'

'Okay, so I had it in my apartment. But I thought of you, huh, George? Huh? Huh?' She was teasing, trying to win me over again.

As I put the T-shirt in my back pack, Dawn said, 'Why don't you come back to my place. If you get up early.'

I tried to sound indifferent as I said, 'I don't know. I don't think it's a good idea. You don't seem in the greatest of moods.'

'C'mon, George.'

'I'll wear it at home in bed.' I was enjoying my moment of attention.

'Yeah,' she sounded sombre, 'it'll probably be more affectionate than me.'

'That's not a bad line for you.'

'You see, I'm not as stupid as you think.' I was flattered she had such a large inferiority complex on my account. 'Oh, go on, George, it won't be any fun sleeping on my own. It's fun when you're there.'

That night, Dawn commanded in a sexy, dirty, Cruella de Vil voice, 'Go down on me.' Afterwards, she said, 'That was really intense.' I explained a few other things that we could do next time but she misheard. She said, 'Okay. The next time we make love I want you to ring me.'

Dawn was the first person I'd slept with whose body I concentrated on when I masturbated. Usually I'd fish some image out of my head of some sleazy man or some *salope* of a woman I'd met and I'd soon come to orgasm and get the tiresome sexual urge out of the way. Now I imagined curling up to Dawn in her bed. I didn't even want some grotesque mind-fuck of being taken from behind in the woods by some smarmy flasher I'd told to 'piss off' earlier that day.

I first realised she was different when I found I didn't want to 69 her, turn her over, stick my tongue up her anus, dribble down her throat and have an impersonal wrench of clitoral bliss in the kind of orgasm that made you feel like the scum of the earth afterwards.

Instead, I loved to bury my head in her cunt and feel it swell and her clitoris stiffen like a bird's tongue and wash my face in her. When it felt right, I could come just by burying my face in her. I felt like I wanted to tunnel my way up into her womb and live in her and my head felt like it would explode and my orgasm wasn't located in my cunt. I couldn't locate it and it was winding, like on a roller coaster. It went up and down and slowly up and faster down and just as you thought the ride was over it turned out there was enough juice to get you up the slope all over again.

I could have gone on for ages more, but I figured that the sight of me squirming around down there between her legs must look slightly ludicrous and I got stage fright.

I couldn't believe I was having such a good time with someone who was so good at making me feel like a 'before' picture. Dawn would often talk about people whom she deemed fat but who I thought were pretty much my shape. The only thing that stopped me getting indignantly out of bed was the thought that I'd probably wobble, and you can't really make a dramatic exit when you wobble.

Sometimes I did want to 69 her and lick her anus and dribble down her throat but there was still that sexy edge of fear that prevented me. She didn't seem all that comfortable with me getting close to her. In the street I used to stand as close to her as I could without looking like a lecherous ninety-year-old flasher on a bus. I would lean the top part of my body towards her so I must have looked like a right-angled triangle.

✻   ✻   ✻

Holly was incensed that I was so smitten with her – he called her leather skin. He was bored of calling me up and finding me in the depths of despair.

'I can't believe you're into someone who wears pink lipstick and who acts like a public health inspector in bed.'

I felt a wedge of anger warm up in my stomach.

'Look, you don't know her,' my voice flailed unsteadily. Then calmer, I added, 'I don't know, it's just this food thing is getting to me. I feel like a pie factory even if I slip a bit of fruit into my mouth when I'm with her. I wish I could be like Ann. She comes home and says, "I'm ravenous" then proceeds to liquidise a dozen carrots and some broccoli and she seems satisfied. Dawn hasn't called all day today and right now I feel like committing culinary hari kiri with a Big Mac and a deep-fried duck pâté sandwich. Even if she did phone up I'd be so fat and disgusting that she wouldn't fancy me anyway.'

'Well, that's all very interesting,' Holly drawled. 'But it's time for me to go to bed.'

'But Holly, it's only three in the afternoon.'

'I know it is, but I read somewhere that you lose 2,000 calories every time you go to bed. I'll wake up looking like Veronica Lake.'

Wednesday, 3 June 1991

Sometimes I turn up at Dawn's apartment and something will put me off. Like the wrinkled backs of her hands or the stupid fake English accent she puts on, or she seems too keen and I think, 'Fuck, how can I get out of this?' And sometimes I turn up and she smiles with the smile she sometimes uses in bed, or she'll be on the phone being invited over to a weekend watch conference in Geneva by a PR friend of hers, and I'll be jealous and she won't seem that pleased to see me and I'll be terrified she's gone off me and doesn't fancy me any more. It's not like with a bloke, because even if they don't really fancy you they'll still shag you. It's more brittle and uncertain with a woman.

Last night, Dawn was lying next to me when she said, 'I'm not freaked out by making love with you. I'm freaked out I enjoyed it so much', followed by 'I think about you. I think, "what would George say about that?"' When I asked if I was okay in bed, she said, 'You're perfect' and added 'I like it that you come quickly.' I think that was a compliment.

Dawn started to call at least once a day. At the end of the conversation she would ask me what I'd been up to. I couldn't tell her I'd done no work all day. No real work anyway, that I was back to teaching English at Madame Bourse's to pay the rent. She'd just get all impatient if I told her about the intensive course I was doing with Monsieur Revault d'Allones, a dull manager at Citroën. He insisted that his lesson started at seven in the morning and all he ever wanted to do was discuss France and the rise of the Fifth Republic.

When I tried to liven things up a little by suggesting a role-play session — me the métro ticket *contrôleur* and him the young student who'd been caught without a ticket — he folded his hands slowly on the desk and said in his creepy, perfect English, 'With all due respect, *mademoiselle*, my conscience forbids me from playing such a role. It is my firm belief that payment of taxes and the entrance fees for all public amenities are indispensable for the proper maintenance of a civilised society.'

I looked at the bright side of his dull nature. At least he never seemed to notice when I turned up with pupils dilated to the size of saucers. But I couldn't tell Dawn this because she'd think I was a failure. So I just used to say, 'Oh, I haven't done much really.'

And she'd say something like, 'You're such a scum bag,' in her husky voice. One day she called up and said she had a plan for that evening. She said she'd call me back in half an hour.

As per usual, when she called back her life had become even more difficult. She had to dash over to the 16ᵉ *arrondissement*; the meeting with her lawyer was taking longer than she'd thought; an old friend of hers had just flown in from the States.

When she finally called at just after midnight she sounded more abrupt than ever. She barked, 'I haven't got much time. There's this thing at Le Locomotive. Duran Duran are playing and there's a party or something. This guy I know has tickets, so I'll have to go with him. He's really excited about my script so . . . but anyway, whatever. I'll see you inside.'

She banged the phone down before I had a chance to remind her that Le Locomotive was a huge nightclub and that there was no way I was going to be allowed access to the VIP party area unless I had an invitation. But that husky voice snaked around my head so I rinsed out a chipped mug, filled it three-quarters full with vodka, downed it in eight painful gulps, and walking through Pigalle at one in the morning felt like a piece of cake.

The door of Le Locomotive thronged with impatient clubbers held off by doormen who milled around with walkie talkies and orange-lined bomber jackets trying to look vital.

One of the doormen I immediately recognised. He was the Sumo bouncer from Le Palace last year, the one who stopped me from lowering the tone of the dance floor.

As I pushed my way forward, I knew that I was going to have to make eye contact. His eyes were roaming around the street like a twisting fruit machine. They went on a whistle-stop tour of several pairs of breasts, a red 2CV, a ten-franc piece rolling along the pavement, a laughing boy in the queue and the orange glow of the night sky. When I'd pushed myself up to the front of the queue his eyes were forced to settle on me. The Etcha Sketch brows rose and a lecherous grin took hold of his features.

'*Toi, alors!*'

He hesitated, then he said, 'I will let you in, but we will talk later.'

At 1.30, Le Locomotive eighties revival night was already chock-a-block with French twenty-year-old girls tossing back long shiny hair and boys in striped green shirts and neat haircuts thinking up good lines to say to them. On the dance floor, a dozen people were doing a listless jive to 'Love Will Tear Us Apart'. About 300 other people were packed around the edges of the floor looking in with lazy eyes. They'd have preferred drunken eyes but at 70 francs for a beer and 100 francs for a short that was out of the question. The wall opposite the bar was packed four deep with eyes both anxious and arrogant. The anxious hoped they would be picked out and the arrogant were biding their time, looking at themselves in the mirror above the bar while they waited.

The most beautiful people seemed to be going upstairs. That was where the VIP room must be located I thought as Teardrop Explodes started pumping out on the dance floor.

But as I was about to head for the stairs, Sumo stepped forward out of nowhere and took hold of my arm. '*Salut, ma belle*. I am glad you have come here tonight.'

I smiled politely and told him that friends were waiting for me upstairs. He nodded and said, 'One glass with me?'

I let him lead me back to the bar. I thought I needed some free topping up on the alcohol front and maybe the delay would make Dawn anxious as she waited for me.

Sumo had a puzzled expression permanently on his face, or maybe he just had it when looking at me. The last time I'd seen him I'd been having near-as-damn-it sex in the middle of a dance floor. Given that this was all he knew of me, it seemed quite strange, certainly novel, that his opening conversational gambit was about light bulbs. 'I wonder how often they change the light bulbs in here,' he said, looking up to the ceiling. And then it clicked: Sumo wrestler was scared of me. Perfect.

'I've no idea how often they change the light bulbs in here,'

I said, chinking his glass with mine. He touched my arm gently and said, 'You will come and dance with me now?' I was going to say that I thought he had the wrong idea about me, but on reflection I wasn't sure that he did. I didn't think too long about it because I still had Dawn in prime position on my mind. I sighed a bored sigh, and said, 'Naaa. I'm going upstairs to see my friend.'

As Sumo called out something behind me, I climbed the metal spiral staircase, tottering past the groups of smoking girls and the kissing couples. The crowd milling around at the top seemed more lively than those people downstairs. Some of them had come out of a door which was evidently the place of the Duran Duran party. But the bouncers were having none of my lengthy, slurred excuses. A twenty-three-year-old with drastically smudged lipstick, cheap black T-shirt, holey jeans and ten pounds of excess fat was not going to make it past that door.

I felt a tap on my back. Turning round I saw Sumo looming up with a big grin all over his puzzled face. He winked over to the man on the door and tugged me gently away from the crowd and down the stairs once more.

'*Alors, on va dancer, non?*' he smiled, pulling me on to the dance floor.

As I wondered if he was expecting me to re-enact my evening at the Gaultier party, I saw Dawn. She was rushing down the staircase and seemed to be heading towards the exit. I broke away from Sumo, fought my way through the crowds of people and dashed out of the nightclub as she rushed towards a phone box on the corner of a street.

I ran past her and stood square in front of her. Trying to sound angry but feeling a bit scared I said, 'I've been waiting for you for ages. I can't even afford a drink. What have you been doing?'

Dawn searched for something in her pocket. Crow's feet were gathering on her brow so I tried to sound a bit more charismatic and devil-may-care: 'God, I've been having this ludicrous conversation with a Sumo wrestler.'

She stopped rummaging and turned her face towards me. Her chin had stubble burn and her red eyes wobbled around like arrows in a compass.

'God, why do you have to follow me everywhere? You're really getting too much. I've got to call up a guy and sort out plans ... God, where's my goddam phone card ... I bet some asshole stole it. God, this country, it's full of ants, they get everywhere. Fucking A, what kind of phone is this ... looks like a shining dragon's wing.'

Right about now I started to feel a sweaty prickle of genuine anger. Some unabashed ire that seemed to be located in my throat and ear lobes. My tongue felt like a big sag-bag stuffed with lead but I exploded anyway.

'Dawn! I think it's a bit bloody rich to invite me to a party and then dump me downstairs to get accosted by a Sumo wrestler while you live it up in the VIP lounge doing drugs with a load of pop stars!'

Dawn had never heard me raise my voice before. She turned around from the shining dragon's wing and contemplated me like I was the rest of it.

'Hey! I mean, chill out. You know? God. I mean, I've been trying to get you in but, you know? It's difficult.'

She hesitated. She wanted to make another point but she couldn't remember what she was talking about. Her face suddenly lit up. 'You know there's this guy in there who said he was really interested in my script. I mean, like, really interested? I was gonna call my agent in LA to tell him.'

Her eyeballs now looked like they had been stretched out and pegged down at the edges with a hammer and nails. They looked utterly manic. She saw, nevertheless, that a little consolation was still in order. Her mouth broke into that sunny smile of hers. 'Don't be mad at me. Look at this great Hermès shirt my lawyer gave me today. He's really cute you know.'

When I looked sulky she said in her irritating English accent, 'Come on, George. I'm here now aren't I? Fancy a joint then, gor blimey?'

I know I should have cringed, but infatuation got the better of me and I smiled helplessly.

Dawn opened her handbag then her make-up bag and took out a ready-rolled joint and a lighter. She wavered as she tried to co-ordinate the flame with the end of the joint. Finally, completing the task, she closed her eyes, inhaled, held her breath for five seconds and exhaled with relief.

Her lips turned upwards in a child-like smile which radiated through the rest of her face like blotting paper.

'Total high.'

Her eyes still closed, she extended her arm to pass me the stubby cigarette.

I watched Dawn who now watched me as I took a big drag of the joint. Roaring desire quickens through my blood and suddenly I've just seen heaven and I know what happens when we die and I know why we die and I don't know where to begin. I want to rush off and tell the good news to the world and then I forget what the good news is but even so, I know it'll come back. I'm lifting higher and higher, on an elevator trip to the light fantastic, startling thoughts spread their wings in my head and words meld together in creamy plasticine. I am Ozi Mandias, King of Kings, look at my works ye mighty and despair.

It is one of the most depressing feelings in the world to be on drugs and to make – what seems to you at the time – a fascinating comment, only to realise just as you have finished saying it that you are talking a load of druggy old codswallop. There is a good chance that the other person didn't hear you, or at least that what you said sounded perfectly normal to them. But that is where paranoia comes in.

Two seconds after I'd said, 'Dawn, you're prancing around on the landing in the shabby house in my head,' it was the turn for my eyes to start flicking round manically. My hand began trembling with paranoia and a burning shard of hash fell out of the joint and landed on Dawn's silk Hermès cuff. Naturally, it burnt right through, leaving a brown-rimmed hole of unmistakable aspect.

There seemed to be a very long silence. The eyes of everyone on the boulevard turned to fried eggs, with hard yolks. They all looked at me, hating me from the depths of their eggy sockets and when I turned to look at Dawn there was just a black hole gaping where a face should have been, with a terrible wind sweeping through it that shrieked: 'Asshole! You stupid asshole! Goddamit, I don't believe what you just did, you stupid asshole!'

When she turned and started walking back to the club, shouting, 'I'm going back to that fucking party and I'm going to do what the goddam hell I want to do without you, you loser, so don't bother tracking me, asshole,' I just saw yellow. All the horrible yellow things that there are in the world – piss and puss and the nicotine colour on the bottom of our mugs at rue de Clignancourt, all squashed up into a horrible yellow mess behind my screwed-up eyelids.

When I finally opened my eyes, I noticed that I wasn't broken. The noise of the boulevard had started again. Sleazy comments became audible from the men who passed by. I could feel a nail from my fake Doc Martens digging into the back of my heel. Another vodka would tip me back into drunkenness.

Then I thought of Sumo. Sumo wrestler didn't have much going for him, but what he did have was gratitude and shock value. I moseyed back to the club wondering what it would be like to sleep with somebody very fat.

Sumo stood at the door as I went to re-enter Le Locomotive.

'Ça va, toi?' he said, with what I think was a wink.

'Ça va,' I replied, looking him square in the face and thinking. 'Why not?'

He followed me inside and asked if I'd like another drink. 'Double vodka,' I said, wondering if my complete lack of interest was what was turning him on.

A short man with a moustache and bomber jacket came over to the bar, slapped Sumo on the back and then turned to look at me. Moustache laughed a dirty laugh, slapped Sumo on the back again and walked away. It was then that I decided to go home and have sex with him. It wasn't so much that I even wanted to see what Sumo was like underneath. I knew that he'd be as strangely revolting underneath as he was on top but there seemed no point in coming this far and merely toying with decadence.

'So,' I crooned to Sumo. 'Are we going back to your place then?'

Sumo seemed startled at the directness of the question. He stood up, zipped and unzipped his orange-lined black bomber jacket three times and stuttered, 'Bah, oui, bah, alors, on y va, oui, non?'

There was an obligatory fanfare of winks from his fellow bouncers as we walked out of the club. We got into his car – a tiny, red Fiat – and drove to a tower block near Place des Fêtes. The apartment was lit like a supermarket and resembled a stale black forest gateau. The chief features were the chocolate-brown corduroy settee which oozed yellow foam and the worn beige carpet – on the walls.

Sumo threw his bomber jacket down on the settee, put Les Négresses Vertes on the tape machine and led me slowly towards some balcony doors which he opened. He looked up at the dark sky where smoky clouds floated over the moon like the silvery film that bobbed on top of cups of coffee at Clignancourt. He chewed gum as he looked at the sky and I felt a wave of maudlin tenderness. But when I started to kiss him he grunted like a rutting pig and the moment passed. Alcohol levels had now reached overload and I was seeing two of him. This, coupled with his sweaty face and his pig noises just made him even more attractive and I led him back inside.

I pushed him down on the chocolate-brown settee. The bulging yellow eyes of foam which shot out of the cushions reminded me of Dawn. I knew I had to stop myself thinking about her so I ripped open the buttons on his orange shirt and felt a growing frustration to get at his flesh. The curtains of orange polyester were parted by a tidal wave of brown chest which wobbled like a pan of simmering cocoa. Sumo could bear it no longer and yanked undone his belt and tugged open his jean buttons. He stood up and the pan of cocoa suddenly boiled over in a most spectacular fashion as tyre upon tyre cascaded down from his descending trousers.

Looking down at him, now recumbent on the chocolate settee, writhing around in nothing but a pair of blue boxer shorts, he looked rather like rampant larvae. Judging from the sweat glistening on his face and his bug eyes which bore the expression of one who has just been told that he is about to be shot, he didn't do this kind of thing very often and I hoped the strain of me jigging up and down on him in space-hopper fashion would not be too much for him. He trembled and moaned like a grotesque baby waiting to be changed. Sitting astride his thighs I suddenly felt utterly gorgeous in comparison and sensed a familiar hotness in my groin and an ache in my lower belly as I moved up to press down hard on his cock.

Except I couldn't feel a cock. Just the soft, spongy buoyancy of a piece of warm girth. His whimpering was growing in volume now and he began fondling my breasts manically like he was trying to tune into his favourite radio station but had no idea where it was.

'*Suce-moi, suce-moi,*' he moaned in desperation, moving his middle from side to side as I pulled down the huge shorts to find out what was happening. His penis was hidden underneath a mini skirt of flab hanging from his stomach. But the vodka made me tenacious as well as utterly amused at the idea of sucking off a man mountain, and I slid down his hairless legs to investigate. I heaved up the fatty skirt and fished around to locate his bits. I tried to tease his groin into life with some mouth action. That seemed to make little impression so I tried some deft finger work. This move meant that my hand could no longer prop up the sweating tyre. It squelched down on top of my head and my fringe got jammed in the damp ledge between his underbelly and his genitals. While my head remained wedged face-down in this wet, airless cavity, I wondered if you could suffocate to death in a fat belly. I thought that probably you could, so I yanked my hair free and sat up feeling a sudden high from the oxygen rush.

The irony of the fact that Dawn was probably now snorting coke off Simon Le Bon's stomach while I was up to my elbows in a sludgy butter mountain of a stomach had not escaped me. But at least Sumo was not a time waster. He grunted as he rose from the floor and turned over on to his knees — turning me on to my front as he did so. The existence of Sumo's penis had, up to this point, been purely mathematical but now it seemed that he was ready to reveal it. As he knelt behind me, he gathered up his doughy sling of flesh in his arms like gathering up a load of washing. With that out of the way, he thrust his groin forward so that I could guide his bits into the right place.

My orgasm took a while in coming because the part of my body that I was most aware of was my back. By the sound coming from behind my ears, Sumo was having such a good time that he had forgotten all about the washing and its full weight had flopped down on to my kidneys. At least it was a new experience.

When Dawn didn't ring for days after the Duran Duran party, I decided to jump over the cliff. I'd make pork and apple casserole followed by treacle pudding and custard. It would give me fewer peaks of ecstasy than Dawn had, but at least it would be nicer to me overall.

She called when the whole of the flat was reverberating with the sound of frying pork chops. The fatty crackling sounds were tremendous, as if the whole world were wrapping up its Christmas presents at once. I lunged to shut the kitchen door and tried to answer Dawn's question 'So, what are you doing now?', in as calm and salad-like a voice as I could muster. I was even more surprised when she said, almost meekly, 'Can we meet up?'

We met in a café near her house. She arrived late. Almost immediately, she said: 'You know, this thing between you and me has been fun.'

There she went, using that word again. 'Fun'. The best accolade a night out with Dawn could receive was that it had been 'fun'. 'Fun' seemed a special Californian space-saving device. You packed a myriad of concepts into a three-letter word and it left you with time to trot off and have even more 'fun'. I'd always thought of 'fun' as a supremely non-sexual thing. It was something you had when you galloped along a beach on a horse or got drunk with your friends. It was not a word to use when you were writhing around in someone's clit.

But I knew what fun meant. Fun was the end. I left the café stiffly and went home to begin a new cycle of staring at the ceiling for hours on end.

Sunday, 30 June 1991

EPILOGUE
If there is a kissed and a kisser, there is also a phoned and a phoner. Naturally I am the phoned and I wait, comforted by a holey brown sheet and a big, fat reefer.

Two days post-Dawn, the phone rings from the bottom of a quarry explosion. Flaccid bellows puff inside, the promise of intense life fumes up and heart beats like a baseball slammed into a leather glove again and again and again and again. Suffer it to ring. Just a little bit longer. How to speak? Self-conscious indolence: 'Yeeees?'

'Hi, it's Kiki. Just called for a quick chat. You'll never guess what this man said to me in the street this morning . . .'

A bee sting in cotton wool, a balloon deflating in blisters. My water-logged spirit tries to sound light and frilly to chirpy Kiki whose shoulder I will be dripping on not so long from now. She natters on and I see Dawn in my mind, somewhere, in grainy textures in sun-faded colours driving on her moped, eyes fixed ahead, psycho Penelope Pitstop, chatting to waiters, all in all self-sufficient. I am drifting miles in the air on a prickly feather cushion far above Kiki and her tales of smutty men encountered at the bus stop.

But I hear my voice speak: 'Oh really? Are you serious? Typical French. Yeah, fine thanks. Oh no, just a bit tired.'

CHAPTER SEVEN

Le Herald Tribune

At last! Luck with the *Herald Tribune*! Today I met a man called Charles Castiglione who wears his trousers hitched up almost under his armpits in a way that, if he were Kiki, he would definitely have thrush by now. Charles Castiglione has been named temporary Features Editor of the *Herald Tribune* while the full-time woman – who, according to him, really is 'more uptight than Elizabeth 1' – has six months off for maternity leave.

He has just touched down from the Upper East side but he saw a piece that I wrote in *Paris Parade* and he phoned up to say that he would like to discuss some story ideas with me. His voice, over the phone, sounded like Elmer Fudd, the podgy cartoon character with a lisp who is always trying to kill Bugs Bunny.

When I take the métro all the way out to Neuilly to meet him in the offices of the *Herald Tribune*, a guard downstairs in a white shirt and black tie glances at my fake DMs and phones up to Charles Castiglione's desk to make sure I really am allowed to go up. I suppose I don't look much like a William F.G. Whitney Jr iii or a Z. Eden Schmitt like most of the people who write for the *Herald Tribune* are called. But I feel even more out of place when I get out of the lift and walk into a big open-plan office. There is no sign of movement and it is really quiet until a man jumps up and says in a very loud, dirty wotten wabbit voice from half way across the room: 'Hey there! Charles Castiglione! How you doin'!' When we turn to walk out of the office together, he says in an even louder voice, 'This place is a goddam journalists' graveyard,' so that the tortoise faces which have been peeking out at us quickly scram back behind their computer screens. Going down in the lift he doesn't say anything else to me, apart from muttering under his breath, 'Goddam stiffs' twice. I am really impressed with Charles Castiglione by this time.

In the *bistrot* next door — a place with red checked table cloths and pictures of 1940s jazz musicians on the walls — Charles Castiglione gets a packet of Gitanes from the back pocket of his hitched-up trousers and lights one. Puffing out a long line of brown smoke he says, 'Gitanes, man. Reminds me of Paris. So fucking civilised, Paris. Fucking New York. You can't even smoke a cigarette when you want to.' He speaks that glamorous New York English that makes you see steaming pavements and illicit games of poker and people having bagels for breakfast. Like he says, 'I was turned on to Paris when I was a kid' when he means, 'I started to like Paris when I was a child', so the fact of him having got completely the wrong end of the stick about Paris doesn't matter a bit.

After we have been there for a while, I see that his clothes have that beyond-ugly look which makes me think that he paid a lot of money for them. As he takes his jacket off, he moves his chair in to let a coiffed woman in a tight skirt through. When the woman has squeezed past him he grins over the menu and says, 'Women in short skirts. Makes me feel young!'

I have no idea what to say. Number one, I am obviously not the sort of woman who would wear a short skirt and number two, Charles Castiglione would probably think it a bit weird if I replied, 'Yes, and I like big jugs too.'

Still, I am probably reading him even worse than he is reading me, because the next thing I say is, 'You know, you sound just like Elmer Fudd.' He momentarily stops chewing his mouthful of *andouillette* and green lentils and he looks very serious.

Then he carries on chewing like I have said nothing. I'm not sure how to put myself across with Charles Castiglione. With Ralph Davidson my American editor at *Paris Parade*, I usually roll out a barrel of obsolete English expressions like 'without so much as a by your leave', 'boiled beef and carrots' and 'gor blimey guvnor'. This way of speaking normally goes down a treat with expatriate Americans but Charles Castiglione seems to think he's having lunch with Jack Nicholson. He licks some lentil juice from his cheek. 'I kind of had to get out of New York. I'm too known there. Wanted to get a job with Condé Nast but I had this thing with this big shot at *Vogue*. She likes being tied up and that shit. You know, typical ball buster woman by day, then it's manacles on the bed posts. Whips and shit by night.'

I wonder if I should mention that I know a man connected to the Monaco royal family who knows a woman who wants to be tied up. But even though we are making light work of a bottle of Côtes du Rhone I think it might not be wise. Maybe Charles Castiglione can bring himself off into his own mouth too. But I don't ask this. I just plod on and say, 'You do know who Elmer Fudd is, don't you?'

'Now listen here, kid,' he snaps. 'You've got to realise that this could be a big break for you. I mean, the *Trib*'s not a real newspaper but people read it and I've got a good in with the editor. We go back a long way. We've slept with the same women – sometimes simultaneously, know what I mean – and I've got a good track record. I'm working right now on a story about a big-time cocaine smuggler in Bolivia. Have to go hang out in the jail quite soon.'

He looks swiftly about the restaurant and as he lowers his voice, his accent becomes even more like his cartoon counterpart. 'The *Twib*'s full of cwappy Amewican whiters. You do me a good storwy and you're weally set. You don't want to be working for *Pawis Pawade* all your life, do you?'

✻   ✻   ✻

On my way home on the métro I decide to give some francs to an eloquent beggar with matted hair holding a crumpled McDonald's bag as a begging bowl. She is saying, '*Messieurs, dames, je suis sans domicile fixe, j'ai trois enfants.* If you could provide me with two or three francs with which to buy a tin of sardines, two or three potatoes ...' followed by a wild dash through the carriage.

I am feeling a bit down in the dumps. I think: little does Charles Castiglione know that I don't even have the pleasure of working at crummy *Paris Parade* all the time. All my boiled beef and carrots have got me nowhere.

It's not that they don't like me at *Paris Parade*. They do. I get to write all the interesting articles. Once I got to interview France's most famous porn star, Brigitte Lahaie who told me that most of the cum in X-movie cum shots is made out of condensed milk and whipped egg whites because men need some extra help. I have become such a staple of the magazine that once a month my mother has to drive around to all the newsagents in Falmouth that stock *Paris Parade* and buy up all the copies in case any of her friends – who always thought I was going to be in the diplomatic service – find out what I'm getting up to these days. Unfortunately, *Paris Parade* won't give me a full-time job because they think I'm too eccentric to ever want to settle down. I've pretty much given up on the idea that naff old Ralph Davidson is ever going to come up to me, pat me on the back and say, 'Welcome aboard!' like Americans say in films. Now I look at the woman begging for money and I think I'm a loser just like her. Now, when I have an opportunity to be successful at last with a real newspaper that people have heard of, I go and spoil it all by pretty much telling my potential saviour, Charles Castiglione, that he's funny-looking.

Walking up the rue de Clignancourt I decide that there's only one hope for me. If I can write a story for the *Herald Tribune* – a good story that will impress people – then maybe my life will change. Then people will wish they had welcomed me aboard and they will rue the day they ever looked with distrustful eyes at my fake DMs. I am feeling quite positive now, but when I open the front door it appears that rue de Clignancourt is going through an introspective afternoon. Holly, Bet and Ann are sitting in the kitchen, drinking mugs of bottled beer from the ED supermarket and eating a packet of *Pims* Jaffa Cakes. They are arguing about which of them has the worst life.

Ann says that she does because she is back to teaching English at the crack of dawn with Madame Bourse. She has to go to a southern Parisian suburb called Evry-Courcouronnes, a futuristic 'new town' filled with vast underground shopping malls and expanses of concrete which smell of sulphur and cold piss and make you nervous after 3 p.m. She is giving an intensive course in an aeroplane factory and to get to the classroom she has to walk through a giant workshop filled with men and pin-ups of naked women. One day she asked which countries the aeroplanes flew to and her class of bright-eyed boys in blue overalls told her that they didn't make passenger aeroplanes, they made missiles.

Bet says that she has won the prize for having the worst life because she has just started work as an underpaid dogsbody in Brentanos book store near Opéra where all the other staff talk about babies and taxes all day long and nobody even dares steal any books.

But then Holly shouts them both down and says that he has the worst life because he has to face shattered dreams every day. 'I want a couture house in a *hôtel particulier* on the Avenue Montaigne,' he says. 'It'll be filled with assistants in slingbacks, white gowns and very expensive sunglasses. Every time I enter the office – dressed like I've been beamed down from Planet Sex – they'll drop everything and rush to hear what I have to say. And my personal assistant will be a Russian aristocrat of 5 foot 11 called something like Anastasia who'll only wear chiffon and have heroin-perfect skin. And I'll say, "Hello gorgeous", as she passes over a box of Godiva chocolates. And she'll giggle and say something like, "Do you think I should go *chignon* or *gamine* today?"'

In reality, Holly spends his working life of two days a week at Parsons School of Design sharing an office with three other alcoholic prima donnas, a broken-down beige swivel chair and an IBM typewriter the size of a suitcase.

When I go into the kitchen I say that being a freelance writer is the worst job of all because you are shut up all day with your grubby, greasy feelings and the only perks are that you are free to get up from your desk and masturbate when you want. And then, come six o'clock, you have none of the job satisfaction that people who've been working in offices all day have. You have the satisfaction of knowing that you've spent the afternoon behaving like an Olde Worlde village idiot who does nothing all day but eat straw and wank in stables.

I take a swig from Holly's mug which is resting on a couple of Fay Weldon novels and Ann's copy of *The Empty Space* by Peter Brook. As I think back to my lunch with Charles Castiglione I glance at the row of firing letters that Bet, Ann and I have posted to the wall of the kitchen. We all display our firing letters on the kitchen wall to remind ourselves that we are meant for greater things than temping and teaching English (and also to make us feel less bad about receiving so many letters that slander our characters). One of them, addressed to me, says in underlined writing, '*Mademoiselle, vous avez causé un grand préjudice à notre société*' which means, 'Mademoiselle, you have caused great harm to our company'. It is from Madame Bourse last year. I hadn't caused her *that* much harm. I just went to Cannes for the film festival because Sophie was going for *Time* magazine and she offered to put me up for free in her aunt's apartment. Bet was supposed to call Madame Bourse and say that I had food poisoning but she forgot. Things weren't helped when I came back a week later with a sunburnt face.

I lean against the door and Bet asks me how lunch with

the *Herald Tribune* man went. I shrug and say, 'Okay. He was wearing funny trousers and we had green lentils.' Then I shrug again. 'I think maybe he thought I was a bit weird.'

'You didn't do your boiled beef and carrots on him did you?' Holly knows me too well.

I go and sit in my room and wonder if I can be bothered to meet my deadline for *Paris Parade*. I'm just thinking of retiring to my bed when the phone rings and it is Henry Flash. He is calling me to fact check. 'Just wanted to check the spelling of "lawksalordy", as in your "lawksalordy, bless my ten toes". God, you Brits have some strange expressions.'

Henry is still nervous when he talks to me but we get on quite well now because he is going steady with a Canadian intern at the magazine. In the course of the conversation he drops the very interesting fact that Jack Lang, the Minister of Culture, has just appointed a Minister of Rock and Roll. Henry has been asked to look into this by one of the editors of the Spanish newspaper where he makes $30 a week. 'Except that when I made some enquiries their so-called facts seemed to be a little lightweight,' he says with triumph in his voice. 'I went straight to the top – even though those asshole shitheads in the press office keep you hanging on the line as if you've got all the time in the world. So anyway, I finally found out that the Spanish guys had got it all wrong. The guy – Bruno Lion he's called – turns out he's no minister of rock and roll. His title is *Chargé de Mission pour Rock et Variétés*. No idea those Spanish guys. No idea.'

Because it is Henry I don't feel too bad when I say, 'Yes, yes, you're right. Dumb Spaniards. Pretty much a non-story,' and then immediately phone up the press office of the Culture Ministry, announce that I am a journalist from the *Herald Tribune* and ask when I can have an interview with Bruno Lion – because *Chargé de Mission pour Rock et Variétés* is as near to being a Minister of Rock and Roll as anyone is ever going to get.

As I expect, the name of the paper works like magic. The

woman on the end of the line says, '*Le Herald Tribune?* But of course! Will tomorrow morning suit you?' in an excited voice that suggests she can see Jean Seberg walking down the Champs Elysées with Jean-Paul Belmondo and a copy of the illustrious rag under her arm.

Bruno Lion's tiny office contains a regulation cabbage-green Ministry of Culture carpet, a scratched old table for a desk, a shiny ghetto blaster still wrapped in plastic, and not much more. Bruno Lion himself has all the requisite components of the charm package: white teeth, easy laugh, good memory for names, piercingly serious stare when called upon and a vaguely insubordinate yet pristine dress sense. He is wearing a shiny Perfecto leather jacket and a pair of black jeans. He is only twenty-six and he seems a little thrown when I tell him that I am twenty-three. But he is very pleasant and he goes out of his way to make out that he is totally normal – even though I have already read up that his father was the head of one of France's major banks. He says that his job is essentially to promote French pop music on behalf of the government and he points to the success of the Gypsy Kings. He also says that just because the government is going to give money to pop groups it does not mean that the pop groups can no longer be rebellious. Under his auspices, a number of French bands recently went to New York to promote French music. He looks at me piercingly and says that the most famous lyrics of one of the groups – Les Satellites – are about sticking sharp-edged objects up the anus of President François Mitterand. I smile obligingly and Bruno Lion laughs again.

When the interview finishes, he smiles, asks when the piece will be appearing and says that, of course, I must come to the *soirée* at the Culture Ministry next week to celebrate this year's Fête de la Musique. The Fête de la Musique is the day when France rally rouses for its music industry. Long-forgotten

English pop groups play in Place de la République and Parisian cafés are transformed into sweaty venues for ill-practised French bands to play to the people. It has existed for the past few years in a small way, but this year Bruno is overseeing it and he promises that it will be better than ever.

I say yes, I'd love to come, but it's not until he escorts me to another office and asks a woman to give me a press dossier and a handful of invitations that my morning really perks up. When Bruno has left, she introduces herself as Carole, Press Officer for the *soirée*. With her cropped hair, her tightly fitting trousers and her pear-shaped figure she looks to me like what I imagine a bull dyke to look like. I gaze at the back of her neck as she bends over to retrieve the press information. When she straightens up, she smiles brightly and introduces me to her assistant, François who smiles like a jolly boy scout.

Although Bruno Lion wasn't as interesting as Brigitte Lahaie, I like him okay so I write up the interview as if we got on really well. I say that he was wearing a $1,000 leather jacket because I have never bought anything leather before and I guess that it would be expensive.

Charles Castiglione loves the leather jacket detail and he puts it as a caption: 'Monsieur Rock in his $1,000 leather jacket'. In fact, he loves the piece. He phones up and squeaks, 'Great story. Nice one, kid.' When the piece comes out, a day before the Fête de la Musique, I feel like it is the best day of my life. When I go into *Paris Parade*, everybody treats me like they're a bit scared of me. My editor says he can't believe they gave it a whole page, the new art desk intern — who acts brash in a sexy, rich American heiress sort of way — invites me to a Prince concert next week and even Henry is pleased for me because, with his quaint, fact-checker's logic, he sees it as a good reflection on himself that he was the one who gave me the tip-off in the first place. Sophie calls me up and says, 'Hey kid, you made it.' A couple of TV stations call me up to pick my brains and on the evening of the Fête de la Musique, Jack Lang clasps my hand when I enter the Culture Ministry. There is something about his show-biz charm, his perma tan and his sharp Thierry Mugler jacket that reminds me of my father's show-biz tap dancing admirer.

In the refined salons of the Culture Ministry it seems like a revolution has never happened. There are no cheese sandwiches or cigarette stubs on paper plates like you'd think there would be at a rock and roll party. This is because Jack Lang's big thing is that there is no difference between high culture and low culture. Nobody has rocked the boat yet because the socialists have the best Champagne in town and they always put on a good spread. When I was here last – when Jack Lang awarded the *Legion d'Honneur* to Sylvester Stallone – my favourite things to eat were the mini chocolate *religieuses* topped with yellow icing and filled with the kind of delicious *crème pâtissière* you can never find on the rue de Clignancourt. The other thing they do well are huge, hollowed-out loaves of brown bread with hundreds of triangular sandwiches inside, packed as tight as carpet and cut as thin as gold leaf. The fruit sculptures tonight are even more impressive than they were last time. The huge composites of caramelised figs, mandarins, cherries, peaches and a scattering of pomegranate seeds, for rock and roll good measure, are done out in shapes more elaborate than the Acanthus leaves and scrolling *boiserie* which swirl all over the walls and ceiling of the Ministry of Culture.

I stride over the red carpet and head towards the wall of Champagne men. I know the ropes now: you look the white-gloved waiters straight in the eye and without missing a beat you say, '*Deux coupes de Champagne, s'il vous plaît.*' When I was at Sly's do, I kept asking for *verres* de Champagne which are the sort of ordinary kitchen glasses you drink ED supermarket beer out of. If you don't even know the right name for a Champagne glass, the white-gloved waiters keep you waiting or pretend they haven't noticed you at all.

Suddenly the room is filled with hushed whispers. 'Meek,' they are saying. '*C'est Meek.*' I turn around to see a wizened man with big lips and skinny legs being led through the main salon by Jack Lang. 'This way, Meek,' he says, signalling to a small door in the corner of the main Culture salon. Mick Jagger and Jack Lang are followed by David Bowie, Iman and the white-sabred Bruno Lion. The door is covered with more undergrowth of Acanthus leaves and scrolling *boiserie* and Jack Lang wants Mick Jagger, David Bowie and Iman to walk through it and enter his private apartments. It doesn't seem very democratic, but then the chandelier lighting in this room is doing nobody any favours. Anyway, the three famous people probably hope that there will be a better atmosphere inside Jack's private chamber. A few people collapsed on the carpet with alcohol poisoning maybe. They must think they've come to tea with the Queen by mistake. It looks like it might be time for the socialists to set up a Tequila Slammer Ministry. No French stars have as yet managed to cause any stir whatsoever, even though I have spotted Mylène Farmer who is famous for her hit video where she strides around in eighteenth century libertine outfits singing, 'My little buttocks are a constant source of inspiration to you.'

But although Lang, Lion and the three stars have now vanished into the private apartments, they have not disappeared altogether. If you go out of the French windows and walk around the grand T-shaped stone balustrade you can see right inside Jack's inner sanctum. Most of the guests are being so discreet that nobody is looking in, but I want to see what they are doing in there so I glue my face to the window and gawp at Meek, David and Iman perched on Louis XV furniture. Jack's chair is placed exactly parallel to theirs and Bruno stands a few paces behind, one minute using his eyes to look piercingly serious and the next, flashing his teeth for amusement effect. It looks like some kind of coronation ceremony or beatification council – or *Give Us A Clue* special, because every few minutes, Jack will spring up from his chair, face the three seats of Meek, David and Iman and start making wild gesticulations with his hands. The only one of them I can see clearly is David Bowie, who sits with his legs crossed and his chin cupped in his right hand as his arm props itself up on the arm rest. Occasionally, he smiles languidly as if he has only a vague idea of what Jack is going on about. Jack is probably doing his old trick of saying that they are all invested with the 'Rimbaldian spirit of liberty'. Whoever Jack Lang courts – rap artists, Serge Gainsbourg, Sylvester Stallone – he always says they are invested with the Rimbaldian spirit of liberty. But this seems to be going right over the head of everyone else in the room – apart from Bruno Lion who wears the joyous smile of Una Stubbs.

Someone taps me on the shoulder and I turn to see the short-haired Press Officer at my side.

'*Salut*, George,' she says cheerfully.

'*Salut*, Carole,' I say, waiting for her to tell me how thrilled she is with my article.

'Everyone here is very happy with your interview in the *Herald Tribune*. I am glad too. François and I spend a whole year organising tonight's Fête de la Musique and now more people than ever will know about it.'

As she stands next to me she leans against the cold, stone balustrade, and looks down at the crush of *hoi polloi* in the Palais Royal gardens below.

'I think people are starting to warm up at last,' I say, smiling at her.

She doesn't keep eye contact with me and there seems to be a trace of relief in her voice when she exclaims, 'Ah, look. It is François. I must go and speak to him. I think he has found a friend.'

I turn round and see that François's new friend is none other than Holly. François's face suggests that Holly is filling him in on the secret of eternal life. As they approach, I can already hear the words 'fashion' and 'Karl Lagerfeld'. Holly seems annoyed when our arrival cuts him off in his prime.

When François begins rattling away to Carole in French, Holly announces to me that his new friend is the best-looking boy in the room. I inform him that the woman with short hair is his boss and that I have designs on her.

'Don't think much of yours,' Holly snorts, giving Carole the once over as she chats to her assistant. When he sees that I have blushed he shrieks, 'What are you saying! This is your big night! I keep bumping into people going on about the "wonderful article" in *Le Herald Tribune*. Bloody hell, George, you've arrived. Me old mate and mucker's arrived. You're not just at the back of the bus, you've got all the seats to yourself. I can't help but think that it's a bit of a funny business wanting to fill them with dumpy middle-aged women. Put Bruno Lion in as your driver and who knows where you might end up.'

It is true. Bruno Lion has come up to me at least three times tonight and said something gratuitous like, 'You know, my leather jacket didn't really cost $1,000!' But the fact of the matter is that I am more interested in the potential of the George–Carole story than I am in the Bruno–George story. So I tell Holly that as François is Carole's assistant he won't be allowed to go anywhere without her and Holly immediately says, 'I suppose we could re-look her.' He goes up to François, interrupts his conversation with Carole and drags both him and Carole off into the huddle of the finally intoxicated guests who have now become part of a drunken *corps de ballet*, criss-crossing their way in shoddy choreography from golden salon to golden salon.

Holly looks back and signals for me to follow but I pretend I haven't seen him. I think that maybe I really should start thinking about my career prospects. I am nearly twenty-four and I still haven't got a serious job. Could Bruno Lion get me one? Maybe I should go and flirt with him. Or maybe I should go and talk to that leader-writer man from the *Herald Tribune* who I've glimpsed in the main room, the one Alex was rude to at the party. But will he even speak to me?

I lean over the balcony and look at the sea of people down below in the stiff gardens of the Palais Royal. I bet all of the people up here have wondered greedily if anything better is going on down there, but of course, none of us dares go down and see, even though I am feeling a bit full up with opulence and glitter. I have brushed past Iman's naked arms and walked along the stone balustrades like Richelieu in his most despotic hour and now I feel a warm flash of light on the side of my face so I turn round to see famous anchor woman Ann Sinclair on the arm of a man who isn't her husband, although no paper will dare say anything scurrilous about it. Everywhere you look there's another diamond chandelier and another mini *religieuse* and more licks of gilt paint and another scarlet mouth choking on another chocolate-dipped strawberry, and more voluptuous laughter that sounds like velvet and orgasms, and more waiters with white gloves proffering half their weight in Champagne bottles. After a while your eyes start rebelling, like you have been staring too long at a bright, bright, gold sun. You wouldn't mind seeing a grubby yellow kitchen floor or even some grungy-looking rock and roll stars. But when long-awaited *invitées speciaux* the Clash start playing below in the gardens they look smaller than your *coupe de Champagne* glass and, anyway, most of the crushed people down below are looking up to the stone balustrade because they think something better is going on up here. Next to me I can hear a performance between an English girl in her early twenties and a handsome man in his fifties.

The girl is wearing a tight skirt and she has a mane of hair that she keeps flicking. 'So I called up the editor and she said, "What on earth do you mean the interviews are going well? Stop writing this minute, go down to the pool, take your top off and wiggle your tits around until you get us some advertising!"'

The man makes a little chortle, touches her proprietorially on the arm and says, '*Charmant.*'

The girl pulls back a whisper and becomes bolder.

'. . . but I thought I'd stay on a few days after the assignment, you know, just to explore Monte Carlo rather more thoroughly, and I thought I'd go to . . . the Youth Hostel!' she explodes as if it is the funniest thing in the world.

'. . . I was in full Christian Lacroix when I turned up and when I got there the man said that there was a big waiting list and he wouldn't be able to tell me if I had a place until midday. God! And it was only ten!'

'*Elle me tue cette fille,*' the man says to the sky as the girl commences the punchline of her tale.

'. . . all I can remember is the horrible stench of dog shit as I sat there in the boiling sun waiting for the man to tell me if I had a place or not. I mean, I had about 10 francs on me in the whole world! And a really boring Swiss boy started telling me that as I was number eighty-seven on the list there was almost no possibility of me getting in. So I finally thought' (cute shrug) 'I finally thought, "I'm going to have to phone that damned art dealer and take up his invitation to have dinner on his yacht." But it was so embarrassing, because he sent round his limo and his private chauffeur to the Youth Hostel! God knows what everyone must have thought!'

The girl and the man are joined by a man with paper-pale skin and crispy blond hair who I recognise immediately as Douglas Thom. He is the Editor in Chief of Fairchild Publications and I once went to his offices on the Faubourg Saint Honoré for a job interview. The first thing he said was that he was suspicious of anyone who wasn't American because he'd recently had a disastrous experience with a French photographer. 'A cultural clash of horrific dimensions.' He took me over to the light box and told me to look at a series of photos that were laid out. 'Sunday Lunch is the brief this guy had,' he said as he handed me the eye glass. 'Cookery section is where this was commissioned for.' In the photos there was a table covered with hunks of rustic bread and various mutilated animals: a dead pheasant with blood-matted feathers, the limp neck of a strangled goose languishing elegantly over a bowl of split figs, a couple of hares with severed front paws. The scene was captured in impeccable golden lighting and I thought the photos were quite interesting in a neo Dutch Masters sort of way. But I obviously wasn't taking the situation seriously enough because Douglas Thom suddenly brushed his lapels briskly as if the blood had seeped into them as well and said, 'It's nothing to smile about. You think Mrs Schmo in Lancaster, Ohio, wants to look at a picture of some fancy French animal morgue when she's deciding between meat loaf and pot pie for the family dinner? Mrs Schmo couldn't handle the sight of a sliver of *foie gras pâté* – even if we dressed it up with a candle-lit dinner and a heterosexual couple wearing engagement rings and saying grace – even that would get me blown sky high out of my little old editorial seat.'

I didn't get the job, at least, nobody ever got back to me. At one point I thought that maybe it was because I had been wearing my cherry skirt on the day of the interview. Maybe Douglas Thom feared it would get him blown even sky higher than a few smutty food pictures.

Now I can feel the hackles rising on the back of my neck and the nails in the heels of my boots growing warm. Douglas Thom is yelling out, 'Oh God! You don't know him? Why didn't you tell me before, you silly thing! Call him tomorrow and say you're speaking *de ma part*. And while you're about it why don't you come by my office next week. By the sound of that English accent you've got an even more impressive address book than I have!'

Bloodless, bloodless, bloodless, I rant to myself as I stomp away from the trio and go back inside the main salon. If this is making it then I don't want to make it. I am not going to stay and be charming and schmooze Bruno Lion at all. I am going to go home with his Press Officer.

Then Bet rushes up and stands before me with crumbs of mascara clogged in her eyes and streaked tears running down her cheeks. This is a look she usually reserves for her birthday night when Sam is sure to say something to really tip her over the edge.

She says, 'Wanker. I fucking hate the little wanker.' More furious tears shoot down her cheeks like pinballs. I put my hand on her shoulder and try to console her by saying, 'Yeah, he's a wanker,' presuming it is Sam we're talking about and wondering if she'll think it really bad if Holly and I now rush off in pursuit of François and Carole. Luckily, Bet says, 'I'm going to get off with a waiter, that'll really piss him off.'

'Good idea,' I say, wondering what my best next move with Bruno Lion's secretary might be. Alerted to our whereabouts by Bet's screams, Holly saunters up with François and Carole. 'I was just telling our good friends here about our fascinating lifestyle,' Holly says enthusiastically as they approach, his arm resting comfortably on François's shoulder. François has fallen for Holly in a big way but not, it seems to me, in a sexual way.

'Yes,' François says eagerly. 'You are bohemians. I suppose I am not brave enough to be a bohemian. Since I left university two years ago I have worked at the Ministry.'

When Bet stomps off in search of a waiter I take Holly to one side. 'Holly, she keeps smiling at me! I reckon this is it. Let's go somewhere – with both of them.'

Holly says that his keeps talking about his girlfriend in Aix-en-Provence. But he seems cheerful enough about his prospects especially if he can get François to drink some more Champagne.

'But what do you think about Carole,' I say. 'Are you sure she's gay?'

'Course she is. Course she is. What straight French girl's going to have short hair like that?'

Holly's logic is impeccable.

At four in the morning we are all wandering through the streets of the first *arrondissement*: Holly, François, Carole, me, and my bicycle – which I somehow remember I brought with me when this evening began. It stands like a chaperone between Carole and me as I wheel it along the street. Holly and François seem much more intimate as they walk ahead of us like clumsy puppets, knocking their shoulders against walls and bumping arms with each other. Every so often, Holly lets out a Basil Brush yelp of laughter or one of his grandiose 'puh!' sounds.

Carole is not the greatest conversationalist in the world. She doesn't seemed very interested in talking about my bike so I decide to use my classic ice breaker.

'Where do you go out at night?'

'Oh, you know, I don't go out much. I work a lot, I—'

But then I crash my bike into the legs of some Fête de la Musique revellers so she doesn't finish what she was going to say, which I am sure would have been something like, 'I've been trying to get over breaking up with my last girlfriend.' But I still feel frustrated as we walk past au Pied de Cochon where newly forged couples celebrate the night's drunken fumblings with bowls of onion soup, plates of oysters and a sense of *déjà vu*. Some sit and stare at each other over cups of untouched espresso, sad that the moment has come for flirtation to become something more. Others drink their coffee in agitated sips, courage slipping away with the approaching dawn.

I feel cold. The first light of morning breaks the spell of intoxication and can turn carefree pleasure into clenched neurosis. Lust not acted on under cover of night goes stale, randy innuendoes turn into irritable civility, bodies start to stiffen and a drunkenness that is warm and frivolous in darkness becomes pumpkin heavy by day. Holly and François have stopped in front of the Eglise Saint Eustache and Holly is creased up with laughter.

'I think he wants us to go in the church,' says Carole, sounding excited. 'I have a friend who should be playing in the orchestra now. I think you will find it something very beautiful and very—'

'Do you like me?' I spit the words out as I turn to face her.

'Do I like you?' she smiles and takes my hand. 'I like you very much. You are very special. And you must remember never to change. Life is too short to worry about what others think.'

Like a damp firework that is about to phut out but which revives at the last minute and fizzes and flashes into starry life, I ricochet back into the early morning, suddenly feeling drunk all over again. Holding on to my bike with my right hand I move 180 degrees to its other side so that I am standing next to Carole. She laughs at my elaborate gesture. Her face reminds me of the nicest things about strawberry Angel Delight and I kiss her, briefly, on the mouth. Then I grab hold of her arm and pull her into the church which seems to be spinning as much as my head. It is only when I am half way up the aisle of the crowded Eglise Saint Eustache that I realise I am still wheeling my bicycle. Three-quarters of the way up, as I wheel past the line of people queuing for Holy Communion, it occurs to me that bikes might be deemed sacrilegious in church. Still, I think, as I bang into a stone pillar, they had a donkey in a stable. I chain my bike to a chair and lean it up against the pillar. Then I keel over into the seat next to Carole slurring a loud, 'Excusez-moi, madame,' to a woman with a grey bun who looks at me like she has expressly come to church to avoid people such as myself. She wears harsh, black-rimmed glasses, a very pink checked jacket with enormous padded shoulders and a thick orange shawl flung round her neck like a boa. The poodle tied on a leash by her feet is nibbling on it. Sometimes it is hard to know whether Parisians are mad or just being in fashion.

Carole seems entranced by the group of men in black dinner jackets and women in long black skirts who are limbering up on their flutes and oboes and violins, waiting for the signal to begin.

Holly makes room for himself on the bench next to François then turns round to me and hisses, 'He keeps talking about his bloody girlfriend in Aix-en-Provence. I should have stuck with the Champagne waiter. At least I'd be biting the pillow by now.'

The church smells of patchouli oil with one part Chanel number something. I wish I was wearing sunglasses. Although it has been at least an hour now since I have had anything to drink I still have the sensation, even in the church, that everything is rushing past me at 200 miles an hour. Oh, what do I care, I reason as I turn to Carole and say, 'So, are you a tits, bum or leg sort of woman?'

Carole looks puzzled. 'Bum? Yes, I suppose I have some troubles with my "bum", as you say. But I no longer eat dessert and now I have joined *Gymnase Club*.'

'Yes, but you know. When you're deciding what to go for. Well, what do you go for?'

'An attractive part of the body for me? *Eh bien*, I suppose I must say that I like *les jambes bien musclées*.'

'Yes, I quite like a muscly leg myself. But you know what my favourite part is? I love cunts. Have you any idea, the awe and wonder of a cunt seen for the first time? The awe and wonder? I mean, have you any idea?'

The orchestra begins to play so I turn up my slurring voice a pitch louder.

'The forgotten erogenous zone, the zone that's sometimes

heard about but never seen — except when its splayed in porno mags so it looks like something that's been in the butcher's window for too long. You know? So many women say that they find the female body more erotic than the male body. But women have been talked into believing that women's bits are mere lumps of flabby *mal odour*. They think that women's bits are dirty while the cock's okay. If a cock's noble and primordial and thrusting, why does it does smell of gorgonzola half the time? Tell me that, Carole. Tell me that if you can. A cunt's much more complex. Much more secret. I bet you're like me. I bet you love the pleasure of lying above the woman you desire and parting her hair and seeing a mound of shy softness just waiting for the off. Am I right, Carole? Am I right?'

Horror and disbelief line Carole's face. She doesn't seem the slightest bit interested in the musicians now. As she opens her mouth to say something, François turns round to her.

'*Ça va? On s'amuse bien ce soir, non?*' He turns back merrily to the orchestra without waiting for a response.

Finally, Carole looks at me and says, hesitantly, 'You think ... you think I am a lesbian?'

'Well,' I say weakly, 'you do have very short hair ... for a French woman.'

'*C'est pas vrai,*' she mutters in anguish. 'You know why I have short hair? You know why my hair is short? I have short hair because ... because I have been in chemotherapy for six months. Last year I nearly died from bowel cancer.'

One lesson I have learnt from the *Herald Tribune* incident is the importance of taking heed of cliché. The main one to remember is that you should never count your chickens before they are hatched. When I finally dare to unearth myself from the shame of my brown sheets the next day, there is a message on the answering machine from Charles Castiglione which suggests that my Bruno Lion piece wasn't as generally well received as

I had thought. Charles has been dispatched back to New York because the editor of the *Herald Tribune* thinks that his section reads too much like *The Village Voice*. 'So, you probably heard the news,' punches out the cheerful cartoon voice. 'They accused me of lowering the tone of the paper! I know, it's a joke – have you seen the fucking hooker ads they run? I told 'em. "Steve man," I said, "if you want to spend your life kissing ass to Orchids Ladies and Venus in Furs so you can afford to run double-page spreads on art treasures in Athens then you just go ahead and do that." What can I tell you? I'm heading off to Bolivia. See what those schmuks are up to.' Then there is a pause. 'Remember, kid,' he says, 'you have a voice.'

CHAPTER EIGHT

Pins

The imposing door of an apartment in the sixteenth *arrondissement* is opened by a ginger-haired woman wearing sunglasses and lapels crammed with badges paying tribute to Coca Cola, McDonald's and a variety of French supermarket chains. A smell of wet dog wafts out.

'Oh yeah, hi,' rasps the voice of my new patron. 'Thought you were someone else. Yeah, come in.' She leaves Holly and me in a room coloured in faded red and textured in threadbare green. Dotted around the room are many useless or broken objects: cracked mirrors, shards of African mask, piles of broken TV sets, juke-box parts and cans and cans of old movie film.

Holly works off his anxiety by flicking through a dusty copy of *Paris Match*, nearly ripping out each page he is doing it with such vigour. I am biting my nails, eyeing the fat pug dog lying in the corner licking its testicles. I wonder if there's any point to all this. We are nervous because we are planning to get into the Galliano show at the Louvre so that I, for the umpteenth time, can try to get a job in journalism and so that Holly, for the umpteenth time, can try to get a job in fashion. We are additionally nervous because we have entrusted Pins with the business of getting us into the fashion show and now we are wondering if she really is the woman for the job.

✣   ✣   ✣

Pins shuffles back into the room wiping her mouth with the back of her hand. She collapses on a stained red sofa and says, 'Bloody Bob, bloody old pervert. Told me he was a film director when I moved in. Never seen him pick up a camera in me life. Seen him make a few dodgy phone calls. Still, just have to cuddle him a bit now and then, know what I mean?' She takes her shades off and lies down. Her eyes are wasted. Like somebody has tossed an old chip pan into an azure pool.

''S better. I'm best when I'm horizontal. Got a bit of chicken in the oven for later.'

Holly starts flicking through *Paris Match* even quicker and I know it's because he realises that we might be here for some time. I'm quite enjoying Pins' company, although maybe that's because I've never met her before. Maybe it's also because I want to put off the hour when I must summon up all my courage, throw my natural cowardliness to the back of my mind, dash through the curtains in the Louvre auditorium, grab hold of John Galliano and get him to give me the most searing interview of his life. Even if I am capable of doing all that, Pins is still the vital cog in the clockwork. If she can't do what she has promised, then two weeks of planning and dreaming and promising various London editors fantastic stories will have all been wasted. Still, without her, there is no hope whatsoever of being able to get in so I might as well just sit here and carry on biting my nails. Pins takes a roach from behind her ear, lights it, and takes a weary drag. 'He shouldn't be long now,' she says, looking into the middle distance. Then she looks at me and says, 'You lived in Paris long then?'

'About two years.'

'Yeah. Better here than England, eh? Last time I was back there I was on the Epping line. Where my parents live. People work in the buffet car are all transvestites. Bloody disgrace. Great strappers in British Rail women's uniform serving tea and toast and being rude to you. Don't suppose none of the punters even notice.'

*   *   *

Pins' life has been one fiasco after another. Ten years ago she left Bethnal Green to go and live in Paris and set up a business in leather T-shirts. Now, aged thirty-five, things still aren't working out for what seem to be an ever-growing string of reasons. On the first day that Holly met her at Parsons School of Design where she works as a secretary, it was down to a cat.

'Cat got in the bag of leather, didn't it. Peed all over it. Ruined it . . . yeah' (drag on joint) 'bloody cat.'

Another reason for Pins' failure in the leather business is her parallel interest in entangling herself in a series of bad lesbian relationships. For the past ten years, she has functioned as the live-in girlfriend of a string of bourgeois women who have made no qualms about turfing her out when they tire of sex with her. Holly says that the most recent was the director of a small promotional badge or 'pin' company. The woman in question, Claudette, must have made a lot of money because it has suddenly become very popular to advertise your company or your film on a tiny decorated piece of metal and for people to collect your pin like they used to collect stamps. I think the craze is sad and pathetic but Claudette certainly made her mark because when Pins isn't talking about leather she is talking pins.

'She does class stuff, Claudette. You should see her Crédit Lyonnais one. She's a class act,' she tells Holly when she collars him, as she always does, in the Parsons canteen.

The door bell rings and Pins puts her shades back on. She coughs, ''bout bloody time,' and goes out into the hall. She returns almost immediately in the company of an Algerian man with an impressive row of blanket stitch across his right cheek.

'This is Asthma,' she says, patting the man's arm. 'Just going to the kitchen for a bit, yeah?'

Holly raises his eyebrows in a grand stage gesture as the two slope past. He lights a cigarette. 'There goes factor X,' he says.

Now that we are here I suppose it does all seem a bit far fetched. Pins has told Holly that since she supplies 'stuff' to one of the guards who staffs Paris Fashion Week, she will have no trouble in getting him — and me — into the show. 'Didier'll be on the gates for Galliano. I'll hand his stuff over and he'll let us all sneak in,' she told Holly. The only thing she wants from Holly is for him to put in a good word to the Parsons head about her giving a course of advanced leather classes. I'm not sure what she expects from me.

A deafening sound of crashing pots and pans erupts from the kitchen. Holly looks to the ceiling again.

'She's probably trying to tunnel into the Louvre from the kitchen. I can see it now — she'll turn up at the gates with smeared lipstick and destroyed clothing and the guards will direct her to the Comme des Garçons show instead.'

It is comments like these that make me nervous about the whole business of fashion. I have had a brief conversation with the fashion editor at *The European* newspaper who has said if I can get any 'stuff' from the Galliano show then she might be in the market for buying it. I'm not sure the kind of stuff that I have access to is the sort of thing she is looking for. All that I have learnt about fashion I have learnt from Holly and Alex and their take is either too arcane or too libelous. For instance, on shopping trips up the boulevard Barbès they will come across what looks to me like an old T-shirt in a basket outside Tati. One of them will pick it up, raise an eyebrow and look at the other who will be registering the same low-key interest. 'I quite like this, in a strange Rifat Ozbek sort of way,' one will say and I have no idea what they are talking about. Or another time, Holly will phone up after a white night out on the tiles and at the end of the conversation will add as an afterthought that when the lights finally came up in the back room of the bar, 'there

I was holding Jean-Paul Gaultier's knob in my hand. Bloody hell, and just when I thought something interesting was about to happen.'

I know all about Claude Montana's layers of foundation, I know that a plastic carrier bag that Holly was given by a boy in Le Swing is not a plastic carrier bag at all but an underground vest made by someone called Martin Margiela which even Alex is impressed by. I am hardly ever surprised now when Alex comes out with another account of how Yves Saint Laurent's wobbly table manners have sent peas ricocheting all round the dining room at the Tour d'Argent. On John Galliano, all I've managed to get out of Holly is that his backers keep dropping him and some hairdressers in Le Swing once saw him throwing out furniture into the rue Vieille du Temple in the middle of a flaming row with his boyfriend.

By now, I have intimate knowledge of what fashion designers do after hours, but I have no idea what they do on the catwalk. I have no idea what questions would be good ones to ask Galliano and Holly is not giving me any help. He is strangely taciturn today and I assume that the shredded pages of *Paris Match* are not simply due to us having linked our day so closely to Pins.

'The cheek of it!' he suddenly spits.

'What cheek?'

'This stonking Russian ballet dancer I met at Le Swing. Almond-shaped eyes and Heavy Metal T-shirts. He sniffs cigarette boxes and he can only get it going if he drinks a bottle of vodka.'

This seems pretty much an average profile of the men Holly is attracted to on his nights out, so I let him go on.

'Things were going swimmingly until some hairdresser starts making eyes at him from across the bar. Next thing I know the bar tender plonks a double vodka and orange down in front of him — courtesy of the hairdresser. And how does the Russian react? He only goes over and starts snogging him! Can you believe it! I was really tanked up at the time too. I stomped over to them both and I said, "Nobody treats me like this, you know!" in a Montgomery Clift sort of way. And the Russian looked genuinely surprised and said, "But Holly, I'm sure that everybody treats you like this!"' Holly looks apoplectic now. 'Can you believe it! "I'm sure that everybody treats you like this!"' He blows out a mouthful of smoke and pauses. Then he says coolly, 'I have to admit, I thought it was quite perceptive of him.'

Now it is my turn to start flicking manically through magazines. Except it's not *Paris Match*, it's a magazine called *Anal Explosions* that I've picked up from a pile next to the juke-box bits. I feel a bit pissed off because Holly always manages to meet people of the same sex who want to go home with him. I never get to meet any women. But reading porno mags just makes me feel even more frustrated, like everyone else in the world is having more sex – and better sex – than me. My favourite page from *Anal Explosions* is one of the advertisements which shows three naked females kneeling doggy style in red high heels and a caption underneath that says: 'Pick a hole and fuck it.'

'Think yourself lucky that you're getting it,' I say to Holly. 'I bet I'll end up like John Betjeman. Eighty-years-old, in my wheelchair, and saying that the one regret in my life is that I didn't have enough sex. Can you imagine how awful that would be?'

With a big 'puh!' Holly stubs his cigarette out. 'All I can say,' he says, 'is that I'd better get my reward in heaven because I'm certainly not getting it on earth. Apparently heaven's filled with lots of male models.'

He thinks for a while before adding, 'Knowing my luck I'll end up in hell which is filled with all your exes.'

Pins and the Algerian man reappear. Pins has a glazed grin on her face and a fresh joint has appeared behind her ear. The Algerian man nods at Holly and me as Pins guides him towards the door. '*Salut*, Asthma,' she says. 'I'll be giving you a call soon, yeah?'

When Asthma is gone, Pins puts her shades on again and says sleepily, 'Right then. Yeah. Bit of chicken?'

We follow her through to the kitchen where she motions for us to sit down at the laid table, half of which is covered in plastic bags, rizzlas and flakes of tobacco. Pins sits down at the table and seems to forget what we have come into the room for. 'Yeah, he does me a good bit of puff does Asthma.' She lifts the joint from behind her ear and lights it. She takes a weary drag then decelerates her faltering delivery to exhale a mouthful of smoke that dissipates around the room just as her mind is doing now.

'Course, this friend of Bob's – film director bloke – he offered me a thousand quid for the rights to me life. That all went up the spout though, didn't it. Haven't told you about the bust, have I, Holly?'

'No,' says Holly meekly.

'Yeah. Sold this girl some hash and she grassed me up. Set up. Went down for six months. First day I come out, go down the dyke club in Pigalle. Place was full of me old prison wardens.'

She takes another drag and stubs the joint out on the lace-edged table cloth. As I catch Holly's eye we both put our hands over our mouths. Then Holly asks innocently, 'So, Shirley, do you think the chicken's cooked yet?'

'Chicken? Oh yeah. Chicken.'

Pins heaves herself up. She picks up a towel and opens the oven door. She removes a dish that holds a small, charred piece of meat, carries it back to the table and bangs it down on top of the rizzla papers and plastic bags.

Pins descends elegantly into her chair and lets out another weary sigh. She picks up a spatula, eases it under the crispy bird, lifts it out of the baking tray and drops it down on the table cloth.

It takes her a few seconds to register that the chicken she has cooked for her lunch party is sitting in the middle of Bob's kitchen table, resting on a shriveled plastic bag with one of its wizened legs stuck in the overflowing ashtray. It isn't until chicken grease starts soaking into the rizzlas that Pins jumps into action. 'Hell's bells! Forgot the bloody plate!'

Pins eventually levers the bird on to a plate. She stares at it, trance-like. Then, out of the blue she says to me, 'You want breast or leg?'

I say I don't mind, but after a few vain prods with a penknife and a fondue fork she sits back in her chair, breathless. She throws the implements over to Holly and tells him to have a go. As he sighs and mumbles, I decide to talk to Pins because I do think it is nice of her to have offered to help us out on the Galliano front.

'So what are your plans for work now, Shirley?' I say.

'Plans? Oh yeah, plans. The leather's having some teething problems. Course, I've got to live with Bob now. Things was different with Claudette. She was class. We went to clubs. We had special tables. Bottle of whisky on the house. Could have made it big in leather. Bloody suppliers. Sent me Romanian pig leather. I told them. "That don't wash with me," I said. Didn't try to fob me off the next time did they? Trouble was, next time there weren't any cash up front. Then, of course, them cats nobbled me.'

She tells her cat's urine story before pausing to say, 'So, George, you want to go clubbing some time?'

She looks at me with a smile that makes her look almost cute, even though she is one of those women who looks like a fifty-year-old who looks like a thirty-five-year-old, when in fact she is simply a thirty-five-year-old. When she has picked at some of the blackened pieces of flesh that Holly has put on her plate she gets up, holding the back of her chair as a support. Her eyes look like a tipped-up tin of spiders. She says she's going to get dressed and then she'll get Bob to drive us over to the Louvre.

*　　*　　*

Dressed turns out to be a mint-green *tailleur* one size too small with a Euro Disney limited-edition pin attached to the collar and a pair of fingerless, cream net mittens. She is confident about the look. 'Maybe go clubbing later. Dressing up feminine. Always works best.'

Holly and I sit in the back of Bob's 1950s Cadillac Coupe de Ville. We know it is a 1950s Cadillac Coupe de Ville because Bob has spent the past ten minutes going into minute detail about the rusty (mint-green also) hull that keeps stalling at every set of traffic lights. 'They don't make 'em like this any more,' he keeps chuckling like a jolly sheriff. 'In 1950s Detroit they used to say "Build 'em mean to make 'em last."' He chuckles some more, until Pins, rigid in the front seat, yells out, 'Shut up, Bob, for Christ's sake,' like a barmaid chucking a drunk out at last orders. Bob looks like an ancient toad and I can't work out how the car is managing to drive itself given that Bob seems hardly able to move. Once in a while the ship-sized Stetson atop his head turns three or four degrees as he cranes towards the mirror.

On the crowded roundabout at Trocadero a red Citroën swerves to avoid crashing into the side of us as Bob suddenly decides that he is in the wrong lane. A peal of horns is heard, followed by a deafening scream from Pins:

'For Christ's sake, Bob, what the frig are you doing!'

'Keep calm, Shirley, will you just give me the directions!'

The Stetson moves six or seven degrees in an attempt to glare at its mint-green pilot whereupon the 1950s cedar-inlaid steering wheel takes on a life of its own and lurches towards another car. It is debatable how long the Cadillac Coupe de Ville can last in Bob's hands, no matter how meanly it has been made.

'For Christ's sake, Bob, what the frig are you doing!'

'Keep calm, Shirley, will you just give me the directions!'

As we circle past our exit road for the third time, I realise that I have never seen Pins this animated. When the car stalls,

Pins — now mint-green and red all over — lets verbal shrapnel fly from her mouth:

'For Christ's sake, Bob, you bloody hephalump old stupid bloody *connard putain* bloody mung bean.'

The car is bouncing up and down now as Pins becomes more furious but even that can't make the 1950s mean machine move forward. Every so often, Bob stops twisting the key robotically in the lock, turns towards Pins with a light coating of sweat on his top lip and remonstrates, 'Keep calm, Shirley, if you'd only given me the directions!'

The Cadillac stops and starts and bounces and jerks its way towards the rue du Louvre and the terrible thing is that Holly and I can't just jump out and run away because in theory Pins is essential to our operation.

As Holly said afterwards, there are fashion accessories and there are fashion accessories but rocking up to the trendiest show of Paris Fashion Week pushing the rusty tail fins of a clapped-out old banger and its amphibious driver is not the sort of thing you want yourself associated with. The car breaks down a few hundred metres from the Louvre but Bob refuses to leave it on the rue de Rivoli and as Pins can't disobey Bob, we can't disobey Pins. Holly and I are too shame- and sweaty-faced to say anything when we finally arrive outside the Louvre gates although somehow, from somewhere, Pins summons up the energy to start belting out, 'Faarking hell, hell's bloody bells,' as she surveys the damage done to her cream mittens. On hearing the spluttering engine and the curses of discontentment, the black-swathed crowd waiting to enter the show — about 200 people — all turn in the direction of the spectacle. A humourless scattering of indolent necks, spiteful eyes and alienating sunglasses grazes the scene for a few seconds until they realise that this is too close to the bone of real life and turn back abruptly.

Holly, whose egg-white cashmere trousers with the 10-inch turn-ups now have a big oil blotch down the front, can bear it no longer. Holly being Holly, he doesn't make a big drama or demand to know why Pins has dared do this to his day. When we finally leave the car behind us and walk under the entrance arch of the Louvre, Holly turns to me, mutters 'Gloriana' under his breath and goes off to lose himself in the crowd. When, a few minutes later, Pins says, 'Where's Holly gone then?' I tell her that I don't know. It is possible, after all, that Holly could have got himself swallowed up in this swarming complex of queues by natural means. The clumps of disgruntled lines bulge and contract as if they were in the throes of a breech birth. Pins has grabbed hold of my arm and is trying to force us towards the front to see if we can glimpse her contact who is going to lift us up like the hand of God and set us down in the front row seats. But it is not easy. It is hard to see over the heads of all these people and the two women in front have already got into one of those frenetically formalised French rows which have 'vous's and 'madame's flying around like both parties are presenting each other with the Legion d'Honneur and it is only the tone of their voices that lets you know they are cursing each other. Holding on to one of the women's hands is a boy of about ten years old who is being jostled around in his plum position in the middle of the birth canal. The boy looks up at his mother as her mouth contorts with tension. He has a look of quiet fear on his face. You can see the traumas slipping into his mind which ten years later she will be paying a fortune for some psycho-analyst to root out again.

The railings divide invitation holders into different categories. Those with cards marked A, B, C, D and E have the barriers pulled back every so often so that the complaining womb can heave its frightening babies through the railings. Those with cards marked 'S' for 'Standing' have to wait amongst a straining rabble of students, counterfeiters, the unimportant, and us. Pins and I have been sent here by a guard from railing 'A' who took offence when Pins called him a '*sale con*' and then tried to placate him by waving a silver foil-wrapped nugget in front of his face. Pins is really getting animated now; she keeps shouting, 'Didier! Didier!' and then sticking two fingers under her tongue and doing that shrill 'come here' whistle that boys know how to do. I am pretty impressed by the inappropriateness of this gesture in the present company but unfortunately the only person who doesn't turn round to look at her is the elusive Didier.

I feel despondent and don't put up any fight as I let myself get pushed back to the beginning of the 'S' queue. I look around randomly for Didier but Pins' only description is that he has brown hair and a habit of twitching his nose from side to side. Then I spot Sophie who is standing just by the entrance of the 'A' railing. She is kind of jumping around, waving her arms at me, shouting 'George! George!' in a horribly cheerful voice. I get worried because I don't know if I can bear listening to her tell me what a goddam mess her life is. Not today. When she called up yesterday she told me that she was worried because she thought her Greek God was smoking too much pot. She took him round the Louvre for the Renoir show and he kept talking to her about weavils. Weavils in the buildings that he was trying to sell. Weavils in his own house. Things coming out of the walls. 'Goddam, I think he's been reading too many Borges books again,' she said. The Greek God has never struck me as someone to read Borges – or to enjoy going round Renoir shows – but apparently he once read *The Garden of Forking Paths* and had a nervous breakdown two weeks later.

I try to look on the bright side as I stroll leisurely over to her. Maybe she can tell me what the show was like afterwards and I can pretend to my editor that I have seen it – although I know it won't be the same. Luckily, when I go up to her she doesn't even mention the Greek God. She's just rattling on about how she was going to call me because her 'goddam asshole' of a boss doesn't know who John Galliano is and she telephoned me before she left the office but I'd gone home but now here I am and do I want the extra ticket? I do momentarily wonder if I should ask if Sophie has a ticket for Pins, or at least go back and tell Pins that I'm going to get a front row seat after all and that I'll meet her later, but the waters are breaking again in queue 'A' and there is no stopping me now.

My invitation says that I am called Monica Humperdink of *Time* magazine. The number on the ticket says that I have a front row seat in the American press section but when I get to Monica's place there is a man with a violently sweating face remonstrating with a well-groomed woman dressed impeccably in black.

'Row D! Row D! You think I've got "idiot" written on my face? I've always been in Row A! Anyone who's got a life is in row A! Christ, the fucking catering staff get to sit in row C so what in the name of Jesus H. Christ are they doing sticking me in row effing D!'

With tight voice and more spiteful eyes, the woman says, '*Je suis desolée, monsieur,*' and walks off. The man collapses into the empty seat next to me, throwing his face into his hands.

Everyone around me seems to be fairly tense. An American voice behind me keeps going on about 'gutsy wellingtons', while a little further up in the row a woman with an English accent like breaking glass is doing some sort of weird stroking action on the big red coat that she is wearing. I think she must be very hot because the lights in the hall are making me sweat in my T-shirt and Tati denim jacket. She fiddles with the collar and the cuffs as she talks to a woman with a pale, drawn face next to her. Finally, the woman in the red coat can bear it no longer. She thrusts a shoulder forward towards the pale woman and says, 'What do you think of this?'

'Who is it?' the woman asks nervously.

'Who *is* it? Come on, you know the form, if in doubt, think buttons ...'

Buttons are pulled out for the pale woman's benefit.

'Oh, I see. Yes, yes of course.'

'I mean, I was going to get MaxMara, but then I thought: Japanese tourists. No, I thought ...'

The coat power trip is getting boring but nobody near me looks like they fancy a chat. The show is already running an hour late and even though all the 'S' people have been let in – a sure sign normally that something is going to happen, according to what I hear the American behind me say – nobody has yet walked out on to the catwalk. At eight o'clock, I hear the woman in the red coat bellow 'Who *is* it?' once more to the nervous woman who has been foolish enough to ask another question. Someone has just stood up surrounded by a huddle of body guards and rushed out of the show. The woman in the red coat finally announces that it is Madonna who obviously couldn't be bothered to wait any longer and she scribbles something furiously in her notebook. Then she puts her pen down, smiles deeply and says, 'She's going to regret it.'

A sound track of wolf howling begins. It seems to go on for ages and after a while the crowd joins in with their own wolf impersonations. Finally, the house lights blacken, a techno beat strikes up, and from behind a thick red velvet curtain, Italian model Carla Bruni rushes out on to the stage wearing a dress based on an eighteenth-century hooped crinoline skirt (that is what it says in the programme) and a look of big-time mock horror on her face. Other models follow, similarly dressed and beautifully traumatised. The programme says that the fabrics of the clothes are organza, shantung and crêpe Georgette but that's the last thing I'm interested in. The models look like pieces of veal cutlet scampering down the runway. Coupled with the music and the mad poses they strike at the end of the podium for the solid wall of photographers whose cameras click like hundreds of electronic butterfly wings, the last thing you are interested in is what they are wearing.

When the last shrieking woman in billowing crinoline rushes on to the stage to join the others in a wave of standing ovation, a small man strides through the curtain in a fake fur Buffalo Bill hat and a pink T-shirt that says 'Gorgeous' on the front. I presume this is John Galliano because the woman in the red coat is screaming 'Genius!' like a guillotine *tricoteuse* shouting 'Off with his head!' I am glad that people are clapping so wildly because it will be a perfect distraction while I rush up to the velvet curtain and slip behind it. Part of me truly doesn't want to do this and I wonder, momentarily, if I really would feel that wretched if I just slunk off home and told the editor at *The European* that the guards wouldn't let me backstage. But I know this feeling of fear. I have been there before. In my heart of hearts I know that there are some things you just have to make yourself do or you feel really bad about them afterwards. Late at night you churn them over in your head and try to see them from different viewpoints — like a pair of terrible trousers you have bought that you kid yourself will look fantastic if only you hold your breath enough and pose and turn in front of the mirror.

In reality, you know that there is only one angle to the story and the angle is that the trousers are a wash-out and so are you.

I know this feeling of fear. The terror now, at the edge of the curtain, is the same as the day I served my first customer. I remember it clearly: 12.05 Sunday morning, Scottish pensioner with a scowl, code name Jock. Always in directly after mass, face like thunder to snap an order of double egg, chips and whiting. Had the low-down from the staff, had Mandy gunning for me by the drinks machine. Stomach still felt queasy.

*　　　*　　　*

As applause continues to inflate the auditorium my fake DMs walk very fast towards the red curtain. I am pretty sure that everyone is still staring at the girls on the runway who glow with smiles and clutch on to John Galliano's pink T-shirt as if they are about to fall. But when I finally make a hell-for-leather dash through the bit of curtain furthest from the runway I still expect to feel a pair of thick arms on me at any moment.

When I pass through to the other side though, there is just a feeling of airiness. Airiness and the sound of a few female voices chatting quietly as they sit by polythene-covered clothing rails waiting for the stampede of veal and paparazzi and camera crews and hangers-on to come bursting back through the curtain. While the backstage remains empty nobody seems to be taking any notice of me so I sit down on some steps that lead down from the runway and watch some waiters open bottles of Champagne on long, white-clothed trestle tables. Wafts of dry ice vapour rise from the corks like silent genies slithering from the lamp.

The stampede starts with a medium-sized sneeze as the curtain blows John Galliano, drenched in sweat, through to the backstage area on to the stairs where I am sitting. I stand up and he looks at me with tiny pin-prick pupils.

Carry on, carry on, though your legs feel like lead, the still small voice of waitress training tells me. So I stammer, 'Hello, I'm a journalist. I wondered if it would be okay if I asked you a few questions?' My pen trembles on my notebook like my biro on my blue-carbon orders pad. Is it to be a 'Fuck off, I haven't got time for this'? A 'Give me double egg and chips and whiting and for Christ's sake hurry up about it'? John Galliano's face reminds me of the song we sang at the convent about the mad lady who had 'one eye in the pot and the other up the chimney'.

He carries on looking at me and his pupils seem to be getting smaller and smaller.

Before I have the chance to say anything else, he opens his mouth. 'If you like, my main character is a kind of trolloppy Becky Sharp who runs away in a tartan gym slip and then she meets a dodgy prince ...'

I hurry to scribble this down and all the while I think to myself: Wary though, go wary. Jock said, 'Steak pie and mushy peas', and then what happened? 'This tea's bloody cold, lass' come dessert time, that's what. Be on your guard, I think. And sure enough, just as I ask John for his opinions on the current trends for grunge clothes, he turns and says huffily, 'Grunge! What do you mean grunge! I put a stake through the heart of grunge. People into grunge will never know the beauty of wearing an *haute couture* Dior jacket. The mindless worship of jumble sale clothes is the death knell for thousands of seamstresses and artisans who have learnt through generations of *savoir faire* in the most skilled workshops in the world ...'

And it is too late to take another tack because a warm white tunnel of light beams through from the other side of the curtain. The red velvet is torn asunder by a whirlwind of movement as streams of camera crews and photographers and chattering people swarm in, led by André Leon Talley. John Galliano, with all the flourish of Jock leaving a measly ten-pence tip, rushes off away from the crowds leaving me clutching a series of puzzling notes.

Now there is no more quiet backstage. Talley has been interrupted on his way to say 'Genius' to John Galliano by acquaintances of his from a TV crew who grab him and say, 'Come on, André, how about a bit of colour, what did you think of the show?' And now, dressed in fullest Chanel hand-stitched leather mac with Henri IV chainmail – as he informs the man with the microphone – the soothing glare of the camera lights persuades him to scatter some crumbs from his impressive larder of sound bites. 'What do I think of that show? I think that show was hot, hot, hot. And as we all know, the most important things in life are food and sex – after that come love and money!' Slow motion laughs. *Thank you André that was great.* Then, like hounds, they're off again. How about grabbing the editor of German *Vogue* and getting some reaction on having her coat ripped outside the 'A' entrance railings? Maybe Anna Wintour could give us a quickie about fashion being all about being an individual?

There are lots of different noises backstage now. There are thick-armed bouncers guarding the entrance to the magic curtains, yelling to the protesting huddles that nobody can enter. There is the sound of Naomi Campbell yelling at photographers to leave her alone, like Jesus casting the thieves out of the temple. '*Bravissimo, bravissimo,*' are the words coming out of the mouth of the legendary fashion editor of *Le Figaro* with chalky blonde hair and scheming eyes as she touches John Galliano on the arm. I wonder if he knows, as Holly has told me, that you can never trust anything she says because she writes typical French fashion journalism, something on the lines of, 'Surely this Yves Saint Laurent dress was ... created by God.'

I put away my waitress notepad and begin accepting *coupes de Champagne* from the white-gloved waiters who pass by with silver trays, their stern faces softened by being in the vicinity of so much milky veal. John Galliano's four PRs dash up and hold hands around him as if they are playing ring-a-ring-o' roses. It looks like they came in the nick of time for John's mouth is twitching like it is the only part of him still left in this world. They escort him away from the clumps of people near the curtain and take him to the area designated for formal press interviews.

One of the PR people puts a glass of Champagne in John's hand and tries to explain to him who the TV crew standing before him is. John is still out of control and suddenly his eyes fix on the furry boom that the sound man is holding.

He tiptoes forward and starts stroking it. 'Hey, cool, cool,' he chuckles. 'This is really furry and nice.'

A Mediterranean-looking woman smiles tightly. Then she coughs and says, '*Alors, John, vous voulez parler un peu de votre collection?*'

One of the PR people, a medium-height Indian man steps forward and whispers in John's ear a translation of what the woman has just said.

But John doesn't see why he should take his attention off the furry boom. He narrows his eyes into slits and spits at the Mediterranean woman, 'Women in the eighteenth century had as much punk attitude as someone walking down the King's Road in 1977.' Then he stomps off behind some more curtains in the wings, shouting as a parting shot, 'They're only clothes, you know!'

I am not too unhappy when John Galliano leaves the scene because the backstage area is still crowded with the veal girls in American Tan g-strings climbing back into their home clothes. In real life, models are taller than normal, thinner than normal with bigger mouths than normal. They have that aura of springy freshness like over-brimming glasses of milk which makes your stomach feel tingly when you look at them. They don't really make you feel sexy but given that it is now 11 p.m. on a Friday night and given that I keep overhearing the gayboys – i.e. most of the people here – saying things like 'Le B.H. is a good club, although it gets kind of weird after two', I feel like a little action too. Thanks to the beverages I have been downing for the past hour, and thanks to the fact that I have succeeded in carrying out my task, I don't feel like a nervous Cornish chip shop skivvy any more. I feel as arrogant and ruthless as a French Champagne waiter.

☆ ☆ ☆

When I emerge from backstage, only a handful of people remain front of house. Cameramen packing bags, journalists gossiping, cleaners – and Pins. Pins is sitting in a front row seat near the top of the catwalk dabbing a stain from her mint-green skirt.

She doesn't see me and I wonder momentarily about sloping off home on my own. But something about her tenacity and her stain makes me walk up to her. She smiles when she sees me and I sit down while she tells me how she managed to bump into Didier soon after the show began. The two of them went and got stoned in the special *Cravate Rouge* portakabins. In fact, she says, Didier has been in the portakabins for much of the afternoon which is the main reason why her grand plan to sneak me and Holly in has been foiled.

She smiles when I say, 'Fancy clubbing, then?'

We go to the Privilège disco where Pins is lively until she spots Claudette, of pins empire fame. When she sees Claudette, Pins' spirits spiral horribly.

'She done me up like a kipper,' says Pins, chucking back gin and tonic. 'Started an affair with the personnel manager of the glue factory in Neuilly. Course, didn't say a word to me. She'd get into bed and pretend to go to sleep. Then she'd leap out of bed in the mornings saying she had deliveries to make. Should have guessed it. All she could talk about in the evenings was adhesive innovations.' She looks over to where Claudette is sitting and sighs. 'You can't blame the girls for being attracted. She's classy and feminine. That's what they like. I remember her telling me, "You've got to wear a skirt, that's what they like".'

I cast a glance at Claudette who looks to me like an old trucky with an over-sprayed bob. But Pins hasn't finished yet. 'When the chop came, it came bitter-sweet sort of thing. She come home late one night. Begging for it by that time I was, I can tell you. So I jumped her, and afterwards she looked up from the pillow and said, "Shirley". "Shirley," she said. "I'll always remember you as the dirtiest person I've ever slept with."'

Pins relives the tender memory for a few moments. 'I thought that was nice. A nice thing to say, you know. Last thing she ever said to me it was. Got in the next day and found a note telling me to pack me bags.'

I look over at Claudette who is now wrapping one of her beefy forearms around a bony woman sitting next to her.

'Look at that,' Pins laughs bitterly, lighting up another cigarette. 'They're bringing her bottle of whisky to her table. She's got her own special bottle of whisky. They keep it for her. Special.'

But my mind is fixed on Claudette's accolade to Pins as the dirtiest person she has ever slept with and when Pins dislodges the line of ash from the end of her cigarette with a furious flick of her index finger, I seem to see her for the first time. Pure Pins. Self-contained Pins focused in on her anger, scornful of what the world might think of her. Now she chews her cigarette like John Thaw in *The Sweeney*. Not being one to look a gift horse in the mouth, I decide to take her home with me.

The next morning, seeing her lying in bed next to me in my nylon Noel Coward dressing-gown, an ashy joint stub behind her ear, a pair of cheap sunglasses jammed over her eyes and a candle stump in her hand, I realise that Pins is encased in a hoary frost of neglect, unlove. You can see where she is coming from. And where she is going to.

The most enchanting part of the night had been when she kissed me. I had expected she would kiss in a raggedy, slobbery, clumsy fashion but she had an expert, velvety kiss that was teasing and more than averagely dirty. A kiss that was to be taken seriously, a kiss, you could tell, that had made hearts weep and bodies tremble. I tried to let myself be washed away, swept aloft on this dangerous mouth, but when it suddenly stopped and said, 'Bloody funeral music in here,' and got out of bed to inspect what better things than Bach were to be had on my ghetto blaster, the spell was broken for good.

She climbed back in the bed with a creaky 'bloody nora', which could have been referring to anything – from the cold, to the lumpy mattress, to the music, to her lack of success in the leather business – and lay supine, staring at the ceiling. Then she rolled over to face me. 'Come on then,' she croaked in a cockney accent held aloft on wafts of beer and cigarettes.

Sex is rarely an unrelenting line of dark, thrusting brutishness. Thoughts may dwell predominantly on death and power and sticky, steamy, slashing and thrashing and drowning and licking and sucking, but banal images soon elbow their way in to make mockery of your so-called abandoned self. You suddenly notice the terrible pattern on the pillow case, the Abba megamix the neighbours are playing next door, your girlfriend's face metamorphosing into a monkey's muzzle thanks to those cheap drugs you bought in the club which means you have to rapidly think of happy things like whiskers on kittens in order to save yourself from having a complete freak-out.

Coming across a bottom you have never stumbled across before is quite startling and has the power to pull you out of any sex trance. Bottoms. You think you have seen them all, felt them all, and then you come across one that feels like jelly and warm lard, and you are astounded – not necessarily because of the jelly and lard texture but because you imagined that someone that tough, that leather-clad would have hard buttocks made of prime-cut beef.

Surprisingly, the unexpectedly mushy piece of anatomy held pleasures of its own. I put my hands below Pins' waist and felt the warm flesh that hung loose from her body. I kneaded it. It reminded me of the smooth, white fish that I used to watch

my father cut up into large, medium and budget-sized pieces
every morning. Cod, plaice, whiting, skate. Afterwards, into a
red plastic tray filled with soft skin and split gut and slimy
eggy underbelly I would place my hands and squidge hard. It
made me close my eyes and grit my teeth with pleasure. My
grandfather always said I should learn to play the piano to
relax but I find that fish has a similar cathartic effect. Even
now, when I come home from a bad party, I'll open the fridge
and take out some fresh sardines or plaice if I have any from
the market, and I'll cut them open and gut them.

Pins started to get suspicious that I was spending so much
time on her buttocks. 'You do a lot of cycling then,' she said,
tentatively feeling my own bottom.

'Yes,' I said, squeezing her bottom once more and feeling
nostalgic for cod fillets.

'Yeah. Had a bike once. Some bugger put glue in the lock.
Couldn't use it no more.' The memory seemed overwhelming
for Pins. She let go of my bottom and lay down on her back
again, staring up at the ceiling. Then she said, 'Not one for
acrobatic sex neither, if that's what you're thinking. Tried fisting
once but it felt all soft and weird. Felt like doing an abortion.
Got better things to do than pummel up against wet membrane
all night.'

That off her mind, she leaned over and began kissing me.
She was good again, and she began breathing more and more
heavily as she rubbed up and down over my body. Her joke
persona disappeared as she touched me and penetrated me
with energy I didn't know she had in her. Then it began.
Like she'd been punched in the stomach, a low moan came
from her mouth which gradually turned verbal. Nascent words
beginning with Os and Zs started coming out and these built
to a crescendo: 'Fu ... fu ... faar-king-ell ... bloody nora ...
hells bleedin' bells!'

Her ginger head writhed around on the pillow as she entered
her low rent orgasm and came out the other side.

A long silence followed. Pins lay motionless on the bed looking like she'd been embalmed. Then, with a spasm, her eyes jerked open. She sat up, dragged on my purple dressing-gown and picked up a candle stub that had rolled under the bed. She went into the cold hall towards the bathroom. This procedure was repeated three or four times in the course of the night. I finally said, 'Shirley. Why do you take a candle to the bathroom with you?'

She looked at the three-inch piece of wax and jumped as if someone had put it there while she wasn't looking.

'Oh yeah,' she said, remembering suddenly. 'I was going to tell you but I thought you'd laugh. Thought if I held it I'd feel warmer. Know what I mean?' She heaved herself back into bed. 'Bloody freezing 'round here. Hells teeth.'

Now that Pins seems to have found some warmth at last in the Noel Coward dressing-gown I get out of bed and go to the kitchen to make coffee. Bet stumbles in, her eye make-up looking smudged in a happy sort of way, and begins to hack at a piece of stale baguette for her and Sam's breakfast.

When she has cut off a slice she looks over to me and says, 'George, why is there a strange woman wandering around our flat with an unlit candle?'

It seems too complicated to explain the lure of lard and accomplished velvety kisses. As I fill the kettle, I gaze at the saucepans in the sink filled with rusty-coloured water and mushy leek threads. I hesitate. Bringing mysterious one-night stands back is one thing. A pretty cool thing. Explaining foibles that suggest they have only come home with you because they are complete lunatics is another.

'Okay. Brace yourself. She thinks that holding a candle warms her up. She says this place is freezing. She's got a point. About the place being freezing.'

Bet, half-alarmed, half-entering the spirit of the Saturday

morning after the Friday night before, says, 'Bloody hell. We don't want her moving in. Do we, George? George, do we!'

'Course not,' I say feebly, watching Bet fling open the kitchen windows to the cold October morning.

Pins calls up a few days later asking if I want to go for a drink with her. I umm and ah pathetically, talking nonsense about a friend who is coming to stay. As I am in the middle of a bit about how, anyway, my bike isn't working too well at the moment, she interrupts with wistful resignation and says, 'Yeah, well. You don't have to say anything else.'

There is no self pity. It is the despondency of one who has seen all, suffered all. The sorrow of tone, the honesty of feeling makes her human for the second time since I have met her. I gaze at the dust clumps on top of the cracked answering machine and I feel shabby.

Pins disappeared like all good urban myths do. I wouldn't have expected it any other way. Holly said he'd heard she'd run off to Créteil with a toilet cleaner. But then he would say that.

CHAPTER NINE

Doctor Love

Holly hasn't paid the rent for six months now. He fritters away all his money on beers and bargains from Tati so Alex has ordered him to get a job from Madame Bourse.

Bet introduced Holly to Madame Bourse who saw instantly that Holly knew nothing about teaching English. But there is something about Holly that slightly frightens Madame Bourse so she hired him on the spot. Her uneasiness probably has something to do with Holly's *soigné* look and the way he scans his eyes up and down her outfit when she talks to him. He has a trick of making sure his eyes linger on her hair or scarf concept (two problematic areas for Madame Bourse) when her conversation turns to telling-off mode.

Madame Bourse is always calling Holly into her office to tell him off. This is because the only thing he ever gives his pupils to read are articles from *Women's Wear Daily*. He spends hours drilling middle management on how Yves Saint Laurent created the modern woman and how 'classic with a twist' is the correct way to dress. He admits that he doesn't care if his students learn English or not; he says they should be grateful to be learning the rudiments of high style.

One day, the managing director of a company specialising in polystyrene drinking cups went to complain to Madame Bourse about the lesson Holly had just delivered on duchess satin and its uses. As punishment, Madame Bourse sent Holly to teach at the headquarters of Hervé Marie Frozen Comestibles in a dismal suburb past La Défense called Courbevoie. Three times a week, Holly was obliged to travel to a yellow slab of a 1960s building with chipped doors and draughty corridors and the damp smell of municipal lunch in the air to give an intensive English course to a secretary who was having a nervous breakdown because her department – Potato Exports – was filled with men who were all sexist and horrible to her. Holly would sit in a drab boardroom smelling of hot, dusty radiators and bite his fingernails as he listened to the secretary's hour-long lament (in French) about how awful life and society were. Every so often, Holly's glassy eyes would tear themselves away from the poster of The Cheeses of Great Britain attached to the room's shiny yellow walls. He would nod sympathetically at Giselle, the secretary, and say with a note of sweetness in his voice, '*Oui, oui. C'est dégueulasse. Dégueulasse*,' before adding that Giselle could go early if she wanted to.

Holly hates teaching at Madame Bourse's more than anything he has done so far. Yet in spite of his intimidating appraisal of his boss's clothes, he prefers to avoid conflict whenever possible by saying yes to Madame Bourse when she rubs her hands together and says she has '*un petit service*' to ask him. That is how he ended up in Courbevoie on Christmas Eve. Madame Bourse booked him to give an hour-long lesson to Serge Racine, a thirty-eight-year-old *informatique* engineer whom Holly had come to know a little during the previous three weeks when he had been teaching him an advanced English course. Serge used to go on at length to Holly about his hobbies of cycling and gastronomy while Holly tried to make out Serge's arm muscles under the folds of his expensive stripy shirt.

Holly says that if you are ever in doubt as to the whereabouts of your libido, all you have to do is go to a godforsaken suburb of Paris and sit in a room with nothing but a scratched, toffee-brown table in front of you and shiny yellow walls surrounding you and people who have dedicated their lives to frozen peas lined up before you. He says that office workers all have dirty minds; it is inevitable. You sit all day in a clammy office having inane conversations with people you don't really like and you get more repressed and twisted by the hour.

'You never hear of nurses or poets going off to have a wank in the toilets at lunch time,' he says, 'but you hear about accountants and personnel managers doing it all the time.'

Many Courbevoie students were ruled out of the sexy category – Giselle was obviously out of the question – and from among all the sweaty sexists in wool suits and chartreuse blazers, Serge Racine was the best of a bad bunch.

During their last lesson, Serge had spoken in fluent English about the best way to boil crabs: 'There is the possibility of placing them in cold water – with onions and rosemary, naturally – and to boil them little by little. The negative with such a method is that to test how long to cook the meat is very difficult. I prefer to drop the crab into a pan of boiling water. The negative of this is that the legs will drop off from the shock.'

Serge then looked Holly in the eye and made a speech about how his girlfriend preferred method number one because it was more humane. He winked and added in a stock phrase of Holly's that 'women are demented'.

Now, sitting at the scratched, toffee-brown table on Christmas Eve at ten minutes to seven waiting for Serge to arrive, Holly reflected that he didn't care if the *informatique* technician made a move on him or not. He had far better fish to fry. After weeks of persuasion, he had finally convinced the most exciting man he had met all year – the Russian ballet dancer – to come round and spend Christmas with him at rue Léon. In only two hours' time, Holly would have a stark naked, recently retired ballet dancer chasing him round the flat, gripping a bottle of vodka tight by the throat.

Holly still had this image in his head when Serge arrived

boisterously on the dot of seven. Serge was gripping two bottles of Champagne tight by their throats. Perfect, Holly reflected. Perfect to make the time fly.

And to start with, the Champagne seemed to make time zoom along. Holly came over all light and airy and felt it was time to launch into his new theory about the 'Helen Keller school of sewing' which had been brought on by a one-off wedding dress commission he'd recently received from a rich student at Parsons. 'This BCBG girl from Fontainebleau with fat thighs,' said Holly, chinking Serge's glass, crossing his legs and pushing a nearby grammar book out of his path. '"I want a dress in organza," she goes. "But I don't want anything see-through." I ask you! Fat girls wrecking my vision!'

As Serge chuckled and poured him another glass, Holly realised that he was getting tanked up rather quicker than normal. On top of his excitement at the thought of the Russian's imminent arrival, Holly put it down to the fact that all he had eaten for the day had been some dried-up cheese rinds and some limp parsley that he found at the bottom of the fridge of the Hervé Marie Frozen Comestibles kitchen. He hadn't eaten much at all recently. Since the gang had gone back to England for Christmas, he couldn't even hope that Alex might bring some *moules* back to rue Léon or that there might be some vegetarian mulch lying around in one of Ann's saucepans at rue de Clignancourt. Holly had blown nearly every penny of Madame Bourse's wages that month on Christmas drinks to greet the arrival of the Russian. Luckily, he hadn't had to buy in much food because the Russian had told him that he was on the pineapple diet. 'It's the classic ballet dancer's diet,' Holly told Serge. 'You eat nothing but pineapple for three days and you look like Margot Fontaine at the end of it.' Actually, Holly had noticed that the Russian had been eating nothing but pineapple for as long as he had known him – that, and sniff Marlboro packets and drink more vodka than he had ever seen anyone drink in their life. It suddenly struck him that maybe he hadn't bought in enough vodka and the Russian would leave after only a few hours. That would be truly terrible. What would he do then?

As Holly tipped back more of Serge's Champagne, he became increasingly paranoid drunk. Why did Serge want a lesson with him on Christmas Eve anyway? What if Serge really did want to shag him? What would he do? It was 7.15 and Holly realised that there was nobody else in the whole of Hervé Marie Frozen Comestibles HQ. All the normal people had gone home early because it was Christmas Eve. Holly felt the shiny yellow boardroom heave with the monster of intimacy.

Serge kept topping him up and going '*chin*', and smiling as he watched Holly tipping another glass down his neck. Holly watched Serge open the second bottle of Taittinger and wondered if the animated talk about his new cycle shorts – and the hand gestures – meant that this was going to be more than just an English lesson.

And he thought how it was just his luck that something exciting might at last be about to happen at Courbevoie when he couldn't do anything about it because he could only think about the Russian. But another voice whispered to him that he had standards to uphold and as Serge opened his wallet to show him pictures of his bicycle and his apartment and his girlfriend's thirtieth birthday party, Holly wondered if he was going to be expected to do it on the scratched, toffee-coloured table.

Holly wasn't sure if Serge realised that he didn't normally make passes at men – that he made himself available and the men were supposed to make passes at him. And then Serge started to ask him about the proper use of demonstrative pronouns and Holly felt another wave of paranoia as he reflected that maybe Serge didn't fancy him at all; that maybe he just wanted to know about grammar and he had only brought the bottles of Champagne because French people were polite and they always drank Champagne at Christmas.

Holly decided to get back to safe territory by grabbing the

English grammar book that was now lying at the farthest end of the scratched, toffee-coloured table. He had known for some time that Serge was keen on learning about pronouns but Holly wasn't overly confident about what a pronoun was. He turned to chapter one which was on full stops and capital letters, but then he remembered that he didn't know much about those either. He always assumed that words like 'vodka' and 'money' had capitals and he wasn't sure if god had a capital 'G' these days or not.

So he turned to a random page which had a selection of sentence translations. But he'd never looked at the book before and it was only when he began to read out question four that he realised it said, 'We had been making love for several hours when her husband suddenly entered the room.'

Holly, whose top lip was sweating beforehand, now felt apoplectic with embarrassment. He finished the sentence as calmly as he could, but what was that sentence doing in the Hervé Marie Frozen Comestibles grammar book anyway? Was it even really there? As it was, his eyes were having trouble focusing on the page. Had Holly made some demented Freudian slip under the influence of a bottle of Champagne?

He could hear the smirk in Serge's voice as he translated the phrase to '*On faisait l'amour pendant plusieurs heures quand son marie est entré dans la chambre.*' There were a few moments' silence and then Serge kicked Holly's foot gently with his shoe and said in low tones, 'Do you not think that the best sex is when you love the person with whom you are making the love?'

Holly instinctively blurted out 'No!', staggered up from his chair as quickly as he could, wished Serge a *Joyeux Noël* and fumbled his way out of the room as fast as his legs would carry him, promising himself that he would never set foot again in Hervé Marie Frozen Comestibles as long as he lived.

By the time Holly made it into the packed *banlieu* train back to the Gare du Nord it was 8.30. The orange, look-alike leather interior of the snail-slow train smelt pungently of stale garlic and the new Kenzo men's cologne which is supposed to smell like oysters but always reminds Holly of cheap rent boys. The painful defrost of his brain from the strangely potent Taittinger had begun and Holly felt dry-throated and achy-headed. The rhythm of the train seemed to hiss 'the shame, the shame, the shame,' and even when he closed his eyes he had flashbacks of being in the room with Serge Racine and he shuddered to think what news would now get back to Madame Bourse. Worse still, Holly knew that his breath smelt sour and that he had no chewing gum on him which would be disastrous if he bumped into the Russian at the rue Léon gates.

He watched a couple of teenagers drawing a cock and balls on the window with a felt-tipped pen and he wondered if it would be okay to burp or if it would bring too much attention to himself. Instead, he looked through the erect penis on the window and out at the clusters of clean suburban bungalows and glum people with supermarket carrier bags waiting at bus stops as the train crawled by. He pictured the Russian and his almond-shaped eyes and Heavy Metal T-shirt and smiled. He calmed down by telling himself that although he had arranged to meet the Russian at rue Léon at 9 o'clock, the Russian always arrived at least an hour late. It would all be all right. Holly had bought ten pineapples at the Barbès market for a special offer of 50 francs. He would probably make it home just in time to cut the mouldy bits off them and arrange them in an artistic formation. He also wanted to fold the linen napkins into interesting shapes so that there would be some sense of occasion at the fantastic moment when the Russian hammered at the rusty metal courtyard doors and Holly sprung out to greet him.

Holly couldn't really remember much about the Russian's visits. Just that he always felt as light as a feather the next day and his skin looked better and he talked slower and he smiled more. And all these effects stayed the same two days after he had seen the Russian — even when the mad couple over the way threw all their piss-stained furniture into the middle of the courtyard; even when Holly got *merguez* grease on his jacket from a burly man who was gesticulating angrily with a *merguez* chip sandwich outside the rue Léon *boulangerie*, even when Madame Bourse smiled horribly and told him there would be more hours for him at Courbevoie after Christmas. All this, Holly took with a pinch of salt because of the Russian.

The only thing Holly remembered clearly about the Russian's previous visits to rue Léon (four in total, if you counted the first night when the Russian came in, smashed a dozen vodka-filled tumblers heartily against Holly's half dozen, and collapsed in a heap on the bed down by the cooker), was that they all involved the Russian drinking at least a bottle of neat spirits, taking his clothes off and performing a series of twists and vaults before grabbing Holly by the neck, pushing him on to the floor and thrusting into him as he roared wildly in Russian. Holly liked date four best when he had seen the Russian's photo album showing pictures of him in his heyday at the Bolshoi.

The Gang used to joke about the Russian but I knew that Holly thought about him all the time. I'd noticed that he was starting to leave bits out of his stories about him. One day he talked about how the Russian 'jumped on me like a bear he was grappling in the woods', then suddenly his voice faded out, like he was embarrassed to go on. It was the first time I'd seen Holly being shy about going into details. I wondered if it meant you loved someone if you censored bits in your stories. Soon afterwards I asked him what he thought about falling in love. He replied immediately: 'Love is 90 per cent about feeling intimidated and 10 per cent about feeling the best drunk you've ever felt when they finally smile at you for a few seconds or kiss you on the neck when you're not expecting it or look you in the eye when they shag you. That's the most exciting sort of love. That's the sort of love I'm interested in.'

Holly was grinning by the time he pushed his way off the train at the Gare du Nord. He walked briskly and arrived back at rue Léon by 9.05. He unlocked the rusty metal gates, walked across the courtyard which smelt of rotten vegetables and skipped up the wooden staircase until he arrived at his white chipboard front door. He dropped his bag in the kitchen and ran to the bathroom where he peeled his clothes off, showered, brushed his teeth, applied a dab of Chanel No 19 to his temples – no time to shave – and slipped into his top pulling-outfit of the moment: a pressed white shirt and a pair of faded 501s tight against the crotch, slightly threadbare on the thighs. The shirt was straight out of the packet from Tati and would be thrown out the next morning. Holly thought he owed it to himself to go the full Great Gatsby – given that the shirts were only 20 francs each and given that he was selling his soul out in Courbevoie for Madame Bourse. (Holly had to throw the shirts out anyway because it was traditional for the Russian to literally rip them off Holly's back every time they had sex.)

It was now 10.30 and Holly knew that the Russian would be due at any moment. He already had a couple of bottles of Côtes du Rhone chambréing on the brunch bar and he thought he'd start drinking to get into the right state of mind to greet the Russian. He filled up one of Alex's blue Moroccan goblets with red wine and took a swig. He looked with satisfaction at the spread he had laid out on the squat brass Barbès coffee table: pink napkins folded into water lilies (a trick Giselle had taught him one day), a filigree fan formation of pineapple rounds clustered together on a Barbès gold plate and an ice bucket stolen from Alex's work filled with ice and two bottles of chilled vodka.

The only lighting in the flat was the ochre glow given off by a dozen night light candles floating in an oval wooden bowl. Competing with the rotten vegetable odour from the courtyard was the glorious aroma given off by the intricate arrangement of white lilies that lined the whole of the brunch bar and which Holly had invested in instead of a decent Christmas present for his mother.

Everything was set. And just as Holly was starting to drum his fingers against the side of his 501s (it was 10.45) he realised with a sudden panic that he still hadn't sorted out the music concept. As soon as he heard banging on the rusty metal doors the plan was to switch Alex's Pet Shop Boys CD to 'West End Girls' so that when he rushed down to greet the Russian – with just the right mixture of charisma and confidence – the two of them would arrive back in the apartment when 'It's a Sin' was starting. The Russian always liked 'It's a Sin' with his vodka.

By 11.30 the Russian hadn't arrived and one of the bottles of chambréing wine stood empty. Holly was sitting cross-legged on the floor, lips stained red, prodding the candles in the bowl, wondering whether he should start on the mountain of washing up that lay under a white linen cloth in the sink.

By 12.00 the Russian still hadn't arrived. Holly had nearly finished the second bottle of chambréing wine and had cracked open a third one. He was still sitting cross-legged in front of the bowl of candles and had begun to tip some of them upside down.

By 1.00 Holly's white shirt was splattered with drips of purply red. He had started lighting matches and stubbing them out on the now desiccating slices of fresh pineapple.

By 2.00 the third bottle of Côtes du Rhone was finished and Holly was crawling round the flat looking for his address book. The thought crossed his mind that the Russian was seeing someone else. Holly has always maintained that feeling jealous is almost as sexy as getting chucked but now the thought was intolerable to him. The only number he had for the Russian was a hotel he was supposed to have checked into at 4 p.m. that evening. But when he called up he realised that he didn't know the Russian's second name and by that time he could only speak in slurred, staccato sentences so that every time he rang up, the receptionist slammed the phone down. That was when Holly started on the vodka.

⁂   ⁂   ⁂

When I returned to Paris from England on 28 December, I listened to the answering machine and heard the following messages:

— 'Hello, George. It's 9.30. Bloody hell, I think one of my pupils from Courbevoie was trying to get off with me. Ha! He'll be lucky! Anyway, just thought I'd leave evidence on your answering machine that I'm about to be flown up to pleasure mountain while you're probably sitting round your parents' dinner table pouring gravy and talking about the Batley fly-over. *Bisou, bisou.*'

— 'Hello, George. 10.30. I can't help but think that I'm looking fantastic. Bit of a white shirt, pair of jeans — nothing too Nelly. Just doing a bit of work on that bloody wedding dress to kill the time. Think I'll turn it into a Bolshoi tutu. Really nobble her.'

— 'Where the fuck is he! It's bloody 11.30 and he was supposed to be here at 9! My candles are going to be all burnt out by the time he gets here. Bloody bugger bollocks.'

— 'George. I can't believe it! He's been really bad this time!'

— 'Oh Georgina!' (sound of gargling) 'George in! Gin. Geor Gin! Guess what! 'M garling ... garling ... say, I'm gargling with Rush's spu ... wi'is spuk. Spuk! Know wh'a mee? Naa. Naa. Joke.' (sound of wine bottle and glasses tipping over) 'Bug, bugger. Bugger Russian.' (howling) 'I'm all alone! All alone on Christmas Eve! Three in the morning, ruddy morning. Mourning.' (chuckling) 'How dare he turn me into Ju, Ju ...

Juee Garland. Bloody Juee Garland . . .' (sound of burping; phone hangs up abruptly)

— 'Fuck 'oody rush . . . rush . . . rush. Show'm. Show'm. Go out . . . pull . . . got stas . . . stasdards, stasdards to keep up . . .'

It was obvious that Holly needed some cheering up. When we met at Le Swing he told me about the pathetic ending to his pathetic evening. After he had drunk the last bottle of Côtes du Rhone he crawled over to the Minitel and tuned into 3615 Beau Mec where the only man who would respond to his stark message of courtship ('Fuck me, someone'), was a man calling himself 'Moustache'. When Moustache hammered at the rusty metal gates on rue Léon, Holly opened them to find that he wasn't bad-looking at all.

'He had quite a kind face. Although it has to be said, I felt like I'd been drunk for a week by that point. When he said, "Are you coming to my place then?" I just went.'

'Where did he live?'

'He said it was a bit of a way out of Paris and he had quite a nice car — so I thought I'd really made it. Thought my ship had come in.'

Holly slumped down and sighed. 'In my dreams.'

He lit a cigarette. 'After about an hour in the car, we drive in through these big gates on to a gravelly drive. He says, "I'm a doctor. I live in an apartment of the hospital." So I think, "Oh well. At least he's a doctor." But then I woke up the next morning and I looked out of the window and saw this bloke in pyjamas walking round and round a tree. It was only a psychiatric hospital!'

As Holly talks I notice that lots of men in Le Swing — even the good-looking ones — keep glancing over at him. I have often observed that men find Holly attractive and sometimes I wonder why he isn't more happy about it. If Le Swing was full of women who kept looking at me like they thought I was attractive then I would never moan again.

'That man's really giving you the eye, Holly,' I said.

Without even looking at him, Holly snapped, 'He's ugly. They're all bloody ugly,' and started lighting matches and throwing them in the ashtray. I did feel sorry for him. Then he said he'd spent Christmas trying to sleep off his hangover and wandering round to haunts that he and the Russian used to go to.

'Holly! You mean you were actually considering talking to him again?'

'Of course I was. Am.'

He made an irritable 'puh!' and continued, 'Maybe his plane was delayed and he lost my number.'

'Holly!'

'He might have got the dates wrong. And he likes Le Swing.'

'Holly! Have we come here tonight in the hope of you bumping into the Russian?'

'Face it, George, I don't fall for pipe and slipper/Val Doonican/Argyle jumper types toasting crumpets by the fire. I wish people would stop setting the moral police on me every time I go for a social outcast. Alex might choose to fall in love with witty, charming boys who know how to make kitchen cabinets and *boeuf en daube*. Bully for him! It doesn't give him the right to sneer at my choice of boyfriends.'

'Ones that sniff cigarette packets?'

'He's Russian, for God's sake!' Holly tutted as he stood up to go to the bar. 'Sniffing cigarette packets is probably the equivalent of shaking hands over there.'

I wondered if Holly really had fallen in love with the Russian. I watched a bland-looking American boy at the bar slide a sly hand down Holly's arm as Holly ordered two *demis*. Holly turned to look at him dismissively, and then did a double-take when he realised he liked something about the boy's face. Or maybe his jacket. His lips melted into a smile and he leaned up against the bar as the boy said something to him and then took a 50-franc note from the back pocket of his jeans which he handed over the bar to pay for the two *demis*.

Then, something happened that only rarely happens in Le Swing. The doors burst open and two women in their early thirties entered the bar, holding hands and laughing. It was as if they didn't even care that the bar was full of jostling gayboys and only one other female apart from them – me. One of them had a blonde bob and the other had a dark, Delia Smith crop. As the blonde one pushed the dark one over to our table, I saw that they were both tottering drunk and yapping away in jolly hockey-sticks English. They were still hesitating about where to sit when Holly came back to the table, frowning, and muttering that two frumpy lesbians were about to get in the way of his conquest of the bland-looking American boy at the bar. 'You've really nobbled me now,' he said, folding his arms. 'They look like Brown Owls.'

In a huff, Holly stormed off to the toilet which was just next to our table. He was soon followed by the blonde woman. The dark-haired one ventured over to sit at the table next to us. She started smoking and pretended to look at the Kronenburg poster on the wall behind me. When I caught her sneaking me a look she stood up, took a big shiny blue wallet from the voluminous pocket of her jeans, looked me briefly, slyly, in the eyes and walked over to the bar.

I watched her from behind. She was wearing horrible ladies-cut jeans that were the wrong colour blue and made her look like a pear. The hems were exactly the right (i.e. wrong) length – so you could see a sliver of pristine white sock between the homely hems and the too-white training shoes whose style was way off the mark. She was wearing a stripy T-shirt which looked like it had been the nearest thing she had been able to find at lunch hour in Marks and Spencers to something she once saw a trendy gayboy wear in the street. When she came back to her table with two gin and tonics I saw that the texture of her forearms was what the French would call *mou* – sort of Rubenesque flabby, like putting your finger in a pink marshmallow and denting it in, then watching it slowly fill out again. Her shade of lipstick was orangy-red. In fact, there were hardly any red tinges in it at all and it put about five years on her and made her lips look thin and clenched. When she was sitting down again with the gin and tonics, she looked shiftily around the room to check if there was anyone cute there or to see if anyone had noticed her Saturday night outfit which she seemed to feel good about. When she had finished her visual tour of Le Swing her eyes returned to their original position on the Kronenburg poster. She looked slightly alarmed – as if the plot had changed and nobody had told her about it.

In the toilet, the blonde introduced herself to Holly with an apparently rapturous response because when the door opened later, a gust of ammonia flew out followed by the two of them staggering arm-in-arm. Swaying back into his seat, Holly smiled at me and said, 'George, this is Sukie.'

'Suzy,' she guffawed, smashing his arm with her handbag as if she had known him all her life.

'Sukie! Good time, Sukie!' He picked up his *demi* and chinked it against her glass of gin.

The dark-haired woman raised her eyebrows at me and smiled.

'God, Luce,' said the frenzied Suzy. 'You should see the bloody bog in there. Remember our school trip to Morocco, you know, when Fatty Forster stopped the bus at that terrible hotel so we could have an impromptu pit stop?'

'How could I forget it,' the dark one said in tones of crystal, flicking her cigarette into the ashtray with a shaking hand. She looked up at me more slyly than before and said, 'Hello. My name's Lucinda.'

I felt shy. 'I'm George,' I said. 'And this is Holly.'

Lucinda chatted about how she'd just started working in Paris as a lawyer and how her friend Suzy had come over for the weekend to help her settle in.

'But we've been trying to find some good bars,' said Suzy, 'you know, bars for women.'

Aside from Pins, I'd never met any women in Paris who were open about being gay. This was interesting.

'Don't worry about that,' Holly said. 'George and I can fill you in on that score, can't we, George, old hands that we are.'

'Yes,' Suzy carried on, 'not that I'm into all that now. Was though. I was, wasn't I, Luce? Lucinda and I had a whale of a time when we were at Roedean together. Hey, Luce?'

Lucinda looked me in the eye again with that look of complicity.

'Cigarette?' she asked, pulling one out of her pack with a still-shaking hand.

'No, I don't, thanks.'

'Lucky you.' She fixed me with her eyes which were now both vampy and sly.

'When I was twelve,' I said, trying to pull myself together, 'I got in with the cool girls in the class – don't know how – just for a couple of months. I'd never smoked before, only seen my father sit in his TV chair at night puffing away, holding his fag like a secondhand-car salesman – between thumb and forefinger. When they saw the way I held my cigarette they all started laughing. They were all holding theirs like Bette Davis with a cigarette holder. I never wanted to smoke again after that.'

Lucinda chuckled and her face seemed to relax. She insisted on buying Holly and me drinks for the rest of the night. In exchange, Holly regaled the two women with tales of cheap encounters he'd had in all the bars they'd spent the evening trying to get into.

I wasn't really listening. I couldn't get over the fact that I'd finally met my first live lesbian in Le Swing. By this time, Holly too had cheered up considerably at meeting such an attentive fag hag and her friend with the big wallet, all on one night. We kicked each other under the table when Lucinda invited us back to her flat for a nightcap.

If it had been cigarette packets for Holly with the Russian, then it was lemons for me with Lucinda. The black leather Doctor Love settee and the mat black electrical appliances were a start, but it really all started with the drinks cabinet. When Lucinda asked what we would like to drink, Holly said smoothly, 'I'll have a gin and tonic, please,' as if he was used to going to houses where he was offered a choice of more than beer or cheap vodka. I asked for the same and Lucinda brought in four thick tumblers filled with gin and tonic, ice and floating chunks of lemon.

It was strong and cold and tasted like going on holiday. The glasses were clean and expensive, the ice was fresh and the lemons – two fat waxy pieces for each person – seemed the height of sophistication. At Clignancourt, never in a month of Sundays would there ever be a fresh lemon hanging around the place on the off-chance that someone might pop in for a drink. Not that we even had any drink at home that you were supposed to put lemon into. We just had home-brewed Spanish *aguardiente* in a plastic bottle, a souvenir from one of our parties which even our slaggy guests refused to drink.

As we drank, Suzy told more tales of her and her friend's days together at Roedean. Lucinda smoked endlessly, holding her cigarettes in the Bette Davis manner. At one point, when she wanted the ashtray, she didn't say, 'Please pass the ashtray.' She cupped her hand under the tip of the cigarette and gestured abruptly with her head to the object at the end of the coffee table. 'Ashtray,' she barked with divine right in her voice and I jumped to it. Holly says that posh people are so confident they dispense completely with a need for the word 'please'.

The thrill of the first encounter with this new person with dark hair seemed to get greater as the night went on. By the time I hit the wall of drunkenness at about 3 a.m. and started thinking about water, I was still fuelled with enough bravado to announce to Lucinda that I was going to investigate her kitchen.

If Lucinda's sitting room looked like the penthouse suite of a residential hotel, then her kitchen was even better. On the main work surface, next to a wet knife and the remains of a lemon, stood a rice cooker, a fish steamer, a set of Le Creuset saucepans and a pine rack filled with assorted mustards: whole grain mustard, tarragon mustard, thyme mustard, mustard that looked like bottled ant eggs, green paste mustard with black bits in.

From a shelf behind a gleaming stainless steel oven, I picked up the glass – another one that was heavy and clean without a trace of a thumb print and with no gritty bits stuck to the bottom. When I'd filled it up with water, I decided to have a look in the fridge. Inside there was a row of five more lemons, a cooked chicken, a dainty china bowl filled with an assortment of olives, some packages wrapped in *Fauchon* paper, a large goat's cheese encased in straw, a half-eaten pink fish with garlic and herbs sticking to its skin and an unopened bottle of Champagne.

I closed the door and my heart started to beat very fast. Wait until Holly heard about this. Not only did we now know somebody who had a penthouse in the Marais, a shop-bought roasted chicken in the fridge, proper gin and tonic glasses and a black leather settee, but these two people – one of whom had a serious, respectable job – seemed to think that Holly and I, scum of the earth, were really interesting, that we were a lucky find.

After the water break, the gin and tonics didn't stop. By 4.30 a.m. I could barely see anything. Sitting in the penthouse living room felt like looking through a car windscreen in the pouring rain and my lips couldn't catch up with my brain any more. Lucinda seemed a slight figure who kept rushing out in front of the car. But I sat back calmly because it had now become clear what my market value was: Lucinda's life was characterised by closing deals, going to business dinners and talking in Roedean tones about her fruity past. But now her past had dried up — just as mine was beginning. As day began to seep in through the sky light, Lucinda learnt that I have a second-hand bicycle, that I shoplift books from an English bookshop on the rue de Rivoli, that I can pass as a native when I speak French, that, thanks to Holly and Alex, I know exactly where you need to go to get a second-hand pair of Levi 501s and that I live my life supping Krug at the Ritz one night and eating bowls of green lentils with rationed slices of bacon in my cold garret the next.

And all of my potted biography was topped off with my fantastic age of twenty-four. I knew that it would only be a matter of time before we went to bed with each other. I felt ten miles high.

By his fifth gin and tonic, Holly was on to the subject of the Russian. He sat there with an insane grin on his face and started talking about the Russian as if he had lived through the greatest love of his life.

'He used to call me Holy. "Holy", he used to say. "Holy, you are too fat. Come here that I fuck you and after, I will show you the pirouette I do for the Banquet of Elizabeth Taylor in 1969." He was so sweet. He used to tailor make his physical jerks to fit the kitchen.'

Holly grabbed the vase of red tulips standing on the coffee table and buried his face in them. 'Oh, Russian, Russian,' he said in his *Coronation Street* accent. 'Where are you when I need you? Where are you when I've got eight cut-price pineapples in the fridge waiting for you?'

Lucinda wasn't sure if Holly was being serious or not, so she said, 'Don't worry. I'll introduce you to my lawyer friend Seth. He had his forty-fifth birthday last week and he's just come out as gay.'

Holly made a big 'puh!' into his gin and tonic.

'He's been seeing this blind pianist in San Francisco for a while,' she said, 'but then he met this man in London in a bar the other week and he did poppers with him for the first time. Anyway, he's been getting quite experimental since then. And he's very loving.'

'Poppers for the first time at forty-five? Doesn't sound my sort. Besides, the last thing I need is another boyfriend who adores me.'

I saw Lucinda smile slightly before she offered Holly, Suzy and me another top up. But Holly swayed his way to his feet and said, 'Thank you, Lucinda, but I'm off to a very, very bad place to have some very, very bad people help me forget my worries. It was a pleasure to meet you.' Holly kissed Lucinda and Suzy goodbye and then stood waiting for me to get up.

My favourite thing about going-home time in Paris is that physical face contact is obligatory. The *bise*, or the kiss goodbye, works like a barometer in ascertaining what friends and strangers think of you. First, there is the anticipation of knowing that you are going to brush cheeks: you wonder if they will be downy or cold or warm; whether you will feel sparks as you angle your kiss so that you do not just kiss air but brush the corner of a warm lip. When that happens, the Gang calls it a *bise* that is more than a *bise*. Ann is now over her chocolate kissing stage and she is quite fond of doing *bises* that are more than *bises*. She says they are good because you go home feeling pure and semi-sated at the same time. As you lie in your bed you wonder about what might be, what might follow. It was through a *bise* that was more than a *bise* that led Ann to go out with her new boyfriend Jean-Christophe, the pizza delivery man.

As I clawed my way up from her leather settee, I could see Lucinda's head bobbing unsurely from side to side as she decided which cheek to go for first. She finally opted for my left cheek, just as I was coming in on her right. I was expecting this and withdrew to avoid a nose collision. 'Right left, right left,' I said, so drunk I now felt sober. 'The French are formal about these things: go to the right first then to the left. You're like some lager lout.'

She looked me lustily in the eye. She moved towards me again. Her right cheek brushed my right, lingered warmly, then the left brushed my left. It stayed there for a second and then she put her hands on my shoulders as if to steady herself. 'That's the good thing about being in France,' she dribbled in my ear in squashed Roedean tones. 'You always get to do a bit of posh snogging at the end of the night.'

A current of pins and needles rushed through me. She was even starting to speak like me.

When Holly and I hit the Marais streets at 5 a.m., I was jumping up and down like I'd just struck oil.

CHAPTER TEN

The Yellow Brick Road

The Marais is another world from Barbès. In the Marais there are romantic restaurants and pink buildings and jolly cake shops with poppy-seed buns and cumin bread stacked up in the window like toys. Some guide books talk about the Marais as the Jewish quarter of Paris but this is not the first thing you notice when you come here. What you see in the Jewish streets around the corner from Le Swing are pale-faced men wearing ringlets and black hats mingling with orange-faced gayboys who strut along as if they were on a catwalk. Holly says that just walking along the street in the Marais you can get laid at least fifteen times. 'It's quite frightening,' he says. 'I think I might come here to retire.'

The main arteries of the Marais – the rue des Archives (Lucinda's Street), the rue Vieille du Temple and the rue du Temple – are home to the beautiful gayboys with excellent posture who come here at night for dates in the underworld. By day, you can hear them pronouncing *oui, oui* as '*ouais, ouais*', in that worldly wise, seen-it-all, done-it-all manner as they lean against café tables talking to pumped-up waiters who eye up the husbands in good leather shoes popping into the BHV *bricolage* annex for panes of glass and strips of wood to run up at the weekend. The skinny streets that run between these arteries are dotted with boys not yet in cruising mode. They sneak glances in the windows of tea rooms and home-furnishing boutiques and tiny transvestite clubs advertised with sun-faded photos in their fly-specked doorways showing merry regulars with chubby faces and bad outfits.

The sexual energy that glugs through these streets is more streamlined and predictable than it is on the boulevard Barbès and this makes it the perfect place to wander when you have time on your hands. For nearly two weeks now I have been meeting up in the Marais with Lucinda. I always arrive a little too early so I have time to take in the sights and adapt to the Clignancourt/Marais culture shock. Unlike Barbès, the Marais is all about keeping up appearances. This hits you as soon as you emerge from the sticky métro at Hôtel de Ville and are struck by the over-egged cake of the Town Hall, glittering with grandeur and 136 shrunken statues of famous male citizens chiselled on to its façade. Way above the big-boned stone women on plinths who play harps on the Hôtel de Ville's spacious square, there is a cluster of poofy, green metal knights twinkling to attention on the roof, looking breezily towards the Seine. I watch them waving their flags before taking a deep breath, turning towards the pollution of the snarling rue de Rivoli and crossing over on to the Marais's very own yellow brick road – the rue Vieille du Temple.

The rue Vieille du Temple is lined with rickety *hôtel particuliers* with big, burping gargoyles carved into pistachio-coloured doors, and waxy green roof gardens that you only notice when you raise your head to see where the birdsong is coming from. Crammed between these rickety old buildings are small bars and restaurants and in a frantic strip of the street not far from the rue de Rivoli you can see Le Swing where I have a date with Lucinda this evening. I am too early, so I pass by and continue on up the rue Vieille du Temple towards the tranquil stretch that leads to Place de la République. When I reach the rue de Bretagne I turn off left into a maze of even smaller back streets where it feels like you've been whisked out of Paris and into a pretty ghost town with hardly a soul. I do a few circuits up and down these streets trying not to think about Lucinda. It is not until I am half-way down the rue Vieille du Temple again that I notice I have bitten several of my nails to the quick.

I have the distinct feeling that something is going to happen tonight. It seems to me that two weeks is a very long time to hold myself back and I don't think I am capable of holding myself back any more.

The signs are good. Lucinda called me up (*she* called *me* up!), five days after our first encounter and invited me to dinner. She suggested meeting at her apartment although when I arrived it felt a bit embarrassing being there sober. We left quickly and I took her to the Petit Gavroche, a cheap, rowdy restaurant just off the rue Vieille du Temple. I go here with Holly sometimes and we joke about how the Roquefort sauce looks like spunk. The Petit Gavroche is an acquired taste and I don't think it was the ambience Lucinda was quite expecting. So I quickly ordered some wine. I don't know much about wine, but I do know that Gamay is the red sort that you keep in the fridge and it is so light that you can drink it like water. Whenever I forget what it's called I just think of gamee leg and I remember it. I look at Lucinda and see a leg with pus coming out of it and then I say, 'Gamay, shall we get?' with a knowledgeable lilt to my voice. I am pleased that Lucinda has obviously never ever heard of Gamay because she hesitates slightly and says, 'Yes. Yes, I should think so.'

When we had drunk a couple of tumblers each I told her the spunk joke and she laughed and the restaurant suddenly became the funniest thing in the world – the man in a tie next to us ripping away at his *pavé* was hilarious, the old *clochard* at the *zinc* drinking a Ricard was hysterical, the waiter's leery smile as he brought us plates of ill-washed lettuce made us look into each other's eyes and forget for a few seconds that anyone else was there.

There were awkward parts too. During dinner, Lucinda told me select facts about her past three years spent working in New York. She seemed at pains to stress that she had a girlfriend there but at the same time she was definitely flirting with me. She was really interested in my Minitel stories and wanted me to tell her all about Sponge and Sponge's body and if I was scared by having sex with a woman for the first time.

When I saw that she warmed to this, I started to tell her choice one-liners from my time with Californian TV person Dawn and leather business Pins. She downed around half a dozen *demis* during the meal and a couple of Cognacs afterwards and spent the rest of the evening taking shaky drags of cigarette and saying things like, 'you have great eyebrows', before ripping photos of her girlfriend in New York out of her Filofax and shoving them over to my side of the table.

The girlfriend business doesn't really bother me. I just see an experienced lesbian who can teach me a trick or two and who will almost definitely chuck her New York love interest when she realises what sort of prowess I have.

When the bill came for the meal, Lucinda snatched it up immediately, put a pile of notes on the table and said she had to get back to her apartment to do some reading for work. I had put on my good underwear and felt a bit disappointed. When we were outside, she hovered in front of me nervously, saying she'd call me soon. And then she didn't say goodbye with the *bise*. She kissed me hard and quick on the lips and handed me a card. The card said 'Lucinda Davenport. Shipping solicitor, Slaughterhouse and April.' She nearly toppled off the curb as she turned to go. She mumbled, 'Shit. Rather uncool. Call me.'

Calling Lucinda is really sexy. On the phone, she is as white hot as the elusive, smartly dressed TV executive I have been fantasising about for two years. When I called her the next day, I could hear the rumble of corporate power in the background. She answered the phone herself with a brusque, 'Lucinda Davenport'. Her voice sounded much further up the posh scale than it did when we'd met in the Petit Gavroche. When I asked her what she was doing she whispered that she was 'closing a deal'. As I sat hugging myself on the windy floor of the Clignancourt entrance hall, playing idly with the thistledown-light ball of fluff and dust and knotted pubes and hair strands which had just blown out from the bathroom, the idea of 'closing a deal' felt really rousing.

After two weeks of speaking to Lucinda on the phone, I have got to know the vocabulary even better. Sometimes I imagine Lucinda striding round her office at Slaughterhouse and April in her Barbara Bui suit, crossing legs on leather sofas and snapping at men at the other end of long, polished tables about closing deals, exchanging contracts and negotiating revolving credit facilities.

Today will be my fourth meeting with Lucinda and I have asked Holly to meet up with us too – to speed things along a little. Holly is always up for free drinks and I am hoping that under their influence he will nobly step in with a distracting back-room anecdote whenever Lucinda is on the point of bringing out her Filofax and showing me more photos of Zelda in New York. I was due to meet Lucinda at eight and now it is 8.20. I can put it off no longer. I hope that Holly will be there already so that he will have Lucinda nicely relaxed and slightly drunk.

When I walk into Le Swing, Holly is making a point of ignoring a smiley boy in a blue blazer who is trying to start a conversation with him. I see that it is Colin, code name The Vicar. The Vicar is a thirty-year-old English accountant doing a six-month *stage* in Paris. He has latched himself on to Holly ever since Holly gave him some encouragement one night when he dragged him off to a group orgy in the Tuileries Gardens at three in the morning in fullest scrape-the-bottom-of-the-barrel mode. When I get nearer Lucinda I can't get her attention because Holly has hogged her to fill her in some more about the Vicar. 'He's a big cliché,' he's telling her as I mentally curse him. 'He's a ridiculous expat who thinks Paris is like what happened in his French text book when he was at school.'

'Sounds rather nice,' Lucinda says, brushing my arm.

'Nice!' Holly squawks. 'He's a complete disgrace. You should have seen him the night we were in the Tuileries. There I was, being nicely seen to by some sordid fashion type. Suddenly, the Vicar comes over and starts pulling at my T-shirt, gibbering on about how he's just spotted some accountant from a company he's always wanted to work at. He says, "I think I'll go and say hello to him," and so he goes up to this poor bloke whose jeans are half-way down his ankles and who's on the verge of shooting his load. He takes his hand, shakes it briskly and says, "Hello, delighted to meet you. I think you know my father." Can you imagine! What a disgrace! And the bloke just stares at him like he's a lunatic.'

Lucinda chuckles and says, 'He sounds sweet.'

'Sweet maybe, but hardly sexy. His catchphrase is: "He's a lovely boy. A lovely, lovely boy!"' Holly raises his eyes in disdain. 'Another time, we were standing in this leather bar, watching a muscle queen in a gas mask being todged to high heaven. In between the sound of the screams you could hear the Vicar – all misty eyed – murmuring, "What a lovely boy. What a lovely, lovely boy!"'

'I think you should go out with him,' I said, bored now of Holly hogging the conversation and wondering how I was ever going to make a move on Lucinda.

'Really, George! *Suggest* I can go out with someone whose fantasy is eating a croissant as the sun goes down over the Seine while simultaneously being shagged by some leather psycho and going, "What a lovely, lovely view!"'

'Having sex by the Seine sounds all right,' I murmur, suddenly remembering my theory. My theory is that talking about sex is an effective way of flirting. Talking about your past exploits is good because it makes you seem adventurous, nonchalant, experienced, attractive to lots of people – and therefore desirable. As you are telling your love interest stories of what you did and how you did it, they will be picturing you in their mind's eye, imagining what your naked body looks like, how you take your clothes off – how you might take their clothes off. Once you have started the ball rolling they will start to observe you even closer. They will wonder if the way you hold your beer glass might be a sign of how you might hold their body; what your fingers might get up to; if you will want to see them the next day. And when, lubricated with drink and anticipation, they retire to the bar toilet, they hug themselves in the cubicle with excitement and they hope you will be daring enough to come in after them, crush them against the partition wall and prove that your technique is even better than what you have been bragging about all evening. And even if you're not daring enough to go in after them (Lucinda would probably not feel very sexy in the toilet in Le Swing; as Turkish loos go it is one of the least savoury I have yet seen in Paris), the few minutes of solitude will have given them the time to mentally picture you doing it to them and when they come out they will be even more desperate for you than they were before they went in.

The only proviso with my theory is that there has to be mutual attraction there in the first place for it all to go like clockwork. Mutual attraction is the tantalising thing that you can never be totally sure about. I am just wondering if I have enough proof that Lucinda is interested in me when I feel a warm tingling on my forearm. Lucinda suddenly seems to be standing very close to me and she is starting to brush my arm in a way that is definitely good enough proof. I think that another short conversation on the subject of the Minitel should be enough to tip this evening into the memorable category.

Holly passes a couple of new *demis* over to Lucinda and me. 'I'm just bitter and twisted I suppose,' he sighs. 'I wish I could meet the people from my school French text book. Monsieur Berthillon the *douanier* from Orly airport. Now there was a fine piece of trade ...'

I realise that Holly must have been in Le Swing for a while because he is starting to sway and get a far-away look in his eyes. This means either he is going to start getting spiteful or he is going to get over-emotional and start reminiscing about the Russian. Luckily, I spot a man sitting at the table behind the pillar who is giving Holly the eye in a very obvious manner. I suggest going to sit down and the man – code name Mick Jagger's Grandad – moves over almost immediately and asks if Holly has ever modelled in a fashion show. When Holly gets going on his Yves Saint Laurent speech, Lucinda turns to me. She suggests going to have an aperitif at her place before we go to dinner which I think sounds pleasantly fishy. We have already drunk quite enough by now.

So we leave Holly to Mick Jagger's Grandad and start a silent walk back to the rue des Archives. When we are standing in front of her door she looks at me and says, 'So, aperitif then?' as if she is saying, 'Shall we start now then?', as if the starting gates are finally about to open and I can at last put all my theory behind me and get to the practice.

But when we are going up in the lift, a centrifugal force of lust seems to freeze us to the walls, stiffening our limbs and paralysing our derring-do. By the time we get into her flat she is back in Roedean mode. She giggles and says she wants to play on the Minitel. I sit on the stool she pulls up for me and she sits in a chair next to me. I can feel that her knee is near mine and in a way I wish we could just kiss and get all this tantalising stuff over with, but I also want to feel like this for ever. I flex my fingers over the keyboard and cue up a favourite service of mine. The opening line reads, '*Salut, je m'appelle Lolita. Qu'est ce que t'as envie de faire ce soir?*' which means 'Hello, my name is Lolita. What do you fancy doing this evening?'

After a few minutes someone called 'Sabine Sexy' writes back: 'I don't know, what do you propose?'

'Typical,' I brag to Lucinda, feeling in charge now that I am in familiar territory in front of a Minitel keyboard. 'They're always really coy and this is probably a man anyway. Still, we've started now.' And I type in, *'Je veux te défoncer très fort.'*

Lucinda's knee brushes mine.

'What does that mean?' she asks, her voice cracking.

I look straight into her soft brown eyes. I start slowly and speak firmly.

'Défoncer? Défoncer's not just little old "I want to fuck you." Oh no. It's more than that. It's more like, "I'm going to take you to the sexy torture chamber where Madame de Pompadour and Madame de Montespan – naked but for mink stoles, high heels and red lips – await with leather belts and quantities of baby oil and a very long phallus that they will ram in and out of you until your clit gulps with pleasure and you start to scream for mercy."'

For a Sloane Ranger raised on cold showers and team spirit by a brisk mother – code name The Wing Commander – the explanation is a red rag to a bull. I feel a meaty pair of hands on my arm and in seconds I am sitting on Lucinda's lap. Our lips have begun to trip the light fantastic by the time the legs of the canvas chair give way and we both collapse in Kiss me Quick postcard formation on the beige carpet.

If I found myself in this situation normally, I would take my clothes off and do it there and then on the carpet. But Lucinda says, 'Come on, upstairs,' in gym mistressy tones which I can't say are so unpleasant. I do find it slightly strange however when we finally find ourselves in Lucinda's mezzanine bed and then she announces that she has to go down to the bathroom because she hasn't cleaned her teeth. 'Sorry about this,' she says. 'Zelda always makes me clean my teeth.'

I wonder what she thinks about me staying in the bed and not cleaning my teeth but she can't think that badly about it because when she wobbles her way back up the mezzanine stairs she jumps on the bed, tears my T-shirt off and starts pawing at my breasts. When she takes her top off I see that she has a torso a bit like a female rugby player but I like it because she is strong and taking charge and she pushes me down on my front and lies on my back and grinds herself against my white jeans like she is a gay boy shagging a brickie. And then I can bear it no longer so I turn over and push her back on the bed and lie on top of her and am about to pull her Barbara Bui skirt off but as I hold it scrunched in my hands I realise that it feels fantastic – crisp and soft at the same time. When I put my hand underneath, the silk lining is cool as water and then I feel her plump bottom for the first time and she moans loudly – and there are so many sensations that I think I might come right here and now in my brickie trousers.

And then she takes charge again. She undoes my belt and yanks it out of the loops so I think she might be about to whip me or something breathtaking like that. But even better, she just rubs it back and forth over my crotch and when I am desperate for her to touch me she passes the belt over my naked breasts and my nipples go hard in an instant – which is quite unusual for me. She pulls my jeans off – expertly – and I wait for her to gasp when she sees I am wearing nothing underneath. She makes a growling sound instead, pulls up her skirt and presses the crotch of her office black tights down on my naked bits. Office black tights are one of the major pivots in my sex-in-a-corporate-location fantasy and as I feel the feverish skin of her pear-shaped bottom against the palm of my hands and the sea-cool silk of her Barbara Bui lining against the back of my hands and the warm friction of itchy black nylon against my wet cunt, I suddenly realise that I am going to come and even though I want it to last longer I can't help myself. I know there must be a look of surprise on my face because as I look at Lucinda's damp forehead I can just see her mouth going, 'It's okay, it's okay. Come on, darling. Come.'

Then everything goes blurred and head over heels and I'm not even embarrassed when I make a large, long wailing sound and when I can see again I can just see her soft brown eyes looking down at me. And I look at them for a while like I don't know where I am any more and then she starts to stroke my hair and I snap back into the present and realise that I should be going to work on her. I think that maybe the hair stroking is just a way of telling me to hurry up and get on with it. But when I try to jerk up and put my hand under her skirt again, she just takes hold of my hand and smiles and says, 'No. It's okay.' And I think how special Lucinda must be because I have never met anyone yet who didn't want to have an orgasm when they have just given one to you. She kisses me on the lips, says, 'You're sweet,' and starts to take her Barbara Bui skirt off.

I wonder what she means by 'sweet' as she gets under the covers and I get in after her. She lies on her left side and pulls me into the hollow of her back. When my knees touch the backs of her legs and my front touches her smooth back and her warm, pear-shaped bottom, she makes a tiny little whine of pleasure like a child. I think I had better say something before we go to sleep. I whisper, 'That was amazing,' and Lucinda laughs gently and murmurs, 'That's only 10 per cent of what I can do to you.' My ears prick up. What an exciting thing to say. The kind of thing I normally say. We clasp hands and fall asleep.

CHAPTER ELEVEN

Tree Climbing

The next morning, everyone on the rue de Clignancourt is beautiful. Even the particularly annoying Algerian man at the Sandwich Grecque stand has something going for him this morning. When he makes his usual snaky hissing sound as my bicycle and I glide past him towards number 27, I reflect that he is at least a man who knows the meaning of the word 'tenacity'. At the entrance door I get off my bike and give ten francs to a one-legged man in turban who is slumped against a gigantic Minitel poster showing a woman balancing a telephone under her ear with a nail-varnished finger and a naked leg. 'Dare the network', the slogan reads. 'Call 36 69 99 99 and listen to women unveiling their most intimate fantasies without taboo.'

After last night, I feel utterly without taboo. In fact, my body feels pleasantly unfamiliar to me this morning. It is not just down to the red bite mark on the left side of my neck. I feel all sort of thrusting and molten. Maybe the truth of the matter is that my body feels familiar to me for the first time ever.

By the time I reach the top of the stairs I feel a wave of hangover nausea. I unlock the door and decide to call Holly. The first thing he says is, 'What sort of body has she got?' I reply, 'It's interesting.' Holly says he doesn't know if he likes the sound of 'interesting'. I realise that I don't want to go into nitty gritty detail about what we did in bed, so I tell him about the deluxe orange squeezer that I discovered this morning in Lucinda's kitchen. 'It's this juicer thing that you put oranges on and you get fresh juice. It's a bit hard to work but it's really good.'

Holly snorts down the phone. 'Well, when you discover where her helipad and swimming pool are kept, don't forget about your old mate and mucker wanking off in a stable and eating straw.'

When I've put the phone down, I get under my sheets. I am too excited even to have room for an apple doughnut or coffee. I look at the clusters of dusty grapes that border the ceiling and I see Lucinda's face. And when I fall asleep I dream of orange towelling and ripped canvas.

When I wake, I see Lucinda's face on the dusty grapes again and then I see a picture that she has in her apartment. Next to a black and white photograph of a man in military uniform with a stiff moustache there is a photo of Lucinda as a child on a beach. This morning, when I climbed down from the mezzanine bed, the photo caught my eye. Lucinda, the child, is turning to look at the lens with a mixture of sadness and defiance in her eyes. When Lucinda, the woman in the Barbara Bui suit, came and sat next to me on the floor, she told me that the photo was taken when she was seven or eight. She said she remembers being on a beach with her father and wanting to walk down to the sea on her own so that she could impress him. But the beach was covered with shingle and stones and she had to walk very slowly so her feet didn't hurt too much. In the end, her father picked her up and put her on his shoulders and walked to the sea with Lucinda howling to be put down. If you look closely at the photo you can see that her eyes are slightly damp from the fury of it all.

As Lucinda sat talking next to me, her eyes shone and she sounded like a tree-climbing eight-year-old. I suddenly wished that she could have been my best friend to go climbing trees with and sit in the bus with and stay the night with, even though Ruth Worthing was okay for a while and in the beginning when I went to stay with her we got to climb down to breakfast via the outside drainpipe as opposed to the stairs. I was in my prime at eight. For a start my mother finally allowed me to cut my hair short. She allowed David – Falmouth's only Vidal Sassoon follower and one of Cornwall's few hairdressers of the 1970s to take annual holidays in LA – to cut my plaits off because it was too painful come hairwash day. When David had finished cutting I looked like a boy and I couldn't stop smiling, even though my mother wasn't too pleased when we left the salon and went to the greengrocer's next door and the man patted me on the head and said, 'Now then, sonny, what would your mother like?'

Eight was the best. It was the time when my class dubbed me 'gorilla' – because of my new, short, curly haircut – and every morning I would arrive in the classroom, put my satchel down, shout 'The gorilla's here,' and chase the squealing girls around the room and give them fireman's lifts. Eight was a good year also because my breasts had not yet started to sprout. By age ten, it was all over. I no longer looked totally convincing as a boy even in swimming trunks and could only pass in the men's changing rooms at the swimming pool if I walked around with my arms stretched in the air so that my budding breasts were flattened into near disappearance.

Lucinda and I would have been great together, aged eight. She would have been braver than Ruth Worthing. She wouldn't have flinched from my orange towelling pyjamas like Ruth did the night I stayed in her bedroom on the fold-up camp bed, the night I managed to have my longest peek yet at life beyond the sleeping bag, at the world behind the curtains.

I wanted to impress Ruth – she might be a Catholic and have straight hair but my pyjamas felt clean as a cotton lawn to the touch and it was obvious they were better than her itchy nylon nightie that you couldn't move your legs very far apart in. And she was impressed, at first. At first she told me to climb up into her bed so she could see them better. She asked if she could try them on and I let her and her tummy didn't go out like mine did and her skin was light brown and soft as bird's feathers. She must have seen what my skin looked like too because I refused to put her itchy nylon nightie on as a swap.

When she'd felt the orange towelling pyjamas against her skin for a while and tried out some Hong Kong Phooey moves in them, she took them off and told me to pretend that I was the man and she was the woman. And it felt funny and silly and we giggled and squirmed and we were all white from the moon because she'd turned the lights out. And then it wasn't funny any more. It was just serious and nobody had told us about this bit in the man and the woman game, and her eyes looked dreamy and a bit frightened and the feeling between my legs felt big, even bigger than the feeling I had in my mouth when I ate Crêpe Suzette in a French restaurant for my birthday.

I suspected that probably, if Ruth's mother came in at that moment, there would have been something about what we were doing that she wouldn't have liked and it would all have been my fault because I wasn't a Catholic. But even though Ruth's mother didn't come in, Ruth suddenly said that we had to stop. She said I had to put on my orange towelling pyjamas again and get back in my own bed. I didn't want to leave Ruth's bed because it smelled like a rubber dingy at sea on a hot day. But I did climb down and when I was kneeling on the camp bed wriggling back into my pyjamas, my knee went through the canvas and there was a big ripping sound. Ruth's black and white shape looked down from her big, tall bed and said it didn't matter – that she'd hide it from her mother and she'd never know. And we didn't tell each other so many secrets after that and gradually she started sitting next to other people on the bus and I knew that we must have done something pretty bad.

Lucinda picked up her eight-year-old self and put it back on the bookcase. Then she turned to me with wide eyes, shrugging her shoulders like a parody of a child who thinks it must have done something pretty bad.

'S'pose I'd better be going,' she said. 'Got some stupid deal to close this afternoon.'

When she got up and went towards the kitchen I thought I was going to evaporate into the air with infatuation. But when she got there, the intimacy snapped and she reverted to a sarcastic Sloane from Roedean. She called from the kitchen, 'Christ! You've left a bit of a mess in here. Didn't anyone ever tell you how to squeeze an orange properly?'

One night, after we had been sleeping together for a couple of weeks, Lucinda said, 'Why don't we have dinner at your house one evening?' I had been hoping that she wouldn't ask this. I knew that one of my attractions for her was that I was wacky and bohemian but I wasn't happy about her finding out how bohemian Clignancourt really was. Still, there didn't seem to be any way out of it, so I said that she could come round the following night. We kissed and I made a mental note to swipe the new blue milk jug that had been in Madame Bourse's fridge for the past four weeks.

I went sick from Madame Bourse's in the early afternoon (with the milk jug safely in my rucksack) and came home to begin the tidying up process to prove to Lucinda that I was serious and sensible and a worthy girlfriend replacement for Zelda. I brushed and dustpanned the entrance hall and then went out to buy some pork chops, some apples and potatoes, some cider and a packet of Omo washing powder from the juvenile delinquent supermarket. It was hard to decide which T-shirt to sacrifice to scrub the kitchen floor with, but in the end I decided on a grey one with a *harissa* stain on the front in a place that couldn't be hidden, even with a jacket. I dipped the T-shirt in a plastic bowl filled with Omo, got down on my hands and knees and scrubbed. I was going for candles as a lighting concept so there was no need to clean the oven.

I gave the bathroom floor a quick once over and felt quite

pleased, although I did think it was a shame that Bet had chosen that day to do her monthly black tights wash. About ten pairs were hanging from the line above the bath, dribbling grey drips and blocking out most of the light from the window. There was no way I could ask Bet to stash them away until later because she had already come home at lunch time and slammed her half baguette down on the kitchen table, leaving heel prints on the wet floor as she went. Before she flung her bedroom door shut she announced, 'Well, at least Madame bloody Bourse won't be doing my head in for a while,' and I knew that Bet and our French employer had parted company again.

Lucinda arrived at the door of 27 rue de Clignancourt brandishing a bottle of Veuve Clicquot with one hand and smoothing down her Barbara Bui work clothes with the other. She was still in Slaughterhouse and April work mode.

'God! It's a bit hairy round here, isn't it!' she said, as if she'd just made it up the Amazon.

I led her into the apartment which I still felt a bit uneasy about – despite the fact that my back was aching from the effort of sprucing it up. In the kitchen she met Ann who was preparing homemade hummus for her evening meal (with the lights blaring full on, and the oven looking dirtier than ever). They both said hello to each other and Lucinda, with a shaking hand, started to pull the foil off the Champagne cork. 'The man in that rather rowdy supermarket next to you seemed to think it very odd when I asked him if he had a bottle of the stuff that was cold,' she said in her best Slaughterhouse and April tones. I looked over at Ann. I'd already warned her that Lucinda was a big Sloane – even though when we met with Holly she always tried to tone her background down to fit Gang guidelines. (To give her credit, she really has thrown herself into learning the ways of 'todge', 'vage', 'licky', 'get it going', 'do it', boosies' and 'bits'.)

But I can see that Ann hasn't been offended by her. Ann and I are getting on very well these days. In the mornings, when I cycle back to the rue de Clignancourt from the rue des

Archives I usually arrive home just as Ann is coming back from seeing her new boyfriend: Jean-Christophe, the pizza delivery man. Jean-Christophe is the first steady boyfriend Ann has had while she's been in Paris and they have been seeing each other for five weeks. We sit in the kitchen drinking coffee and we talk about love.

Jean-Christophe's main plus point is that since he is French he has friends and family in the south of France where there is sun. The down side is that since he has a serious job (although when Ann first told us he was a pizza delivery man we all thought it was pretty funny) he thinks that being a juggler is too risky for Ann. He has offered to pay for typing lessons so that she can be a secretary. Another down side is that he is still in contact with all his ex-girlfriends and he expects Ann to make dinner for him most nights. His catch phrase is, *'Mais, il n'y a pas d'entrée?'* which means, 'But where's the starter?' because a meal without a starter – a humble *salade aux tomates* or a *crottin de chavignol* – is inconceivable for a French person. Ann says she puts up with all this (and even makes him meat dishes sometimes) because the sex is exciting.

Sometimes I can hardly wait for Ann to finish her sentence about Jean-Christophe because I want it to be my turn. I want to talk to Ann about Lucinda – tell her about her child's eyes and her tree-climbing voice and her cellulite which wobbles endearingly as she climbs down from the mezzanine bed in the mornings. I usually do get time to get all this in during our morning conversations. This morning I learnt that Jean-Christophe likes Ann to wear a leather corset when he is doing it to her and Ann learnt about Lucinda's posh orgasms ('Oh bloody hell, oh Christ Almighty, God, God, for God's sake').

Lucinda continued to fiddle with the Champagne cork and my body suddenly froze as I realised that we had no glasses – let alone any Champagne flutes. All we had were four tiny Algerian tea glasses that cost 15 francs for half a dozen. They are nice to look at but risky to drink from ever since I used a couple of them as turps pots when we were repainting the kitchen its current custard-yellow. Bet and Ann haven't noticed anything odd yet even though no matter how hard you wash them, the turps never seems to disappear entirely. The only way you know which are the turps glasses is that you get a shiny film of mercury-like bits on top of whatever it is you are drinking. I was going to suggest using some plastic cups that were left over from a party, when the phone rang. The phone was in Bet's room and I heard her pick it up and talk briefly. When she came out of her room she looked quite bemused. Lost for words almost. I had rarely seen her like this. To Lucinda she said, 'Oh, hello. You must be Lucinda,' and then she jerked her head at me. I presumed this meant that I was to follow her to her room. When I was in her room with the door closed, Bet held her hand still over the receiver and muttered, 'Sorry, George. But he said he had some work for you.'

I had never seen Bet so apologetic but when I picked up the receiver I realised why she was feeling the need to grovel. It was a raspy, American voice.

'Hey, who's that kinky woman I was just speaking to? She sounds kind of strict. You might want to bring her round to my place later tonight.'

It was Chester. The man with the green anus. I looked at Bet in exasperation but she was now listening in on the phone's spy piece, avoiding eye contact. I couldn't see Bet's eyes, just her red mouth, which kept wobbling up and down as if she was about to burst out laughing. There was nothing for it now. I had to talk to him.

'So, Chester,' I said briskly, 'my flatmate tells me you have some work for me.'

'Yeah, think it might be right up your street. You're like me. You like all that kinky stuff. I was doing some business with these guys in Monaco the other weekend. You know, just the soft end of the market. They're good payers – if you're looking at what other companies offer for this kind of stuff.'

I looked over at Bet who was now pointing at me with wide eyes and mouthing the words 'porn star'.

It had crossed my mind too that this was what Chester was talking about. I was shocked to find that I was quite interested in his proposal.

'Chester. Can you try to be a bit clearer. What sort of work are you talking about?'

'Voice. I need to hear your voice. See if you're fluent.'

'What do you mean, see if I'm fluent?'

And then something really bad happened. Lucinda wandered into Bet's room as part of a guided tour of the apartment that Ann was giving her. She was drinking Champagne from one of the Algerian glasses and she handed me and Bet two other glasses, neither of which had silver bits floating on the top – which meant it was highly probable that Lucinda was drinking from one which did. My stomach started to feel really queasy. What would Lucinda think if she knew I was on the phone to a man with a green anus trying to get me sex work in Monaco? I knew that I should save my pride and just slam the phone down on Chester. But a part of me couldn't help wondering how high the money was, and an even smaller part of me wondered what kind of stories I might be able to tell afterwards.

'You still there?' the raspy voice panted.

'Yes, I'm still here,' I said slowly as, horrified, I watched Lucinda perch on Bet's wooden stool, the one she'd found in the street, as if she was settling in for the night.

'So look, sweetheart,' the voice gasped. 'Just tell me. Tell me what you got up to this afternoon.'

I decided that the best way to deal with the situation was to carry on talking as if there was someone completely normal at the end of the line.

'Well, I went to the supermarket and did some shopping.'

'Yeah? Like it. Shopping. What did you buy?'

'I don't know. Some potatoes. Some apples. And two pork chops.'

'Apples and potatoes and two pork chops, huh?' Chester breathed hard.

'Yes, and then I had to leave the checkout queue and go back and get a bottle of cider.'

'So you did, huh? Naughty little girl forgot her cider, huh?' Chester's voice was starting to sound over-excited.

'And then when I'd got everything I went into the street,' I went on in a monotone. I couldn't imagine why Chester was so interested in this conversation. 'There were these two poodles having a fight.'

'Real rough and tumble stuff, huh?' Chester seemed suspiciously excited by this point. I could hear him repeat 'rough' under his breath several spirited times before he said, 'And then what did you do?' as if he was about to expire. Bet looked at me like something really strange was going on and I looked at Lucinda – who alternated between smiling at me and looking puzzled into her glass.

'Look, Chester,' I said, 'I really have to go now.'

'And then what did you do?' he panted.

'Look!' I'd really had enough by now. 'Then I took my apples and potatoes and cider and pork chops and I pressed the *code d'entrée* and I walked up seven flights of stairs!'

Chester groaned, 'Yeah, yeah, yeah,' until suddenly he made a deep, long groan. Bet scrunched her nose up and took the spy piece away from her ear as if some horrible liquid was coming out of it. Finally there was a 'Great. Talk to you soon', followed by a click as Chester hung up.

I felt slightly squeamish when it dawned on me that Chester had been having phone sex over my supermarket expedition. I wondered what I was going to tell Lucinda. People like Chester are all supposed to be part of my past now that I have met her. The thing about a disgraceful story like Chester is that you can only ever tell it once. Chester re-emerging from the woodwork in the cold light of day could put you in a very bad light indeed.

But Lucinda didn't seem to have noticed anything out of the

ordinary. She just stood up and said, 'I say, George. I think I've got a bit of a dirty glass,' before going back out into the kitchen. When she had gone, Bet said, 'Poor me. I feel a bit *malade* after all that.'

I went back to the kitchen and started reheating the pork and apple casserole that I'd prepared earlier in the afternoon. By now, the thought of pork and apples was making me feel a bit nauseous but I carried on robotically, hoping that in some shape or form unbeknown to me I was succeeding in impressing Lucinda. She didn't seem to have noticed how stressed out I was. She sat at the table sipping her turpsy Veuve Clicquot, talking about her university days at Bristol when she too had lived in a house that looked like a squat. As I laid the table, I hoped she wouldn't start making jokes about the bendy Dan Air cutlery.

In the end, our first evening spent together at Clignancourt was perfect. Lucinda did laugh at the bendy Dan Air knives and forks but she didn't mention Zelda all night. We talked about our friends (she was very impressed with Bet and Ann), our pasts, where our favourite places were to go on holiday. She said that she'd take me to a place in Asia where the hotels were the most luxurious in the world and we'd spend all day sitting round in lush, white bath robes and ordering up room service and having sex. It was even okay when Bet burst in to make a cup of tea because she was being amusing about how she was going to have to go back and work in Place Vendôme in the horrible offices of Oliver and Sullivan where the space between the photocopier and the front desk was too narrow and gave rise to problems with *Maître* Foucault, the lechy head lawyer. She was cut off mid-sentence by the sound of a man gobbing outside. This was followed by the furious voice of the Yugoslav concierge yelling bullets as she sloshed expletives and a pail of water around the courtyard and we all laughed, and then Ann came in juggling and offering a joint round.

When I got into bed, Lucinda came back singing from the bathroom. Springs pinged as she jumped in and she giggled about the trouble she'd had brushing her teeth when the sink ledge was covered with Bet's gummy mascara wands and the basin was filled with Tati T-shirts bleeding black dye. 'Just as well I went to Roedean,' she teased, pulling me to her. 'Used to the rough life and all that.'

She was quiet and then she said in her tree-climbing voice, 'It's nice that your life is so different from mine. You make me feel relaxed. Zelda's always so stressed about everything.'

It was the first time I had heard Lucinda say anything bad about her girlfriend in New York. In a chorus of boinging springs she rolled over to face me. Up until now, Lucinda had acted quite boisterous in bed: rough and hard, hot on the ramming and scant on the kissing. It was okay because I figured that she must have imparted about 60 per cent of her bed knowledge by now. But that night, something better than even 100 per cent bed knowledge happened.

She kissed me slowly and tenderly with her eyes open. I could see her eyes in the wan light coming in from the yellow HLM building opposite. I looked into them as she looked into mine and I didn't even think of sex. I just thought of being with her always and never flirting with anyone else and never sleeping with anyone else and never being cheap again or playing the court jester ever again or never slamming the phone down when someone like Chester called up. Life was all about staying in this room with the broken springs in the bed and the dusty grapes on the ceiling and looking at her, belonging to her, being happy, making her happy, being locked in this moment. The ultimate. And while her tongue still searched in my mouth and her crotch rubbed against my leg she mumbled, 'I love you. I love you, George, I love you.'

I think I might have gasped when she said the word 'love'. Sunday, 12 January 1992, 2.30 a.m., 27 rue de Clignancourt. Fruit-crate bed. It felt like the height of my life and I grabbed the brown sheets to make sure I wasn't dreaming.

CHAPTER TWELVE

Eggs

Lucinda and I are taking a bath together one morning. As I recline against the smooth end and Lucinda lazes with her arms around her knees at the tap end, we talk about what to have for breakfast. Suddenly, the water begins to eddy and the tranquillity of the morning is broken.

'I don't really see there's much point in me putting in chopped parsley if you like them all dried up,' Lucinda snaps, kicking the water with her foot.

I sit up slightly.

'I can have them dry if I like them dry,' I smile.

She is really snarling now. 'God, I don't believe that you want to be a food journalist. You didn't know what pesto was until I told you. Frankly, anyone who likes dried-up scrambled eggs shouldn't be writing about food.'

She begins scrubbing her back vigorously, whisking the water with her legs.

'What happened, did your mother make you eat fish and chips for every meal? Yes, chips and spam every meal time was it?'

I take my feet out from under her. 'Lucinda,' I mumble, 'if I like eating dry scrambled eggs instead of wet ones, then that doesn't make me some kind of worse person than you are.'

Scoffing: 'Oh, you think so!'

Stammering: 'I enjoy food, it just so happens I don't like wet eggs.'

Sneering: 'Yes, my darling, it also "just so happens" that you like sweet and sour pork. I mean, Christ almighty, that alone speaks a thousand volumes about your level of food appreciation.'

Wobbling lower lip: 'I can't believe you're being like this.'

The bath is now churning round like a Jacuzzi. Lucinda hauls herself up in a terrible roar of water suction and splashes her feet down on to the soaking bath mat.

'I'm just pointing things out to you. God, has nobody ever told you a few home truths? You know, Zelda might be neurotic but at least she knows a thing or two about food. She'd laugh at your taste in scrambled eggs!'

Sometimes I feel like I'm in a bit of a 'let's have a look at the old score board' situation with Lucinda. Although I am not very experienced about relationships I do know that rows like the scrambled eggs one are not really about scrambled eggs. Sometimes, Lucinda will go for days without even mentioning the name of Zelda, and then I will leave too much mess when I use the orange juicer or I'll order sweet and sour pork in the Chinese restaurant, and she will get that aloof, defiant look in her eyes or she'll flare up and ask me how I can possibly expect to have a girlfriend when I have no idea about good taste. And I know that Zelda has just been given 50 points and I've had 100 taken away, and the thing is that there's not much time left to catch up now. Lucinda and I met at the end of December and now it is the beginning of April. Zelda is due to arrive from New York at the end of the month.

When Lucinda has dried herself she goes into the dressing room and starts swiping the corners of the ceiling with a feather duster. I mope on the carpet of the sitting room by the beach photograph and when she finally calls out, with irony in her voice, asking if I'd like eggs or toast for breakfast, I tell her that I don't want any breakfast. 'I told you at the beginning that this was only a fling,' she says, coming into the sitting room with her arms folded. 'We've had a really nice time but there has to be an end to it.' Then she unfolds her arms and says awkwardly, 'I'm sorry I was mean to you. I suppose I feel guilty about Zelda.' She kisses me gently and says, 'Why don't we just try to have a nice time together for the three weeks we've got left?'

I am deciding whether to carry on sulking or not when the doorbell rings. It is Holly. He springs up the stairs like the Six Million Dollar man to announce that he is about to become the new Karl Lagerfeld. Throwing himself down on the leather settee, he says breezily, 'I always told you, George! Didn't I always tell you?'

'Tell me what?'

'That the three Rs would take me places!'

As Holly is dancing round the flat singing 'rogering, rooting and rimming' to the tune of 'Bamboleo' by the Gypsy Kings, Lucinda comes out of the kitchen with a big glass of orange juice. 'Come on then,' she says, handing him the glass. 'Tell us your good news.'

Holly takes a triumphant gulp of juice to lubricate his mouth for what he is about to say. He looks at us both to check we are rapt enough and then he begins.

'Guess who I just bumped into in the rue Vieille du Temple?'

'Alan Whicker,' I murmur, not really in the mood for good news.

'George!' Holly warns. 'If you're not going to say anything nice ...'

'Who then?'

'Only the Russian!'

I make one of Holly's 'puh!' sounds.

'Shut up! I'm coming to the good bit!' He takes another slug of orange juice and begins again. 'He comes up behind me and puts his hands over my eyes, and when I turn round I'm thinking, "Oh my god. He's back!" I fix my eyes on his AC/DC T-shirt so I won't have to have any contact with the winsome almonds. But then I forget all about the almonds when he starts saying how he's been looking for me all week because a Japanese business friend of his is desperate to find a fashion designer to back. I fit the profile perfectly, apparently. The Russian says this bloke's loaded and he's got the best contacts . . .'

If there is anyone in the world who seems least likely to be able to put Holly in contact with a serious business backer then it is the Russian. Lucinda is obviously thinking the same thing.

'That's great news, Holly,' she says, 'and I don't want to put a dampener on the occasion but . . . are you sure this Japanese contact is legit?'

'Legit!' Holly jumps up and starts stomping round the room too outraged to speak.

When he becomes verbal again he snaps: 'Did Andy Warhol make his mark on the twentieth century by staying in on Friday nights swotting for his A levels?'

He makes a little *moue* then sits back down on the settee, crossing his legs.

'You've got to understand something about the *profession libérale*, Lucinda. It's not the early bird who catches the worm in the *profession libérale*. It's not 7 o'clock power breakfasts and golf on Saturday mornings.' With a debonair flick of the thumb he lights a cigarette as he thinks hastily about what it is exactly that catches the worm in his line of work.

He puffs a coquettish wisp of smoke from his mouth and decides that the winning bird is the one who 'rises at 2 in the afternoon, drinks a gallon of heroin-strength coffee, picks up some pinking shears for an hour, takes an early aperitif and then throws himself into a bit of night-life action before waking up at noon the next day to begin feverish sketching — inspired by the perforated tassels on the pair of shoes he was licking in some sordid back room the night before. That's who scores in my line of work.'

Holly suddenly seems bored at being called upon to justify his good fortune.

'Look, the fact is that the Russian met Rudolf Nureyev a few years ago on his travels to the bottom of the barrel. And Nureyev's crowd all used to hang out in Paris with Jagger, Loulou de la Falaise, Saint Laurent, Lagerfeld, and Warhol . . . that sort of thing. This Japanese guy — Koji he's called — he hung out with them too.'

He uncrosses his legs and sinks, as if exhausted, into the leather settee. 'I can't help but think it's about bloody time I stumbled across the Gay Mafia.'

Lucinda decides to be effusive in the face of the new twist in Holly's fate. 'Wonderful! Brilliant,' she whoops. 'And just think of all the other perks of fame and fortune — like beautiful lovers.'

That comment makes me decide definitely not to come out of my sulk. To make matters worse, the phone then rings. I can tell by Lucinda's tone of voice that it is Zelda. She looks shifty as she takes the phone downstairs saying that she'll be back in a bit. The *moue* has come back into Holly's face.

'Thanks a lot for the encouragement, *chérie.*'

'What?'

'I think you'll find that I've just had the best stroke of luck ever. You're supposed to congratulate me for being about to be the next Karl Lagerfeld. And here I am, visiting me mate and me mucker in her posh new garret with her posh new girlfriend, and she can't even tell me how fantastic I am.'

'It's not that, Holly,' I sigh. 'I'm really pleased for you. When are you meetng this Japanese bloke?'

'Day after tomorrow. We're having lunch at Le Crillon.'

'Cool,' I say half-heartedly. 'Now you've got a lover and a job. I haven't got either.'

'What do you mean? What about Lucinda?'

'I don't know. I don't think I'm going to have a girlfriend for very much longer.'

'Don't be ridiculous,' Holly says, picking up Lucinda's feather duster and twirling it in his hand. 'You're probably just having some strange paranoid allergic reaction from hanging out for so long in a clean apartment.'

'I'm serious, Holly. I'm not posh enough. I bought Lucinda a jasmine and peach air freshener that I nicked from Madame Bourse's the other day as a present. And all she could say was "Why do you think I've got a box of matches in the bathroom?" Turns out that if you light a match after you've done it, all the smells vanish.'

Holly turns his nose up and says that he didn't come round to talk about bathroom smells but I carry on regardless.

'Air freshener smells of Opal Fruits. It's for suburban people who twitch lace curtains. Lucinda says.'

Holly opens his mouth to tell me to shut up but at that moment we are forced to look downstairs because Lucinda has raised her voice by several notches. 'Look, I'm doing the best I can,' she's going. 'I know I haven't organised your office yet. I've been busy. I'm sorry. What do you mean, "Am I seeing someone else?" What an absurd thing to say.'

Then she lowers her voice again and Holly raises his eyebrows.

'Lesbians like arguing quite a lot, don't they?' he says, settling himself down on the leather settee. 'Anyway, Zelda sounds a pain in the neck. That's perfect for you. All you've got to do is make out you're a really confident and cool person.'

'But I'm not confident and cool.'

Holly thinks for a bit. 'All right then. Here's your trump card: you announce to Lucinda that when Zelda arrives in May you won't be able to see her any more.'

'Not see her any more?' I feel cold. My first thought is how will I survive without the sex. I am beginning to realise that having sex on tap can take a lot of the stress out of your life. And it can make you feel proud about bits of your body that you never knew you had. Like a good bum. Lucinda has told me that I have a great bum, like a boy's bum. So now, when I look at it in the mirror, I feel proud. But if I suddenly have to stop having sex with Lucinda I'll think what a waste. Twenty-four with a great bum and nobody to admire it in its prime. I will have to go out night hunting again, except that now I think I want to go night hunting for women and I'm not exactly sure of the ropes.

Anyway, I don't want anyone else. I have never had such good sex as the sex I have with Lucinda. Yesterday, after a Saturday afternoon's walk along the Seine we went back to Lucinda's flat and she fucked me with her hand as I lay on my back, body writhing, face twitching, looking out of the skylight at the blue sky and the fluffy clouds. When I told Holly about this he said it sounded like the scene in *Drugstore Cowboy* when Matt Dillon takes heroin and sees blue sky and fluffy clouds everywhere. And I think he has a point. Being with Lucinda is what I imagine taking hard drugs feels like. Like taking drugs you can't quite remember what the experience felt like afterwards, but you know it was nice and you want more.

Holly is still thinking about his plan. 'Better still than the threat of never being able to see you again,' he says, 'is the threat of never seeing the Gang again. She's never going to chuck you if she thinks she'll lose the Gang. She might know about posh air fresheners but her dress sense and her social life were in tatters before she met us.'

Then he looks at my stripy T-shirt and says, 'On second thoughts I think I might have to advise you to chuck Lucinda altogether. Your dress sense has suffered terribly since you've been seeing her.'

It is true that I do have an overwhelming urge to wear the same clothes as Lucinda these days. Our current look is the stripy T-shirts and sunglasses one. My stripy T-shirt comes from Tati and has holes in by now – even though I make sure not to wash it too often. My sunglasses are scratched and the stretched arms mean that they keep falling down on to my nose. Holly found them in his pocket one morning after a night out in Le Swing. Lucinda bought her stripy top from a mail order offer in the *Sunday Telegraph* and her shades are Ray Bans. But she has now invested in a pair of second-hand brickie white jeans from Clignancourt market – just like mine. She has also started chewing gum and wearing a leather shoelace around her neck like me. In my better moments I feel sure that this is proof I am going to win out in the Zelda/George war.

'Have you found any letters yet?' Holly asks suddenly. I know he is referring to Zelda's letters to Lucinda. Of course I have found them.

'They're very Virginia Woolf,' I say.

'Go on then. Read one.'

I look swiftly downstairs to make sure that Lucinda is still on the phone. Then I pull out a large cigar box from under the bookcase. It is filled with sheets of typed paper. On the top of each sheet it says: AP New York. Business. Hard Copy.

'She's a journalist for some news agency,' I say. I pick one out of the box but then I feel bad about reading it. 'I suppose it's not good to read people's private love letters.'

'Well, it's not great. Let's just say that the old score board wouldn't be too happy if it knew.'

'You think so?'

'Oh really!' Holly says, irritated. 'I read my best ever personal tribute once in some dullard boyfriend's diary. He'd started off writing, "Holly is the most shallow person I've ever met." But all you've got to do is scan read for a few pages. They wouldn't be writing about you if they weren't obsessed. I finally saw a line that said, "But he's the best performer I've ever slept with."' He hits the air triumphantly with the feather duster.

'Makes you sound like a seal,' I say. I start to read:

Dear Lucinda,

Preparing to leave these past few weeks has been a tear-stained blur. A nightmare. I hover around the borders of sleep. I rage inside, torn between all I am afraid of and all I want to know, like an endless, insane debate. Last night I was becoming unstuck . . .

Holly cuts me off with a big 'puh!' 'Spare us, Virginia!' he snorts. 'We don't want *her* in the Gang.'

We hear a click as Lucinda puts the phone down.

'Just remember,' Holly whispers. 'Confidence and cool. You'll have her eating from your hand.'

Lucinda sounds all jolly hockey sticks as she walks up the stairs.

'Come on then, George,' she trills. 'How do you fancy a spot of lunch at the Café Beaubourg?'

'Actually, George is coming with me,' Holly drawls, as if Lucinda has just suggested taking me to the Women's Institute bring and buy sale.

Holly catches my eye and nods at the door. 'We have to go and buy a birthday present for Alex.'

Lucinda is disappointed. 'Oh,' she says. 'I didn't know it was Alex's birthday, George. I thought we were going to spend the day together.'

I glance at Holly then shrug at her. I can hardly bring myself to say it. 'Sorry,' I say, unconvincingly. 'Forgot to tell you.'

I feel betrayed and grumpy as I sit in the métro with Holly who is now telling me that I have to buy him breakfast to thank him for his sterling advice.

'What do you mean, "sterling advice"? You're just trying to nobble me. Now that you're going to be rich and famous, even more people are going to fancy you. You won't have any time for me.'

Back at rue de Clignancourt, we eat coffee *religieuses* with lumpy *crème pâtissière* in my bedroom. A medley of Cheb Khaled ballads crank in through the window from the HLM opposite and Holly flicks through an old copy of *Paris Parade*.

'I could be choosing between eggs benedict and smoked salmon by now,' I sulk.

'You don't like eggs,' Holly murmurs.

'I'll be on the shelf for ever,' I say gloomily to the soggy pastry.

'You've got a point there,' Holly says, jumping up. 'Let's get you down to the flea market and sort you out a new look.'

Later that evening, just as I am wondering if my new belt with the Thierry Mugler-inspired Flash Gordon buckle is going to make up for having no girlfriend, Holly's plan starts working. Lucinda calls up and apologises again for her breakfast behaviour. She offers to take me to dinner at Chez Omar, a fashionable couscous restaurant on the borders of the Marais. You can't get posh about couscous and I see Lucinda's choice of dining venue as a thoughtful compromise between our lifestyles.

In the restaurant, I show Lucinda how to mix in *harissa* with the ladle of vegetable stew and Lucinda tells me how confused she feels. How she feels that she has just started a life of her own in Paris and now Zelda is coming over and she's not sure she wants it all changed again. 'I feel I'm different now,' she says slowly. 'In New York, Zelda used to mother me and in return I'd calm her down when she started getting all panicky and nervous about her work. It was okay in New York.' She sighs. 'I don't know,' she says. 'Part of me is dreading her arriving in Paris.'

'Look,' I smile. 'I'm sure it'll all be fine when she arrives. It's just a question of getting used to her again.'

Lucinda looks surprised. 'You think so?'

I force myself to go on. 'Of course. And I agree that we should have a great time for the next three weeks,' I stop. 'Because after Zelda comes, I won't be able to see you any

more.' Lucinda puts her fork down. 'And neither will the Gang.'
She stops chewing.

Over the next three weeks, I make sure I am very confident and
cool. We go to Normandy to stay at Alex's boyfriend's house
where the Gang pokes gentle fun at Lucinda and she and I
pretend to have sex in the sea and I write 'I Love Lucinda'
in the sand, even though I feel sad as I do it. When we get
back to the city we go to Le Privilège disco where I do my
cool trunking dance (keeping my upper torso quite still and
thrusting my pelvis from side to side) and we both flirt just a
little bit with other women to make us fancy each other even
more. When we walk back to the Marais in the early hours,
as the last traces of black have drained from the light and the
sky is a soft-focus golden white, we amble over to the Place de
l'Hôtel de Ville and look down in silence at the waters of the
Seine. For the first time since I have been living in Paris I find
that the city is beautiful.

On sunny evenings I meet Lucinda when she comes out
of work at a bar on the haughty Place Trocadero which has a
view of the Eiffel Tower. We drink Kir and she kicks me gently
under the table with her stockinged foot because presumably
she's worried that holding my hand over the table would imply
more commitment. One day, she introduces me to a lively friend
of hers from Slaughterhouse and April called Cheryl. Cheryl
looks slightly like Miss Piggy. She wears very high heels on very
small feet and she has dry blonde hair and a habit of flicking it
back over her shoulder when she feels uneasy.

Holly has been introduced to Cheryl too and has already
converted her into a drinking friend. He likes Cheryl's capacity
to drink him under the table and her compulsion for shopping.
When Lucinda introduced them, Holly warmed immediately to
the cockney geezer trapped inside the Nicole Farhi lawyer drag.
'She's so desperate to make out she's a real lawyer,' he said.

'"Yeah, well, can't make it tonight," she says. "Going to the Opera." "Oh really!" I say. "Get Bianca Jagger!" When I know very well she'd rather be going down the Coach and Horses.'

Some evenings the four of us meet up and knock back Kirs until we are drunk. As we breathe in the early summer air and the fumes from the *coursier* bikes, I look at the *seizième arrondissement* couples with their bobs and their good leather shoes packing up their Peugeots to prepare for a weekend in the country and I wish that Lucinda and I could be a normal couple like that. I wish we could do ordinary, boring things that ordinary couples do. But for the moment we are still a normal couple. The aeroplane has not landed yet. I knock back the last of my Kir and think it would be nice to add on a new service to my Philippe Starck control box – the one with the buttons that you press to make The One appear and disappear when you want. I would add another button which would make moments like this stand still for as long as you wanted.

Even when Cheryl and Lucinda start talking to each other in a strangely quiet way so I know that they are talking about Zelda, there is always Holly to keep me amused. He knows that they are talking about Zelda too, so he will tell me a Cheryl story to make sure that I continue to live in the present. Holly says that Cheryl invites him out to dinner whenever she's just bought a ridiculously expensive item of clothing that she looks terrible in. Apparently, she spent £800 on a Hermès leather coat not so long ago that made her look like Myra Hindley.

I play the confidence and cool game so well that the night before Zelda is due to arrive in Paris there is a knock at the front door of Clignancourt. When I open it I see Lucinda looking bedraggled and tear-stained. For some reason, I am not surprised. This morning, when Lucinda and I shared our last freshly squeezed orange juice, Lucinda was quiet and I felt sick and jubilant at the same time. When I left, Lucinda said that she wanted to run away.

Seeing her now on the doorstep — motionless, frightened, doe-eyed — I know I have to take her in and spend just one more night with her. We don't even have sex. We just hold each other very close. She pleads again to be allowed to see me when Zelda arrives and I say — like a wise owl with a violently pulsating heart — that it is best to end our affair in its prime. The next morning at eight, I walk down to the boulevard Barbès to get her a taxi to take her to Charles de Gaulle airport. I'm not sure if I feel shock or just exhilaration as I watch her stare blankly through the window like a kidnapped child as the taxi drives off down the glinting boulevard, already buzzing like Marrakech.

When I go back home, Ann has just returned from a night at Jean-Christophe's house. She is sitting in the kitchen with a pile of clothes on her lap. She tells me that the previous night, when she arrived at his house, Jean-Christophe greeted her with an armful of dresses — from his ex-girlfriend. 'Lord! He went to visit her and she seemed to think it the most natural thing in the world that I'd want her old cast-offs.'

'Do you think you're going to wear them?' I ask, looking dubiously at the tailored jackets and short skirts and thinking they are the sort of things Lucinda might wear to Slaughterhouse and April.

'Shouldn't think so,' she says. 'But they might have potential as clown costumes.'

When I tell her that Lucinda has left for the airport, Ann says, 'Oh, poor George.' She gives me a hug and I bury my face in her blonde mane and make sure I breathe sharply through my nose so that no tears come. Then, seeing as it is Wednesday, she suggests going down to the Barbès market to buy some food.

Ann is on good form this morning. As we walk down the boulevard Rochechouart towards the Barbès market, she tells me that one of her friends from her juggling group has expressed an interest in meeting me. 'She's a really good stilt walker,' Ann says. Then she adds quickly, 'Not that I want to rush you or anything. I mean, with Lucinda only just out of the picture.'

But I am still feeling high from lack of sleep and at 9 o'clock on a sunny May morning it even seems a good idea to quit while I'm ahead with Lucinda, move to fields afresh. I am just having pleasant thoughts about what fields afresh might look like when I hear a man hiss, '*Eh! Ça va, la blonde?*' and I know that we've arrived at the market.

On Wednesdays, street badinage goes into overdrive at the Barbès market which is a haze of noise and jostle and sheep's feet and spicy sweat and incense smoke and black women in bright robes with children tied on their backs, and Maribou fortune tellers, thrusting slips of paper into your hand to tell you how to attract love or put a curse on your employer. Every few minutes the bedlam of the market is obliterated by the sound of the Porte Dauphine-Nation métro line which thunders and screeches overhead.

Some days, the market is too hectic and I prefer the anonymity of the juvenile delinquent supermarket where you don't have to think up cute-but-firm repartee every time you buy a kilo of potatoes. But on those days when you feel like losing yourself a little as you shop, then the Barbès market is the perfect place to be. The main thing to remember as you are wandering around is not to eat anything too obvious or Algerian men will come up to you muttering '*bon appétit*', like you are about to put their cock in your mouth instead of a nice *pain aux raisins* or a fat, juicy peach.

Even at 9 a.m. the market is in full swing. Old men who look like they live in haystacks are selling gnarled lemons and bunches of coriander the size of hedges. At the cheese stand is a woman who looks like she stepped down from the Minitel advert. She is shouting '*goutez, goutez*' about some brie *en promotion* that she is trying to shift. She is attracting more customers than a lap dancer but not as many as the boys who flex their bodies and cry *'eh, chérie!', 'eh, ma biche!'* from behind mounds of strawberries and apples and leeks and asparagus as you quickly try to assess which wares are the least damaged.

I make a bee-line for the fish stall. It's good to get here early, before the blooming morgue gets too old and the eyes of the fish sink despondently into their heads. At this hour of the morning they still look iceberg fresh. Plaice are on special offer this morning and they lounge in perky, rubber-lipped couples on beds of crushed ice – 10 francs for two. *Promotion.* As I wait in the queue I watch the woman serving. Her face is painted like a parrot and her lacy apron is brown and red and yellow from hours of wiping spilt guts all over it. She waves a bloody knife in the air, brandishing a handful of chipped cherry nails and a wedding ring smeared with sticky fish threads. To a man in the queue she shouts, *'Mais c'est pas possible! Un poisson sans tête et sans queue est comme une femme mal coiffée et mal chaussée!'* which means 'Don't be ridiculous. A fish without a head and a tail is like a woman with a bad hairdo and bad shoes!'

Everyone in the queue laughs and the man blushes but he goes home with two fine plaice with faces and fins.

I go home with two plaice, a large bunch of coriander, two kilos of peaches, a kilo of strawberries, a large plastic bag of lettuce (10 francs for four), two kilos of tomatoes (which will be good for roughly one more day), 500 grammes of brie, 500 grammes of Comté and three baguettes. On top of this, Ann has bought a few kilos of fruit and vegetables and we lug them all the way home, ignoring the various offers of help from wizened men and cheeky boys in bomber jackets who we encounter along the way.

As I make lunch at Clignancourt with Ann, I tell her I can feel that burrowing feeling coming on. My week's shopping has only cost me 120 francs (more or less). I am going to concentrate on self-sufficiency and coming up with some brilliant ideas so I can get a job and maybe at the weekend

I will meet up with the lesbian stilt walker and teach her a thing or two.

And then the phone rings and it is Lucinda. As I listen to what she has to say, I feel as if I am watching myself having a phone conversation with her. A few hours ago I had thought I would never speak to her again and now she is telling me that she wants to see me. She says, 'I'm sorry. I'm really sorry to call you. I couldn't help it. Zelda and I went to have a drink in Le Swing just now and I saw a white bike chained up outside. I was so excited because I thought it was yours. I thought you were going to be inside. And then you weren't . . .'

She sounds a bit of a mess. I can hear some sort of banging in the background.

'Lucinda, are you okay?' I ask.

'George. Look. I know I shouldn't have done this, but I did.'

'What did you do?'

I hear her breathing for a few seconds, and then she says, 'I told Zelda about you.'

A wave of dizziness passes through me and I sit down on the pile of telephone books next to the answering machine. When I consider it, I can't really understand why I'm not overjoyed. If Lucinda has told Zelda then it means that she is serious about me. All along I have been telling Holly I want her to chuck Zelda. And now that it seems she is on the verge of doing so, my palms have come over all sweaty and I have suddenly lost my appetite. Ann peeps her head round the kitchen door, looking worried. And when I look at Ann all I can think of is the stilt walker who wants to meet me and maybe I'm not free to do that sort of thing any more.

I hear Lucinda's voice on the other end of the phone again. 'Are you still there?' it asks timidly.

I take a deep breath and say, 'What's going to happen now then?'

A blade of jolly hockey sticks enters her voice and she says, 'I don't know actually.'

I like that better. Now that she sounds more reassured I feel my libido and my hope rise once more. 'Well look, if you need anything you can always call me. I'll be here for you. Okay?'

I finish frying my plaice in the kitchen and tell Ann that I need to be on my own for a bit. When I am tucked up in my bed with a plaice sandwich and a pile of French magazines on my lap, I start to relax a little. After all, from the outside, this looks like the perfect situation. The woman that I love is flinging herself at me while I remain all in all self-sufficient: here I sit, in my bed, eating food that I have earned from the sweat of my brow by getting up at 7 in the morning to teach at Madame Bourse's. I take a big bite of the sandwich, flick through the magazine pages and start to think that the old score board is looking very much in my favour. I smile as I think again about the new service on my Philippe Starck control box.

But unfortunately the box has still not been invented and the doorbell rings, and when Ann opens it Lucinda is standing there. She looks like she has spent a week shopping in the Barbès market. Her face is sweating and her clothes look dishevelled. Throwing my arms around her is not what I really feel like doing, but I do it anyway.

As I hold her to me, my first thought is that my plaice baguette concept is ruined. It will go cold if I make Lucinda something to eat. And if I make her something to eat then my stocks of self-sufficiency will be diminished and I won't be independent any more.

I find it slightly worrying that I am even thinking like this. I think I am being selfish so I try to push the importance of the morning's shopping to the back of my mind and hug her a bit tighter. Her body starts shaking and swaying and I realise that she is sobbing. I'm not sure whether to say, 'Just cry, it's okay, just cry,' or to say, 'Don't cry, it's okay, don't cry,' as I lead her down the hall into my bedroom. I take my plate of fish sandwich and very ripe tomatoes off the bed and she collapses in a heap.

'It's terrible! Terrible!' she wails. 'She started throwing all my things round the flat. My fruit bowl from Kenya. It's ruined. My Japanese prints, all torn up. The whole place looks like a bomb hit it!'

Although this is all obviously very tragic, I do find something quite funny in the thought that Lucinda's apartment, which once looked like the penthouse suite of a residential hotel, now resembles a mock-up of 27 rue de Clignancourt – though most of the chipped and broken objects in Lucinda's flat come from Kenya and Japan as opposed to Tati and Taiwan. I stroke her hair and say that it's all right but this seems to make her infuriated and she stands up and starts pacing round the room, saying, 'It's not all right, it's not all right! She was banging her head against the wall when I left her. Banging and banging. And when I tried to get her to stop she flung her arms at me and punched me in the eye.'

Lucinda is forced to stop pacing my room because there is the sound of a broom handle hitting a ceiling from the men underneath and muted cries of *'Putain! Arrête putain!'* Lucinda stops and looks at me head on and I see a cut in the corner of her eye. And suddenly an ache of love comes over me and I leap up and take her in my arms and pull her to the bed. She just buries her head in my neck and sobs and I hold her tight and start crying too. And then I kiss her to make it better and her warm, salty face rolls over my hot, damp mouth and the gasping sobs give way to rhythmic deep breathing and thick aroused moans, and soon the broken bedsprings shake and the anguished cry of orgasm fills the room until we can't even hear the broom handle any more. And afterwards, when we have been silent for several minutes, listening to the sounds of rubbish bins being brought out to the courtyard and the light thumping of beanbags hitting parquet as Ann practises juggling in her room, Lucinda turns my face to look at her.

'You know, in spite of everything,' she says. 'In spite of everything I think some good could come out of all this. I knew as soon as I saw Zelda at the airport that it wasn't going to work. That I wanted to be with you.' She strokes my side. 'I'm just going to have to be calm. Sort things out with Zelda. Maybe she'll want to go back to New York. I don't know. It'll all sort itself out.' Then she sits up. 'The main thing is that you should know that I want to be with you. I'm doing this for you.'

At first, this feels fine. It makes me feel ecstatic. It is only afterwards when I am in the kitchen, frying the other piece of plaice and making a large bowl of salad that unease starts to creep in.

'This lettuce has seen better days, Georgie,' Lucinda says cheerfully as she stabs her fork into some of the provisions that Ann and I have braved hell and high water to hump back from the market. I know I can get a little over-sensitive about my Barbès shopping, but in my opinion this lunch, with all the trouble and care that has gone into bringing it into being, has reached the status of a work of art in my eyes and she has failed to appreciate it.

Lucinda is filled with an almost irritating post-trauma chirpiness. 'We can do everything together now,' she says in a voice filled with bustle. 'When you come and live with me in the Marais I promise that all the lettuce will be slug-free and you'll never have to eat a bruised peach ever again.'

Shit, I think. How can I get out of this one?

CHAPTER THIRTEEN

Procrustes' Bed

Holly says that fast food is cool and modern. Part of me thinks that he only says this because until recently he was forced to live almost exclusively on hot dogs. He could have lived on green lentils and pork chops like me, but Holly believes there is no point in being poor unless you do it with style.

He said his lunch times were very The Factory. The concept was to buy a tin of frankfurters for 4 francs 90, a bag of six soft white baps for 4 francs, a bottle of ED beer for 4 francs 50, and then put his boxer shorts in the washing machine for a boil wash. When they were pristine, crisp and dry he would put them on — and nothing else — turn up the heating full blast and lounge in Alex's crisp, white bed — hot dog in hand — before calling me up, starving hungry, to tell me that he was being cool and urbane in a Joe Dallesandro sort of way.

Then, suddenly, Holly stopped being poor. Koji gave him his first wage packet and it was even better than a wage packet: it was a thick wad of 500-franc notes bound with a twist of purple taffeta. He went straight to Le Swing where the evening proceeded, he said, much like the 'I'm Getting Married In The Morning' scene from *My Fair Lady*. There was camaraderie and cheering and everyone wanted to take him and his wad off into the night. But he ended up going home with an unremarkable boy with a pock-marked chin who, when Holly first offered to buy him a drink, replied with sincere bewilderment in his voice, 'But ... you don't even know me.'

'How touching was that!' Holly sighed nostalgically the next day, lighting a cigarette. 'If only we'd known that it doesn't matter not being back of the bus stock. If only we'd known that you can always buy a Gang.'

Holly was lighting cigarettes every few minutes that morning. This was because when he left the boy's flat at 10 a.m. he went straight to Cartier on the Place Vendôme and spent 10,000 francs on a platinum gold lighter. After he'd done this, he called me up and told me to meet him at the McDonald's opposite Tati on rue de Clignancourt. By 11 o'clock, we were both tucking in to four rounds of Big Mac, large fries and diet coke. Holly said it was best to start at the bottom and work upwards when it came to luxury. 'Can't have white gold and two Michelin stars all in one day,' he said, cramming his mouth with posh, clean chips.

Holly was in fullest Joe Dallesandro mode that day. As we looked at the brown plastic trays of fried food I could see him wondering if they were working as a concept, but soon, the reassuring texture and bland flavour set him at ease and he settled down to enjoy the treat. And it was a treat: American fast food doesn't come cheap in Paris. A Big Mac alone costs 19 francs – a third more than the price of a Sandwich Greque from the couscous stall next to number 27. I've only ever eaten in the rue de Clignancourt McDonald's once before – a couple of years ago on the day of moving into the apartment. As I walked out of the shiny, plastic premises, I clutched the warm, brown paper take-out bag like it was an attaché case. And as I swaggered my way back to the flat with my 87 francs' worth of strawberry shake and brightly coloured straws and individual cardboard boxes I thought, this is what they do in America; this is what American TV execs in LA look like after work when they drop into a fast-food restaurant in their fast sports cars to pick up their tea.

When we were fed up with fast food Holly said he fancied buying an antique table. So we walked to the Clignancourt flea market – but not to the murky part under the bridge where old people sell off their life belongings for 10 francs: a mothy blanket here, a 5-franc chipped horse figurine there. (Once I got a pair of old men's pinstriped trousers for only 3 francs which I later sold off to one of the clowns for a 6 franc profit.)

We proceeded directly to the upmarket *brocanteur* end but when we got there Holly couldn't make up his mind which antique table he wanted. All he did was light his cigarette about 10 times a minute and stare blankly into the packed windows of the shops. My eyes fixed on a distinguished-looking man with *harissa* and lamb fat seeping out of the corners of his mouth from the Sandwich Greque he was eating. He lingered for a long time in front of an odd-looking table before licking his wrists and moving on. I wanted to go home so I decided that this was the table Holly should buy. I didn't like it much. The man in the shop said it was an eighteenth-century rococo design in patinated bronze but I thought it was frightening-looking. It had garlanded goat's limbs for legs – knobbled and cartilaginous – like the bandy legs of an old lady wearing a hitched-up skirt and heels that are too high.

Holly needed a hair of the dog so he didn't need much persuading to buy it. When he dug his hands into his pocket he saw that there was now more purple taffeta than there were 500-franc notes. There were just enough to pay for the goat table and so we couldn't afford a taxi home and had to lug the horrible, heavy thing back to rue Léon by foot.

We put the goat table next to the idealised peasant on the brunch bar but once Holly had drunk his hair of the dog I really got told off for making him buy it. He said that the last thing he needed in his life was post-baroque trellising and shell motifs. 'I'd have been much better off with an art déco ice bucket,' he grumbled, digging deep into his pockets. He soon became even more grumpy when he realised that he'd run out of cigarettes and he was now back to being skint again. 'I'll have to wait until Koji decides to give me another wad of notes now,' he cursed. He spent the rest of the afternoon flicking viciously through back issues of *French Vogue*, occasionally setting fire to pages that irritated him with his new platinum lighter.

Holly has two new catchphrases these days. The first one is, 'Don't even ask!' The other is, 'I can't even get excited until four in the morning!' He says this as an excuse for always turning up late for every single Gang event. He is already three hours late for this one. Tonight's gathering is to celebrate Lucinda's thirty-second birthday and present guests so far include Bet, Ann, Alex, me, Lucinda, Cheryl and a twenty-eight-year-old man she fancies who works in systems at Slaughterhouse and April. His name is Dave. Dave has a boxer's nose and he sits bolt upright, his arms folded like steel, jaw grinding away nineteen to the dozen as he stares cryptically at me. I know why he is looking at me but it still makes me nervous. I'm hoping that Lucinda hasn't noticed because she doesn't like Dave. You can't blame her. The other week, when he was over at Lucinda's apartment with Cheryl and me, he kept putting new rave records on Lucinda's record player and they sounded like dentists' drills. Lucinda didn't say anything but I could see her neck go strangely tight. When Dave finally slumped down on a chair, his eyes skimmed past Lucinda's beach photograph and then came to rest on the black and white photograph of the man in military uniform with a beaky nose and misanthropic eyes. Dave sat bolt upright and said, 'Is it all right if I turn that picture round to face the wall?' As the picture was of Lucinda's father, Brigadier Fraser Cranley Davenport, who had died only twelve months ago and whom both Lucinda and the Wing Commander had worshipped like a god, the ice in Lucinda's gin and tonic glass began to rattle in tune with the dentists' drills. She snapped, 'No you can't.'

After that, Lucinda's drinking hand calmed down and she carried on chatting to Cheryl about how hilarious it was that all French girls wore their 501s hitched tightly up their bums. Through the corner of my eye I saw Dave stand up, go over to the photograph, take hold of the elaborate silver frame and turn it round to face the wall. He only gave me the briefest of smiles as he came to sit down again on the chair and it was not until the following evening that Lucinda realised that Brigadier Fraser Cranley Davenport had spent the night contemplating her hessian mat wallpaper from extremely close range.

Luckily, I don't think Lucinda has noticed Dave's meaningful stare because she is drunk and is gabbling away to Cheryl whose face is growing so red it is beginning to steam with enjoyment. The drunker she gets, the more she resembles Miss Piggy. Her involuntary flicking back of her blonde fringe with a pale, whimsical hand is getting more frequent as the night proceeds.

Lucinda had specified a lively night out to celebrate her thirty-second birthday and our nine-month anniversary so I booked a table at a restaurant in a street where sleazy Barbès becomes touristy Montmartre. In the event, even a fondue restaurant that specialises in serving wine in baby bottles with teats on and a clientele composed mainly of Swedish students and Belgian backpackers seemed to go down well. It made a change from getting food poisoning from Chicken Maffei on the rue de la Goutte d'Or and the birthday guests seemed perfectly happy with the ambience of a Munich Beer festival. When they ran out of boozy conversation they amused themselves drawing genitalia on the paper table cloth with blue biros, only breaking off to pick up their baby bottles and suck red and white house wine through rubber teats.

✴   ✴   ✴

Just as I am sure that Lucinda is going to twig any minute why Dave and I are staring at each other, the door of the restaurant bursts open and Holly staggers in. He is now three and a half hours late. He staggers up to our table and says, 'Sorry everyone but I can't get excited until four in the morning.' Then he picks up Ann's baby bottle, squirts some red wine into his mouth, says, 'Sod this,' yanks the teat off and sloshes the rest of the contents of the bottle down his neck. Finally, he topples into a seat next to Lucinda, bids her a brief 'happy birthday', before turning to Alex and spluttering under his breath, 'Don't even ask!'

A few seconds later, the door bursts open again and a short man in his early forties wearing a beautifully tailored emerald-green velvet suit and dark sunglasses, walks into the restaurant like he's performing a Marcel Marceau routine. When he gets to our table he stops and collapses on to Ann's lap. He takes the baby bottle from Ann's hand, sucks wantonly on the teat and starts to swing his legs to and fro like he's a little boy. Then, he takes his free hand and places it on her left breast saying, as he gleefully squeezes it, 'Big titti mama! Good time lock and loll!' In the nick of time Holly comes over and pulls the man to his feet, announcing, in town-crier fashion: 'Everyone: this is Koji. He's very pleased to meet you!'

The whole table suddenly sobers up a little. Nobody says anything. They just stare at Holly's eccentric new business partner who has now broken away from his protégé and is gazing punch-drunk at the naked bodies all over the table cloth. Neither Ann, Bet nor I know any Japanese people. Recently, the Prime Minister Edith Cresson caused a stir by saying that they were all like ants. But Koji doesn't seem like an ant although he does keep itching himself – like he's got ants, or itching powder down his suit. He alternates between being very energetic and very lethargic – one minute he bangs on the table screaming for a biro and the next he stops and stares enthralled at the bubbling fondue pot.

The only thing he does constantly is talk *sotto voce* gibberish. Holly has said that Koji used to hang out with people like Andy

Warhol and Mick Jagger but I wonder how he got on if he couldn't communicate verbally. When the table has recovered from its initial shock and recommences its regular drunken chatter, Koji pulls his gaze out of the fondue pot and looks over at the far wall as if he has seen a vision there. With taut eyebrows and a gaping mouth he shoots to his feet, nearly upturning the fresh tray of baby bottles that the waiter, standing behind him, has brought over to our table.

As Koji is drawn inexorably over towards the toilets, the fraught waiter bangs the wobbling bottles down on the smutty table cloth in front of Cheryl. Cheryl smacks Holly's hands as he makes a grab for two of them. She passes one bottle to Ann and one to Alex. Then she makes a point of cupping her hands over her mouth and squawking to the man grinding his jaw at the end of the table, 'Hey Dave, we should have ordered you some baby's milk shouldn't we! I say, we should have ordered you some baby's milk!'

Dave looks edgily at Cheryl who is winking at him now. He is doing his best to behave, but he doesn't drink alcohol and he doesn't fancy Cheryl in the slightest. He only has one thought on his mind tonight and it involves me. When he can't get my attention, he tries to distract himself by attempting conversation with Bet. He has already used his best line on her and it went down like a lead balloon. His best line is, 'I want Mick Jagger's body. Not Mick Jagger 1966. Mick Jagger 1965. By '66 it was already too late'.

Dave's body looks more lumpy pillow-shaped than Jumping Jack Flash skinny but in any case, Bet isn't interested in Dave. She is even less interested in him now that Koji has entered the scene. Dave is too wrapped up in his own thoughts to have noticed that Bet and Ann only have eyes for Koji, and Cheryl and Lucinda are too drunk to have noticed much out of the ordinary with Holly's new mentor.

Alex is the only one who can read Bet and Ann's thoughts perfectly. He turns sternly to them both and says, 'We've got to be patient.'

This immediately sends Bet into a strop. 'What do you mean, "be patient?"' she snaps. 'Ann's just been sexually harassed by Holly's ludicrous business partner and you tell us to be patient!' She glances over at Ann, demanding back-up.

'It has to be said, Alex,' Ann ventures, tossing her blonde hair back nervously, 'I'm pretty fed up with men making comments about my breasts all the time – let alone touching them.'

'I touch your boosies sometimes!' Alex protests, pretending to prong Ann's nipple with his fondue fork.

'It's hardly the same thing,' Bet snaps, folding her arms against her chest.

Alex puts his fork down and his voice becomes serious again.

'What I mean,' he says slowly, 'is that we should be glad that Holly's found some success at last.'

Bet makes a Holly 'puh!' sound.

'All right then,' Alex concedes, dabbing the corners of his mouth with a serviette. 'To hell with the success. To be honest I'm just glad he's started to pay off the back rent he owes me. I want him to keep going so he can start making some headway with the Minitel bills.'

'How much does he owe you?'

'Don't even ask. And that's not the end of it. I've been paying astronomical electricity bills too. I think it might have something to do with the washing machine. My bedclothes are always freshly laundered. Every day. I know he's getting up to something.'

At the other end of the table, Holly's voice is getting louder as he holds court about his new life as a successful person. He says he arrived late for Lucinda's birthday party because he was sent by Koji to Versailles for the day to entertain a Japanese couple called Mr and Mrs Soya and their daughter Yoko.

Lucinda barks: 'Entertainments manager, eh? I thought you were supposed to be a fashion designer. You didn't tell us you'd become a geisha girl!'

Holly misses a couple of beats and his blue eyes go slightly moist. But he recovers himself.

'Geisha girl!' he camps. 'It's even worse than that, Lucinda Luvie! They wanted me to marry Spoonhead!'

'Spoonhead?' Cheryl burps into her bottle.

'Yes! Their daughter – Yoko. She kept smiling at me and Mrs Soya kept wanting to take our picture together.'

'What about Mr Soya?' says Lucinda.

'He just stood there all chubby and soft in his Burberry mac and umbrella, looking at me with the expression of someone who's just been bludgeoned over the head with a lead pipe.'

'What did you talk to them about?' asks Cheryl.

'Couldn't say anything, could I? None of them speak English. I just smiled the whole morning and when my cheeks started to ache I took them to lunch and got Mr Soya drunk.' Holly lights a cigarette. 'He's even better at drinking than me. We ended up communicating like a house on fire. He kept bowing and nodding his head and so I kept bowing and nodding my head.' As he lights his cigarette a second time he suddenly remembers another detail. 'Bloody hell, I think he taught me some Japanese at some point.' He starts to look a bit worried. '*Kekkon shimasho* or something. And he kept putting my hand on top of Spoonhead's.' He shrugs as he exhales a stream of smoke. '*Kekkon shimasho.* I'm probably married by now.'

Further analysis of the morning's activities are interrupted by the voice of Dave which sparks up from the end of the table. 'You haven't answered the question, Holly,' he says antagonistically. 'What were you doing trotting round at Versailles if you're supposed to be a fashion designer?'

I can feel my palms start to sweat. Nobody has talked to Dave for ages now and obviously one of his rucking moods is coming back on. Dave used to be a boxer at school and he seems to lose his rag quite easily. He is always talking to me about his rucks and the times when he has punched people's lights out.

This time Holly has no witty rejoinder. He looks Dave in the eye and says coldly,

'Fashion's not just about pink organza, you know, Dave.

There's schmoozing to be done. Mr Soya was in talks with Koji earlier this week. They're . . . sorting out a . . . money deal for . . .'

His sentence peters out and he turns to Koji for assistance. Everyone else turns to look at Koji who is now back in his seat and looking no more alert than before. He is pulling a string of gruyère further and further out of his mouth like chewing gum. On his bit of paper table cloth he has drawn something that looks like a banana.

Dave bangs his hand down on the table, making everyone jump – apart from Koji who sees the thump as a signal to slump down into his plate of melted cheese and fall asleep. 'For fuck's sake!' Dave hisses, glaring at me and smashing his right fist into his left palm.

Dave might sometimes come across as a bit of a psycho. But he is not only interested in punching people's lights out. Or rather, he is, but he has other more interesting strings to his bow. Greek mythology is his speciality. When we hang out together he tells me how Apollo – the god of poetry and boxing – is his favourite deity. There is a similarity between Dave and Apollo; when Dave is not having rucks he has some very observant things to say about life. My relationship with Lucinda, for instance. When I had been seeing her for two months he announced that she was like a mythical Greek character called Procrustes. Procrustes was a robber posing as an inn keeper. His victims lay in their beds at night and Procrustes came in and hacked their limbs off if they were too big for the bed and stretched them out if they were too small.

Dave learnt all he knows about relationships from his last girlfriend, a French woman he split up from last year. 'Lucinda's trying to make you into something that you're not,' he said. 'And the dangerous thing about Procrustes is that when he's had his way with you and you find yourself back in your own bed, you can't even recognise yourself any more. You're so used to being chopped up or stretched out that you don't want to be with someone who lets you be yourself. Given your way you'd willingly get back into that bloody bed and offer yourself up for some more mincing and mangling. It doesn't matter that your arms and legs are just bloody stumps by now. The bed can be the size of a postage stamp and you still want to get back in there and fit.'

Maybe Dave is just bored now that he doesn't have a girlfriend. I think he was slightly irritated when I beat Zelda on score-board points – just – and she went back to New York leaving Lucinda and me together. Although I do feel slightly shrunken by Lucinda sometimes – especially now that it's just me and her in the picture – I think that Dave just wants me to finish with her because he wants someone to go to raves with. That is why he is putting up with this birthday party for a woman he doesn't even like much. The fact of the matter is that I have kind of promised to go to a rave with him later tonight. I am still wondering how on earth I am going to go about talking Lucinda round to the idea.

When Cheryl gets up to wander off to the other end of the table, Dave comes over and sits down in her chair. He leans back into the Myra Hindley coat and begins by watching Holly entertaining the rest of the table with a story. Then he leans over to me and says under his breath, 'So, when does the real birthday party begin then?'

I glance shiftily at Lucinda and then say quietly, 'I told you, Dave, we're going to have to tread easily on this one.'

'I know about treading easily. I just don't want to get stuck treading on Lucinda's toes at the naff disco I know Cheryl wants to go to.'

'Don't worry,' I say, aware of trying to impress Dave. 'I'll get round her. She'll be fine once she gets there.'

Lucinda kicks me under the table. I think she's going to tell me off for talking to Dave. But she doesn't tell me off. She just kicks me playfully under the table and sucks hard on her baby bottle, grinning. She really seems in good spirits. The baby-bottle wine seems to have made her only too happy to have all manner of juvenile bedlam break out at her birthday table.

'You okay?' Lucinda asks, those gentle brown eyes gazing at me.

I gulp and nod.

Lucinda looks at me again and smiles and I realise why I've lost my heart to her. Again, I see Ruth Worthing running around with me in the autumn leaves and then I see myself running around with Lucinda Davenport in the autumn leaves and my breath comes quicker and I think that this is definitely what love must feel like.

In the background I can hear voices talking about sex.

'French men are all mouth and no trousers if you ask me,' Cheryl is saying. 'The first French bloke I ever pulled put so much energy into buying flowers and taking me for meals in restaurants, by the time I got him into bed he was a right washout.'

'What happened in bed?' Alex quizzes.

'Oh you know,' Cheryl honks, 'a bit of buggery and Bob's your uncle.' Then she adds in an even louder voice, 'Not that Bob *was* your uncle that night, thank you very much. I might be broad-minded but I'm not having buggery. Trouble is, it's bread and butter for every French man I've ever been out with, do you know what I mean?'

'Oh,' says Alex in his disgusted little old lady voice, 'I think we do, don't we, Ann?'

'Alex!' Ann shrieks, and then there is the sound of Bet's archive handbag hitting Alex's head.

Lucinda kicks me under the table again and grins. The right side of my mouth curls up in a sheepish smile as I see that she is looking at me with a lust I have never seen before. While Cheryl tries to goad the table into a sing-song of 'Happy Birthday', Lucinda passes me a screwed up serviette. 'This is the best birthday I've ever had,' it reads. 'I really trust you. Don't ever leave me.' I like the first bit. And the last bit. But the middle bit makes me feel a little queasy.

If Lucinda knew what I'm burning to do tonight she probably wouldn't trust me so much. I'm going to have to introduce the idea to her in a round-the-houses sort of way. Lucinda comes over all trembly at the mere mention of late-night warehouse parties and she has even made it obvious that our relationship will be on the rocks if I ever go to one. There is nothing like talking about a rave for making Lucinda feel really unsettled.

Lucinda seems quite unsettled in general these days. Ever since Zelda finally walked out of her life at the end of the summer, Lucinda has started becoming possessive. We have to do everything together: go to parties together, go shopping together, go to dinner together. If I want to spend a Saturday on my own, there had better be a valid reason. And this kind of behaviour makes me feel unsettled too. I am plagued by anxieties that I might be missing out on something new.

To tell the truth, it is not so much the raves themselves that I am interested in, although Dave insists that rave is the best thing that has happened since Punk and that we will regret it for the rest of our lives if we miss out when the French scene breaks. My main interest is in taking ecstasy. Dave too is looking forward to ecstasy because, being a boxer in his youth, he never experimented with drugs or drink. Now that he is looking for Mick Jagger's 1965 body the moment is ripe. Everyone I know in London has taken ecstasy and they all lose weight and say that it has changed their lives.

I just wish that the mere mention of class A drugs didn't scare the living daylights out of Lucinda. When I told her about a really good rave which was happening in a warehouse in the suburbs on the night of her birthday, her body became tense and she sat down to light a cigarette with trembling hands. She said she didn't know. She'd have to think about it. She was a lawyer and couldn't just spend her weekends at illegal gatherings, could she now? And when she finished the cigarette she stubbed the end hard in an ashtray and put a shaking hand on the leather shoe lace round her neck. She fixed me in the eye and said, in a voice that seemed rather dramatic for a sunny September afternoon, 'If you ever take drugs – ever! – then everything between us is finished.'

I watch Lucinda swigging back her third Cointreau, joshing with Holly and Alex as Cheryl prods Dave with her car keys and asks him what we're going to do now. By this time, Dave looks like he is really desperate to punch someone's lights out. But he keeps his cool and says to Cheryl, poker-faced, 'I know of a really great party.'

'I fancy a good party, Dave, but not one of your weird parties,' she says, taking the bill and fanning the Turkish bath of her face.

Dave looks at me quickly and then turns back to Cheryl. He says, 'Cher mate, you'll love it. And you know, I'd really like it if you were there,' which causes Cheryl to perform a delighted Miss Piggy hair flick. Then, gesturing with the bill towards the still-sleeping Koji she says, 'I'm not taking that weird Japanese bloke with us.' Dave just says, 'Don't worry about him. That weird Japanese bloke's not going to be able to get out of the restaurant let alone to Villeneuve Saint Georges.'

'How will I know how to get there?' Cheryl winges sweetly, enjoying the attention now.

Dave tells her not to worry. He says, 'Just drive to the centre and I'll give you directions from there.'

I whisper, 'What about Lucinda?'

Dave replies, 'Just tell her we're taking her on a magical mystery tour.'

He gives me a wink. I chew on my teat, uneasy.

CHAPTER FOURTEEN

Ham

And now, here we are, on the proverbial road to nowhere. There are no human voices, only the *shish, shish, shish* of personal stereos and the sound of feet crunching along the ground. The day has just started to dawn, but it is not a pretty sight; a mushy grey light jacks open our eyes and fills them with a vinegary sting. No beautiful countryside, just a concrete road and some brown grass and these people with jelly eyes and dinner-plate pupils walking, cut off in their own worlds. It is classic O-level stuff: the bleak landscape surrounding us reflects our bleak, blank minds.

They're not blank enough by half in my opinion. Just when you're concentrating on getting to the end of the road, your mind tips your body off that it's freezing cold. So cold, the sort of aching cold that sends you to a fantasy time zone to be plagued with dreams of lying in hot baths and huddling under duvets.

Only four hours ago we were all dancing princes breathing satin and sugar, inhaling calm and beauty, clothed in rose leaves, housed in a space age Taj Mahal. Now we are cold, druggy ravers leaving a damp, spent warehouse, trudging through some horrible housing estate on the outskirts of Paris, trying to find the métro but seemingly stuck on one of the more tedious rings of hell.

I itch with irritation and the terrible need for music to plug my ears and take me back to last night, but all you can hear is the *shish, shish, shish* of techno coming from other people's Walkmans. Right now, a stick of gum would go down like a gift of gold.

Somehow, we get to the train and I try to remember how you're supposed to sit on train seats and what facial expression people who sit on train seats are supposed to have. Half of me doesn't care and drops into half sleep, then out of nowhere I see cornflakes and cornflake boxes and green and red chickens with curly plumage squawking, 'Are you ready! Are you ready! Are you ready!' in shrill lines that loop round and round and tie themselves up in a big red pussy bow that wraps itself around me and turns me into a big box of chocolates with a Sega picture of Renoir's *Umbrellas* on the front.

Too hectic to doze I open my eyes and look at Dave but he is still connected to his Walkman. When our train pulls up at Saint Lazare station, I follow Dave towards a taxi. When we are inside Dave shouts, 'Les Halles,' to the driver and then takes his headphones off momentarily to mumble in my direction, 'We'll have breakfast in Café Beaubourg.'

When we walk in through the heavy velvet drapes of the Café Beaubourg I feel like I have stepped out on stage and I know that I don't know my lines. I follow Dave over to a table by the window.

Our waiter seems to have the speed and dexterity of a street hustler playing Chase the Lady. 'Where's the dice? Where's the dice? She under this one? She under that one? Roll up, roll up, where'd she go? Now you see her, now it's no,' he seems to say as he swishes the cloth, wipes the tray, pours the coffee, bangs the table, whirls his hips and glides to the kitchen. He stares at Dave every time he comes back with another piece in the puzzle which constitutes our Café Beaubourg brunch.

When he brings us the scrambled eggs – mine are too wet – he eyes Dave's jawy grin as he grinds his teeth wickedly to the *shish, shish, shish* coming from his headphones.

I am glad Dave ordered for us. It would be easier to choose between living in India and living in Africa than it would to choose something from the menu. I look at the runny eggs and they glisten like King Solomon's Mines – yellow and shiny, with hollows and dells and a sprig of parsley for an oasis. One lick of the end of my fork and the shiny spoils of the mines start doing the *cha cha cha* round my blood stream. I put my fork down. The idea of lifting yellow and green stuff into my mouth is absurd. It is too complicated. Eating is like reading Chinese. Dave shovels mechanical forkfuls of bacon and pancake into his mouth, staring mesmerised at his plate as if he sees the afterlife there.

I look out of the window at the tourists with swollen rumps and white training shoes, staring up at the Pompidou Centre. Dregs of magnanimity are still sloshing round inside me. I feel like rushing out and telling the tourists that they should all just sit down with me and Dave so that we can talk some sense to them. A big, buzzing lady in slacks and a straining elasticated waistline looks nice. I want to go and tell her about how taking a pill will soothe away all her cares in her world. She will stop buzzing around and leave her husband and leave her washing up and take to the road and then she will be really happy. Really happy like me. I think I am happy.

I am about to leave the café and go over to her as she rummages through a cow-sized picnic bag by the newspaper kiosk, when Dave puts down the knife and fork, takes off his headphones and looks me in the eye.

He has hardly spoken since we left the rave. His eyes look like chicken eyes, a tiny pinprick of a pupil and a cold, yellow colour to the rest. The acid tab he took a while ago on top of his ecstasy pill seems to have made him even more woozy than I am eight hours after taking my ecstasy tablet. There he goes again. He's started saying 'Foxy minky' all over again. He has been saying it at intervals all night.

'Yeaaahhhhh,' he drawls with a gargoyle smile. 'Foxy minky. Foxy minky. Foxy, foxy, foxy minky,' and his chicken eyes turn into glazed fish eyes. 'That Marie-Christine bird, you know, she was so cool, man, so cool. She was like Artemis with her hunting arrows in her bag. With her retinue of nymphs. Bitchy look in her eyes even when she was on E. Fucking brilliant. Foxy or what? Minky or what? Foxy minky, minky minky minky . . .' His index fingers start techno dancing in the air, now pointing to the ceiling, now diving towards the half sausage and puddle of egg still remaining on his plate.

The swinging door at the entrance to the beautiful garden of drug-altered perception suddenly swings back on to the sordid backyard of paranoia and I start worrying if the world of Lucinda has been well lost, if Dave is all I have placed in her stead. I begin to think of Lucinda's house, just around the corner from the Café Beaubourg. I wonder if she went to sleep after last night. What if she really doesn't want to see me any more? What will I do? Who will cuddle me now?

Dave said that ecstasy would put Lucinda in a brilliant mood. Not that she was in a bad mood when we left the restaurant and Cheryl drove her, Dave and me on a cramped magical mystery tour to the dayglo rave warehouse in Villeneuve Saint Georges. Lucinda was fine at first. Then she realised that this very big musical party was not just a funny disco. It was a rave party and she was in the middle of it. As the space became more crowded she began to act insane. She kept digging her nails into me and hissing, 'Why did you bring me here, why did you fucking bring me here!' as if I'd taken her to the international paint-drying championships rather than the most throbbing, slinky, starry evening that Paris had yet managed to come up with. I had to do something about Lucinda's mood and as they weren't serving vodka at the bar – only miniature bottles of Evian – when Dave appeared from out of the crowd with a handful of tablets the size of big aspirins, I took one.

I slipped it into my mouth and the sky didn't fall on my head. In fact, half an hour later I still felt the same as we wandered round looking at the giggly, smiley people who all seemed to be waiting for something to happen.

Then Lucinda started shouting, 'You've taken some of that stuff, haven't you! You've taken some!' until we thankfully bumped into Cheryl whose face now resembled a big red balloon.

'God, there you are,' she slurred. 'Bit weird here, isn't it? Bit druggy. All right, though. More lively than most of the dos you go to in Paris. You seen Dave? Last time I bumped into him he was milling around talking to lots of dodgy blokes in anoraks.'

Lucinda had begun twitching again and pacing back and forth. 'She all right?' Cheryl asked under her breath when Lucinda was out of earshot. I was about to answer in the extremely negative when Lucinda marched up to us both.

'What's happening?' she barked.

Cheryl was taken aback.

'You all right, Luce?' she asked gently.

'How could I possibly be all right?' she hissed back as though she hated every fibre of Cheryl's being.

A spasm passed through Cheryl's body. I thought she was going to give Lucinda a Miss Piggy chop. But she just put her hands on her hips and said, 'Look, I'd actually just come to ask you if you wanted a lift back to Paris. What are you two going to do then? Hang around here?'

I shrugged weakly.

Cheryl flicked her fringe back dramatically and said, 'Well, I'm buggering off. Dave obviously doesn't fancy me, bloody loser.' She gave Lucinda another dubious look. 'You sure you're all right, Luce? I'd put your head under a tap if I were you.'

I shrugged again and Lucinda resolutely said nothing. Cheryl wiped her forehead (her face was now looking like a sauna) and gave us a knowing smile, like she was glad to be getting out of that place. When she had left, Lucinda said, 'You enjoy ritually humiliating me, I see,' so that by the time Dave arrived I was more than willing to follow his advice. His advice was: 'Go on, go on. Give her an E. They used to use MDMA as a marriage-guidance drug during the war.' So I took the half pill that he was holding out in his hand and when he vanished into the crowd I gave it to her. She snatched it from me, swallowed it immediately and ten minutes later she was walking round like a psychotic sleepwalker, knotty with tension, mumbling nonsense: 'You had this all planned, didn't you! Didn't you! Oh, I can see it all now. Ages of knowledge. The moon is bloody and threatens destruction.'

Luckily, I was now starting to feel pleasantly light headed. My body was feeling buzzy, as if swarms of buzzing ants had rushed to the ends of my arms and legs. The revellers on the dance floor attracted me like the Moonies and the stress of coping with Lucinda floated from my mind. If, at that moment, Dave had started to nail Lucinda up on a cross, sticking a placard saying 'Pain In The Neck' in Latin at the top, I would have been helpless to do anything about it. I would have thought it was nice. I would have thought: Oh well, she can do some meditating while she's up there, she'll be learning to love those nails and anyway, her body looks great stretched out like that.

Lucinda dug her nails in my arm and said, 'Stay here right now or I'll never forgive you. You walk away now and I'll never have you back.' And I wandered over to the twitching dance circle, attracted by a John the Baptist look-alike, with a purple tie-dye top, spiralling manically round with a withered yellow rose in his teeth and a dark-eyed boy in a gold paper crown making rabbit leaps around the floor. This was coming home to somewhere happier than I had ever known. I looked at the beautiful friends who were with me and I touched their cheeks gleaming with a sweat that looked like dew and I knew that Lucinda would understand the sacrifice I had to make. When I occasionally looked back at her I saw a tightly huddled ball shaking on the floor; legs crossed, arms folded, brows giving the evil eye to all the world and his wife.

When the waiter comes up and asks Dave if he would like anything else, Dave raps back in cockney French: '*Chha, Chha, Chha, c'est grave quoi, c'est vraiment grave!*' When the waiter turns on his heels, Dave starts laughing. 'I know what he's on,' he says, jellyfish pulsating, 'he's on really bad acid. I'm telling you, all waiters are on drugs on Sundays. That's why they're all like Josef Mengele!' He says the last two words in an extra loud voice and when the middle-aged couple dressed in *décontracté* Sunday casuals turn round and look, Dave points his techno fingers at them, moves them in piston-like shapes and hisses, '*métro, boulot, dodo*' at 135 beats per minute long after they have turned back to their cups of *crème*.

There seems nothing left of the intelligence that attracted me to Dave in the first place. I need to move. Dave has snapped his headphones back on and I head for the loo. As I go down the steps, all the voices in the café sound muffled, like they are coming from behind a closed door and I am the only one left out in the open. When I arrive in the designer toilets, the number of doors seems to be endless: more King Solomon's Mines. Trick doors and dark marble and sharp corners and infinite mirrors and water trickling from holes and crevices. Nothing to grip on to: a handle here, a door there, now a toilet with Cleopatra's burnished throne inside. But closing the door, the throne becomes a metal box, a pressure cooker, a big encompassing metal grin. My hands flail around searching for the catch to get me out of this cold smirk, away from the surfaces that suddenly feel as hard and unloving as my life now is without Lucinda.

I feel all right once I am safe at home. I take no *beignet aux pommes* and no cup of coffee with me to bed. Just a mug of water and some very loud dentists' drill music. As usual, once I am flat on my back on the fruit crates, tucked inside the brown sheets I feel as right as rain. At moments I feel righter than rain. I feel like I'm sitting on a flying carpet, gently buffeted over a vista of endless green hills. I drift in and out of sleep. My mother phones and by mistake I pick the phone up. She says I sound funny.

'Have you got a cold?' she asks. I haven't got a cold but the continuing effects of the ecstasy come in fits and starts. I felt like a well-oiled sports car just a few hours ago. Now I am beginning to feel like a car that keeps stopping and starting, chugging and jerking. I am Bob's clapped out Cadillac Coupe de Ville.

'Oh, no. I'm fine. I went to a party last night. It was a good party. A really beautiful party.'

'What do you mean, "a really beautiful party"?'

'Ma, can I call you back tomorrow?'

I sleep some more and am wakened by the tip tap sound of Bet coming home. Her shoes – which tip tap quite benevolently – come towards my door. She enters, sits on my bed, expresses interest at the size of my pupils, chats a bit about the row she has just had with Sam, sighs at the thought of teaching the present continuous to a class of fifty-year-olds at 7 a.m. the next morning, picks up the phone that lies by the side of my bed and says she's off clubbing now and she'll see me later. What she means by clubbing is that on Sunday lunch time she takes to her bed. Here, wrapped up in a few black cardigans, she writes a nightclub page for *Paris Parade*. She sits with the phone next to her bed, phones up a few clubs and writes reviews on the strength of what whoever answers the phone – usually the cleaner – tells her. She says it's the only option open to her because Paris nightclubs in the flesh are crap. She asks me about what it's like going to a rave but she can't get any sense out of me so she stands up and says, 'Well, I'm going to call Sam. Can you imagine? Refusing to help me carry it up because he reckoned it was covered with urine. Urine! Pathetic! I kept telling him it was rain water not urine!'

'Rain water. Cool. That's really cool.'

Bet narrows her eyes and tells me that I'm sounding like a hippy. Then she walks into the hall, saying, 'How often is it that you spot an armchair covered in green corduroy in rue de Clignancourt? Bloody never, that's how often. I'm going to call him up.'

She comes knocking on my door a few minutes later saying that Holly's on the phone for me, sounding urgent. I tell her that I can't even get out of bed so, with slightly harsher-sounding heels, she brings the phone in on its hair-entwined extension cord and it is true that he does sound quite urgent.

'George!' his voice shoots down the phone.

'Hey, Holly,' I say lethargically. 'Good night at that rave last night. That base, you know, it was really amazing. It just went through you and like, became part of you. You know? It was—'

'George, stop talking druggy nonsense.' He sounds very brisk now. I'm not sure I'm up to this.

'Look,' he carries on, still brisk and, if my druggy mind's not mistaken, very muffly of voice. 'Look, I can't say much now but basically Lucinda's in the next room holding some sort of machete to her throat and if she doesn't chop her head off with it, she's liable to jump out of a window at any minute.'

'What, are you at Lucinda's flat?'

'Well, I'm not cruising the Seine on a *Bâteau Mouche*.'

I try to register the situation but I don't really want to register the situation. Sounds like Lucinda really is nailed up on some cross and the thing is that I couldn't care less. What I care about is closing my eyes and skiing through the air, charioteered by a thousand snow leopards and a retinue of silky, bendy, fluffy things. But I sigh because I know that under the fluff, something is wrong, something bad is happening. Worse than that, I know that if anyone has the power to compel me to do something in this beautiful lackadaisical state, it is Holly. So I try saying, 'I caaaan't,' long and drawn-out until Holly says:

'Now listen here, young Georgina, I was dragged from my bed at eight o'clock this fine Sunday morning by your' (low voice) 'nutty girlfriend. And if I'm going to be forced to play Florence Nightingale I'm damned if I'm going to let you play some drugged-out Timothy Leary figure. So, love child, get yourself down here before I'm forced to do something really drastic.'

There was a silence and then I made a very long groaning noise.

When Holly arrived at the rue des Archives, Lucinda's first words to him had been: 'She hates me, she hates me, I can't take it any more.' Subsequent events have become immortalised as one of Holly's favourite stories. How he dragged himself away from his vaguely conscious bed partner and turned up at the apartment of the lawyer with the 20,000-franc leather sofa, to be greeted at the door by said lawyer looking like an IRA hit-woman. How she was wearing grubby clothes from the night before, holding a butcher's knife in one hand, a washing line in the other and how her face looked like she was about to do some serious knee capping. And then how she burst out crying, stopping from time to time to blubber the phrase, 'I've broken all the rules, I've broken all the rules and now I have to pay,' in tones of such camp tragedy that Holly blushed with embarrassment.

Lucinda finally sat down. She looked more like a frightened animal than an IRA terrorist – a lugubrious, chubby fieldmouse trapped in a Victorian melodrama. Holly was highly amused. As he always says, the good thing about being a gayboy is that you don't have to go around feeling guilty all the time. You chuck one, you move on to the next. You don't hang round like a lesbian torturing yourself, begging them to remain friends with you, willing yourself to believe that you are a terrible person, and then make ridiculous financial arrangements with them to salve your conscience. For Lucinda wasn't just being metaphorical about her 'paying'. Holly soon gleaned the juicy bit of information that Lucinda had phoned Zelda in New York and actually agreed to pay her palimony because she felt so guilty about chucking her for me. 'Palimony!' he spluttered later. 'A dodgy one-year relationship with Virginia Woolf and she gives her a year's salary!'

Lucinda soon started rocking backwards and forwards on the carpet, wailing, 'She's betrayed me, betrayed me, don't you see? I'm so foolish to have ended things with Zelda, so foolish. I broke the rules and now I have to pay.'

But Holly is not as hard-hearted as people think. He said that the whole situation, especially the sight of Lucinda sitting there rocking back and forth, stabbing a carving knife in and out of the carpet reminded him of his mother the evening she came back from chopping 'whore' into the door of his father's fancy piece. He sat down next to Lucinda, just as he'd sat down next to his mother on that terrible night, and he begged her to give him the knife because he was terrified something terrible would happen to his outfit. And like his mother, Lucinda was so overwhelmed by the sight of Holly's pleading blue eyes that she parted with the weapon — but not the washing line which she continued to twist around her wrists whenever there was a 30 second break between cigarette lighting. Holly put his arm around her shoulders and stopped her rocking.

'George hasn't betrayed you. She loves you.'

'No she doesn't love me.'

'She does love you, she thinks the world of you.'

'No she doesn't. She cares for drugs more than she does for me.'

'Of course she doesn't.'

'Yes she does, she's really superficial.'

'No she's not. She might come across as shallow sometimes, but underneath the surface I know she's a really sensitive person.'

As Holly said these words, a ray of light flooded into Lucinda's eyes. But then the doorbell rang and in I walked, giggling like a village idiot, before stumbling into the coffee table and rolling over on to the floor like Ann does much better in her clown shows.

'Wow,' I said, sitting up and rubbing my head. 'That was pretty weird. Weird and sort of floaty.'

The mad look began rushing back into Lucinda's eyes. She tightened the slack on the washing line around her hands so that it left red welts on her wrists. Then she leapt up like a spring and ran off towards the bathroom, shouting, 'I knew you were shallow. I knew it would be like this. You're shallow, you're so fucking shallow. I want you out of my life. Out of my life!'

When the door slammed shut Holly said, 'Bravo, George.' I flopped down again on the carpet and made another very long groaning noise. The bike ride down the hill from rue de Clignancourt to Lucinda's apartment had felt like a strange out-of-body experience. Like being a spacy kite, disconnected from earth and flapping wildly in the fresh air of the late morning. Now I was just a pile of stagnant kite. There seemed to be no more fresh air left.

'Holly,' I said finally. 'I don't think I can handle this. I know I've been bad. I know I shouldn't have taken ecstasy but I just wanted to try, you know? You know me: try anything – try everything!' My weak laugh petered out into a sigh. 'And now I've made her go all mad.'

'Oh, don't be silly,' he said, sitting down next to me and stroking my hair. 'You didn't cause all that,' he gestured towards the bathroom door. 'That was there long before you. Who knows who put that there.'

'This must be a really pleasant way for you to spend a Sunday morning,' I said, sitting up.

'Oh, I don't really mind. I quite liked all that knife and rope business. I just wish she'd stop the "gone, gone, and never called me mother!" bit.'

'I think it's the E. She insisted I gave her some. Dave said that when you don't relax enough for it to work, it makes you all tense up. Then it turns you into a ham actor.'

'Well, I don't really mind any of it. All of it was more exciting than dragging Koji back to my place last night.'

'Are you shagging him as well then?'

Holly thought about this for a few seconds before saying, 'Not really. To be honest, I can't imagine him shagging anything. You've seen what he's like. It has to be said though, he's taken a bit of a shine to Ann.'

'Big Titti Mama, you mean.'

'Yes. He kept asking when she'd come to dinner with him.'

'Think he might be waiting a bit of a long time.'

Holly lit a cigarette. 'Mmm. That's what I thought.' He started pacing the room and said, 'Thing is, it'd be really good for my career.'

We heard the sound of clattering objects coming from the bathroom. 'He *is* obsessed with breasts,' Holly continued, as if he'd heard nothing. 'We went to Les Ambassadeurs the other night – two star Michelin restaurant, honey-coloured marble, eighteenth-century chandeliers, frighteningly professional waiters leaping about all over the place, three 7,000-franc bottles of wine. It was all looking pretty good – Koji was sitting there harmlessly, talking double Dutch to his fork – until the waiters came over with our *entrée: Saumon fumé norvégien à la crème aigre*, painstakingly prepared on two splendid silver platters and covered with two domed silver lids.

'So the waiters are hovering at the table – one on his side and one on mine – for that vital synchronised moment when the silver mounds will be lifted off in one dramatic, simultaneous, abracadabra moment. Only when the moment of lift-off finally comes, Koji goes mental. He leaps up from his seat, shrieking like he's giving birth, and he makes a grab for the silver lids, shouting, "Big titti! Big titti!" And he's trying to wrestle with the waiters to get them to put the silver tits back on the bloody plates! How embarrassing was that! I can't even begin to tell you. I wonder what he's on sometimes.' He stubbed his cigarette out.

'Oh well,' he brightened. 'It's all a means to an end, no?'

He yawned. 'I'm getting out of here. I've done enough being grown-up for one day. I can feel the cowardly lion coming back. Say goodbye to Lucinda from me. I don't think I can bear another round with slasher.'

I went with him to the door. After we did the *bise* goodbye he said, 'The machete, by the way, is in the top drawer of Lucinda's underwear chest. If your girlfriend's mind is anything like the state of her lingerie then it's probably just as well that you've been chucked.'

I closed the door, sat on the floor again and stared at the matt black bookshelves. When ten minutes later she still hadn't emerged, I went and knocked on the bathroom door.

'Lucinda, please can we talk. Please? Talk to me?'

There was silence and then her voice: 'Why should I talk to you? You abandoned me, you left me all alone.'

Pause.

'I'm sorry about that. I, I don't know. I couldn't stop dancing.'

'You took drugs! You promised me. You promised me to be truthful, truthful always. You broke my trust.'

I sighed. 'I'm sorry. I'm sorry, I'm sorry, I'm sorry. I made a mistake, I didn't know how upset you'd be. I hate the thought that I've hurt you. I love you.'

More silence, then: 'Where's Holly?'

'He's gone home. He said to say goodbye.'

More silence, followed by more ham: 'Holly only likes me for my money.'

When I'd thought about that one I concluded that, yes, Holly probably did quite like the fact that Lucinda had a lot of money. But what was I supposed to say? Lucinda's big thing has always been about telling the truth and now that I was experiencing the after-effects of what Dave, in the Café Beaubourg, termed the truth serum drug, I figured that now was a really good moment for the truth.

'Well, Holly said the other day that it was a good thing you were rich or we probably wouldn't have been nearly as interested in you.' Then I hastily added, 'But I would have been interested in you because you hardly ever meet any lesbians in Le Swing.'

The sound of a shattering mouthwash glass came from the bathroom. Then the sound of more objects — toothbrushes, bath toys, soap — being hurled at the mirror. I sighed and went to sit on the black settee. When the bathroom door finally opened, Lucinda walked into the sitting room, sat herself down cross-legged on the floor and lit a cigarette. She looked calm. Her hands weren't even shaking. She was still wearing her rave clothes but the washing line was no longer round her wrists.

She looked at me, or rather, she looked through me. After an age of silence she said blankly, 'You want something to eat? There's chicken in the fridge.'

CHAPTER FIFTEEN

Elvis

Sometimes I think of my sleeping-bag dream as I lie here holding the brown sheet in a line over my mouth and below my nose. Only now I'm not on Dartmoor rolling around in a sleeping bag with my English teacher. Now I feel like I've been cut loose from the earth; I'm all alone, bobbing around in space in a cotton brown cocoon.

It's still warm. It's like being in warm water. Like a warm swimming pool. I'm just managing to keep my head above the water. I know it would be easy to put the sheet over my head and go under the water, drown. Turn off. I know there is some sort of ledge lying out here in the blackness of the deep end but I'm not sure exactly where it is. Maybe the deep end will suck me down anyway. But that seems impossible. Where would the energy come from?

Sometimes, the brightest spark of inspiration that comes to me all day is the decision to go to the toilet. But usually I rethink. I can't be bothered to stand up, then I can't be bothered to turn over, then I think I can't be bothered to breathe. Suicide is a joke. Something that well people have the energy to do. It's too much like maths to work out how to do suicide. Then Lucinda's cellulite wobbling down the stairs of her mezzanine bed in the morning fills my eyes, and my ears are filled with the sound of her posh orgasms ('Oh bloody hell, oh Christ almighty, God, God, for God's sake'), and I start to cry.

I hide under my brown sheets and I wonder if my tears wetting them will make them smell any different. Smell is all I am aware of. Smell and self-pity. With all that has eked into my sheets in the past month I bet there is more substance in them than there is in me. It seems a shame they can't get up and walk about, but I don't want them to leave, they're all I have.

I've done it all – gaze hungrily at my crying face in the mirror, wake in the morning feeling queasy and then feel the queasiness explode with the clear, sharp splash of a stone hitting the water after a terrible black trip down a well shaft. The clear, sharp splash is remembering, when the full force of pain rises up in all its bluntness and I know I have a day of pain in front of me. I have done it all – been to the opera, taken ecstasy, had more sex than most people of my age I know, fallen in love, and now I am experiencing the most intense thing of all – rejection.

Lucinda left me after the rave saga although we stayed together for several more weeks. We never spoke any more about what had happened that night. We never spoke about anything much after that. And the more aloof she was, the more I yearned to be close to her. Soon afterwards she started spending her weekends in London. Something about getting back in contact with old friends. When she returned from her London trips she would kiss me on the cheeks instead of the lips and she would spend weekday evenings pacing the room saying, 'What shall we do now?' or 'I feel so sad and I don't know why,' when she knew very well why. I knew the end of the road had come when she didn't want to argue with me any more. Then she didn't want to have sex. Whenever I rolled closer to her in the bed she insisted that she had to go Christmas shopping the next morning for the Wing Commander so she had to go to sleep now. She didn't even go on about me leaving too much orange flesh in the orange juicer any more, although one Sunday evening she sneered loudly that 'the smell of Roquefort makes me feel sick,' as I sat on the Doctor Love sofa munching a Roquefort sandwich. By this time, I'd even started calling the leather settee a sofa in a final desperate attempt to win her back.

It is dark everywhere. The blinds are shut and different shades of white, black and grey filter through, depending on the time of day. Maybe it would be easier to suffer in a more salubrious place – like the Marais. Thoughts of masturbating flash through my head but one of the worst things about being chucked against your will is that you can't even think of anybody to wank about. Your thoughts are consumed by your ex and it's fatal to masturbate to a still-desired ex. You always cry afterwards.

Even when I forget that and I turn on to my stomach and pull my T-shirt up, I can't be bothered to wank any more. I lie still, my face in the pillow, and all the towers in the world crumble down over my head. The brown sheets get another drenching.

I can't get over the fact that I've been rejected. Nobody has rejected me before. Even Dawn was more of an experiment and chucking at her hands was a temporary setback. The confidence and cool ploy was a waste of time and even my fabulous technique – my brilliant, Holly-honed, much-praised, fabulous technique – has come to naught. I was so sure as well. So sure that if you knew the three Rs properly, if you could rim, root and roger with skill and derring-do, then that was it. Nobody would ever be able to bring themselves to leave you.

'As you say, some of them do seem to be on a thin line between glittering heroics and over-the-top pyrotechnics.' Radio 4 is the other thing I have. It is irritating and comforting and most of the presenters trill away with posh voices like Lucinda's. What's wrong with me? If I'd been a lawyer with a posh accent, I'd have been successful. I could have had a black leather sofa and had lemons in my drinks and cooked chicken in the fridge and Lucinda would never have chucked me. Stupid brown sheets. I hate everything that is mine. The Conran shop settee that she gave me looms in the corner of my bedroom. I am afraid of it. It says too many things. It started out with Lucinda pressed into every last atom of it. Now, day by day it dries out.

When Holly finally comes round to see me, I must be looking pretty rough. For two weeks now, to punish myself, I have been wearing an off-white T-shirt and I haven't washed my hair so the curls have all fused together like a big tangled Rasta mat. Round the wooden slats of my bed lie torn métro tickets, shredded cigarettes and tobacco flakes. Sometimes I think that maybe I'm turning into Pins.

He slumps down on the bed as though everything is shipshape. He gives me a *bise* that smells of whisky. It is midday and he says he has just escaped from the flat of a German diplomat. At six in the morning the German diplomat handcuffed Holly to the bed and came back three hours later when Holly was almost hysterical with outrage and excitement, and on the verge of wetting himself.

Holly is still on his post-promiscuity high. 'Yes, I suppose it was all a bit sordid-making really,' he grins. 'Still, nothing that a good white wash won't put right.'

He rubs the red marks around his wrists and says that the experience with the diplomat was worth it anyway because his apartment was so impressive – a 300 square metre loft in République furnished only with one bed and one clothes rail (half pinstripe suits, half leather). 'I've always fancied a bedroom that looks like a Joseph Beuys exhibition,' he announces, spreading himself out on my bed and then recoiling slightly as he feels crumbs all over the mattress.

'Bloody hell, it's like a bread bin in here,' he says.

I wrap the brown sheets around me closer, worried about

my smell of cheese, stale sweat and something that's like acrid daffodils. Even more worried that it might escape. It is mine. I have been nurturing it for the past two weeks; I have scarcely left my bed, let alone my bedroom. The sweet and sour smells reassure me that I exist; the odour is the pique of my body refusing to be forgotten.

'You're like Elvis,' he says. 'Lying in bed surrounded by joint butts and cheeseburger wrappers.' He picks up a camera from the mess on the floor and asks, 'Is this your chucking present?'

I tell him that it is. I tell him about my penultimate trip to Lucinda's apartment on 20 December — almost exactly a year after our first meeting. Lucinda hadn't kissed me on the lips for days and when we went to the Privilège she kept telling me that women were looking at me and why didn't I get off with them. It was true that I was starting to get to know a few of the faces there — even dare to speak to some of them — but getting off with anyone else was the last thing I wanted to do. I just wanted to pretend that Lucinda's birthday night had never happened and go back to the days before, which had been idyllic in my recollection. I kept telling her how different I was now that I'd got raving and ecstasy out of my system but she kept making eye contact with the barmaid and then she turned round and said coldly, 'I have to be honest, George, I don't care if you've changed or not.' We walked back to her apartment in silence. When we got in she started to do some dusting and then about fifteen minutes later she came to sit next to me on the settee. She said almost cheerfully, 'George, I think it's over, don't you? I think that we're too different to be together. We want different things. We can try to be friends, can't we?' She smiled and her eyes gleamed.

My mouth went dry and she carried on to say she thought we should exchange Christmas presents anyway. I thought this must be normal behaviour when you got chucked so I went off for a big panic-attack shop in the Mouton à Cinq Pattes discount clothes store along rue de Sèvres. With a sweating top lip and moist palms I handed over 190 francs for a figure-hugging top from a discontinued line of Junior Gaultier that I really wanted myself.

On chucking presents day, I made a final trip to her flat. Lucinda looked surprised when she took the top out of its wrapper but immediately slapped on a smile. As soon as she put it over her head and was pulling it over her breasts I realised that it was going to make her look fat and I felt sorry. She pulled it down and turned to look in the mirror. She grinned and said, 'Great!' Then she peeled it off, left it on the floor and slipped back into one of her baggy silk jerseys that she bought in bulk when she worked in New York.

She handed me a wrapped box. I opened it and found a camera inside. The thought of its cost flashed through my head. About £100 pounds. For a second I felt angry. She knew I wanted a computer. 'Oh, thank you,' I said slowly, hoping she'd realise that I hated it. Maybe that was customary maximum value for chucking presents – £100. But then the respite of bitter thoughts passed and I sank into a horrible hole again. Lucinda took the camera from me and began showing me how the buttons and switches worked. She handed it back to me and I slipped further down on her leather settee. There was an uncomfortable silence, so she came over playfully, took the camera and said, 'Time for a Christmas photo'. I smiled weakly for the photograph, although she might just as well have kicked me in the face with the Doc Martens she'd recently bought on a trip to London – even though she'd once expressed interest in buying a fake pair from the shoe cash and carry off the rue de Clignancourt.

Holly seems delighted with the camera. He picks it up, looks through the viewfinder and turns to point it at me.

'Bloody hell, the only chucking presents I get are sweaty pairs of underpants.' He clicks as he says, 'Looking good, George. I think you've lost some weight, you know. God, that's what I need. Being chucked to make me look gorgeous. Course, I'd make sure I suffered in a half decent interior décor.'

He clicks some more as I roll a joint. I imagine that I will look bewildered if I ever get round to developing the film. I'm not an Elvis in the true sense of the word. All I ever eat every day is one cheeseburger — nothing else — and on the rare occasions when I cry into the mirror, gorging on my tears, I notice that my bone structure is looking fantastic.

'I suppose at least you're being a bit different,' he says as he squints through the viewfinder, training the camera round the dishevelled room. 'Most lesbian taste is stripped pine and dried flowers. Or, like your good lawyer friend, it's the stern headmistress study look, done out in leather and chrome.'

I feel a ball of heat explode in me when he refers to Lucinda. I try to make it go away by changing the subject. 'So, what's gayboy interior décor like?'

'A funny business,' he says. 'They either have homes that look like baroque knocking shops or they have very good taste.'

Holly puts the camera down and smokes some of the joint. He starts to tell me about his fabulous studio on the Place des Vosges. It is true that the Places des Vosges is the most beautiful square in the whole of Paris. Any old banker can live in the *seizième arrondissement* but this part of the Marais was the artistic and literary centre of seventeenth-century Parisian life; here it was that Madame de Sévigné used to stomp around throwing fantastic *soirées* for any aristocrat with a good line in brilliant conversation.

The Place des Vosges itself is an airy cloister of pink *Ancien Régime* apartments. On all sides of the harmonious façade there is an arcaded gallery which houses prestigious boutiques selling art and antiques and Japanese clothes. Behind this po-faced stage, on the other side – the court side – each pavilion has its own architectural personality, its own mysteries and secret uses. Residing in the Place des Vosges can make you feel proud to live in Paris.

Holly tells me that he usually has to spend the whole day hanging around in the studio because Koji is very concerned that he should be there to sign for any packages that might arrive. After two months of working for Koji and the receipt of several thick wads bound in purple taffeta, Holly has still not started work on any clothes. I can see that this worries him slightly but he says he can't do anything about it because he is still waiting for fabrics to be delivered. 'Funny really,' Holly says, rummaging round in his bag. 'The only time Koji makes any sense is when it comes to signing for post. "You be here, all time. Post important,"' Holly says, mimicking Koji's trance-like English. 'He knows we can't make any money 'til the frocks are done and dusted. He's not as dumb as he looks.'

I am still waiting for some word of support from Holly, something to make me feel better about my terrible post-Lucinda life. Bet and Ann feed me practical advice hourly. All Holly can do is be funny. Be funny and talk about Koji. He avoids talking about emotion, as though any real emotion would set him off on a flood of tears that would never stop. I want to make him say something. I put the joint down and lunge to the foot of the bed to grab the camera out of his hands. It is the most energetic thing I've done in days. But lifting the camera to my eye is the most I can do because when it is there another pain ball goes off inside me. It even feels painful to breathe.

'Holly, Holly. What am I going to do? I don't want to feel this bad.'

My eyes start to water and Holly says, in the same tone as when I told him someone had stolen my bicycle saddle, 'Poor

George.' He takes off his blue bandanna and passes it to me. I blow my nose.

He is silent for a while, then he speaks more gently. 'You know the best thing,' he says. 'The best thing is to sit it out in bed a bit longer, and then when you start feeling really pissed off with the old bat, that's when we put the master plan into action. We'll go and sit in that dodgy bar opposite her apartment with a huge siphon aimed up at her window, and as soon as we see her stick her yuppie head out in the morning, we press the button and splurge her with a dozen bin loads of dry scrambled egg.'

Holly finishes rustling his bag and pulls out a package wrapped in pink tissue paper.

'For you,' he says. 'Better than a chucking present.'

I feel tears well up because I feel so touched. But when I open the package, I find a cream satin blouse inside. Cream satin with green flowers sewn on the front. I feel like I felt when my mother — usually a source of first-class presents — gave me a frilly Laura Ashley dress for my eleventh birthday. The tears start rolling down my cheeks because I think that Holly is making a sick joke.

'Holly! I don't want a stupid satin blouse!'

Holly looks incensed. 'What do you mean, "a stupid satin blouse"?' He snatches the silky garment back in a huff. 'That blouse, thank you very much, is a replica of Loulou de la Falaise's taupe lamé kimono with red and green appliquéd opium poppies — as worn during Saint Laurent's historic 1978 Opium perfume launch on a Chinese junk moored next to the Brooklyn Bridge!'

'I don't care what it is!' I am bawling my head off by now. 'Why didn't you get me some army boots or some mud guards? You think I'm just some girl! You're supposed to know me! You're supposed to be my friend!'

I search into the blue bandanna, looking for somewhere dry to blow into but there isn't anywhere. I must look a pitiful sight because Holly abandons his high horse and starts looking a bit more sheepish.

'Well ... well, you could make it into a headscarf concept,' he suggests. 'Sort of a pirate look — kind of feisty. Very Radcliffe Hall. Androgyny ... Androgyny! Yves likes a bit of androgyny,' and he hastily starts bandaging my head with the horrible kimono thing. When he has finished, he makes a big point of standing back and clasping his hands together as if I look really fantastic.

'My god! You're right you know, George, it looks much better on you like that — Marlene Deitrich the pirate. Now I come to think about it, I know a couple of dykey girls in Koji's group who wouldn't say no to one of these.'

Then Holly confesses his real reason for making me the present.

'Thing is, George,' he says, still twisting at the head-dress, 'I've got a favour to ask you. It's just that Koji ... fancies a bit of a party ...'

'So?'

'At rue de Clignancourt.'

'Holly!'

'Koji suggested an Opium party tribute ...'

I push Holly away from my head.

'Holly! What do you mean? A party here — for Koji! Bet would go mad. What's wrong with Place des Vosges?'

'Well, that's the problem unfortunately. It's strictly forbidden to have parties there. It would have been fine but Koji has, well, alienated the concierge by some ... anti-social behaviour. Can't think what it could have been.'

Something is dawning on me. 'Does he want to have his party here because he wants to get his hands on Ann's breasts?'

'Well,' Holly is squirming now, 'he'd probably quite like to see her ...'

'Holly! I'm not being a pimp. Anyway, Bet would go mad and ...'

Suddenly, Holly sees a way in. 'Bet would love it!' he says, slowly and emphatically. 'Just think of the glamour: ultra splendour in Paris's most louche *quartier*. And, *entre nous*, I can't help but think that "opium" as a theme – think opulence, think white orchids, think Diana Vreeland in a pagoda jacket sitting on a pile of empty Champagne bottles snorting coke – I can't help but think that kind of theme is more attractive than your current "squat" theme – think crumbs, think dust weevils, think the eternal, tell-tale smell of tinned tomatoes cooked with onions in a bent frying pan. Plus – and this is a big plus – Koji is willing to pay for Champagne on tap all night.'

The idea does seem quite interesting. But then I remember that I am suffering.

'No, Holly.'

'George! What happened to your spirit of adventure?'

'No, Holly.'

'I could get Koji to bring some of his dykey friends . . .'

Now I sit up a bit. Holly could be lying, as he usually is when it comes to lesbians. But he might be telling the truth. I tell him I have to think about it and hand him back his soggy bandanna which he tries not to look too disgusted about.

When Holly has gone, I feel restless. I get out of bed and go and stand in front of the half piece of mirror that you can only see half your body in which I found in a skip. In spite of my anxious face, Holly's kimono bandanna concept is actually looking quite good. Also, I can't help noticing that, as Holly said, I have indeed lost weight. I pull up my off-white T-shirt and look at my stomach. It looks small and unfamiliar. A wave of sad pleasure floats through me. Elvis ate cheeseburgers in his bed and went to the toilet and died. I eat cheeseburgers and emerge as an anxious-looking swan with a small tummy. I feel some more energy creep back into me.

I go back to bed but I feel restless again. I want to go back to the mirror. When I get out of bed and go to the big, cracked shard I think that my hair looks a mess and my off-white T-shirt makes me look ugly. I open the cupboard and rake through the pile of cotton garments which lie scattered on three flowery wallpaper-covered planks and which have turned freezing cold in the January chill of the room. I pull a pair of chilly white jeans from the cupboard and step into them. They feel loose around the waistband and I can pull the belt to the fourth hole.

I am pleased. I think I look like a rent boy. I switch off Radio 4, put on 'It's a Sin' by the Pet Shop Boys and start doing my cool trunking dance in front of the mirror. '*It's a, it's a, it's a* . . .' I sing, trunking to the left. My face begins to flush and my body feels warmer. Maybe a party would be a good idea. I'm not bad-looking, I can dance pretty well. If you have a party in your house everyone is obliged to get off with you. Maybe I'll end the night with a beautiful girlfriend and one day we'll walk into a bar somewhere and Lucinda will be there and she'll want to speak to me and I'll refuse to speak to her, '*. . . it's a sin*'.

The song finishes. I don't like the next one. I look at the pile of clothes on the floor. It feels too quiet in my room.

The next morning when I wake up I only cry for a few minutes. A new breeze seems to be blowing through me. Still sluggish and grey, but with a glint of blue. For a while, I consider getting out of bed. When I do, a few hours later, I go to the bathroom and run a bath. I lower myself into the hot water and sit, hunched up because the bath is a half-length French tub standing on four lion-paw china feet. Through the hole in the window there is a corner of cold blue sky and a gung-ho man driving a chariot. Even in Barbès there is no stinting on naked statues. The man has a six pack chest and the chariot that he is driving is crossing the top of the back entrance of the Banque Nationale de Paris which stands on the rue de Clignancourt. He raises a powerful arm to lash his horses.

Wearily, I pick up the soap whose brittle skeleton is etched with dirt-filled lines. Tears roll down over my breasts and plop into the water. It seems vaguely ridiculous to be crying into water. You can't see the fruits of your labours like you can when you do it into sheets. The salt water disappears under the suds and simply becomes part of more water. I think of the bit in *Alice in Wonderland* when Alice's tears are so big that all her animal friends go swimming in the huge pool and then have to run a race afterwards to keep themselves warm. Lucinda's favourite book was *Alice in Wonderland*. But I shouldn't have thought of that because now the tears are really starting to fall.

When I manage to stop, I pick up an orange plastic Bic razor lying by the edge of the bath. I lift one leg out of the water and rest it on the side. I soap it and shave it slowly in long, straight strokes. I have just enough energy left to do the other leg. When I have finished I feel a sense of achievement.

Sophie called today. I only let her talk for a little while about the Greek God who apparently is still talking about worms crawling out of walls. Only now there is a new development. He keeps making strange connections and talking about weird coincidences. ('Your shoes are size 42? At 4.20 yesterday I realised that my apartment is 15 kilometres from the nineteenth *arrondissement*. And if you add 1 to 9, you get 10. And 10 was the age when my mother told me to keep it unpredictable by being unpredictable: to be unpredictable by doing too much. And too many.') And then he does a strange, impish grin.

Normally I would have told Sophie that it all sounded fine and maybe he was just having a stressful time at work. But today I couldn't be bothered. These days I can't bring myself to even think about the worries of anyone else. The only thing that exists is Lucinda, or the lack of her. Just as I feel the need to keep jumping out of bed to look in the mirror to make sure I'm still here, I need to talk about Lucinda to make her live again.

✻   ✻   ✻

I cut Sophie off and told her that I'd written an angry letter to Lucinda. Sophie said that that was a really bad idea. I am not sure about this advice because the letter is quite good. In it, I have used the opening line of a Stevie Smith poem which goes, 'I have no respect for you'. Then I have paraphrased the last lines, telling Lucinda that she has 'a light mind and a coward's soul'.

Sophie seems to think that the best thing is to play games and just not contact Lucinda. The history of Sophie's love life hardly qualifies her to tell me what to do now, but at least we were talking about Lucinda at last.

Sophie continued that I must certainly not give Lucinda the pleasure of letting her know how miserable I was. I said, 'What's the point of playing games now that it's over?' She said, 'You just have to.' Then I thought about the rest of the letter. I thought about how it would have sounded to me if somebody had written saying, 'I woke up this morning at 6 a.m. and tried to get back to sleep because I couldn't bear to face the day without you. Then I started to cry inconsolably for an hour, then I got up.' It would have made me feel guilty, and then I'd think that there must be something quite cool about me if I could devastate somebody like that.

Tuesday, 19 January 1993

Holly's front door slammed behind me. I walked like all my bones were made of hot metal. I had burning metal instead of blood and the gasping breath of a cross-country runner. I scudded along like I could plough through a brick wall, sustained only by the thought of you. Of kicking you. Kicking you in the stomach, hitting you in the face, kicking you and kicking you and kicking you. I'll break into your house and rip up your books, tear up each individual page and not leave before I've filled your curtain railings with fresh fish which will decompose and fill your house with nauseous smells and it will take you weeks to work out where it's coming from.

She sounded sleepy when she picked up the phone. When she heard my voice she sounded tetchy. I panted, 'I want to know why you lied to me.'

Lucinda said, 'I don't intend to discuss this now. It's two in the morning and I feel ill.'

I said, 'So do I.' It seemed quite a dramatic thing to have said but I couldn't stop now. 'Holly's just told me about your new girlfriend!' I'd always suspected this but now the truth seemed to be out. I waited for a reaction. 'Cheryl told him you've got a girlfriend!'

'I don't intend to talk about any gossip you may have heard from Holly.'

'I feel rejected. I've never been rejected before.'

'You'll get over it. It's nothing to do with you. There's nothing wrong with you.'

'I never want to sleep with anyone else again.'

She laughed gently and said, 'Of course you will.'

'Don't you miss me in bed?'

Now she was angry. 'I made this choice for a reason. I was very unhappy when we were together.'

'Do you still love me?'

'Of course I still love you.'

I told her too much. I told her I ached to phone her sometimes. But she switched to a different tack. She said it was foolish to remain silent; that we got on in so many ways and that now we should be friends. This might be my first heart break, she said, but take it from her, it was more painful to remain isolated and stew in one's own pride.

I wanted her to say 'I miss you'. 'I want to cuddle you again'. 'I don't know if I made the right decision.'

She didn't say any of it so I asked her if she'd thought of me over Christmas. She said 'sometimes', which I reckon means 'rarely'. All she said was that she thought of me at Gatwick airport when she saw an ad for 'George's Steak Pies'.

When she heard my stunned silence at the other end of the phone she seemed glad because it gave her a chance to round up the conversation. She said, 'Look, one day I'm sure we'll be really great friends. You must understand that I care for you very deeply.'

I just hung on to those words, and when I put the phone down I felt some sort of relief. I was eight years old again, I'd had a good day in the trees and I went to sleep happier than I had been in months. Safe sleep, like child's sleep.

The next day I woke with whiplash.

Bet came and sat by my bed. She drew up a mental chart for me.

'You've got to think of it like this,' she said. 'Nothing worse could happen to you now. A) Lucinda lied about her feelings during the last weeks of your relationship. B) She chucked you. C) She chucked you for another woman.'

She held my hand and said that I'd been through the worst, that the only possible factor to top this would be if we ever slept together again. According to Bet, that leaves you feeling like you want to die the next morning.

CHAPTER SIXTEEN

Tintin

The Basilica of Sacré Coeur looks like a big white-washed wedding cake. It stands on Montmartre's highest hill and looks down serenely over the whole of Paris. I like to go to the Sacré Coeur at dawn, after I've been clubbing, before the tourists arrive. I'm surprised more people haven't cottoned on. You're just coming down from the night before, the new day's still shaky on its legs and you want to hang out just a little bit longer before you go home and tuck yourself up in bed. I like to walk in through the doors and see Jesus splattered on the domed ceiling, a huge gold and white painting of him, arms outstretched like he's giving you a big hug or saying, 'Come in. What'll it be today – nice bit of haddock? Piece of skate fresh in from Hull this morning?' His spotless robes are as comforting as fryers overalls and the frankincense of Sacré Coeur is as calming as salt and vinegar forcing its way through warm bundles of greasy paper.

This morning I'm not here on my way back from a club; I'm here because I couldn't sleep last night. I couldn't sleep because after a two-month-long period of not seeing Lucinda, I agreed to go to rue des Archives following a series of calls from her telling me that she really wanted to be friends now. The meeting was terrible and when I left her apartment and came back to rue de Clignancourt I was so worked up that I started banging my head against my bedroom wall until Ann knocked at the door and asked me if I was all right. I don't know if her flushed face was to do with shock at my actions or shock at being interrupted in the middle of another corset clamp session with Jean-Christophe.

When she came in I was hissing and screaming like a mad firework: 'Everyone's crap; you seeing Jean-Christophe's crap, Holly's crap for shagging loads of people all the time and looking surprised when I say I'm lonely and Bet's crap for pretending to be at constant loggerheads with Sam when we all know she'll probably marry him and she couldn't hack being alone for two seconds.' I couldn't seem to help what flew out of my mouth and I tried to come down to earth by watching the shadow of Jean-Christophe's legs shifting nervously behind my bedroom door.

Things feel different here in Sacré Coeur, the toy town of suffering. The Catholics are good at fast despair, the kind of beautiful sadness you feel when you see a good episode of *Little House On The Prairie*. The pestilence and the torture and the grief and the fear that loom from every statue and every stained-glass window are converted into boulevard Barbès candy floss by the face of the kindly fryer above.

Business is slow at this hour. There is just one girl of eighteen or so who sits and rocks her body on the other side of the aisle. Her miserable movements can only mean one thing. I wonder how many young girls are sitting at this moment in churches all over the world praying like mad with a picture of a writhing new-born on one side of their head and a picture of a big, mocking penis on the other. And the nagging questions: How long was he inside? Did he come a bit inside? How could I have been so careless? Please God, please God, please God. Until sex replay footage takes over the mind and the rocking prayer motion accelerates.

*　　*　　*

I don't think it is prayer that brings me here. I don't think I'm here to ask for salvation. I feel at home and maybe part of that has something to do with the kindly fryer. I look at his calm face on the domed ceiling and then I see Lucinda's face.

Dave told me that the first time you fall in love and are chucked 'you're fucked for two years'. The idea of Lucinda's face popping up out of nowhere for another two years is frightening, but the truth is that my sadness ebbs and flows. These days I try not to spend the whole of the day in bed and I've been crying less. Last week, when Bet asked me how I felt, I told her that I felt angry. Bet said this was a good sign and advised me to write a list of all Lucinda's bad points so that I wouldn't be tempted to get nostalgic about the relationship. My list begins:

1.   *She blamed me for not being able to give up smoking.*
2.   *Sometimes, when I listened to her talking to her friends on the phone in her Barbara Woodhouse accent I thought, 'I'm embarrassed to be associated as the lover of this woman.'*
3.   *She withheld sex from me as a weapon. Once when we went to Normandy with the Gang she refused to have sex in the train toilet with me. Like Holly says, one of the bonuses of going out with a lawyer, apart from their high wage packet, is their capacity for being dirty in bed.*
4.   *She first told me she loved me while we were having sex. How shallow is that?*

But last night I didn't feel quite so strong. Or at least, I did to begin with. For the last couple of months I have been thinking of a pale face with floppy hair and a ragamuffin smile and now I find that I've been mourning over somebody quite different. I was almost happy when I arrived at Lucinda's apartment and saw that her face was looking fat and she had a terrible new short haircut. She was tanned though, which unfortunately made up for the other disasters — like her outfit which looked like she'd recently done a sweep in the rue Saint Bon branch of Marks and Spencers.

As I walked after her into her apartment — glancing quickly at the section of carpet where, a while back, I'd seen her knotting washing line round her wrists — I forced myself to concentrate on the spare tyre on the back of her neck (newly revealed by her short crop), so that I wouldn't see anything beautiful about her. When we got to the Doctor Love sitting room there were lots of other different things to concentrate on. The room had changed completely. Lucinda had said on the phone that she was feeling 'content' and the stripped-pine bottle rack on the wall, the floral scatter cushions on the floor, the bowls of pot-pourri and the Tintin bric-à-brac nestling in every corner certainly screamed of sluggish contentment. The Doctor Love settee was still there, but its pervy sex vibes were diminished in a room so gripped by a morass of soft furnishings.

Trying to keep my tone casual, I said, 'What's with Tintin then?'

A hint of irritation clouded Lucinda's face as she replied that Agnes had bought them for her birthday. Agnes then was it? It must be love if she'd managed to change Lucinda's tastes so radically in such a short space of time. Only nine months ago Lucinda had been begging me to take her to Clignancourt flea market to buy her second-hand 501s and leather shoe laces to tie around her neck. Now she seemed delighted to have Snowy and Captain Haddock mobiles dangling from her ceiling. I felt embarrassed for her. Then it struck me that my whole back of the bus theory was a lot of nonsense. My back of the bus, live-as-near-to-the-edge-as-you-can philosophy seemed to have driven Lucinda away from me completely. What a come-uppance. My bohemian ways were obviously so frightening that they had driven Lucinda into the arms of a woman whose world of Tintin egg cups and Captain Haddock mobiles seemed a much more reliable and comforting prospect than I could ever be.

We went to eat Chinese and I ordered sweet and sour pork for old times' sake. When the plate of pork fritters covered with a glutinous, bright orange sauce and garnished with pineapple chunks arrived, I made a great show of putting a huge piece in my mouth to demonstrate that I really didn't care any more. It was blistering hot but I thought I'd look really stupid spitting out bright orange pork in a restaurant and Lucinda would think how repulsive I was and what a good thing it was she'd finished with me. Besides, I couldn't afford to dirty my clothes. I had just spent three-quarters of my month's earnings on a Helmut Lang jacket and a pair of men's Helmut Lang trousers from the Mouton à Cinq Pattes in Saint Michel. Holly said it was a good investment because Lang will soon be famous (although already after a week the trousers were smeared with bike-oil stains around the right ankle). I thought that if I wore designer suits like Lucinda I'd be her sort of person and she'd want me again. But she didn't seem to have noticed.

I gulped back lots of water, swallowed the burning pork ball and ate the rest of the meal with a burnt tongue and a raw roof. She chattered away, jovial and distant, like she'd known me twenty years ago. She constructed crispy duck pancakes, sipped red wine and talked about the holiday to Italy that she and Agnes had just returned from. She talked about the pros and cons of the ticket buying system at Naples train station, detailing minutely what the 'greasy little man' behind the counter had told them and how they'd had to enlist the help of a 'funny little woman' to point out to the man behind the counter that they did, in fact, have first-class tickets and that they'd paid jolly good money to have them. When she finally arrived at the punch line ('and after all that we got to the platform and discovered that the train had left five minutes early!') she stopped and there was a silence. As

I was thinking how boring she'd become she suddenly said, 'I've given up smoking. You must think I'm really boring now. But I suppose, really, I just feel content.' Content.

We walked back from the Chinese restaurant to her apartment where we stood awkwardly in front of the main door waiting to say goodbye. When Lucinda initiated the *bise* I held my breath so I couldn't smell if she had changed her perfume – swapped to Opium or Charlie under the influence of 'Agnes'. She stood at the door as I walked over towards my bike and then, just when I was nearly through it all, just when I thought I'd managed to hold in all my sadness for a whole night, something snapped and all the ache and the misery came rushing out again. I turned back to look at her as I waited on the pavement to cross the road and she had this look of affection on her face, affection or pity, a look that seemed to say, 'Good old George. She's so mixed up, so hung up on being cool, I hope she finds someone nice one day.' But she just shouted over, 'You're looking a bit posh tonight, Georgina,' in that voice, that stupid baby voice, that stupid, fucking, tree-climbing voice and I felt annihilated, like I was holding up the passage of the world just by standing there, worthless and superficial in my back-of-a-lorry Helmut Lang suit on a dog shit pavement waiting for the cars to pass.

A year of love came flooding back and I felt like Tintin, like a bland cartoon character with a roughly sketched face. I felt foolish, I knew I must look foolish in my new outfit, even more foolish than Tintin. I had silly sprigs for hair and twigs growing out of my ears with little chunks of pork stuck on at the end and I had chins down to the ground and my face was like the ugliest Toby Jug in the whole world. I had no right to exist and now I should just disappear, withdraw back into a hole, a dark, warm rabbit's burrow where nobody could get me. I could feel it already: my face, my features, evaporating away in condensation bubbles, my particles floating through Lucinda's skylight like a balloon: numb, light, just a thing filled with air. If I didn't manage to cross the road soon, the only thing left of me would be an O where my Tintin mouth had been drawn in and a stupid Snowy dog woofing away for me, not knowing I'd vanished to a place where I could feel no more pain and never be hurt again.

And just when I thought my lungs would burst from holding in the typhoon that strained at their walls, the cars parted, I crossed the road, unlocked my bike and cycled off to the rue de Clignancourt without looking back.

At six in the morning the streets of Paris are as clean as your soul. As clean as your soul is ever going to get. The green *Propreté de Paris* dustbin men sweep vigorously through with their hoses and plastic brushes. They waterblast away all the scum of the night before and leave channels of water chuckling along gutters, washing the city's slate clean once more. If you close your eyes it sounds like you are walking by a mountain stream. When you open your eyes the pavements are mercury shiny and a glow starts to warm up the dawn white sky.

Six to seven is the best hour to change your life. By 7 a.m. you are a worry bomb once more. The rawness goes and it feels like a layer of polish has been sprayed on the surface of the city. The smell of commerce hits the air, the fat flies wake up and bird song sounds whorish.

But it is now six-twenty precisely. I leave the pew. I leave the rocking girl and I walk down the aisle, past the Sacré Coeur warden in his cheap suit and loosened tie, through the heavy, stiff church door and into the light. The breeze up here on the hill pumps quickness into your veins. I walk into the morning at a mad pace, as if to slow down would be to lose my decision. This is not an agitated Surrealist amble or a Baudelarian *flâneur* stroll. My mind is too set for that. I am not going to let fate take its tortuous course; I have a purpose, I feel inspired. I know what I am going to do. I march down the hill from Montmartre, along the tiny cobbled Doisneau streets, down the 126 steps of the hill that is the rue Utrillo, past Madame Valence's house on rue Muller and into the rue de Clignancourt. On the corner of the rue de Clignancourt and the rue André del Sarte there is an Arab café which is filled at this hour with the sound of clattering chairs and rattling beer crates. 'There's a pretty little *boudin*,' says a man in a blue overall who stands at the door gulping at a *demi*. I just smile at him and say, '*Merci, monsieur. La vie est belle!*' And he shouts back, half laughing; '*Mais qu'est-ce qu'il y a de si belle?*' What's so beautiful about it? But I am too far away for him to hear my reply.

I'm starting to feel a sharp pang of hunger and when I go into the *boulangerie* for a *beignet aux pommes*, I even get a smile out of Madame Dupont.

CHAPTER SEVENTEEN

La Misère Sexuelle

When Holly finally touches down at the rue de Clignancourt Opium party, he is tense. In spite of white orchids spilling out of porcelain bowls to disguise the ugliest fittings and dirtiest crannies of the flat, in spite of rows of Chinese *objets* and perfumed candles and pony-skin throws and red velvet drapes and pink crystallised fruits ingeniously arranged on silver platters – by the hands of Holly and the wallet of Koji – so that rue de Clignancourt really does resemble a glamorised opium den, Holly has the cheek to complain about the calibre of the guests. By this, he means Ann's guests.

When he arrives, the hallway is awash with clowns, stilt walkers and a stoned but perky French juggler calling himself '*Le Satyr*.' This orange-legging-clad figure feels compelled to block Holly's path and tell him that the secret of love-making is not 'in-out-in-out penetration but in-out-in-out penetration followed by a swift side-to-side movement'. Holly makes a big 'puh!' and storms past the juggler with the intention of making a theatrical entrance into my bedroom to scold me soundly for letting the clowns nobble his posh party. But he finds the door locked. He starts banging and only when I hear it is him do I open up. Inside, he finds Bet, Ann, Alex and me sitting on my fruit-crate bed. Bet is glaring at him. This disarms him somewhat.

'What's wrong with you?' he says weakly.

Bet's face could turn a dairy sour. 'What's wrong with me!' she exclaims. 'I think you'll find that our flat – Ann's and my bedroom, to be precise – has been taken over by a lot of strange Japanese people who think we're servants. We've had to lock them out.'

Holly tries the offensive. 'You should be grateful that rue de Clig's got a facelift at last,' he says, brushing the leg of his cream cashmere trousers with 10-inch turn-ups. 'And look at the free Champagne Koji's provided.' He points to the gold-necked skittles dotted around the room.

'Grateful!' Bet shouts, incensed. 'I think you'll find that I didn't get much of a say in the matter. I should be getting minder money for keeping Koji's hands off Ann. I bet that's why he wanted the party here, isn't it?'

Holly pulls his cream smoking jacket tighter round his chest as if he has suddenly become cold.

'I've told you before,' he says, looking at his feet. 'They think it's louche here. They like it.'

Then Bet mutters under her breath and says, as close to the wind as flatmate treachery can get, 'seems like the only purpose of this party is to get George laid.'

I suppose I do feel a bit bad for agreeing to let Holly have his Opium party here. I knew Koji would be a pain in the neck, but I also know that the Gang has seen me in too much of a state recently to dare protest too much about my actions. Anyway, tonight my grand decision has been made flesh. Any minute now my stupid suffering over Lucinda will be over. I have decided that much of my current mopey state has been caused by a malady which the French term *la misère sexuelle*. This means more than sexual misery. *Misère* means poverty and so *misère sexuelle* means not getting it at all. Someone suffering from *misère sexuelle* is the opposite of a *mal baisée* because if you're one of those, then sex would, in theory, relax you a whole deal but you're just not interested. I thought I wasn't interested, but now I know that sex with a new person is the answer to all my problems. By hook or by crook I am going to get it tonight and when I have been flattered and gratified I will finally be able to put Lucinda behind me and get on with my life.

If what Holly has told me is true, tonight will be as rich in licky opportunities as it is in hot-house flowers. I just hope that my Helmut Lang suit and army boots and my pirate turban are a good enough look. Holly hasn't even commented on my look yet. He seems preoccupied.

Holly picks up Bet's Champagne bottle and takes a swig. 'At least those "strange people" know what glamour is,' he says quietly, 'which is more than can be said for those clowns.'

Bet tuts in exasperation. 'Glamour! Some ancient Japanese woman with black lipstick and a complexion like a rice pudding with skin over the top—'

'Black lipstick?' Holly interrupts.

'Yes. If that's glamour then I'm Inès de la Fressange.'

Holly looks really nervous now. 'Was she with two tall Japanese men?'

Bet thinks for a moment then says that yes, the woman did arrive accompanied by two very tall Japanese men carrying an embroidered screen and some brown parcels.

'You won't believe the old codswallop she was talking at the front door when I opened it,' Bet adds.

Holly bangs the bottle of Champagne down on the floor. 'How big were the parcels?'

Bet starts chuckling at Holly's serious face. 'Why? Expecting some more orchids, are you? More gold lamé? God if I see any more gold lamé . . . I think I might be getting nostalgic for our fusty sheet.' She and Ann laugh but Holly cuts in and says urgently, 'How big were the parcels? How bloody big?'

Bet and Ann fall silent. 'Holly,' Ann says softly, 'are you sure you're feeling okay?'

'Yes,' Bet slurs, passing him the bottle, 'maybe you should have another drink.' But he still looks tense so Bet thinks back to the tall men and says, 'I don't know. I suppose the parcels were about the size of ... pillows?'

Holly turns white as a sheet but he tries to snap back to his old self by grabbing the Champagne bottle from Bet and saying, 'I think you're right, Bet. I think I need to relax a bit. The past couple of months have been a bit exhausting.' He takes a few swigs and seems to calm down a little. He says he's still recovering from an interview he gave that morning to an important Japanese fashion journalist of Koji's acquaintance.

'I took her to the Deux Magots for breakfast and ordered a tumbler of neat vodka. I said I always drank a tumbler of neat vodka for breakfast because it was the purest way to start the day.' Holly's face breaks into a smile for the first time all night. 'When the interview finished I shook her hand, gave her the *bise* and went to the loo to chuck up.'

'Poor you,' Ann says.

'Poor me nothing,' Holly beams. 'I'll now be known as the whippersnapper designer who drinks neat vodka for breakfast. Image, angle, that's what it's all about.'

'Why did you say you were inspired to be a fashion designer?' Alex asks.

'Oh, you know, the usual roll-out-the-barrel gayboy stuff: the smell of my grandmother's talcum powder, watching my mother dress up in her cocktail frock before she went out for the evening – omitting to tell her that my bastard father would never let her go out in the evening anyway.'

Holly seems to be getting back on form now. 'Come on then,' he says, draining the last of the bottle. 'Let's go and mingle.'

But Alex points out that nobody is really doing any mingling at his Opium party. That they're all shut up in Bet and Ann's room, lounging around in harem pants and Jerry Hall jewellery, while in the kitchen there is a strange rapport going on between his boyfriend Raoul and Jean-Christophe.

Then Alex remembers that there's someone here called Mr Soya who has been asking for Holly all night. Holly goes white again.

'Mr Soya! What's he doing here?'

'Don't ask me,' Alex says, bored. 'He's with some Japanese girl with a smiley face. She seems pretty keen to see you.'

'Fuck!' Holly mutters. 'Spoonface!' But Ann has already opened the door of my room. A Japanese woman in a red satin tunic darts in like an eel, grips Holly by the arm and whisks him off in the direction of the excited rumble coming from the big bedroom as Holly stammers, 'But Mrs Soya, I think I might need a drink first . . .'

It is now 1.30 a.m. I feel restless and I can't relax because rue de Clignancourt has been turned into the Ritz and invaded by people I don't want to be here. The only people I do want to be here are the glamorous lesbians Holly has been telling me about but – what a surprise – they haven't shown up yet. I walk into the kitchen where Jean-Christophe and Raoul are both holding Champagne flutes up to the light. Raoul is talking about the beautiful 'robe jaune' (yellow dress) of the liquid and Jean-Christophe is talking about the fine 'jambes' (legs) that it has. When I hold out my half-filled glass for a top-up, they look back at me, horrified. Then they look at each other and laugh patronisingly and say that indiscriminate mixing of wines is just the sort of thing the English excel at. I am feeling very sensitive tonight and think I might start to cry, so I gulp down the rest of my glass and then hold it out again.

The Gang seems to think that it's easy for me just to have sex and be as right as rain. They seem to think that I'm enjoying this – killing Lucinda off once and for all. Well, maybe I am enjoying this – but only when my glass is topped up enough.

Otherwise I seem to wobble, like a boat that might capsize at any moment.

While I down the glass with the yellow dress and the great legs, the two French men start to talk about other great wines they have drunk in their lives. The pizza delivery man starts talking about the wonderful white wine called Puligny Montrachet he drank the other day and I reflect how much I like the word Montrachet because it is rough and guttural and the word Montrachet sounds like 'cravache' which means a crop. After I think of crop I think of *god* which means dildo in French and then I think of Doris the Double Header. I am starting to feel just about ready for the arrival of my date and I wonder where she can be. It must be the drink making me feel like this. Holly says that Champagne makes him feel sexy, but the dirtiest I have ever felt was when I bought a bottle of 13-franc Vin de Table Blanc *Special Fruits de Mer* from the juvenile delinquent supermarket with a picture of some greenish-looking oysters on the label. It was supposed to be for sea food but when I drank it – Lucinda was in my bed at the time – the idea popped into my head that I wanted to piss all over her. It was strange because I had never even thought about sex with urine before. But there I was – the exciting new thought turning my lower body into an articulated lobster's tail that thrashed around of its own volition.

My new puppet-on-a-string body was ready to do it there and then all over the bed, but luckily Lucinda suggested that we went to the bathroom. We got out of bed and rushed down the cold hallway, but when we got into the bathroom it was like Blackpool illuminations and the coldness and hardness of the yellow floor tiles nearly brought me to my senses. But not quite. My sphincter acted a little oddly to start with but then Lucinda started groaning and suddenly it all came out and I thought of a warm white squid and a big black dick, a T-shirt mop and a velvet vulva ship, and there soon followed the familiar refrain of *OUAIS!*

OUAIS! OUAAAAIS! And afterwards, I loved Lucinda even more than ever.

Now though, as I look at the dry, pony-skin throws all over the floor I curse myself for even thinking about her. I wish I could get her out of my head. And then, at last, the doorbell rings.

When I've managed to fight my way past the clowns I open the door to see four people wearing huge sunglasses. Two of them are gayboys and two are women in their early thirties wearing silk pirate head-dresses, lipstick and leather jackets. The one that I have my eye on has short hair, stilettos, a PVC mini skirt and a huge piece of pink gum in her mouth. The two gayboys are wearing lycra shorts and navy-blue bomber jackets. They are doing little disco dances on the door mat as they wait to be let in. There is actually a third one on the staircase but he is hovering between the sixth and the seventh floors, talking to one of the men who lives in the apartment below us. He is American. He is calling my neighbour a 'piece of trash' and pushing his crotch out towards him. He is giggling so much that I hear Ship Ahoy on the third floor come out of her flat and shout, *'Mais, ça va pas, non! Je vais appeler la police!'*

But I don't care about Ship Ahoy, or the gayboy on the stairs, because I am just watching the woman with heels and pink chewing-gum.

She takes her shades off and does a slight wince with her eyes. 'Sar . . . vah?' she says, with a thick American accent. *'On est là pour Koji.'*

Now her eyes are flickering over my head, darting down the corridor to see if she can spot him. The eyes of the whole group are now straining over my head, bobbing down the corridor. I think this is a little rich, given that strictly speaking, this is my party and one of the women is supposed to be sleeping with me and should be giving me eye contact.

'This is my flat,' I say proudly, trying to sound casual.

The woman with the pink gum ignores the comment. She is looking at the perky *Satyr* walking down the hallway on his hands, singing 'Lemon Incest'. 'Cool,' she says, slowly. Then she adds, 'Thanks, sweetie. I figure we'll just walk on by.' And with that, she gives me the *bise* and saunters on down the hallway, spiking fleshy white orchid petals on to her heels as she goes. I watch with my mouth open as her friends follow her down the hall towards the main bedroom. I am just thinking how I will go about strangling Holly when my neighbour from downstairs pops his head round the door and gushes, *'Putain!* I didn't know you were in the *milieu artistique!'* And he gives me a wink. He introduces himself as a big Madonna fan – pronouncing it Mad-onna in the French way – and asks me how come I know her dancers. He insists that the American boy on the stairs was one of Mad-onna's dancers who is currently in Paris for her *Blonde Ambition* tour. He says that both the women were also in the singer's 'Erotica' video.

This piece of information interests me slightly and yet it is also a pointless piece of information because what is the use of having famous celebrities in the flat when they don't want to go to bed with me? Sex with me certainly doesn't seem to be on those women's minds. I think of how Holly has betrayed me yet again and my chin starts to wobble uncontrollably.

I am only prevented from bursting into tears by the sound of some more footsteps on the stairs. It is Sam who has come to collect Bet to take her back to his place. He bids me a curt 'hello', and then drags his feet down the hall into the kitchen where Bet is mixing her Champagnes. When I walk into the kitchen shortly afterwards, Bet and Sam are snogging and when I go into my bedroom, Ann and Jean-Christophe are there, slamming back Champagne *culs secs* and snogging. Raoul and Alex are standing outside the bathroom, ravishing each other and it all makes me so furious that I push past the stupid clowns and fight my way into Ann and Bet's bedroom to find Holly and see what he's got to say for himself.

When I push open the door, I see that the room is filled with lots of Japanese people sprawled around on the floor, puffing on cigarette holders. By an embroidered Japanese screen in Ann's corner of the room, I see the two women in leather jackets. They are not exactly snogging, but they are lying listlessly together on a pony-skin throw, eyes closed, indolent smiles on both faces. From under the screen, two Chelsea Boots are peeking out as if they belong to a corpse.

The only person in the room who seems to have any energy at all is Holly. He is gripping a half-full bottle of Taittinger and jumping frantically up and down to 'If You Go Away' from my Shirley Bassey CD. When he sees me, he puts on his gleeful *Coronation Street* accent – as he always does when he is embarrassed or on the verge of passing out – and he shouts out, 'Eh, George, you all right then, chuck? Hey, guess what! Koji's off his head on some weird pills. I've taken six of them already!'

I say, 'That's how people commit suicide, isn't it? Champagne and pills?'

Holly seems to consider this possibility for a moment. Then he slurs, 'Lorra rubbish,' and starts to do the Pizza Dance. Doing the Pizza Dance means deluding yourself that you are the sexiest person in the room, whereas you are really just drunk and dancing in a really embarrassing way. Holly coined the phrase when flinching at some photographs Sophie had taken at one of her formal, expat media parties. In the photos, Holly looks like the pervy uncle at a child's birthday party. He has a slice of buffet pizza shoved into his mouth, tomato paste streaked down his cheeks and his chin contorted into grotesque double folds – the consequence of the series of horrible beery hip thrusts he was performing at the time.

* * *

And then the Pizza Dance stops. The pair of Chelsea Boots that has been lying vertically under the screen suddenly disappears. A few seconds later the two boots are standing firmly on the ground a few centimetres in front of Holly. Above them, there are two trunks of emerald-green velvet and at the very top of that there is a head that belongs to Koji. This time the head does not look like it belongs to a wacked-out idiot. The lips on the face are puckered and cruel and when Koji slowly removes his sunglasses, his eyes look like scorpions; like someone has double crossed him and now they are going to pay. His eyes are drilling into Holly, making Holly's Adam's apple bob up and down in his throat like a cistern.

Koji suddenly grabs a silver-tipped cane from a tall Japanese man standing at his side. It is hard to tell if he does this to steady himself or to look even more menacing. In any case he manages to achieve both objectives; the people in the room have begun to gawp at the two figures. The only voice left speaking is Shirley Bassey's, quavering, 'I'd have been the shadow of your dog if I thought you might have kept me by your side,' but that is soon eradicated when Koji makes an irritated gesture towards my ghetto blaster and one of the tall men turns to switch it off. Now all you can hear is the sound of Holly's heavy breathing and a slow, rhythmic tapping.

Koji seems hypnotised by the end of the cane as he hits it incessantly on the floorboards.

'Silly boy,' he says in a monotone. 'Big silly boy.' And it all seems really ominous because he just carries on doing this tapping and saying 'silly boy', 'big silly boy', over and over again for what seems like ages. And just when Holly thinks it's all a big, dumb, Koji sketch, Koji suddenly throws the cane down on the floor with a bang and turns his shiny eyes on Holly like suction pads; he sucks up Holly's big, blue, baby eyes with his shiny, slippery, snake eyes. They're the kind of eyes that wouldn't be averse to slaying children, instigating torture, severing heads off crowds of beggars pleading for mercy. And now the same eyes look at Holly and the room gets darker.

'Mr Soya,' he says. 'Mr Soya. Important man. Mr Soya want Holly marriage to Yoko. Yoko want marriage to Holly. *Shimasho!* Mr Soya. *Shimasho!* Important man.'

Holly starts brushing his cashmere trousers. Then he flicks his head left and right and cautiously surveys the room to see how many people are observing this scene. Everyone is.

'Mr Soya angry!' Koji shrieks the phrase and brings Holly's terrified head back to face its inquisitor. 'Mr Soya say Holly agree marry Yoko! *Kekkon shimasho ka!* Mr Soya angry! Mr Soya be obey all time! Destroy Holly! Destroy! Destroy! Destroy!'

Actually, Koji doesn't say quite all that, but it seems as if he does because he is getting so worked up that he sounds like a dalek with a short circuit. He has started vibrating round in a circle like a mad clockwork toy. A woman wearing black lipstick comes up and puts her hand on his deranged shoulder to try to calm him down, but Koji just sees the white orchid on her collar and he gets freaked out by the stamens of the flowers that look like snappy insect jaws – I've never been a big fan of orchids either – and he starts trying to club the woman's breasts with his cane until the two tall Japanese men come over and put their arms round him. They put their arms round him and hug him like he's a baby. They stroke his Paul McCartney hair and they whisper '*Daijobu, daijobu,*' in his ear until he slumps to his knees, closes his eyes and drops into another of his deep sleeps.

The last noise that happens is the sound of the embroidered Japanese screen crashing to the ground as Koji kicks his legs out in a final little tantrum. With the screen lying on the floor you can see what a big mess there is behind it: there are scratched trays and scorched knives and bits and pieces in plastic bags. Lying down by Koji's shoes is a large piece of silver foil with wavy brown lines all over it.

The woman with the black lipstick and the two tall men glance at each other quickly and then heave the screen up again. There is a sense of nervous movement in the room – Koji's little scene appears to have roused a fair number of them – and as chattering and giggling spring up once more, Holly grabs hold of my arm and pushes me towards the bathroom. Once we are inside, he locks the door and goes over to look in the mirror. He gasps when he sees how pale his face is.

Part of me wants to smash Holly over the head with my Champagne bottle. Number one – my so-called shag of the night has turned out to be completely non-existent, and number two – Bet, Ann and I seem to be hosting a party stuffed to the gills with real-life opium eaters.

Holly is talking to the face in the mirror.

'He did used to hang out with Andy Warhol though,' a numb voice mutters. 'He used to supply drugs for The Factory. He was a bit of a figure in those days, apparently.'

Lucky for Holly, I am still very drunk. I just look at the floor and say, 'Tell me immediately what this is about or I'll piss all over you.'

Holly looks a bit taken aback, but at least it makes him feel at home. He takes one last look at the drained face in the mirror before going to sit down on the bath's edge.

There is a silence and then he gives a deep sigh and says, 'I believed him, George. I really believed him. It all seemed so plausible – waiting for the postman, signing for the parcels. I did think it was odd when he'd never let me open any of them and I did wonder when the fabric was ever going to arrive. Then one day it did arrive. Reams and reams of it. Triple the amount I'd ordered. I got so used to opening these brown paper packages that one day I opened one of Koji's by mistake. There was this big plastic bag full of grey itching powder stuff.'

He looks at me. 'Heroin.'

Our eyes meet for a few moments.

'Anyway, this was all a week ago. When Koji found out

that I'd opened his smack he went mental – did a little scene like that one in there.'

He pauses.

'I just feel stupid. I thought he was an eccentric Japanese fashion type. I thought Mr Soya was some dopey frock merchant who liked a bit of karaoke. I didn't know they were all drug barons. I didn't know that Places des Vosges was all a front. I can't believe I've been turned into a cog of some Tokyo mafia ring. Not even a cog, a husband! Me and Spoonface!' There is another deep sigh. 'Poor Spoonface. Oh well, at least she'll get a decent wedding dress.'

He gets up and looks at himself in the mirror again. 'Maybe Dad was right,' he says despondently, pulling at the skin under his eyes.

'Right about what?'

Holly brings his face closer to the mirror, contemplates some blackheads for a maudlin while and then makes a disgusted 'puh!' sound. He turns his back on the face and leans against the sink. The platinum lighter makes another appearance.

'My alcoholic patriarch of a father used to take me and my brothers camping to Lloret del Mar every summer,' he says, lighting up. 'You could describe him as a man who got passionate about life. Every other word was "fucking" ("I fucking come from fucking Yorkshire"), with the occasional "bastard" dropped in for good measure. I used to worship him in those days.

'The highlight of the week came when he'd take us all to a bull fight to "toughen" us up. It was debatable how much toughening up happened at the *corridas*: my father saw five bulls hacked to death by the sword every Saturday afternoon whereas I saw an arena filled with a dozen men in pink boleros and black ballet pumps strutting in poses that outlined their cock and balls to the best advantage.'

He puffs away distractedly on his cigarette and tells me how, every night, he and his brothers had to meet up with his father, stepmother, two uncles, two aunts and three cousins at the family barbecue where pockets of wine-soaked conversation would ricochet around the campsite:

'We haven't got a British film industry and the French have because they've got good light in the south of France.'

'Chatting women up? In my day you just had to say, "Can I walk you to the bus stop, ducks?"'

'You go there, you get three courses for three pound: you get starter, main and sweet. Sweet's always ice cream or cream caramel but three pound for the lot.'

'My dad's a rat's cunt,' (from Holly's younger brother).

'It still makes me shudder,' he says. 'I remember one day a couple of years ago. It was the last holiday I had with him. We were at lunch and Dad got so irate that his walnut tan started flashing red. He was doing one of his diatribes, I can't even remember why he was going on about it: "Bloody stupid idea Britain entering Europe," he's ranting. "I'd rather be the fifty-second American state than bloody part of bloody united Europe." I knew Dad was a big xenophobe. He even made a point of pronouncing *peseta* "peseeta". He might occasionally have to speak foreign words during his four-week holiday on the Costa Brava but he was going to do his damnedest to say them in a Yorkshire accent.'

Holly's eyes glaze over and one side of his mouth curls upwards at the distant memory. 'So, my younger brother Michael starts flushing red too. But it's a different sort of flush; he knows he's on the verge of the perfect opportunity to put my father down in public. Michael's the youngest. Me and him were still living at home when Mum and Dad split up. He was fifteen and I was seventeen when we drove Mum to the door of Dad's new lover's house and watched as she hacked the words "whore" in the front door with an axe.

'Anyway, so Michael said in his best sneer, "Sure Dad,

that's not what the young generation think any more." That really turned Dad's tan a funny colour. "I don't want to know what the younger bloody generation bloody thinks," he goes. "Besides, I've been talking to that Dutch lad in the tent next to ours. He bloody hates the bloody Germans."

'Everyone in the dining room froze. All you could hear was the nervous sounds of clinking glasses and OAPs choking on calamare fritters. Suddenly, I heard myself saying, "Actually, I know a Dutch fashion designer who hates the Germans too."

'God I can't believe I said that. Of course, Dad didn't care less what I thought even though I was trying to come to his bloody defence. He mumbled into his paella: "I don't care what bloody Willy Woofters bloody think."'

Holly falls silent. 'Funny really. Michael had a friend with him who was in the Marines. Scottish nutcase, code name "Slasher". He was quite nice in a piss head, psycho sort of way. He'd been listening quite passively to this conversation but he suddenly threw his knife and fork down on his plate and shouted in a very loud Glaswegian accent that Dad was a neo-fascist. I think my Dad quite liked it. At least it was a full-blooded heterosexual who was telling him.'

Holly starts fiddling with his cream trousers. 'Maybe Dad was right. What does a Willy Woofter know?' He takes a last drag on his cigarette then stands up straight. 'Oh well. He always thought I'd end up in debtor's prison. At least now everyone in jail will think I'm Matt Dillon in *Drugstore Cowboy*.'

'Holly!' I say, exasperated. 'You're not going to end up in prison. You're . . . you're Holly.'

But Holly points out that he has personally signed for around twenty pillow-sized parcels of heroin. 'I'm one of them now. If I run away I might wake up one morning in some hideous Comme des Garçons concrete overcoat.' He goes to unlock the bathroom door.

'Where are you going?'

'To Le Swing,' he says gloomily. 'When Koji comes back into consciousness he's going to have my guts for garters. And Mr Soya's probably going to crack me over the head with the same lead pipe he's been bludgeoned with.'

He staggers out of the bathroom. When he gets to my bedroom he picks up a couple of Champagne bottles and moves towards the door. 'Where are you off to?' Alex slurs, peeking out at Holly through Raoul's hair.

'To Le Swing. Special performance of "I'm Getting Married In The Morning".'

I don't think Alex can have heard properly because he just carries on snogging Raoul. But I can't stop to alert him about the drama that's happening because Holly has already opened the front door. I rush after him just in time to plant the *bise* on his cheeks.

'*Hasta luego*, chuck,' he says. 'Maybe.'

I try to stop him from leaving because he doesn't look safe — he is still really out of it — but he just shakes my hand away and stumbles off down the stairs. I am thinking about going after him when I hear Ann's voice behind me.

'George! George!' She is shouting. 'I've got some good news for you. Good News. You're going to get laid tonight after all!'

I step inside immediately.

CHAPTER EIGHTEEN

Marianne Faithful

Ann says she has a stilt walker lined up for me — the same stilt walker she was hyping the Wednesday we went to the Barbès market together. Alex immediately asks what she looks like but Ann just raises her eyebrows. She turns to me and says confidentially, 'She's very experienced.' This is all I need to know.

The bell sounds like the jingle of the warder's keys come to unlock my ball and chain of *misère sexuelle*. But I have trouble getting to the door because a huge bottleneck of clowns has formed in the hall, dozens of them — a mass of big grins and flexing flesh and sun-faded, loose-fitting clothes — leap frogging on to each other's shoulders to ogle some spectacle on the landing. The excited bodies only part when *Le Satyr* strides through them doing a chicken impersonation. I watch him walk into my bedroom, flap his arms around in wing formation and announce to Ann, in his irritating clown way, that '*T'auras du poulet pour ton dîner!*' which means, 'You've got chicken for dinner!' but which also means, 'There is a police officer at your door.' I start to feel queasy because I think the police have come to the door to arrest me for my electricity trick.

Strictly speaking it is Bet's electricity trick. She said she was fed up with living in an ice box and that if I didn't put a piece of wire in the metre immediately then she would have to move out.

I think she's going to move out and live with Sam anyway, but it seemed easier to stall for time. Luckily, 27 rue de Clignancourt is so ancient that the metre is situated inside the house and is encased in a plastic box instead of a modern metal one. As Sam showed us, all you have to do is drill a tiny hole in the top of the box and then slip a piece of fuse wire in to stop the numbers going round.

I push the clowns out of the way and try to work out what I am going to say about the sabotaged electricity metre. But when I finally catch sight of the two *poulets* my brain wakes up from its Champagne stupor and I realise that I've got two pillow cases of heroin and a room full of stoned Japanese criminals in my house. I can see Ship Ahoy bobbing behind them on the landing in a particularly racy polka dot blouse.

'A neighbour has called the *commissariat, mademoiselle,*' the first chicken says. 'She claims also that many suspicious people have entered the building tonight.' I momentarily think about denouncing Koji, but then I think how that would just get Holly into more trouble. Plus, Ann, Bet and I would probably all get evicted so I merely point apologetically at the clowns and try to get some eye contact going with the chicken who's talking so that he will decide not to investigate any further. I make a point of saying very loudly to the clowns that they've all got to go because they're making too much noise.

As some of them start to troop out of the flat, the two *poulets* turn to look down the stair well because a terrible racket is coming from below. The din intensifies and echoes as it approaches the seventh floor. Then a huge sea creature comes into view. At least, it looks like a sea creature because the light on the landing has just blown: we can see the shadow of a big, bulbous body with several tentacles of varying thickness, and hear a plashy, spluttering sound.

When it gets closer, the shape turns out to be that of a woman who is panting heavily. She is bigger in build than the sumo wrestler and clad in a black leather waistcoat and shorts.

Two of her tentacles turn out to be stilts and she leans them against the wall. She extends a damp flipper to me and says in a deluge of Texan accent, 'Hi, I'm Sherry. Sure have a lot of stairs here. You must be George, the writer. Gee, I think that's just so amazing that you can be a writer.'

Sherry turns out to be an American who really does say 'gee' all the time. We've only just met and already she is jabbering away about how she majored in English and volley ball at the Southern Methodist University in Dallas and how, although she likes to express her body now by walking on stilts, her favourite thing is to write 'poetry about liberation'.

The only good thing about all this is that the *poulets* seem really ready to leave. With a final stern word of warning – saying that I should invite my neighbours next time if I want to avoid this kind of *galère* – they start trooping down the stairs. When Ann comes out on to the landing to say goodbye to all the departing clowns, she sees Sherry and gives her an affectionate hug.

'Glad you're here,' she beams. 'I see you've already met George.' And she looks at me like she's just given me some kind of fantastic Christmas present.

Sherry grabs hold of the fish tail of my pirate head-dress and gives it a heavy-handed tug. 'Of course,' she chuckles flirtatiously, 'you could say that I come from a bohemian background myself. When I was eight years old my father used to put lemons in the bathtub . . .' But I don't hear what she's going to say next because there is suddenly a stampede of Japanese people shoving us out of the way.

Having got wind of the police visit they have decided to take flight. Like a bucking bronco rearing up and tossing off its fancy new saddle, 27 rue de Clignancourt hurls the line of agitated bodies out of its sight. Embalmed faces with cigarette holders and helmet-head bobs and prominent sunglasses walk past clutching Chinese *objets* and silver platters and pony-skin rugs. The two women in the tight, leather jackets totter past with the embroidered screen, followed finally by Koji – propped up by the tall Japanese men and clutching some brown paper packages.

Not only has Koji not thanked me for saving his bacon, he and his friends are running off with all the party decorations. Just before he begins the trip down the stairs he stops before me and I think he is going to offer to let us keep the Japanese screen but his face breaks into a scowl and he starts shouting, '*Kekkon shimasho! Shimasho ka!* Bad boy, total big time, *mo sugu yudetamago ga dekiru yo!*' until one of the tall men has to pick him up and give him a fireman's lift down the stairs.

The last person to go is Ship Ahoy. She is still on the landing, probably having her most exciting night out in years. The Champagne is still buzzing round my veins so rather than stare her off our territory I decide to take hold of the sea creature's leather waistcoat and pull her huge breasts towards me. I am quite surprised to find that their feel against my six-months-chaste body is an enormous turn-on. I forget all about the presence of Ship Ahoy who now stands even more transfixed than before.

I am so delighted by the waistcoat embrace that I pull Sherry inside the apartment, jostle her into my bedroom, throw her on the fruit-crate bed and slam the door.

'Woa, you wild little thing,' she says breathlessly, hurriedly loosening the laces that tie her waistcoat flaps together. 'You writers are horny little things, huh?' But I don't care about her irritating comments because the only thing that exists in the room is the trinity of her hands, the leather laces and her breasts. I am keeping my hands purposefully off the waistcoat so that when the floodgates open I will appreciate them all the more. The flaps are a while in bursting open because she is holding a bottle of Champagne in one hand. She tips it back like it is water. 'Oh yeah, baby,' she says. 'Yeah baby, yeah.'

This is perfect. This is what American women say in porno films and I know that I will be able to completely objectify her when I finally get it going with her. It will probably be even better than the golden shower evening with Lucinda and she will drive Lucinda out of my head like a rocket through a roof. And just as she is about to undo the last lace of her top, she stops and looks at my bike. She says, 'I used to have a bike but I never rode it. I just strapped my lovers to it.' I think that my guardian angel must definitely be with me tonight and as she undoes the last lace of her waistcoat I hover dangerously near to dirt saturation point. Hooray, I think, someone is going to teach me about sado masochism at last. And when her breasts boil out of her leather jerkin, like an avalanche of steamy ski slopes, I put my face and hands and nose and tongue in the warm crevasse and I paddle frantically a while in the warm fjord – doggy paddling in a place so warm and watery and endless that I want to choke on her breasts and spit on them and bite them and my tail turns into a thrashing lobster once more and rubs against her shiny, wet tail while in the background her voice goes, 'Yeah baby, yeah,' just like in the porn films.

And then I panic. The premature ejaculator overtakes me and I come like the snapping of fingers. I come and I want her to go away and I wonder what on earth I am going to do now with all this passionate, embracing flesh on my hands. She still has fire shooting through her loins and I can feel my chin start to wobble because Lucinda hasn't been blasted out of my head at all. My cheapskate orgasm with the sea creature makes Lucinda flood into the room to laugh at me for having presumed that I could forget her just like that. But then I have to stop thinking about Lucinda because the woman named after an alcoholic drink has suddenly started saying, 'Ride the wave.' Over and over again she is saying it, 'Ride the wave, I want to teach you to ride the wave.' When I open my eyes I see that she has the Champagne bottle poised over my neck – as if she is about to pour it all over my face. 'Hey, sweet thing,' she says in a voice that sounds much drunker than it did a few minutes ago. 'This is all about giving and trust. I want you to ride it baby, ride it all the way.' And the next thing I know is that she is chucking a load of cold Champagne all over my stomach. She seems to be really getting off on this and I realise that she must be trying to do a *Nine and a Half Weeks* sort of scene – drip, drip over a quivering body sort of idea – but she's being so ham fisted that she might as well be sloshing a bucket of cold water over my head. I try to push her off but she just slurs, 'No, baby. No. You better take it. You better play the game. You better . . . ride the wave.'

And so there I have to lie: riding the freezing cold, sopping wet wave until the whole of the bottle is empty and she has finally flopped down on her side next to me. It is only after about two minutes of panting that she suddenly feels the sheets and says, 'Gee, it's kinda wet here, right?' But when I tut in exasperation she just gets fire in her loins again and starts moaning and grinding.

I think that the best thing to do is to bring her off and then I can ask her to leave. But when I sit up and kneel in front of her and start to put my hand up her bits, I can't do it. Well, I can, but the trouble is that there is so much fat pushing on her hulking frame that I have a great deal of trouble squeezing my hand in in the first place and when it is inside, her silky, warm, sticky walls do battle with my wrist, like I'm being crushed by a huge sea creature and I take my hand out because I suddenly can't bear it any more. I can't see the point. I can't even see the point in telling the story tomorrow to the Gang. Because I know that I'd tell the story but I'd edit out the parts when I start to cry and she strokes me with her maternal fins and says it's okay and asks me how big my feet are because she wants to give me her cowboy boots to cheer me up (and how I lie about my size for obvious reasons). And I wouldn't tell them how I spend the rest of the night clinging to her salty cellulite flipper because at least it is something to cuddle and not just me and the brown sheets on our own again and at least it offers me affection, even though it doesn't belong to the right person.

At the same time that I was wondering if I would ever again be able to find someone, something, anything to connect to, Holly was lying dead in the flat below.

He was not really dead, but he said it felt like he was because when he opened his eyes, his cloudy vision beheld a series of twisty, gothic shapes like the illuminated Es and Ss in his mother's best bible. He said that he was quite surprised to find that he'd gone to heaven after all, but on gazing at the swirling calligraphy for a few minutes longer he realised that the holy forms were not dropped letters at all but dropped pubes and that he was lying face down on a cold yellow floor with his arm wrapped around a toilet bowl.

The next thing Holly wondered was why he was wearing false eyelashes. He couldn't remember having put any on. But then he rubbed his eye and realised that the glue on his lids was not eyelashes but shards of sticky orange carrot which, in the space of a terrible groan, he worked out to be vomit, and he was lying in the rest of it. It took him a few more minutes before he managed to peel himself off the floor and emerge groaning into the bedroom. The layout of the flat was the same as our flat upstairs and he only realised it wasn't my bedroom when he flopped on to the bed and saw before him a wall of posters of Madonna gone green and hideously distorted thanks to the presence of a large algae-furred fish tank on eye level with the bedside table.

Things got worse when the Mad-onna fan sat down next to him on the bed, slowly unslid Holly's zip and put his hands down Holly's flies while simultaneously charting Mad-onna's rags to riches success story. Lucky for Holly, his body had become jammed. The effects of the drink and Koji's strange pills were still working. His whole being was buzzing like he'd taken something much too strong. It was like an out-of-body experience: he could see himself lying there on the man's bed – alive and conscious inside his head – but he couldn't move anything or open his mouth to say anything. All that he could think of to think was, 'another fine mess'.

Three hours after leaving 27 rue de Clignancourt, Koji's body was found half-way through the windscreen of a four-wheel drive which was wrapped around a tree trunk on the outskirts of Versailles. The only items in the wreck which remained intact were two large brown paper packages.

It was shortly after hearing this news that Holly announced he was going to become Marianne Faithful. 'Sod Holly Golightly,' he said. 'Sod Holly scrape-the-bottom-of-the-barrel-at-3 a.m.-in-a-clammy-nightclub-when-you're-looking-for-a-husband. I'm going to run away from the city and live in a remote cottage and make buns and get some topiary going and spend the rest of my life with a labrador making wedding dresses for local girls with fat thighs.'

I told Holly to stop being ridiculous. People would think he'd gone mad.

'I don't care what people think,' he said. 'They can think what they like. They won't see me anyway – I'll be tucked safely under my topiary hedge by three in the afternoon – shears in one hand, bottle of gin in the other.'

Holly was in a bad way. We were standing in the cheap dry cleaners on the boulevard Barbès where Holly had come with his party-damaged trousers. The place smelt of sweaty incense and we were being pushed around by other people in the queue. This atmosphere, coupled with his Opium party hangover and the worrying news that Koji had survived the car crash, had sent him careering off form. Koji had called him that morning from the American Hospital in Neuilly where he was lying strung up in a bed with pretty much every bone in his body broken. Naturally, the police – both French and Japanese – were baying to get into his room and question him about the packages found in the car. At present, his injuries were so serious that he had escaped questioning but Alex's answering machine was chock-a-block with near-incomprehensible messages from Koji ordering Holly to call him immediately. Alex had already told Holly not to worry. Practically everyone he worked with was Japanese. Alex was sure that his company was so highly respected that it would only take a letter written by one of them to explain to the Japanese police that Holly was entirely innocent. Naïve but innocent.

But Holly was dubious about this. He said that anyway, there was no reason for him to stay in France. He was skint again, he was twenty-six next birthday and if he went to live in the provinces he'd look good in comparison with everyone else. He saw my glum face and said, 'Don't worry. It's not as if I'm going to give up my bad ways altogether. I might have to pop down to some care-in-the-community style nightclub from time to time – just to set my mind at rest that it's all unutterably dull.'

He gave a big sigh and added, 'Thing is, George, I always think that someone else is out there – and they are – except that when you get to know them you wish you hadn't.'

I tried to think of something to say but you can't really ask Holly too many questions. Sometimes he's like a big rickety bookcase. You might take one book out and it would upset everything else – bring everything else toppling down to the ground. By now we'd reached the front of the queue and Holly was opening the Tati bag and placing the precious trousers on the counter under the nose of the crumbling woman who sits behind the desk. This woman used to resemble a crumbly piece of chalk statue; every time you saw her, some other piece would have chipped off and fallen. Now so much has come away that her face looks like an old squat where you're not sure which floorboard to tread on in case it might be a rotten one that might send your foot crashing through to the ceiling below.

The crumbling woman knows Holly well. She is extremely *au fait* with his cashmere trouser stains. There is a look in her eyes this morning that tells me she's really going to nobble him. And so she does. She takes one look at his shifty face and then she unfolds the crumpled garment and holds it up to the light in front of the assembled shop of customers. '*Mais, c'est quoi, ça?*' she hisses.

Holly goes red as a tomato and lowers his eyes to the floor. 'Vomit,' he mutters.

'Vomit!' her miserable voice scoffs as she brandishes the mucky trousers in the air like a severed head. 'We don't do vomit here!'

Everything in the shop seems to glare at Holly – the crumbling finger from behind the desk, the faded Mitterand on the wall, the bricks, the mortar – every winking pot and pan on boulevard Barbès, every zigzag pattern of every Moroccan robe on every corner of the eighteenth *arrondissement*, all glaring at Holly, all at once. Holly looks sadly at the once so cream cashmere trousers and he realises that the end has come. All that remains for him to do now is make a decent exit. So he stands up straight, smoothes his bandanna, snatches the trousers back, folds them up ostentatiously, and with a gargantuan 'puh!' he turns on his heels and takes his leave.

CHAPTER NINETEEN

Curtains

I have decided to pack my Helmut Lang suit, my books and diaries, two tins of green lentils and two holey brown sheets. On the top of my rucksack there is a one-way coach ticket. Because I am twenty-five, I have purchased it at a special reduced rate of 395 francs called a *Tarif Séduction*.

There is a strange atmosphere in rue de Clignancourt tonight. Bet is in the kitchen being bright and breezy with Ann. She wants to take the Barbès liquidizer with her as she invested 80 francs in it. If she can't take it with her then she says that Ann and I could give her 40 francs each to buy her out.

This is not the most tactful time to start such a conversation. Because I am moving on and Bet is moving out to live with Sam, Ann is looking for a new flatmate. A Swedish student has just been round to view the apartment. She seemed keen on the place although she told Ann that she'd like to instigate a 'cleaning kitty', whatever that is. Alex, who has been serious and mature in work all day, just sits at the kitchen table like nothing is happening. When things look like they are getting too near boiling point, he prods Bet on a nipple with the claw of a stale croissant and says, 'Get yer boosies out.'

I sit on my fruit-crate bed and look at my rucksack. I think about the letter I received this morning, postmarked Yorkshire. It seems that Holly hasn't become Marianne Faithful just yet. His total lack of funds means that he has been forced to temporarily relocate to his mother's house. She would only have him back on the condition that he got a 'useful skill' under his belt – meaning a computer studies course. I sigh when I think of him sitting sketching evening wear at the back of a draughty classroom as some man in a bobbly polyester jumper drones on about megabites and ram.

Suddenly, I grab my Walkman. I shout to the kitchen that I'll be back later, I slam the door behind me and I race down the stairs. Then, once I'm cycling down the boulevard Barbès with the wind whistling though the holes in my jeans and the Stone Roses jangling away in my ears, the magic happens: all words fly from my head and all I can think of is sky blue. I can't help but smile. The feeling of being myself starts to creep back into my bones and when I breathe in long, deep draughts of cold night air it revives like sea air. I just want to sail along on my metal friend for ages, scud along, taking life for what it's worth, stage diving down the boulevard Barbès.

When I make a stop-off at the Privilège my happiness keeps on growing. As I am locking my bike up, a man stops and asks me the time. When I tell him, he replies, 'Mademoiselle, you are very sensual when you move your mouth,' and I smile again because it sounds so ridiculous. Then he says, 'So, mademoiselle, what is it that interests you in a man?' but by this time I am starting to feel a bit chilly so I say, 'His wife.'

When I finally walk into the Privilège I realise that I know quite a few people here after all. I know Yvonne who runs the bar, I chat with Mylène the Algerian who has a good figure and wears leather chaps, and then that stoned Argentinian woman who fancies me comes over with her two friends. The perfect back of the bus moment arrives when Laure, the trendiest, most beautiful lesbian in the whole of Paris, walks over to join in – without me even having to make my usual lap-dog run over to her. Afterwards, the Argentinian says, 'Mais, tu connais tout le monde ici!' which means, 'But you know everybody here!' and I shrug and say, 'ouais' in a casual sort of way.

I get on the dance floor and start doing my trunking dance and as I do it I watch naff, Dawn-type lesbians doing stupid suggestive thrusts against the pillar. I think how unimaginative they are with their tight jeans and their expensive haircuts and how funny it is that they think themselves so beautiful and attractive – but I think all this in an amused way. And I know that I don't have to go home and account for myself, turn my Walkman off when I get into bed and have my spirits smashed by my lover being grumpy or refusing to do it with me. I feel better than I have done in weeks. It all seems to fit into Dave's theory that social life is miserable on the whole, and then one night out of ten you go out and everything falls into place.

And then, just as I am turning to go, there is a glint in the room and I see Frédérique. Frédérique bubbles and sparkles like Champagne in army boots. I have seen her on and off for the past year; smiled at her; exchanged a few words sometimes. She is so confident that she makes me feel gauche when I stand next to her, and I knock drinks over her and flick ash on her by mistake. She is a fashion photographer and she wears the boots I love and a suit that's much more striking than I'd dare to wear. I even love the way she can't dance very well and to hide it she does a clownish butt-fuck simulation dance on the other girls. In my more objective moments I know she looks a bit like a rat – but she is an alert, seductive rat with a big red smile and big white teeth. These teeth probably also add to the rat likeness but, as Holly would have said, she *assumes* her rat likeness. I love her teeth and her big red smile; when she smiles she fills the room more than 2,000 people. And best of all, she is right out of my league.

They say you live and learn, but maybe life hasn't scared me enough yet. I look at her and I want to throw her high in the air and wolf her down like a triple-decker Scooby snack.